PORTIA H.

Tale of Philippa

A Legends of The Unbound Novel

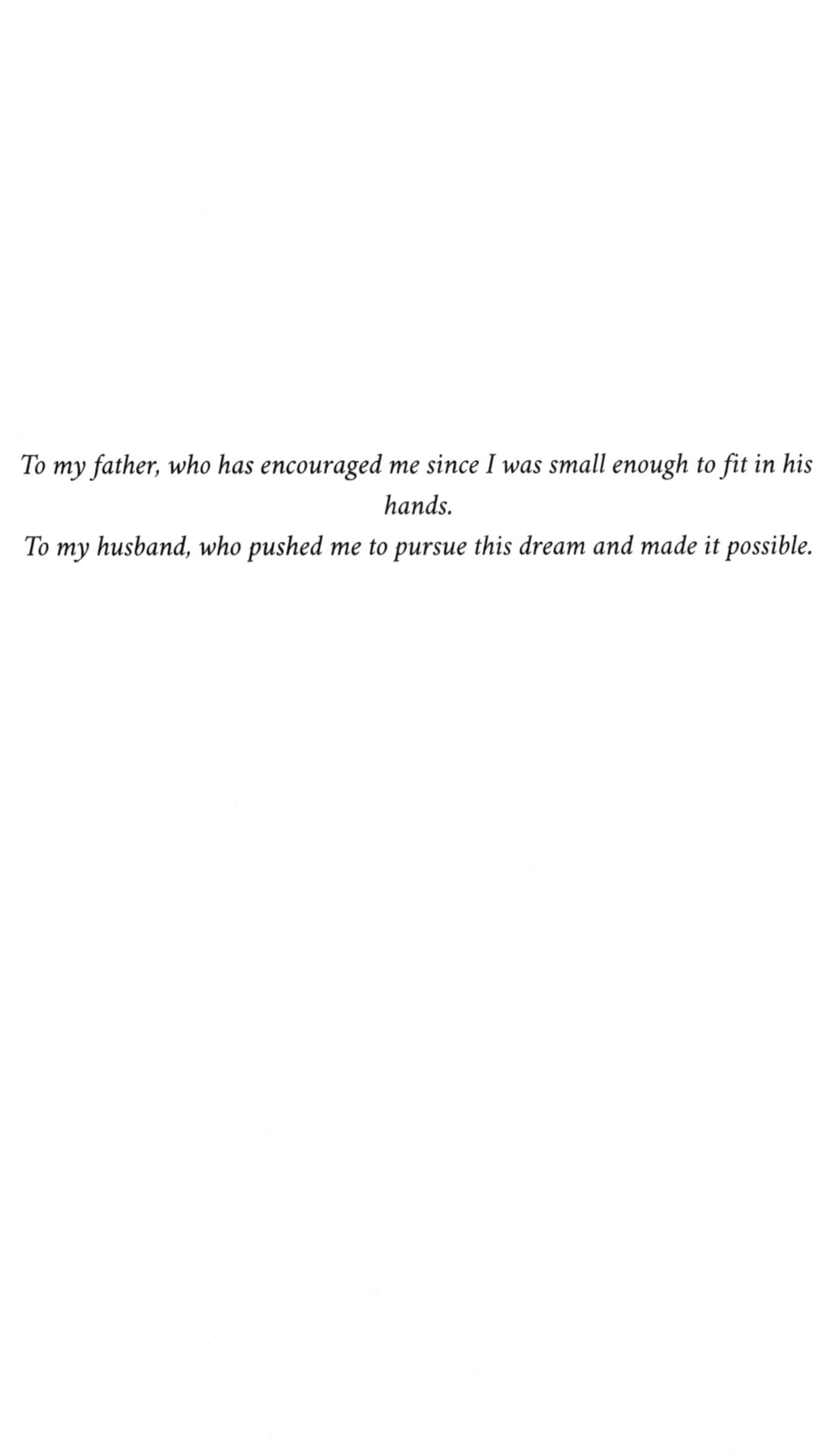

To my father, who has encouraged me since I was small enough to fit in his hands.
To my husband, who pushed me to pursue this dream and made it possible.

PROLOGUE

Her eyes wouldn't open. The blood was too thick. It wasn't even hers.

Small feet pounded against jagged stone, she fought to keep up. Tried to keep her eyes off of the blood, off of the bodies.

Ever a picture of calm, Philippa's mother moved with a fluid urgency through the streets of burnt libraries. There was very little time to get the children out, even less to explain that she could not come with them. The worry came in waves of her mother's tightening palm, the sweat that trickled into Philippa's own hand.

Disbelief still settled in Philippa's chest between ragged breaths. She did not dare cast a glance back, not at the burning homes, not at the storefronts that had been freshly painted, not into the smoke where their father had left them.

Her parents had their differences, but today was the first time in Philippa's life that she'd heard Mother scorn her Father's name.

A fool, Mother had called him as he left, *a fool to think he would leave his ways for us.*

Those were words that Philippa would remember forever. Words had power, memory, magic in their own right. She had always sensed it when mother spoke, recognized the thrumming of it when her father wrote with his massive hands. But magic and words had caught up to them. Magic typically had a cost, but scribing took a toll. It was what divided her parents' peoples in the first place, all those years ago. It was what led them here, now.

When her mother came to wake her and her sister in the middle of the night, they had asked *why*. Why did they have to leave?

Cressida Aporo had morphed into more than just their mother at that moment. Her dark brows knit in a way that told a thousand stories from long before Philippa was born.

Her father's people, she had explained, the Scribes who yearned for more, were artful in their destruction. They assumed there would be no retaliation for what they had done.

Philippa no longer thought of the two sides of her family as one people. There were those with magic who wanted more than what they were given, and there were those here, in Soffer, who had fled to live with what they had.

Morgana, her older sister, went careening to the ground as her foot was caught in a part of the road that had been blown apart. Their mother shoved Philippa forward, urging her to keep going.

"Hurry, hurry," Mother whispered, hauling Morgana up by her armpits. Mother's eyes were alight, frantic.

But Philippa did not run. Her muscles froze, the way a deer locked up when it realized it was prey. If she had kept going, she would have run straight into the maw of a man-beast. Storyless monsters, without myth or legend. They simply were, simply existed.

Her little hands shook. He - *it* - hesitated, drool slipping from its disturbingly human mouth. Its curious eyes swept over her, lingering as if it recognized her smallness, her helplessness.

As if it has a conscience, she thought, fear tightening around her.

The whine of a dagger being drawn caught its attention. Philippa's own fingers tingled at the sight of her mother with a blade as long as her forearm, rising against the beast.

"You will back away," her mother said, voice steely. She wobbled on her feet.

The beast smiled. "You do not command me with mere words."

Mother returned the smile in kind, death written upon her ashen lips. Her eyes flitted to the ground.

"You will back away," she repeated.

The monster's eyes widened as he reluctantly obeyed the command that she had traced into the dirt with her bare toe, sealing it with her voice. He retreated ten steps, fury palpable.

There was no time to feel relief. The expression of magic was draining their mother. She had been making these small alters since dawn, and had been racing towards the bay that they could only now see past his sinewy wings.

Philippa ran to Mother, gripped her side as if in hiding. She tried not to look like she was holding Mother up.

She was.

"You will yield," her mother breathed deeply, taking in enough air for the last sprint.

A lump formed in Philippa's throat. Even if they ran as fast as they could, they wouldn't get out. There were more monsters. Some who did not wear the face of men, who wouldn't hesitate to kill them.

Morgana had moved underneath her mother's other arm, meeting Philippa's gaze. Her full lips were set in a determined line. An unspoken conversation passed between the two sisters. They would get their mother to the beach at any cost.

They would save her.

They each took their mother's hand and forced their legs to run like they never had before. Darting around the beast, even as he furiously clawed and snapped at them with sharp canines. But their mother's magic held his feet in place. The silver tongued writing in the dirt would only hold him for so long, and it did not stop him from bellowing to his brethren that they were getting away.

The girls' shins hit the longboat awaiting them. It would take at least three days to make it to the larger continent. There was a sanctuary for lost souls where they might be safe.

Beating of wings drew closer, like a wolf howling to mark its prey.

Their mother knelt, her knees sinking in the mud of the shore. She took this brief moment to remember every inch of their beautiful faces.

"Do not be afraid," she told them, her voice steely despite the storm in her eyes. "Seek safe haven. Grow up strong, it will serve you longer than your beauty. But do not grow up hard. Show mercy. Give it when you can. And when you cannot, if the world beckons you to slay mighty dragons or venture into the wilds, you show the world such ferocity that the ground quakes beneath your feet. But above all, above *all else*, look after one another. You *must* do this. Nothing else matters if you cannot protect each other."

Morgana covered her mouth to bite back a cry, and reached to squeeze Philippa's small hand to steady them both. Philippa could draw little comfort from her sister. They both knew their mother's encouragement was a goodbye.

With the comfort only a mother could possess, Cressida squeezed her daughter's noses and pinched the points of their ears, as if nothing was wrong in the world.

Gray eyes shifted to Philippa, who did not cry, but met her mother's gaze head on. They had always called her unwavering like their father. Her stomach was in knots, her mouth dry. Magic roiled in her veins rising with each crashing wave of fear.

She opened her mouth, "I am not afraid."

With a sob, their mother embraced them, right before shoving them backwards into the longboat and drawing her dagger once more. She held a finger to her lips.

"Mama!"

Mother turned at the sound of the cry.

Philippa and Morgana stared at her with wide open eyes. Neither could look away. Philippa's mind *pushed* for her mother to understand why they couldn't tear their gazes away from her.

Worthless, worthless, worthless, Philippa's mind was screaming at her. Why couldn't she do more?

We aren't worried about us!

With a whisper of time left, their mother pressed her lips to each of their foreheads.

"Close your eyes," she instructed as she pushed the longboat from shore, "you're still brave when you close your eyes."

In a heartbeat, they were gone.

In another heartbeat, she shifted from mother to warrior. Some would say there's no difference between the two.

By the time clawed feet hit the shore, muddying their crimson-stained talons, their mother was standing tall. The boat had vanished. Her inscription in the small vessel sent her girls far, far away.

"Where are they?" Growled their leader.

She smiled, tears streaming down her soft cheeks. She had no more words for them, not a single one. Her magic was depleted. The ink that seemed to thrive in her, able to change and create, had gone silent. Fear drummed in her ears. Utter, all consuming fear. *Live.* She had commanded her daughters to *live.* Their father no doubt had something prepared for this to ensure their safety. She prayed no one else would be at the expense of it.

With nothing left to say, her bones heavy, she willed herself to charge. Cressida Aporo held the line on the beach against three monsters before a fourth one came to overpower her.

She lasted a few moments after that, until a fifth one came. Until they subdued her arms and legs, hoisting her from the earth, as she strained to be let free.

Blood pricked at her skin as tooth and claw held her in place.

The fires of her home burned in her eyes. She let her head fall limp, to see the upside down vision of the bay, where her daughters were now safely sailing towards the unknown. She heard the tang of a sword being unsheathed.

She looked into that upside down hope, right up until her eyes became unseeing as the sword fell across her neck.

CHAPTER ONE ✦

Salty water blossomed over Philippa's bare feet as she waded into the gentle surf. With each step, the sand shifted, sinking, pulling as if the ocean was trying to reclaim her. She stood still, letting the tide rise and fall, breathing with it. Once, she had fought against its current with gasping breaths. Now it welcomed her like an old friend or perhaps a patient beast waiting for her to stop resisting its pull.

She avoided small crabs that scuttled past her toes. When the sand under her feet shifted from soft to coarse, she held still. Seconds passed in countless breaths, a gentle rise to her chest as she lifted her arm into the air. The familiar, gentle weight of her spear steadied her.

A shimmer of bright scales dazzled under the hot sun.

Thank you, little one, she thought as she swept one of her feet behind her in a sort of death dance, before tossing the spear into the water. The blade, sharp and true, punctured the fish. His purple eye bulged with awe. As she hoisted him out of the water, crimson droplets fell, exploding like ink falling onto parchment. Slugging the large catch over her shoulders, Philippa dragged the spear through the water as she swayed into shore.

Sand crusted to her feet, the smell of the sea curling around her like a fine smoke.

"Are you going to eat that all by yourself or do we get some?"

Philippa turned, a smirk playing on her lips as she passed Shanti, who wore a serpent's grin.

"For a trade? Sure, Shanti," she said with a sigh as she heaved the fish onto the block. Shanti plucked a butcher's knife from her belt. Philippa squeezed her eyes shut as the woman brought it down, stilling the once writhing creature. Blood spattered onto her arms, which she tried to ignore.

"Trades are my specialty, dear," Shanti purred. "Be glad I never traded you and your sister for a sack of flour."

She wrinkled her nose, "I don't think I'd fetch a high price."

Shanti's fingers curled around the dead fish's tail as she stilled. Though without title, the older woman carried an air of power in Levanta, despite there being no one assigned Lady or Lord. Levanta was a place of immigrants, travelers, and those whose reputation they'd rather bury.

But it had always seemed Shanti was none of those things. Ever since they washed up on that shore, Shanti had been there. Respected as well as feared. She rummaged in her pocket for coins, before flipping them across the table. "You'd be surprised what you'd go for if I was involved."

Before Philippa could ask her what in Istoria that meant, the older woman's eyes crinkled with more than age. A tinge of disgust played on her lips. "There is an *out of towner* here today."

Philippa shrugged, dropping her coins into her hidden pocket, casting a glance around the waterfront. Nothing seemed out of order. She clasped her black toga over her shoulder and unfolded her trousers to cover her sea-kissed calves.

"We have travelers often," she said by way of parting.

But Shanti's eyes flickered with more than human wariness. Philippa had always wondered *what* the woman was. She was no elf, like herself, and not another creature like most of the others in Levanta. All wary from a life they didn't care to share. That seemed to be the only similarity between Shanti and the rest of the souls in Levanta.

"She smells of soot and smoke."

The words landed like a stone in her stomach. Smoke.

It was just a traveler. Just laced with smoke from the fire the night before. The desert was cold at night. Just the scent of something distant, something harmless.

But her fingers curled into her palms, nails pressing deep into her flesh.

The back of her mind was whispering, cooing of burning timber and screams swallowed by the roar of flames. For a moment, she was small again, barefoot on a scorched beach and her father's ink burning into her shoulder.

She exhaled sharply, shaking the thoughts away. Philippa rubbed her hands together, grains of sand cascading onto the stone street. "Likely from the fire they used last night," she offered. In the back of her mind, she saw ash covered stones and smelt burnt hair in the distance. As if she could still feel the embers rolling under her hurrying feet.

The old woman simply shook her head and scoffed, as if it was ridiculous. But Philippa knew better than to question her any further. Shanti had her secrets, perhaps even gifts, that seemed to give her understanding.

Philippa tried not to dwell on the thought of a stranger that smelt like disaster, like another lifetime.

She rolled her neck as she strolled further into town. *You are not in danger,* she reassured herself, a coaxing whisper in her mind.

But that nagging was there. A constant itch on the base of her skull. A tingling in her fingertips. A thrum in her blood.

Diving between two shops, she pressed herself against a coral painted wall, and cast her eyes to the sky. The lattice connecting the two buildings blotted out some of the sun, marred by hanging leaves and bundles of fresh lavender that draped down low enough to touch.

Wrapping her hand around a bundle, she buried her nose in its soft, herby scent. Earthy. Safe. Normal.

But the shade of purple in her clenched fist reminded her of something else; the hue of ink when bled onto parchment, shifting fate with a single stroke. It reminded her of the magic in her blood, the voice in her head that never left.

What she had tried to forget.

She could write this feeling away, if she tried hard enough to remember how.

I'm here, I'm here, I'm here, the voice in her mind curled in her head like fresh incense.

Worthless, worthless, worthless...

No.

She was *here.* She was *alive.*

Live.

She had never forgotten the command. Not since almost drowning when the waves threw her from the longboat. When phantom hands hoisted her onto land, even if her sister always claimed that she must've washed ashore. She had never been so lucky. Something followed, saved her life so many times, something perhaps from Soffer.

The land of their mother. Of their true people.

Philippa gulped down the memory. It never seemed to get easier to forget what happened. To move on.

If she could just bury herself enough in this life that she had lived for twelve years, she could let go. The panic would leave her chest. The call for *more* would die away like a diseased limb.

This was enough.

It had to be.

As if called from a trance, she turned back to town. Fresh bread was being set out for the day's sale, and the children who had already finished their morning chores were screeching in the streets about going swimming. A smile played on her lips as she ran a hand along the pebbly wall.

Her life.

A breath of life had been blown into the streets of Levanta.

Donkeys brayed in alleyways as her neighbors dragged them towards their market stalls. Children chased chickens and dogs through the corners and around fountains. Morgana nudged her shoulder, smirking as she pointed at two of the children dangling upside down from a wooden archway.

A boy with glasses that slid halfway down his nose was casting a lazy smile to the girl beside him. Everyone swore those two could have been siblings in another life. Philippa wondered if maybe they were supposed to have been written that way, but something separated their books by just a page.

Her nephew, Raff, was inseparable from young Elodie. Both no older than six, and yet they seemed like they had known each other for decades.

Philippa looked to her sister, whose smile had been twinged with a faint sadness.

"What is it?"

Morgana shrugged, adjusting the pack of harpoons on her shoulder. "Nothing."

With a roll of her eyes, Philippa planted her feet in front of her older sister. She may have been shorter than her sister, but she was stockier, entirely planning on using her body to block her path until she coughed up what was bothering her. She wrinkled her nose and crossed her arms.

"Pip—" Morgana started.

Philippa held up a hand. "I have *all* day to wait for you to fess up. You, on the other hand, look plenty tired carrying those harpoons around town waiting for the boat to come back. I wonder how long you'll last while I block your path?"

Her sister ground her teeth and tossed a lock so dark it was almost purple over her shoulder. Philippa remembered a time when their hair was simply black and brown, not tinted by the sea life they ate.

Morgana was stubborn, but her eyes were carved with weariness. Philippa almost felt bad about forcing it out of her sister. Almost.

She saw the moment she gave in: Morgana's shoulders drooped and she nodded towards a corner. Philippa obliged, following her out of ear shot from the young children.

"Out with it."

Morgana wrung her hands together and smiled warily as she touched her locket. Philippa's pulse thrummed in response, as if she were on a precipice. *Run, run, run.*

Strange. She only ever felt that way when trouble was near. A warning. A shadow of something lurking just out of reach. Suddenly, she feared that her sister may have something more serious to say than she had anticipated. An apology was already on her tongue, when her sister cut her off.

"It's just Raff," her sister murmured. "Every day, he looks more and more like…"

Philippa's ears shivered slightly. "His father?"

Morgana nodded. It was true, though. Raff didn't resemble much of Morgana or Philippa.

His ears were only half pointed, such as perhaps a fae, not an elf. He had thick curls like his mother, but his dark freckles peeked through ruddy skin that lacked the pigment of Morgana's. Philippa remembered the boy's father, how handsome he had been, and how it looked like the sun had kissed his olive skin with a peppering of golden freckles. He didn't look to be of that world in the *least*. But in a flash, he had been gone, leaving Morgana without ever knowing she was with his child.

"It's only a matter of time before he starts asking questions. What will I tell him? That his mother was foolish enough to fall for a man too eager to leave in the night?" Her voice dropped lower. "That his father does not love him?"

Philippa's chest tightened. She squeezed Morgana's hand, willing some of her strength into her. "Just because his father doesn't know about him, doesn't mean he wouldn't love him. If you could send for him somehow…"

"And if he doesn't come?" Morgana's voice was brittle. "What then? You know the ships stopped coming when he left."

Philippa hesitated. Her blood sang louder in her ears. *Help her, help her, help her.* The truth was, she didn't know. Raff's father was a mystery, a man who had drifted in and out of Morgana's life with the tide. She remembered when he was suddenly gone one morning, without a goodbye, as if whisked away by magic.

"You don't know that he wouldn't," Philippa said softly. "Your story didn't think it was necessary for him to stay, but that doesn't mean he wouldn't have wanted to."

Morgana pulled her hand away. "You sound just like those old scholars in Soffer, prattling about fate as if we have no choice in our own lives."

Philippa exhaled through her nose. She knew better than to argue with her sister about life stories, about the books in the great library that dictated their lives, or at least recorded them. Morgana had never found comfort in them the way that Philippa had.

To Philippa, it was easier to believe that nothing could be changed at times. No matter how much she wanted to; and there were many great things she would change if she could. The two notions were constantly at war in her heart. On one hand, changing things for good sounded beautiful, tempting even. But magic was never without cost. Changing a fact for the betterment of one, often meant the downfall of someone else. It was too risky to change meaningful things.

"I don't find peace in knowing that every choice is out of my hands, and that it is permanent," Morgana whispered. "I would rather my son have his father."

The only way to change what had already been penned by magic was with scribes, who were all but extinct. Philippa very much doubted any of them existed anymore. The gift had died with her people in Soffer. Deep in her bones, though, Philippa knew that she would've written a hundred stories to keep Morgana's love from leaving. It was drawn all over Morgana's face how much she hated knowing that Raff's father may never come back from the Shifting Sea. He'd never come to visit after Morgana became pregnant. They'd talked of getting married. He was a steady man, who'd come see her anytime his ship was near port. Then one day, he was gone. Vanished into the sea without a goodbye, as if pulled by an invisible string.

Philippa's magic stirred beneath her skin, but she bit the inside of her cheek, forcing it down. "You know I'd do anything for you." she said.

It was true. She would, even if it was easier to believe that there was no way to change things. There was convenience in this basic half truth. That lives were going as they should, and that no one was left to alter them. No one had the power to make each other suffer again.

Her blood screamed at her now.

Liar, liar, liar.

Morgana's gaze snapped to hers, sharp and unyielding. "Don't. Don't even think about it."

"I could just…"

"No." Morgana's voice was quiet, but the force behind it was unshakable. "We were given this life by our mother's sacrifice, and I will not have you throw it away chasing *what-ifs*." Her expression darkened. "I love you too much to lose you, Pip. Or would you rather end up like Calix?"

Philippa flinched. "I'm not like him."

"No?" Morgana arched her brow. "And if someone found out?"

Philippa had no answer. The weight of her sister's worry settled between them like a stone.

So instead, she forced a grin and nudged Morgana's shoulder. "Fine, fine. No grand gestures. But if I did try, maybe our Guardian would come to save us like they always do."

Morgana rolled her eyes and her signature smirk returned to her full lips. "There is no unnatural force that is constantly saving you. Somehow you just end up in trouble and work your way out of it."

"Aha, but that's where you're wrong. I have three proven experiences with our Guardian. If I had my life story, I could prove it," she continued as she rounded the street corner, ducking under a large crate of fish being heaved up by ropes that seemed far too thin to hold the platform up above heads to put atop a rooftop restaurant, "the boat when we arrived here, when I fell out and hands drug me to shore, that is the first."

"That was me for all you know, Pip," Morgana chuckled.

"What about the house fire when I was sixteen? I saw a blur and suddenly the window burst open and I was safely laying on the sands while the neighbors rushed to help."

"A lucky neighbor who got there in time," her sister reasoned. They watched as the crate was heaved higher, straining men and women yanking on the pulleys with all of their might.

Philippa hummed. "Then what about the bandits that tried to rob me when I ventured into the groves beyond Levanta to hunt for pelts, and a shadowy figure rescued me *and* left me two extra pelts?"

Morgana whipped her head around. "You have never told me anything about a *robbery*. What else have you kept from me?"

"Oh, lots. But I never had a secret boyfriend," she purred. *That* earned her a yank on the ear from her sister, followed by a sullen laugh. Even if Morgana never believed her, Philippa knew that something was there when she was at her most defenseless. Each time her life seemed to truly be in danger, a blur and a plume of feathers left in its wake seemed to appear. It was always faster than her eyes could discern, but she knew that she could recognize her rescuer somehow, if she had to.

Her very bones seemed to sing to her then. *Look up, look up, look up.*

Unable to disobey, scanning the streets they had been avoiding while the workers loaded crates onto the flat rooftops. A bad habit from the past, but she had learned to listen when her body warned her.

Her nephew Raff was running towards them, hand-in-hand with Elodie. They were smiling. Unharmed. That only made the dread curdle in her stomach.

It was nothing. Just the memory of the Guardian. Just her own mind playing tricks.

Then, the first rope snapped.

CHAPTER TWO ✧

Two men slammed into the cobble road with a sickening crunch. Blood burst from their faces as the impact shattered them. Shouts erupted. The remaining workers strained, struggling to keep the platform from tilting.

Morgana threw the harpoons to the ground.

"Raff! Run!"

The boy's head snapped up. His glasses slid down his nose as he caught sight of the teetering crates. He didn't hesitate. Grabbing Elodie's hand, he bolted towards his mother.

Philippa's blood roared in her ears as Morgana tore down the street to meet them. The platform was falling. She was frozen.

Three massive stacks, each hundreds of pounds. Philippa had worked on these docks and streets before. It took ten people to sturdy a single side.

Not enough hands.

She lunged. Seized a rope. The burn was immediate, slicing into her palms, already slick with sweat.

The crew opposite her was losing their grip. Slipping. The rope dragged inch by inch through their hands, pulling them forward.

"Wrap it around your arms!" She screamed. "Hold! Do not let go!"

Philippa's skin splintered. Blood warmed her fingers. She ground her teeth.

Morgana reached Raff, yanking him into her arms. His glasses were cockeyed. He still clung to Elodie's hand.

Another snap.

Philippa's vision tunneled.

The platform tilted. The weight shifted. She knew - *knew* - what would happen next. Morgana did too.

For a single heartbeat, their eyes met. Philippa saw the panic, the impossible choice.

Morgana chose.

She turned. Shielded Raff with her body as she threw herself forward to avoid the crate.

Elodie screamed.

The crate struck her leg, and Philippa wouldn't ever forget the sound. Her arms buckled. The rope wrenched from her grasp. The platform fell.

Raff was crying. "Go back! Please go back!"

Philippa ran. Elodie was still screaming when Philippa's knees hit beside her. The child's small frame was unnaturally twisted. The crate had trapped her leg, pinning her to the ground. The sobs had turned silent. Shock settled in.

No. You will not fail.

Philippa's fingers scraped the stone as she shoved her hands beneath the platform. She pushed. The weight was crushing. Her body screamed. Too heavy. Too much. What she was trying was impossible.

Others ran to help. Shadows beside her. *Lifting.*

Shanti, despite her age, was there, grim and unwavering. The woman nodded. Above them, another rope snapped.

Every Levantian there *pulled.*

Philippa dove.

Dust burst around her as she seized Elodie and *yanked.* She could only cover Elodie with her body. They hit the ground as the platform slammed down. A gust of air shoved them aside. The world blurred. Someone took Elodie from her arms. She didn't know who. She'd been too late.

Worthless...

Her chest seized. *Too tight.*

She clawed at her top, trying to breathe, but it felt like her skin was choking her. Her mother's face. Her father's hands. A blur of color fell before her eyes.

White. Gray. *Feathers?*

A plume of them as a shadow fell beneath the world.

Then—

Darkness.

———————————————————

A monster clawed at Morgana, talons as long as scythes. Calloused hands stained in black ink dug a fang into her shoulder; her sister's hand was intertwined with her own.

Her mother smiled.

A head hit the beach.

Philippa awoke in a mess of sweat and salt. It couldn't have been more than a few hours, but for her, it felt like time had passed in seconds. She could see blood on the road in the back of her mind and hear the screams of children.

RAFF!

She bolted upright, straining against her bed, nearly falling to the floor. Morgana was suddenly there, steady hands pushing against her shoulders.

"Pip, you're okay, you're okay," her sister murmured against her hair. "Everyone is okay."

"Where is Raff?"

"He is with Elodie."

Philippa brushed her hair from her eyes. Elodie. "What happened?"

Morgana pursed her lips and shook her head. Something like disgust shone in her eyes. She wasn't telling her everything. But when she met Philippa's iron stare, her shoulders fell with ease.

Philippa listened intently as Morgana explained that the ropes had been tampered with. Cuts made by what could only be described as incisors of a beast so great that they dared not speak its name. A beast made of words and nightmares. The ones that she dreamt of when the wind howled a little too loudly or when the ocean sounded particularly visceral.

No one in their right mind would have sliced through those ropes. Everyone in Levanta took great care in making the city safe. Incisors sounded right, Philippa decided. Teeth and nails, not swords or daggers.

Why did they still want them, after all these years?

Her expression must've been plain, because Morgana gently stroked her sister's forehead and gently squeezed her nose.

"We don't know for sure if it was… one of them, Pip."

Philippa narrowed her eyes. "Who investigated the ropes?"

Morgana needed not answer. "Shanti."

She would have made no mistake. "Where are Raff and Elodie?"

Her sister clicked her tongue, "Love, you were nearly crushed. You don't need to think about this right now. Raff is fine."

"That's twice you have told me that. Where is Elodie?" Philippa's voice cracked. Part of her already knew. The distinct wrinkle in Morgana's brow told her more than she needed to know. But she had to hear it, to know it was true; that she had failed. That nothing she did had saved the girl. Not even the puff of feathers that she swore had saved her. Maybe her luck only applied to her.

After all, it had been that way the day their mother died.

She grit her teeth.

Morgana sighed. "Elodie is at the apothecary. She hasn't awoken since the incident. Her father is on the prowl to find out who cut those ropes, and why. He has half the men in town with him."

The breath escaped her chest. Elodie was alive. She was safe.

"I want to see her," she breathed.

Morgana reluctantly agreed. She warned Philippa that she may not like what she was going to see. But she had to know if there was something more that she could have done.

By the time they reached the dimly lit apothecary, a crowd had gathered inside and out. In the furthest room, lit by candles and oil lamps, Philippa found Elodie and her family. Shanti was overseeing and doing her best to comfort Elodie's mother, Lucile.

Philippa didn't know her all that well, but she was a good parent. Kind. Baked sweets for Raff anytime they had extra sugar.

Shanti's weathered hands were clasped around Lucile's shoulders, thin lips murmuring prayers and words of encouragement. It was like looking through time. Once, she had been between those wrinkled fingers and heard the words of a hardened old woman who begged a higher power to offer protection. Shanti was many things, which was precisely why she was here.

Here with dying Elodie.

Raff was nearby, staring at his little friend's head, which was the only exposed part of her body. The rest had been covered with a sterile sheet, but the shapes were not right underneath the purple silk. Where two bumps of knees should have been, there were ridges and lumps of malformed legs. There was hardly anything to contradict that her little chest was likely in similar shape.

Philippa covered her mouth. Grief filled her throat with a trapped sob. Who would do this to a child?

Monsters of midnight and ink quills.

She pushed the thought away.

Shanti's eyes found hers, and she offered a knowing shake of her head. The girl would die tonight.

You didn't help her, help her, help her, her body whispered.

Save her, save her, save her.

"What can be done?" She asked in a whisper.

The Apothecary, a thin man of barely fifty years and already losing tufts of his purple hair, stepped forward. "My medicines would help her heal, and I could set her leg, if she awoke. But I fear that the damage to her head is too great. The trauma likely traveled through her entire body when she was thrown to the ground. The legs, I could take, if they didn't heal. Craft a wheeled chair. But the rest of her I cannot heal tonight, which is all she has."

Though he spoke in a whisper, Elodie's mother released a sound of such mourning that Philippa's blood boiled.

Someone had done this.

Save her, save her, save her.

Morgana went to her son, pulling him away from the table and cradling him to her chest.

"I would do anything," Lucile cried, "anything!"

Philippa's ears twitched. She had seen what the power of the people of her past could do. Had watched trees be felled with the swipe of a hand and ink. Had read of armies swept aside with the finest of parchment and the will of a few loving people.

If all that destruction could be made from the magic that was supposed to flow in her veins, couldn't she do something *good* with it?

Slowly, Philippa lowered herself to her knees. Morgana was going to *kill* her. Trying could only make a fool of herself or put a target on her back. But she had to try, even if the entire town was outside waiting to hear what became of the child.

She grasped Lucile's cold hands and met her heartbroken stare.

Her own mother had looked at her just like that, once. When she thought she was sending her children to die.

"Anything?"

Confusion filled Lucile's eyes, but she nodded nonetheless. Shanti shot Philippa a glare that could cut.

"Morgana, take Raff out, okay?" Eyes filled with tears, Philippa cast a glance over her shoulder. Tension settled in her chest. She hoped Morgana would buy the idea that she was just worried about having Raff see his friend like this.

Her sister would never have left if she had known what she was planning. But she tried to sound natural, only worried about the little girl who they had loved like family. Morgana gathered Raff up in her arms, whispering into his bouncing curls.

When they were gone, the room felt eerily quiet.

"I cannot promise you anything, but I can't walk away without trying," she whispered to Elodie's mother, who only nodded in her grief.

Philippa turned to the Apothecary. "Get me the finest vial of ink you have."

He looked at her with scrutiny. Real ink was expensive, and hardly ever imported to such a small town. She doubted he had even used an entire vial of ink in a year to preserve it. But when he eyed her, his face paled. He was not a simple man, the Apothecary. He knew of what she was implying. At first, he looked like he was going to object. That is, until Elodie's mother spoke.

"Please," Lucile begged, "for Elodie."

That was all it took in Levanta. A place of welcome and love.

Somewhere the most undesirable could live.

Philippa had no idea what she was doing as the Apothecary turned towards his desk and began to rummage below herbs and well kept bundles of plants. She had only ever seen these things performed when she was a child. But she had known the power of a simple word on the day their mother saved their lives.

She could not ignore what screamed in her veins any longer. Her body begged her to use what was there, and she had pushed it aside today, for what? For Elodie to die?

The Apothecary gingerly handed her a vial. It was shaped like a stem of lavender, its contents a deep indigo. Barely half a vial. Unused for years, as the bottom was filled with what had settled.

Shanti grabbed Philippa's wrist as she approached the girl's bedside.

"You better know what you're doing," Shanti whispered with venom.

In her mind's eye, she could see their father instructing them as they scrawled on parchment. She couldn't remember anything miraculous happening. But she knew the steps, ones she had followed in her head anytime she fished or hunted deer.

The death dance.

One of glass and inky blackness. It took something to create, to give.

"I know this may not work for her. I have to try."

Golden eyes flashing, Shanti whispered, "That is not what I mean."

There was something more in the older woman's words, but before Philippa could ask any further, the Apothecary handed her a sharp quill. "Hurry, she doesn't have much time. Her breathing grows more ragged the longer we wait."

Gently lowering herself to her knees at the girl's bedside, she asked the

Apothecary to remove the sheet. Lucile was glued to the scene as the sheet was lowered to the girl's mangled feet. Philippa felt bile rise in her throat. She was utterly destroyed. Where should she even try to start?

What was the most important part of her to save first?

She wasn't an apothecary, or a physician. But she loved her nephew, and she loved her home.

With shaking fingers, Philippa uncorked the small vial with a *thunk.* The quill nearly missed the neck of the vial as she tried to dip into the ink. Somehow, this felt wrong. Sacrilegious.

Yet, familiar.

She could almost feel the weight of her father's stare.

The nib filled up with ink. Philippa set the vial on the bedside table.

Slowly, she lowered her hand to the girl's destroyed legs. The bone inside had been snapped clean in two. She hoped what she was doing wouldn't hurt Elodie more.

The nib touched ribboned skin.

Philippa sucked in a shaking breath, and closed her eyes. She could be afraid and be brave, she told herself. She had to be.

Ink bled onto the girl's skin as Philippa wrote in swirling letters she had practiced for days at a time with her parents. A swirling *H* bleeding into a looping *L.*

Heal

She felt nothing. Lost nothing.

Peeking through her eyelids, Philippa felt her shoulders droop. Not a thing had changed.

Elodie's mother held her breath.

Philippa grit her teeth and closed her eyes again. Once more, she swirled the letters onto the girl's body. Nothing.

She scrapped her flowing, flowery lettering for distinct, obvious characters.

H E A L

Shanti scoffed. The Apothecary sighed with disappointment. Lucile hadn't breathed.

"I'm sorry," she whispered, and lowered the quill.

Shanti opened her mouth, likely to scorn her for even trying something that the law strictly prohibited, when Elodie's mother reached out and snatched Philippa's wrist in her hand.

Her brown eyes were wild, brows knit in desperation. Lucile seemed to tower over her as she dragged her hand back to Elodie's body now covered in small bits of handwriting. Philippa had never noticed how big that little woman could feel. Then, she spoke with such reverence, as if she were speaking to a deity.

"Use what you are. *Be* what you are. Save my daughter, Philippa."

Belief. Lucile spoke with belief. Philippa had heard of those who still believed in the magic of Scribes. Levanta was probably the place to find such ones.

She could promise nothing, she wanted to say again, but the fire and terror in the mother's eyes froze her lips shut.

Philippa could only nod and say, "Help me."

Lucile looked as if she would move the sea to do so. Philippa took her hand, having her mother guide the quill. She recalled her father's voice:

"The mind and heart must be one to make a significant change," Titus Aporo *said with authority.*

His large hand guided her pudgy, fat fingers across the parchment.

"You could change someone's thoughts or opinions with the snap of your fingers, if you tried hard enough," his voice echoed, *"but if you practice enough, you could scar very flesh into obedience."*

Philippa allowed the mother's hand to guide her to Elodie's chest, right above her heart. Through the strongest tears Philippa had ever seen, Elodie's mother pushed the quill to her daughter's chest.

"What do your mind and heart want to change more than anything else?" her father's voice sang in her skull, strengthening her bones for a power that was someone already leaking out of her. Philippa swore she saw sparks of light at her fingertips, but her mind was hardly her own.

She turned to Elodie's mother.

"Write what you want more than anything else in the world," Philippa whispered.

Heal her, heal her, heal her, her own mother's voice whispered in her blood.

Lucile stood in shock, but forced the ink to move under Philippa's hand. A single letter.

Not written in beautiful penmanship.

A second letter.

Not scrawled in desperate, bulging writing.

A third.

Not worried about anything else other than this moment. An unhurried word.

Four letters.

LIVE

Her body became alive and decaying, present in the fullest degree, and farther away than it ever had been. Something cemented in her mind. A mother's love, desperate to save her child. Determined. Believing. Elodie's mother *believed.* A whole mind and heart, and Philippa's hand was the embodiment of a miracle.

Power thrust from her body, heart, and soul from her fingertips to the ink that now lay permanently on Elodie's chest. Sparks flickered in her palm as all the blood in her body fell to her feet.

The vial on the bedside table shattered, sending ink all over the floor; a bleeding heart in the apothecary.

She felt people surrounding her, and wasn't sure when so many had entered the room. Her throat felt raw. Had she been screaming?

Weightless. She was weightless.

The last thing she saw was Elodie's chest rising and falling at a steady pace.

CHAPTER THREE ✦

Philippa halfway wondered if passing out would become a part of her daily life at this rate.

She had awoken to dozens of familiar faces hovering above her, as if *she* was the one who had been nearly killed. Morgana had marched her home and ordered her to rest, but it wasn't until a crowd continued to follow that she realized something was amiss.

They knew.

Everyone in Levanta knew.

Her sister had thoroughly chastised her for two days, all the while forcing her to eat to regain strength and being careful that Raff didn't hear. None of it mattered, though. Elodie was *alive,* and according to her father, who had come by with tears in his eyes, she was going to stay that way. When Philippa had asked about her leg, he had gone quiet. Elodie would likely never walk without assistance ever again, or ride a horse, or run with the other kids, but she was alive. That's all Elodie's mother had wished for. It didn't matter beyond that at the moment. She had just wanted her daughter.

After the two days, Philippa's ears still twitched anxiously when she thought about facing everyone. But when her bare feet hit the stones, she was met with the quiet bustle of the morning. Trading and bartering. Arguing. Kids playing. The brush of the ocean in her ears.

Everything was normal.

No one stared at her or asked about the bags underneath her eyes. It was as if the entire ordeal had never happened.

Philippa still felt the shift. Everyone was trying so hard to act normal, that they were painfully obvious in doing so. No one could forget that a beast had torn through the ropes as if it had known someone would get in the way. It would also be remembered how Elodie had been saved by a woman with *magic.*

Though forbidden, Philippa had never really considered what scribes could do to be magic. Growing up, it had been talked about like the blessing of their bloodline. Then it had become an ugly curse writhing in her veins, sought after by only ill intended criminals.

It didn't matter what she thought of it now that everyone knew it was inside her.

Philippa rubbed her temples as she waded into the warm ocean, her mind unraveling at the thought.

Slowly, she sank into the water, letting it rush up to her waist and swirl over her thighs. Closing her eyes, she pressed her fingers into the shifting sand beneath her, as if anchoring herself in the moment. As if time had no weight, only the pull of the waves, the hush of the tide. Her hands skittered through the foam, shaking hands with an old friend.

You and I go way back, she thought to the sea. *Save me now.*

The ocean's only reply was a kiss of salt on her brow and the fraying of the hair around her face. Even if everyone else around her remained quiet, her mind was a cacophony.

Her father's hands were curled around her spine. A talon pressed at her heart. A quill dripping with blood in her hands. Over and over she heard his commands.

"Write, Philippa, write."

"There is power in your hands, from your heart."

"Morgana may not be able to do this, but you, little one? You will be the greatest of us all. Now write."

Her fists filled with wet sand and she set her jaw. Hot air filled her chest as she bit back a yell of indignation. Magic had never flowed from her hands this strongly as a child in Soffer, so why now, when she was so far from her training? When she couldn't save her family?

And what did I give away?

The thought had plagued her even in unconsciousness. Elodie had lived, but at what price? What did she give to save someone's life?

Her bones were tired, her appetite insatiable. But she could argue that the latter was always true. She could come up with nothing that was equal to the price of a life.

Somewhere, deep in her mind, her mother's voice called to her.

A salve to her soul, she listened.

"Close your eyes."

They immediately snapped open. Someone was calling her name, but in a whisper so low she could have mistaken it for a breeze.

Shanti's slender form stood like a mountain in the winds that were picking up.

"The stranger that smelt of smoke has returned."

Philippa narrowed her eyes, scanning the woman's face for clues. Shanti's brows were creased, creating a deep *v* on her forehead. Lines that hadn't seemed to be there before around her mouth drew worry all across her face.

Shifting in the sand, Philippa drew a shaking breath. "Does this have something to do with—"

"Elodie's mother is dead."

CHAPTER FOUR ✦

Your fault, your fault, your fault.

Philippa couldn't silence the thrum in her body. She had killed her. Taken whatever desperation from that poor mother and drove it into Elodie like a cure to a wound that could not be healed.

There was a reason that the ruler of Istoria and his new wife had made sure to pass the laws further into outlawing Scribe magic. The prices were too high, too unseemly, too unpredictable. Sobs were echoing through the streets as she numbly stumbled down them. She passed her home like a ghost.

Waved through the crowd of family and friends like a whisper of air.

Eyes were on her, bodies parting as if she was the plague.

Only Shanti was brave enough to stand beside her, and likely not out of love but out of duty. Someone could lawfully sever her head from her shoulders. Philippa wasn't sure that she would try to stop them. She had taken a girl's mother from her.

Her hands shook as she pushed open the door to their home. Elodie's father Marcel sat at his wife's bedside, face sunken and grave. The child was nowhere to be seen.

As the Apothecary covered Lucile with a sheet, Marcel's eyes slid to Philippa in the doorway.

It was his right to kill her.

But she would not run. She couldn't bear the thought.

Marcel's breathing seemed to come to a stop as she crept into the house, Shanti blocking the crowd in the doorway. There was so much of this that she did not understand, that she had forgotten in her childhood.

But you knew there would be a price, her bones sang.

I thought I would pay, she answered.

Words had failed her when she was trying to save Elodie, and she would not make that mistake now. There was only so much she could say to this man who had nearly lost his daughter, and now had his heart being covered with a sheet so thin you could still make out the point of her nose and the curve of her lips.

Her knees gave way as she sank to the floor a few feet from Elodie's father. He still hadn't moved an inch since he saw her.

"I am so, so sorry," she whispered, "I was so desperate to save Elodie that I didn't think of the price. If I had known that this is what it would have cost you, cost Elodie, I … I would have …"

"You would have *what?*" his voicc shook the house.

Philippa did not wince. She braved the man she had stolen from with wide eyes and open palms. Morgana would be so heartbroken. Raff wouldn't understand. But that is why she had come immediately to the house, not home. She could not hide from this any more than she could hide the fact that magic roiled in her veins.

"You would have let my daughter die?"

Her ears flattened to her head. "No, I … I don't know. But I am here, because by law it is your right to do with me as you will. I won't fight you." Tears threatened to spill over, and she swallowed the lump growing in her throat. Shanti would scorn her for being so emotional about something that she had done. "I have stolen from you, and I—"

He held up a hand to silence her.

Marcel stood up so quickly that the chair fell over, and his grasp fell away from his wife's cold hand.

The Apothecary took a step back. He would be witness to the lawful murder.

"You stole from me."

Philippa's eyes were unblinking. Fear thrummed in her neck, and she swore a vein would explode.

"You saved my daughter."

She swallowed. "Your wife saved your daughter."

He paled at her statement, and he slowly drew his dagger from his hip. Philippa became deathly still. It would hurt, but not for very long. She hoped Raff would not see, and that Morgana could forgive her.

Steel touched her cheek as he settled onto the floor in front of her, the blade dangerously close to her eye.

"By law, I can do with you as I see fit," his voice shook with such immense grief Philippa thought she might shatter, "death, or stealing of equal value."

She blinked.

"Sir, I—"

"You will not speak," he whispered, gray hair falling in front of his eyes, "my wife made her choice. Elodie always came first. Always. I cannot thank you enough and I cannot hate you more than I do now. But I can't kill the woman who saved our child."

Philippa bit back a sob, and anxiously gripped her salt covered legs as she lowered her head. He wasn't going to kill her.

Gratitude seemed inappropriate, so she turned back to Shanti in the doorway, who stood like a sigil in the fading daylight. The woman did not look proud, or relieved. She looked... remorseful.

Philippa's ears lowered ever so slightly as she rose to her shaking feet. Elodie's father had backed away to right his chair, sinking into it like it was keeping him from floating away.

She approached Shanti tentatively, and when she reached to walk around her, Shanti blocked her path without meeting her gaze. Somewhere in the crowd that was stirring with worry, Morgana's voice called out like a war trumpet.

Again, Philippa tried to look past the older woman, but Shanti stood firm. Philippa narrowed her eyes and tilted her head in question.

For the first time in her life, she saw Shanti look ashamed. "I told you, girl," she said with a disturbing lack of emotion, "I hoped you knew what you were doing."

A hand was over her mouth before she could scream. Thick, acrid smoke flooded her nostrils, burning with such intensity that, for a moment, she thought she was on fire.

Sweat soaked leather pressed against her back as firm arms drug her, not towards the gathered crowd, but to the back door.

Philippa thrashed, kicked, and screamed. She threw her head from side to side as she tried to break free, but the door burst open and she was dragged outside. Desperation surged through her. She worked her attacker's thumb between her teeth and *snapped* down - hard.

A sharp, pained whine cut through the air, the taste of copper blooming on her tongue. The grip loosened just enough. Philippa wrenched herself around and found herself staring at the tallest woman she'd ever met. Thin, chapped lips blew her a kiss as their forehead collided with hers. Stars bloomed and darkness touched the edges of her vision, but she would *not* allow herself to lose consciousness.

A language she did not understand floated from the assailant's lips as she shoved Philippa with so much force that her back cracked against the wall. Without missing a beat, the mountain of a woman grabbed a fistful of her hair and dragged it across the wooden structure until she could push it against the window.

Panic flared in her chest, but she couldn't muster a scream. Somewhere in the distance, Morgana was yelling with a fire that only a mother could possess.

Philippa was waiting for talons and wing beats to fill the air. They were going to feed her to the monsters that had chased her nightmares since she was a child. They had found her, because of her foolishness.

But the sting of punctures never came, and the skies were eerily clear and dark.

Her attacker pressed a leg between hers to keep her immobile, and dragged her head to face inside the window again.

Cracking open an eye against the glass, her breath caught. Elodie was asleep in her bed, fresh lavender and newly crafted toys on her mattress. She was still alive, unburdened by the knowledge of her mother's passing.

The woman spun Philippa to face her, lowering her hooded head.

Again, she spoke in a language that Philippa did not understand, but the words were the same.

Tentatively, the woman removed her hands from Philippa's hair and arm, and turned her palms upward. She raised and lowered them slowly until they fell evenly, then she pressed a finger to Philippa's forehead, and finally rested a finger on Elodie's window.

Realization settled in her chest like ice, a stark contrast to the smoldering stranger.

This was the equal price. Not a death sentence, but a payment. A deal had been struck.

A life for a life.

CHAPTER FIVE ✧

Despite Philippa being dragged through the back streets, she could see a crowd forming towards the border of Levanta, people murmuring and darting through alleys to keep up. They carried torches that cast a wavering light on…

On the oncoming band of warriors.

Her skin crawled.

The strangers stood like stone just outside of the overgrown archway of thick fronds and creeping vines that lead into town.

Their feet, bare like her own, were planted firmly against the ground. The only word ringing in her mind was *immovable.*

Her magic had fallen silent, as had her conscience.

This was the price for her sins. She had killed someone. The words felt foreign in her mind. A person whom she had seen almost every day for over a decade. A wife. A mother. A woman who would soon be laid to rest in the sea.

Her ears laid flat against her head. She wondered what the last page of the woman's book would say. In her mind's eye, she saw a quill being laid to rest as the mother's book was closed, and Elodie's remained wide open, with scrawling red ink demanding *life.*

Bile rose in her throat.

Not ink. Blood.

Philippa gagged, and tattooed arms grasped her firmly again as she was hauled to the border.

"Take your filthy hands off of my sister!"

Philippa snapped her head up as the grip on her forearms tightened. No, no—

Morgana stormed through the crowd, Raff following at her heels. Her braids whipped madly behind her as she plowed over anyone standing in her way; but no one stopped her, no one even spoke.

Her captor stalled for only a moment, before yanking Philippa behind her, as if to protect her. Odd.

Her sister steeled up to the warrior woman, and though she was an entire head shorter than her, she met her gaze with a ferocity that Philippa had seen before in her memories. A fighter's shine in her irises, like she would set the world ablaze in order to keep her sister safe. But Philippa would do the same for Morgana. It had always been that way.

"Release my sister! You have no rights here!"

The warrior smirked, and replied in the same language as before.

Morgana didn't miss a beat. Drawing a harpoon from her back, she dug it up under the chin of the warrior and *pushed.*

The woman did not move a muscle, and it became abundantly clear that she wasn't caught unaware, but that she was allowing Morgana to do this.

Rage filled her sister's voice as she looked past the tattooed warrior, eyeing the small band of intruders who, all things considered, seemed quite set on *not* intruding past the border. "I know one of you has to speak the common tongue! Explain yourselves before I gut this wretch like a fish!"

Raff covered his ears, his eyes the size of saucers. If only he knew what other "adult" words his mother knew.

The band did not breathe, did not speak. They were one body, one mind. Philippa squinted in the night, trying to make out these people.

They were not elves, like her and Morgana. But they did not look entirely human, either. Not a single one of them was *small,* each towering over every Levantian, corded muscles and large feet. Tattoos in intricate patterns floated from their arms, to their bare chests, down their legs and necks, up their heads if they had shaved them. They carried no weapons that she could see. Her skin prickled, every hair standing on edge.

Philippa whipped around, grabbing her sister's hand, which the warrior also allowed with a grin. She knew that she was understanding every word. Philippa wouldn't have been surprised if she spoke the common tongue, too.

"Morgana, stop!"

"I mean it!" her sister bellowed, shoving the harpoon further until a line of red began to trickle. The warrior did not even loosen her grip on Philippa's arm.

Before she could speak again, movement snatched their attention. The entire town's population held their breath collectively as one figure broke from the crowd.

Heavy beads swung around her neck, and her breasts were covered by armor that seemed melted to her body in a substance so black that she became the night. A pair of loose, yellow dyed sirwal sat low on her hips, and a chain of chunky gold adorned her waist. The chest piece she wore left her shoulders bare and arms mobile. Philippa got the sense that she did not wear it for protection.

"You do not have the heart to kill," the armored warrior's voice could shake the walls if she raised it any higher, "or are you a murderer, like your sister?"

Morgana blanched. Her grip shook fiercely as she met Philippa's gaze, eyes pleading and confused. The spokeswoman of the intruders tilted her shaved head, watching them with an eerie resemblance to a snake in the grass.

"What happened was not your fault," Morgana whispered and gritted her teeth, "I told you to never try."

Philippa's throat threatened to close, her eyes welling up with tears. She didn't have to say it out loud for her sister to know that there was nothing stopping her from trying to save Elodie.

The armored leader surveyed the crowd without any of the humor Philippa's captor seemed to have.

"You may not have her," Morgana said firmly, lowering her harpoon.

Something glinted in the leader's eyes as she stared Morgana down.

"I was told there was a Scribe among you. Am I to believe that this woman is the one? Will we have to burn it out of you all?" The leader spoke with a sneer, obviously goading them into defying her.

At the word *burn,* the entire company of intruders burst into flames. Their tattoos glowed like living embers, and wherever ink had touched them, fire bloomed in a deadly dance.

The Levantians shuddered and cried out, crouching to miss the onslaught of flames that danced above their heads.

The leader strode forward, crossing the border of Levanta, with a clicking of claws on the stones. Beside her, standing *above* her head, was a creature so foul that Philippa heard more than one person faint to the ground.

A gnarled, black and golden face of a dragon sat atop shoulders that rotated just underneath leathery skin as it prowled beside its master. Its wild, black eyes roved about the crowd, with an unnaturally long torso that bowed out in distinguishable ribs, before narrowing into simply sinew and bone, followed by large, thin hips that faded into horrific claws. Its tail slid along the ground like a serpent, but it did not rattle like the snakes in Levanta. No, it was deathly silent, save for the click of claws.

Her neighbors gasped behind her, and there was the distinct sound of running on stones as some fled.

The creature prowled right up to Philippa, and lowered its head to meet her gaze.

Instantly, her heart was in her throat. Past its crown of three horns of cartilage, were two curved horns of bone that somehow held a single, flickering flame in place above its head. Philippa didn't have to look further to know that it had wings folded against its unnatural body.

A creature of talon and wing, of ink and terrors. She knew of this creature. Had known where it came from before it cursed the land.

Written into existence by her people, her *true* people.

The leader strode forward, spreading her arms out wide as if addressing subjects.

"I am Herunavira of the Wahanar tribe! You foolishly may know us as

Fire Brutes. Our territory has been here before any of your bones have been laid to rest in Sapria! We have been kind in not laying claim to your little town on the border of our lands," she projected, completely unafraid of the creature beside her, "but now we lay claim! Our generosity has run out! There is a Scribe among you. Give them to us, and your town stands. You will be rid of us. If you refuse…"

With a lift of her hands, Herunavira's entire face became ablaze. Philippa hadn't seen a tattoo on her cheek before, but it rose from her skin like a hawk and screeched over the crowd. Herunavira's fire alone was the size of the entire company she brought with her.

Herunavira was testing them. She knew it was Philippa, but at the chance to prove Morgana a liar, she took it.

This was a woman who knew what she was doing. Philippa wondered how many times she had done this before.

She waited for the uproar to take her, to rid them of her sins. With a heavy heart, Philippa looked back to the monster. The flame between its horns reflected in its large, domed eyes. How many fates had it written in flame and ash? How many books were closed because this monster had been written into existence?

But it did not move to hurt her, as she expected. It was not her executioner. As Herunavira's fire died down, and she was able to look back to her home, her breath left her body.

The monster did not look at her with hunger, but understanding. Her home was not afraid of the sinewy creature. They were afraid of *her.* She was their monster written into skin and bone.

This was *their* Soffer. Their fire and terror while mothers hid their children.

Monster, monster, monster, the thrum sang in her mind.

Muscles tense, she knew the screams were coming to cast her out and demand that her blood be spilled elsewhere. But there was only silence.

Philippa turned again, tears spilling over as she swallowed a sob. The Levantians stood as one, like the Wahanar tribe. Unyielding.

Herunavira's gaze slid over to Philippa, devoid of any mirth. "Guess they care about you too much to give you up. You're more popular than I thought."

For a fleeting, cowardly moment, Philippa wondered if no one spoke, would Herunavira leave with her people and never return? But the threat had been clear. Fire awaited those who did not answer her.

"It's me," Philippa said, her voice barely above a whisper.

Herunavira narrowed her eyes, brushing a hand over her shaved head. "Not everyone knows what you are. Say it louder."

Summoning every ounce of courage, Philippa turned to face the people she had called her own. Her eyes locked onto Morgana, who stood inches away. "It's me. I am the Scribe!"

Whispers washed over them. Some had known. All had kept quiet. But none spoke in her defense.

Morgana let her harpoon clatter to the ground.

"Then it is settled," Herunavira announced with about as much fanfare as a bored princess, "we leave now."

Her captor began to drag her.

"Wait, wait!" Philippa cried out, her hands clawing for her sister.

Morgana fought to chase her, but as soon as she neared the woman dragging Philippa, Herunavira blocked her path. It was the worst sound in the world to hear her sister's knee *snap* under the weight of Herunavira's unshod foot. Philippa screeched and felt about as unnatural as the monster striding alongside them. She twisted hard, but the woman had her locked down tight.

She screamed her sister's name until her throat was raw, fighting to not be taken across the border. Shanti was at her sister's side, trying to pick her back up onto her feet. Her mouth was moving, undoubtedly telling Morgana to just let her be taken.

"Hey!" A little voice shouted.

Everyone stalled.

The scraping of metal against the sand littered road made her ears twitch in anticipation.

Morgana's tears stripped her voice, "Don't!"

The harpoon sat heavy in his hands, his little body swaying under the weight. His feet struggled underneath him as he hoisted up the makeshift weapon that his mother had so boldly picked up.

Raff stood alone in the thirty feet between Philippa and her home.

His glasses had slid halfway down his nose as he tried to point the harpoon at Herunavira. "Let her go!"

Philippa screamed a warning to Raff, but was silenced by a smack to her face by her captor. Herunavira stood, frozen, surveying.

He took three steps towards Herunavira to close the gap, and stumbled. But he picked up the harpoon again. Strode forward three more steps before almost falling over.

"You will release her!" He cried out.

Her captor, evidently done with the antics, kicked Philippa's feet out from under her and strode towards Raff with a hand alight in flame from her inky black palm.

Philippa scrambled to her feet, as Morgana crawled towards her son, her leg bent awkwardly.

But Herunavira held up a definitive hand. The warrior stopped.

Herunavira took it upon herself to close the distance between herself and Raff. He angrily swung the harpoon, spinning all the way around with its weight, but he did not stop. Herunavira simply held still.

"You cannot have her!"

"I cannot?" Herunavira asked. A question. From the one demanding her life.

"You cannot *have her!*" He screamed, and finally the harpoon struck Herunavira in the armored torso with a clang. "She is mine! She is OURS!"

Philippa felt frozen in time. She wished she had ink, because in that moment, she would have written Herunavira out of existence to save her nephew.

Though the face of the leader was hidden, Philippa could see a muscle in her neck twitch. She saw the way her hands flexed, control being spread through her body.

"Bring the Scribe to this boy. Let him say goodbye." Herunavira tilted her head, regarding Raff. She nodded at him, ever so slightly.

As she was hauled to her feet, confusion flooded Philippa as she was half dragged, half scrambling back to Raff. He let the harpoon lower as she was released.

Philippa dropped to her knees and scooped him up into her arms, forcing him to drop the harpoon.

"Get that nasty thing out of your hands!" She cried out, wrapping her arms around him as she carried him back towards Morgana.

Raff stared up at her with as much fire as Herunavira's army. Words would not be enough for him.

Morgana enveloped her son in her arms, tears streaking down her cheeks.

"You can't go," he whispered.

Philippa pushed his glasses up with a single finger. She couldn't let him be afraid.

"Raff," she said, having to steel her voice, "I have been where you are. You must let me go. I will come back." She didn't even believe her own words.

But Raff's owlish eyes widened with recognition and understanding. He believed in her.

"It's your job to give mama a hard time while I'm gone. It's a sister's job, but I need you to do it for me." she said, forcing a smile. Philippa couldn't meet Morgana's eyes.

He nodded slowly. Philippa reached out and squeezed his nose, then his ears.

Out of the corner of her eye, Philippa could see Herunavira waiting impatiently for her to wrap things up. The way Herunavira looked at them churned Philippa's stomach. It was like she was trying to make sense of wanting to say *goodbye* to her family.

Her sister grabbed her shoulder. When Philippa finally saw her sister's expression, she thought she could fall over dead.

She could've sworn she was looking into her mother's eyes. Somewhere, beyond words, she knew Morgana thought the same of her. She covered her sister's hand, and when words utterly failed, melted into her arms, Raff tucked safely between them.

Silently, Morgana lifted the locket from her neck and slid it over her sister's head.

"I promised her that I would look after you," Morgana whispered, her hands gathering in Philippa's hair. "I warned you not to be like Calix."

Her sister's words thrashed around in her mind. The lie she had spoken only days before, and Morgana *had* warned her. *You will have to leave if someone finds out.*

Philippa chewed on her lip to keep from falling apart. "I made the same promise."

"Time is up," Herunavira announced.

Desperately, she clung to her sister and to Raff, as arms gathered her up to take her away.

"Close your eyes, Raff," she called out, trying to smile, "you're still brave when you close your eyes."

He aged a decade in two seconds. "I am not afraid."

His eyes never left her as they took her away.

CHAPTER SIX ✧

Soft sand had turned into thick, heavy dunes as they traveled through the night. Philippa stared up at the purpling sky that had faded to the color of Morgana's hair, deep and luminous in its intense lack of light.

There was no moon.

Philippa cradled her breath in her hands, a plume of white slipping through her knuckles. The gravity of her situation was settling into her chest. Her eyes roamed the party as they walked effortlessly over the dunes, only illuminated by the sparks between their creature's horns.

If they were comfortable with those things, then they must have been just as dangerous. The same monsters had been there on the day that fire became her worst nightmare and had consumed her world.

She shook her head to rid the thought. It wasn't their fault that they were written into existence, and in the way that they were. But the bitterness on her tongue refused to leave anytime she caught a glimpse of one of those creatures. As for the few hours that they had been walking, they seemed to sense that she wanted nothing to do with them, and gave her a wide berth.

Certainly a wider berth than her initial captor. The woman had lost her hood along the way, and had stripped down to a similar outfit as Herunavira. Well, maybe less. Without it all, Philippa saw the blotchy vitiligo around one of her eyes, which was a lighter gray than the deep black of the other. Her body was a honed weapon, and Philippa had tried desperately to look away when she had said something in their language, causing a ruckus of laughter, and pulled down her armored top to reveal a scar.

Philippa hadn't been able to look away fast enough. She couldn't understand what she had said, but it was clear they were exchanging some kind of war story. Her captor wasn't showing off her body as she had initially thought, but a gnarling, twisted scar over her chest.

What could have done that to such a strong woman?

Philippa wasn't even able to pry herself free from her grasp. Who could have gotten close enough to drag a blade across her chest?

A distant, braying screech sounded from the front of the party. Not who, but *what*.

Herunavira held up a fist to halt the journey. Almost lovingly, she dragged her other hand down the reptilian neck of the monster.

A monster like you, now, Philippa's mind whispered.

Philippa rubbed her temples. Her captor smacked her hands away with a grin. What was her problem? They had her! What else could they gain from her? Humiliation? The knowledge that death awaited once they reached their destination?

A pit hollowed out in her stomach. These people were called brutes, but they were the robbed natives of the continent. A scribe would be the perfect way to buy back their lands from the King and his new wife. It was whispered about by visitors and travelers that the Brutes were finally making a scene about losing their lands into Sapria's growing reaches. Decades ago, the king took the central city, Aresef, when Scribes were outlawed, after he reclaimed the libraries at the end of the Scribe Wars. A once celebrated claim of land had stretched too far. The Brutes were not going to give up their native lands, and so far, their efforts had kept the reach of the king from their homes.

But once Soffer was burned, things had changed.

Philippa's gut twisted. What if the king had hired the Brutes for their fire to burn her, as they had burned all the other Scribes?

Maybe this halt in their journey *was* the destination. She wasn't going to stand trial, or be questioned before an execution. This was plain old, cold blooded murder in the sand.

Oh, stars, what would Morgana think?

What would Raff do?

Look up, look up, look up.

She listened. Herunavira was striding towards her. The monster was not far behind, its claws deathly silent in the sand.

Darkness cascaded around Herunavira's face, and the tattoos that had bitten at Levanta faded into the night. The warrior woman suddenly took hold of Philippa's hands, forcing them towards the leader. Philippa bucked backwards, trying to stay as far away from the monster as possible. Herunavira's eyes narrowed in cold calculation. She spoke in her native language at first to the woman holding Philippa in place, before inclining her head towards her.

"You do not like my friend?" Herunavira asked, crooning.

Friend? Philippa couldn't believe what she was hearing. But Herunavira did not seem like she was the type to joke. Suddenly, Herunavira's hands were on her face, dragging her gaze to the creature, her "friend".

Black orbs stared her down. The flame between its horns burned brightly as it leaned down to press its scaly, surprisingly warm skin against her face. Panic flared in her chest. Philippa muffled a sob that threatened to flee from her lips, her jaw about to pop from the scorching pressure of Herunavira.

Nothing could stop her eyes from meeting the monster's.

"Nazheris," she whispered in fear.

"Titus, they sent the Nazheris!" Her mother's voice screamed in her mind.

Herunavira released her. An unspoken conversation passed between the leader of the Wahanar and her guard. Anger surged within her as the woman kept her wrists firmly outstretched, forcing her to touch the twisted creature.

"Let go of me," Philippa recoiled. Her heartbeat was in her throat. She had to get away from it. If this was where she was going to die, she didn't want this to be *how.* Not ribboned and scorched until she faded into horrific oblivion. Pages whirled in her mind, drops of ink exploding onto books as windows burst with white-hot flames. Louder this time, she whirled her face to meet the Wahanar leader, her captor, her executioner, "tell her so she understands that I said *let me go!*"

All Herunavira had to do was nod. She fell backwards with an unceremonious thump in the sand, crawling backwards like a child as she dragged down uneven breaths.

The leader of the Fire Brutes knelt in front of her, observing her like a hawk. "She knows the common tongue. But she does not answer to *you*."

Philippa sent an angry glare up to her captor, who only smiled like a child who just won a game of cards by cheating.

Herunavira snapped, drawing her attention as a flame lit between her fingers. "Tazmireth won't hurt you. She's as harmless as they come."

"Tell that to the bruise on my cheek." She couldn't believe she said it until it was too late.

The warrior before her didn't seem to notice the disrespect. Philippa thought she looked too tired for her age. Instead of highlighting Philippa's attitude, Heru just leveled a glare at her. "You fought her. You were told not to."

"In a language I cannot speak!"

Herunavira chuckled darkly. "True. But now you know her name, and now you are connected. Such is the way of friends, yes?"

Friends. She had called the Nazheris a friend, and now this lethal woman was supposed to be what, her guard?

But the way the leader spoke somehow eased the panic in Philippa's chest. She was being honest. The flame between her fingers danced and extinguished just as quickly as it had ignited. Herunavira looked to Tazmireth, and though Philippa didn't understand the words, she knew a dismissal when she heard one.

Tazmireth nodded and cracked her knuckles, blowing another mocking kiss in Philippa's direction as she sauntered towards the band of Fire Brutes that had settled into the sand.

Something inside her snapped as she remembered being dragged away from her family, her face being smashed against the glass of Elodie's home. Philippa couldn't stop herself from sneering, "so I'll see you later, *Taz?*"

If names were important to them, then she would weaponize it. Stars, she sounded like her father.

The Fire Brute stilled, her back turned towards them. Her inky black palm ignited in a fire so hot that it turned *blue,* as she waved it over her shoulder and walked away without a word. A silent reminder of who was in control here.

"You are very stupid."

"Excuse me?"

"Look around and tell me that I am wrong." The Wahanar leader, for the first time since knowing her, smirked. For whatever reason, Philippa *did* take in her surroundings. She was alone among strangers who wanted to do her harm, the creatures that her people had brought into existence and turned on them, and it was growing increasingly cold. She chewed on her cheek. Stupid felt right. But there was something that had been nagging the back of her mind since they left. Herunavira hadn't spoken directly to her since they set out past Levanta and Philippa had taken those fateful steps.

"Thank you," she said, which earned her a raised eyebrow, "for letting me say goodbye."

Herunavira straightened. She extended a hand to Philippa, and pulled her to her feet. The gesture seemed so… natural. As if she wasn't going to kill her when she saw fit.

"I am not so cruel as to deny a woman her child."

Philippa chewed on that. "You don't seem cruel to me. You seem desperate."

That, she found funny, evidently. Herunavira tapped her own cheek, mirroring where Philippa's bruise was.

"I've seen real cruelty. You hurt my sister and you hurt my family's hearts. But I've seen worse." Her tongue felt dry in her mouth. Unwanted memories began to call for her, and she shook her head to clear the thoughts. "Your friend, however…"

"Tazmireth is my cousin. You should keep calling her Taz. Frustrating her will make your journey feel faster."

Her ears twitched. "There's *more* journey?"

Herunavira smiled, and now Philippa saw the resemblance between the two women. Taz was older, but their smiles were the same. Crooked on one side, but it brightened both of their faces. Herunavira seemed to need convincing to smile, though. Taz threw them around like punches.

"You are thinking I will kill you tonight."

Her blood turned frigid. It took everything in her not to start trembling. *You're a grown woman, act like it!*

She nodded slowly.

Herunavira ran a hand over her shaven head and sighed, her smile already a thing of the past. "I grew up with the stories of what happened in Soffer. That is how you know Nazheris."

Philippa startled. Her question must have been written on her face, because Herunavira slid an arm around her shoulders and began guiding her towards the circle of Wahanar.

Voice heavy, and her Nazheris following at a respectful distance, she began to explain. As Herunavira spoke, it was easy to feel like their dynamic was not that of captor and captive. Easy to lose sight of what was happening, because that's how Herunavira *wanted* her to feel. Philippa's skin crawled, trying to discern whether or not she should lean into the comfortability that this woman was trying to display.

"Scribes wrote Nazheris. Gave her scales and horns, with a flaming heart in her chest. But they did not write her to have a choice. Now, that is power. To take an idea and ink, and forge a life that can only obey. But Nazheris, she is stronger. She followed the orders of the new king, burning Soffer into ash. A beautiful death." Herunavira's eyes were glazed as she stared into the fire that her people had made in the center of them. They were talking, laughing. It felt so *familial.* There wasn't an ounce of mindless blood thirst like rumors said. Just a family who wanted to enjoy their evening. Philippa's heart sank. She believed too much of what she was told about others. "She decided that she does not like ordering death around at someone else's whim. Nazheris was lonely. So, with more power than a Scribe, they left. Swimming across the Shifting Sea, some fizzling out in the waves, for a chance to choose. Nazheris found the Wahanar tribe first. My people did not see a monster. They saw someone who had been robbed. We know a great deal about being stolen from." Her voice became heavy with a rasp that had not been there before.

Philippa almost reached out and grabbed her hand to hold it.

Herunavira removed her arm from Philippa's shoulders and steeled herself. "Nazheris chose us. This one here, she is part of my family now. Raises our children like a mother. She is not docile, or wild. She is herself. She *chose*. Now, Nazheris is written into the laws and history of my people. She is a part of our people. She told us what they had to do in Soffer. That is how I know your fear, and why Tazmireth knew to send for our Nazheris when she was in your town. It is unfortunate we had to steal you. Your leader did not give us much of a choice."

"My leader?"

"Your old woman with eyes of gold. The unbound one," Herunavira sounded like she was explaining, but all she did was confuse Philippa. Unbound? What in Istoria did that mean? Before she could ask, Herunavira grabbed her by the face again. Philippa gasped, yanking backwards, but Herunavira pulled her forward, like she weighed nothing.

"I am sorry your people died. Stealing you saved your little family. Now you will do exactly as the chieftain says when we arrive in Wahanar." Her black eyes glistened like stones of onyx, baring into Philippa's soul.

"Wait," she whispered through pursed lips, courtesy of Herunavira's tight grasp, "you call Nazheris 'she'. This is the same one as in Soffer?"

Herunavira chuckled without humor. "You *are* very stupid. You do not even know about your own history. Scribes wrote all Nazheris to be female. They have no power to reproduce. The number they were, will only get smaller. Cruelty and stupidity ruled the Scribes. Unfortunately for both of us, we happen to need one. That is you. You were worried before that I would kill you tonight. I said I would not. But listen to me with those big ears…" she leaned forward, so close that their noses touched. Herunavira and her cousin had no concept of personal space. "I will not kill you tonight. But I will spill every ounce of magic in your veins should you disobey."

With a sudden force that felt unnatural, she tossed Philippa to the sands. Whatever understanding she seemed to have with her, was gone. *This has been Herunavira playing* nice.

With a clap of her hands, Herunavira called Taz back over to stand watch over Philippa.

Taz said something that dripped in disdain and humor.

Philippa was going to hate asking someone else to translate for however long this lasted. She sent a pleading glance up to Herunavira, who was once again a statue.

"She says you should thank me for not removing one of your fingers," Herunavira paused, thoughtfully, but narrowed her eyes, "she does not joke about this as she does other things."

Swallowing whatever pride she had, Philippa pushed off of the sand and stood up straight, bowing her head. "Thank you, Herunavira."

Her voice wasn't strong.

"You cannot pronounce it. Call me Heru. It annoys me less."

Three days and nights passed at a snail's pace. Philippa had seen hatching turtles move faster than it felt they were going. Morgana's locket was a weight against her chest.

There was no way to tell how far they had gone, or how much further there was to go. A dune sea spread out before them. Hot air settled on Philippa's skin in a way it never had before. Being away from the sea felt like losing a part of herself. Specifically, the part that allowed her to breathe without sand trickling down her throat.

She would've killed for balm to rub over her cracked lips.

You have killed, don't you remember?

Philippa dug her nails into her palms. It was one thing when the voice in her head warned her about danger, but this attitude it was growing would drive her insane. Herunavira hadn't spoken to her since the first night.

Questions swam in her mind. What did it mean that Shanti was "unbound"? Who was Heru reporting to that pulled rank over *her?* She didn't seem like the type to take orders. When Philippa had asked Taz, she had simply smiled and tousled her hair. She was going to keep calling her Taz until it killed her. It was the only power play she had against that mountain of a woman.

Her only solace was that the Nazheris had kept its distance since the conversation had happened. But never too far behind, and ever watchful. Her chest ached anytime she met its eyes.

Her eyes. It was a she. They were all female.

Were Scribes really only ever there to pummel others beneath their feet? Did their existence do anything *good?* Philippa's usage of her power had only ever caused harm. Elodie's mother was likely to have been sent off to sea already. The thought weighed down her feet. Did Raff hold Elodie's hand at the funeral?

Taz, after pointing and laughing at her face, had reached under the layers of her bottoms and fished out a small jar. Philippa gagged at the thought of from where. Inside was a small amount of rich red dirt. In her other hand, Taz held what she'd been wishing for most: water. They'd only given her enough for each day, which felt like nothing. Her muscles ached and spasmed for what felt like hours every night.

Philippa held out her hands, realizing this entire time they had never bound her hands or feet together. For some reason, she was a little insulted.

Taz, however, did not pour the water into her palms as had become their custom. She placed the jar of dirt into her hands, and then added some precious water to it. Her mouth dropped open at the sight. What was she doing to do, make her drink *dirt* as punishment for sunburn?

Then, Taz wrapped Philippa's hands around the jar and shook it once so she got the point. Philippa shook it slowly. She wasn't going to make this easy.

With a huff, Taz snatched it away and thrummed it violently in the air, until a thick sludge was inside. She uncorked the jar, grabbed Philippa's hand, and poured the mud into her palm with an ugly *plop.*

Philippa just stared.

Taz looked ready to kill her. She tapped Philippa on the cheek to make her turn, towards nothing but sand, and when she looked back at Taz, she slapped her own palm right into her face. The mud splattered over her cheeks, caked her eyelashes, and dribbled into her mouth.

Her body tremored. If she didn't die today, she would make this woman's life miserable.

Taz laughed and pointed at her to everyone around, who joined with chuckles of agreement. But then Philippa felt it. The soothing. Her hot skin was radiating through the mud. However she must have looked, she didn't care. Finally, relief.

Heru yelled back at them in the common tongue. "Stop mucking around back there! These dunes are *zharok!*"

She didn't know what it meant, but a sense of danger crept up the back of Philippa's spine. Taz rolled her eyes and pulled Philippa by the wrist as they kept walking. The jars had mysteriously disappeared again, no doubt under her layers of fabric again.

The creeping came up to her ears, now.

Push her, push her, push her, the whisper demanded.

Philippa ground her teeth. Since when did her sense of danger order her around to hurt people? She would do no such thing. Even if the idea of Taz face planting into the sand did sound enjoyable. More than enjoyable. Delectable.

She should have listened to her instincts.

Taz was still laughing with her friends as the sand opened up wide underneath her feet.

Philippa went flying down with her, and did not fail to notice that if she *had* pushed Taz, they both would have made it on either side of the opening world. Taz grunted in effort, somehow winding Philippa underneath her, and pressed her to the surprisingly firm side of the opening. Philippa clung to Taz like her life depended on it, a scream stuck in her throat, even though they'd stopped tumbling.

She looked up, arms wrapped around Taz's shoulders as the Wahanar came to gather around the edge. Maybe *zharok* meant *big gaping sinkhole that will juggle your insides.*

Heru was a bald silhouette in the sun. "Climb up, rat."

Taz scoffed and grunted, pulling herself up the sandstone wall with hand holds that felt far too small for her massive fists. Wait. Sandstone? This had been carved. The sand gave way like a hunting trap that all Levantian children learned to dig.

What dug a sinkhole this big?

Heru suddenly crouched down low, mumbling something Philippa couldn't decipher. But she felt Taz tense. Heru was encouraging her, it seemed. But there was panic lacing her voice. A worry that she hadn't heard before. They were cousins. She was talking to her like this was urgent.

Philippa dared a glance down into the darkness. It was moving. Undulating up the wall at a steady pace, interested and hungry.

Climb, climb, climb! She expected to hear the voice. She didn't expect the second, which sounded vaguely more like her own. *Save her, save her, save her.* Were the two warnings mutually exclusive?

Clicking. Chittering.

Scorpions. The size of camels. Taz yelled something up to Heru.

"She says you're heavy! Let go of my cousin and climb on your own!"

Philippa couldn't be offended. They were going to die there. But she had seen Taz spar with her friends, had seen her tackle a Nazheris playfully, and had felt what fighting her was like. She was strong enough to lift them both out of that cavern. Searching, scanning for anything to help, or a way to turn around so she *could* climb, all she saw was red.

Crimson blood gushed out of Taz's thigh, which pressed against her waist. She already looked tired. She was losing too much.

Philippa felt herself starting to lose her grip on reality. She knew it in the way her breath hitched, the way her fingers trembled, caught between fright and inaction.

No.

Her Guardian would come. They always came in times like this.

But they did not come when the Wahanar took you.

Heru barked an order and flames erupted overhead, likely to burn away the scorpions. But their hard, tan shells didn't even recoil at the sight of the fire. There was no way flames could hurt those beasts. They were thirty feet away now.

"No!" Taz screeched. Philippa startled, not sure if she had heard her correctly or not. She would have at least liked to *see* if the fire did anything to stop them!

"She's right. We'll burn the Scribe," another Wahanar said.

Heru looked lost. Conflicted. Her hands curled around the side, like she was going to climb down there with them. But that would only allow her to haul one of them back up. It wasn't a choice she could make.

The Wahanar leader's eyes hardened. "Tazmireth. Drop her."

Philippa's whole body clenched. Taz tensed around her and shook her head at her cousin.

"We will find another Scribe," Heru explained quickly.

The warrior keeping her against the wall sighed with a tired smile, shaking her head at her cousin. The scorpions were fifteen feet away now.

Tazmireth looked down at Philippa, used a hand to instruct her to hold on, and she began to climb. She rose with strong arms and shaking legs. Philippa's weight wasn't the problem, she knew. Taz was barely pushing off footholds. Her arms would give out before they reached the top.

When they reached a slightly wider foothold, she turned Philippa around in front of her and forcefully placed her hands onto the protruding stones. No, no!

She could feel what Taz was doing. She was going to get her up, and use herself as bait. That's why she knew her Guardian wasn't coming. Because Taz wasn't going to let her die. Philippa banged her fists on the wall, almost shoving them both off.

She whipped her head around, meeting Taz's glare. Taz wouldn't let her die because they needed her, but something else reflected in her black, lightless eyes. Something more. She liked her. Liked teasing her. She may have been the one to steal her away, but Tazmireth didn't choose that. She followed orders. Heru's orders. Which she was now disobeying to drop her.

For all her brashness and rough edges, she wasn't cruel. Philippa understood by looking at her, the drawn lines on her face, the worry in her eyes, that she didn't want to do any of this to her.

Philippa wasn't going to kill anyone else.

Freeing a dark blade from Taz's side, Philippa cut the skirting off of Taz's good leg and wrapped it tightly around her wounded thigh. Blood began seeping through immediately.

Philippa met the warrior's gaze and jolted at the sight of how pale the woman was becoming. "Climb, or I will throw myself." Taz scoffed and grabbed her wrists again, but Philippa wrestled free in the small space. "Now I *know* you can understand me! Now get your sorry hide up there, before I write you into being a writhing little worm!"

Tazmireth's hands gripped the wall. She climbed right over the top of Philippa. Then, she reached a hand down, and hoisted her up to the next foothold. She could smell the must of the earth, the decay of blood on the scorpion's mandibles as they approached at a quickening pace.

Something slithering touched her foot, and she recoiled, suddenly flying up the wall like a spider.

Taz somehow laughed, and then screamed.

The bite of stone made her look down, and Philippa almost dropped from the wall. The dagger-tip of the scorpion's tail had dug into the sandstone wall - right through Tazmireth's injured leg. The mud on her palms became slick with sweat.

Without thinking, Philippa simply let go. She dropped fifteen feet, not able to scream. Landing on the hard shell of the scorpion, her hands squirmed for holds as she slid down its smooth back. Her hands caught ridges.

You will not fail.

She wouldn't.

The scorpion screeched, ripping its tail free from Taz, who sank against the wall. Tazmireth ripped her small blade free again, swiping madly at the scorpion, who only seemed angered at the slashes on its outer layer.

Philippa's chin split open as she bounced against its exoskeleton, begging to keep purchase on its back. She found the strength to let go with one hand, frantically writing on the giant insect.

S L E E P

She had no ink. The scorpion stilled. Its legs rested into the wall, just below Taz. Not waiting to see if it truly worked, Philippa fought gravity, yanking her way up its back. She wouldn't let Tazmireth die on her watch.

Philippa knew she wasn't strong, or very brave, but her terror fueled her. She had seen too much death already in her life, and had tasted it with the salt of the sea as a child. Hauling herself next to Tazmireth, she promised herself that she would not taste it again today.

Her limbs shook, fear thrumming throughout her body.

Dizziness overwhelmed her. Stars bloomed in her vision, the world starting to fade to black. Strong arms steadied her, and she blinked away the gnawing need to sleep.

Something taken.

Her energy, into the scorpion. But the threat was not over. More were coming. To sting them, tear them apart, poison them, if they could. Shaking her head to clear it, Philippa turned to Taz, whose skin was pallid and slick with sweat. Eyes drifting down, Philippa winced at the sight of Taz's knee, which had been blown apart by the scorpion's tail, the fibery ends of tendons laying about like ribbons adorning what should've been her joint.

She met her eyes. Dared her to give up without a word. Taz nodded, finding the strength to smirk. More would come. But neither of them were leaving each other.

Heru had ordered fire to rain down on the scorpions below.

Philippa pressed herself against the wall, her arm pressed around Taz's torso to keep her from falling backwards. Each time the flames died down, they would climb. One reach at a time. Philippa used her shoulders to boost Taz when she could.

She couldn't remember the last time she had been so exhausted when her back hit the sand above and the Wahanar's voices faded into oblivion.

They had only moved a day's journey when Tazmireth had finally lost consciousness. She had seemed determined not to be assisted on their escape from the giant insects, but there was no choice, and each Wahanar took turns carrying her limp form across the desert.

Which was no small feat. She was just as tall, if not taller, than any of the men with them.

That night, Heru came to her in private. "You didn't leave Tazmireth behind. Thank you. I saw your power in that catacomb, and I need to see it again tonight."

Philippa was heavy with exhaustion. It took almost all of her strength to explain that even if she tried, it may not work, and the last person she had tried to help had ended up dead. Herunavira, listening intently, only furrowed her thick brows, as if not understanding. Or, more likely, believing.

"Make no mistake, your kind disgust me. But for my cousin's life, I will get my hands dirty. Even if it condemns me to Nyxveil. Show me your healing power and I will return you to your home after our chief is done with you."

There had been no further argument. Philippa would've done anything to go home.

Taz had been laid out to rest on a leather stretch that they had provided, moaning in her sleep. Knees sinking in the sand, Philippa couldn't help but brush the stray hairs from Taz's impassable face. She didn't realize a warrior could look so... small.

The Wahanar had no ink to give her, but they had the fine red dirt and water, which would have to do.

Herunavira had wanted privacy, obviously uneasy about asking Philippa for help, but their traveling party made it clear that they wanted to watch. The murmurs from the gathered Wahanar were indecipherable, but Philippa got the sense that they were torn about what was happening. Some looked on in clear disgust, curling their lips and clicking their tongues when Philippa held up the leather bag of red dirt. Others were intrigued, whispering to their friends like schoolchildren. Philippa turned her attention to the leather bag, peering in at its contents.

Philippa inhaled the scent of it deeply, trying to picture where it had come from. Ink held power in the fact that it was used for writing. What made this substance so special?

Clay and the scent of freshly wet earth mingled in her nostrils. This was from somewhere far away. Somewhere fruitful and decadent. But that didn't give it power. Philippa had given it power when she wanted nothing more than to save someone else from dying on her behalf.

Green eyes wincing, Philippa looked at Heru, who stroked Tazmireth's head in an almost motherly way. She couldn't stop herself from asking, despite the Wahanar warrior shooting daggers at her.

"You hate me. My kind. I know you love your cousin, but why trust me with this? You know I could scribe something to hurt her, rather than heal her."

Herunavira did not blink. Her hand stilled on Taz's forehead. "I owe my cousin my life. I would not sully my hands with you if I did not have to repay her. Not even for those most dear to me."

Wistfully, Heru hovered her hand over Taz's scarred chest before continuing to explain. "Nazheris are not always kind. I... upset one, once. As children. Tazmireth took the blow for me. I would have died. Now, I repay her. You will heal her. You will not fail."

Philippa took all of Heru in, trying to read into that hard expression on the Wahanar's face, past those dark brows and tattooed lines. Behind all of her sharp edges, Heru cared about her family. That care had limits, as she'd insinuated with Taz's life debt, but Herunavira was willing to dirty herself with Philippa to even the odds.

A woman like that was dangerous. Because once this was over, Herunavira would owe Tazmireth nothing, and Philippa could outlive her usefulness.

Philippa tucked a lock of her wavy hair behind her shoulder, her fingers dancing as they ran into the cold metal hung around her neck. For Morgana, Philippa would have moved the stars. Heru was asking Philippa to move them for Tazmireth now.

As Philippa wrote a single word onto Tazmireth's exposed leg, careful not to shove the mud into the gaping, open wound, she pictured what she wanted more than anything. Though the word *heal* had nothing to do with her, Philippa would've given anything for a chance to go back home. To be with her family.

But something else inside her was louder. More violent in its need to be heard.

She would give anything to help someone else. Anything. She'd been given too much in her life, and had taken too much. Had seen the worst of what the world had to offer, and was desperate to find more out there than death or isolated safety.

What Philippa would give anything for, was *life.*

A single word cemented on Tazmireth's leg, the only light the fire from Heru's face as she hid Philippa from the rest of the Wahanar who were already fast asleep. The mud faded underneath the warrior's skin, disappearing without a trace.

This time, the altering didn't take Philippa's energy. It sapped her mind, leaving her delirious and without concrete thought. She felt drunk, and a strange sense of longing for something she hadn't experienced before. Heru forced her to lay down, eyes wide with awe, and put a hand over her eyes until she fell asleep.

CHAPTER SEVEN ✦

Tazmireth had healed overnight. Though Heru had initially wanted to hide the practice from the rest of the traveling party, she had credited Philippa for her cousin's miraculous healing. Philippa knew why Herunavira hadn't wanted to tell them of what she wanted Philippa to do the night before. If it hadn't worked, Heru would have been blamed for finding a Scribe that couldn't suit their needs, whatever they were.

But Heru had whispered to her that the promise would be kept. For healing Tazmireth, and for fulfilling the chief's needs, she could go *home*.

The word was heavy on her heart. No desert, sea, or mountain could get in the way of her getting back to her family. But after having been outside of Levanta's borders for almost a week, something was stirring inside her. That incessant thrum in her body was strangely at peace, or rather, in connection with what was going on around her.

It wasn't simply threats that she felt coming her way. There was a sensation in the world around her, as if the voice inside was growing a personality and speaking to her more frequently than it ever had.

Or, Philippa considered, she was crazy from magical exhaustion and heatstroke.

"Stop."

Philippa startled. Taz had been uncharacteristically quiet since the incident. Hearing her voice at all, let alone in the common language, felt like a reprieve from the sun.

Clicking her tongue, she turned away. Her scalp burned, and her skin was on fire. The dunes they had been traversing had felt like mountains.

Yet, the Wahanar tribe maneuvered them as if they were waves of the sea, expertly sailing over them without tiring.

Taz then reached out towards her face, at which Philippa promptly stepped backwards. Surprisingly, Taz let her move away.

Slowly, Taz continued to reach for her, but without as much force. Philippa stood frozen, watching as her inky black fingers touched both sides of her face and turned it to face Heru at the front. Well, that was probably the gentlest that this whole ordeal was going to get.

Heru raised her hands towards a particularly massive dune in their way. Philippa inwardly groaned at the thought of scaling *another* cursed pile of sand.

But then Heru's face began to faintly glow. A gentle firelight that competed with the sun. The entire traveling party stepped towards the dune, extending parts of themselves towards it with a quiet hum of fire. Taz was the last to join them, taking Philippa by the elbow.

Probably as softly as she could, Taz grabbed Philippa's hand into her own, the uninked one, and placed it on top of her tattooed hand. Tazmireth then raised it to join the others, only emitting flames from her palm, thankfully saving Philippa's own hand. Philippa began to pull away, but Taz kept her hand fixed against her own. Her dark eyes glinted down at Philippa.

Then, Taz gestured to the rest of the Wahanar. She scanned them, all focused on emitting their fire onto this single dune. Whatever they were doing, they were doing it together, and Taz was including her. She couldn't bring fire, couldn't join, but she could be present.

It felt like a gift. Or, a last meal before an execution.

But it didn't feel planned, not with Heru shooting daggers at them. Maybe she wasn't supposed to see this part. Taz held firm, not quite meeting Philippa's gaze.

Philippa had chalked it up to a matter of pride. The warrior hadn't thanked her or made mention of the scorpions or the healing since it had happened. Philippa considered the set of her jaw, the gentleness in her grasp, and fought to understand this woman whom she couldn't even speak the language of.

Though brash, Taz had never been overtly cruel. Her ways were just different from Philippa's own.

Maybe this *was* her saying thank you.

As if to answer her question, Tazmireth gave her the same look as when she had tried to explain to Philippa that taking her would balance the scales. To Taz, they were even now.

Which meant she really should be paying more attention to what was happening.

Under the firelight from their tattoos, the dune began to glow red, then yellow, and finally, a white so bright that Philippa had to cover her eyes. Taz held her firmly in place.

Squinting to see, Philippa's mouth fell open.

The white hot sand became a warped, cascading surface. The dune was turning to *glass.* Each Wahanar then moved in unison, warping the giant glass orb to their liking. Philippa had never seen fire so beautiful.

They were one flame, burning in the desert. They were not consuming, they were creating. Smoke didn't fill the air, thick, hot coals were not underfoot. But the whine of countless grains of sand slipping into the molten core they'd created shone in colors Philippa had only ever seen in a rainbow.

Tears sprung in her eyes.

It was the most stunning thing Philippa had ever seen. Her chin quivered, her body trembling as one hand clasped over her mouth.

These people were gorgeous, and all she had ever heard about them was their need to chase away strangers, to stomp about like *brutes.* That's what she'd called them. Never again. She couldn't bear the thought.

Slowly, their flames died down into a subtle glow, the glass fading from red hot into a clear, solid structure. Taz allowed her to back away, head craned back, as she took in what they'd made. The dune had become a giant, intricate doorway. Carved columns that were formed by the hands of many, glass that reflected herself in a dozen colors that she couldn't even name.

As if it couldn't get more stunning, Heru clapped her hands, and the fire ceased all together. Philippa's chest pained that the show was over. Whatever it had been, she was amazed.

Tazmireth's shadow fell over Philippa, shielding her from the sun. Philippa couldn't even look up at her.

Tears still brimmed her eyes as she took in the massive doorway that they had created. "How often do you do this?"

Taz answered in her language, her voice lilting and filled with humor.

Heru chuckled from the front, her hands planted on her hips as the beads around her hips swayed.

Nonchalantly, Herunavira gestured to the glass door. "Anytime we need to go home."

Without another word, Heru walked into the glass and disappeared with a ripple like a stone on a stagnant lake.

CHAPTER EIGHT ✧

This was how the Wahanar kept their lands safe from the king and his new wife in Aresef. They hid their entrances in glass doorways that only they could find, because only they knew how to make them.

Philippa's reflection warbled as she approached the doorway, and inside she could see the line of Wahanar already walking away like wraiths in the distance. Tazmireth gave her a shove, and she melted into the glass.

It was frigid. Her breath became white plumes, cascading around her as she shivered with each step to follow them. They each had gathered around each other, standing on a crystalline floor.

Stones and gems, budding crystals and precious materials glittered beneath their feet. When the last of the Wahanar entered, Taz gripped her shoulder roughly.

That, she had come to learn, was never a good sign. At a signal she'd missed, one of the Wahanar men loosed an arrow towards the glass doorway they had made. It shattered in an instant, trapping them in the crystal caverns.

Philippa stared down at her bare feet, her toes curled in as far as they could be on the cold floor. The cool sensation was like icy fire on her blisters. She had never known such frigid conditions outside of being underneath a wave. Her purplish braid had come undone in every which way, fraying around her face in a mad manner. She wondered how long it would take being away from eating the sea life in Levanta that her hair would fade into its earthy brown color. An emerald colored crystal sparkled, reflecting off her eyes, but she couldn't tear her gaze away.

A week away with people she had learned she was so wrong about, and she looked no different. If she was being honest with herself, she didn't feel all that different either. She'd been so willing to go, to save her family, but a secret part of herself was hoping that she would…

That I would what? *Become something more? Find something more?*

The thought was asinine. She was still a prisoner. A captive. This wasn't a journey that would heal the part of her that ached and spoke like another voice in her head. This was the adverse effect of not listening to her sister. Of killing someone.

Worthless…

Her soul settled low in her heart. This was not a place where she should be in awe. This was a punishment for her sins, for what she was.

Cutting off the thought, Heru barked an order.

Each Wahanar suddenly leapt into the air, and landed in a low crouch with a response she didn't understand.

The crystalline floor shattered beneath her feet. Her stomach lurched into her throat. She was falling, hair coming undone and floating in tendrils all around her, and then—

She was upright in the wet sand. A tree shaded their arrival.

She was on solid ground, the world no longer spinning. Her skin was wet. Her hair was damp against her head. Taz next to her was wringing water out of her half shaved hair. Slowly following their shadows, she looked up, and was met with the gaze of hundreds of faces, as if they were waiting for them.

Screams erupted as the crowd charged them.

Instinct had Philippa's hands protecting her face. The rush of bodies plowed over and around her, nearly dragging her into the sand below.

Hardly anyone noticed her. Everyone ran straight for Heru. They hoisted her up, throwing her into the air as she scowled. Philippa peeked through her fingers, watching from a crouch as the Wahanar kept tossing Heru's body up. Her heart hammered, but the realization that they didn't care about her in the least allowed her to calm down enough to see that Herunavira was fighting a smile. As much as she pretended to hate what was happening, she couldn't help but be happy to be home.

Longing filled Philippa. Home. Where she hoped she would soon return, as soon as she completed whatever task their chief had for her. Her ears laid flat against her head as she thought about the hope in her chest. She would only go home if Heru hadn't lied to her.

So far, she had been truthful enough, but who was to say that things couldn't change?

Taz carefully grabbed Philippa's shoulder, guiding her away from the crowd. Colorful tents were arranged in a horseshoe shape, that centered around the oasis they had somehow appeared in front of. Philippa cast a glance over her shoulder at the large mass of water, surrounded by curling trees and thick brush, and noticed the shimmer of scales beneath the sunlit surface. This was a paradise in the middle of an unforgiving desert.

As Tazmireth guided her through the lines of tents, she took in just how *massive* their camp was. It wasn't just the inner *U* of their homes, but rippled in alternating designs as the tents became further away. A maze. Their encampment was a maze to protect their inner circle.

Her mouth fell agape at what she was seeing. These people were no different than her own. Other than that they greeted each other with a warm welcome. Levanta was a quiet place, where silent hands would grant you entrance if you washed ashore. But that was the difference between other cities and the lands of the Wahanar, which she'd been lied to about for years. The Wahanar were one huge family.

She followed as Taz quickly showed her many of the tents in the inner part of their home, where some were smoking meat, others were stitching new cloth together, and children were play wrestling in the shade of their tents. Her heart sank at the sight of a little boy with a mess of half shaven curls atop his head. There was no time to get lost in her mourning, as she tried to peek into the next tent, Tazmireth stopped her rather forcefully.

Philippa met her gaze and narrowed her eyes. "I thought we were past the whole shoving me around thing, Taz."

Her constant companion rolled her eyes, but did not speak. Something was wrong with her. "Listen, I don't know if you're mad that I helped you,

you seem really capable, but you were hurt. I'm sorry."

Taz looked at her like she was insane. Then, she smacked her upside the head. Philippa clutched her skull, as if that would stop the throbbing.

She looked up at Taz incredulously, wondering what in Istoria she'd said wrong. But Taz wouldn't meet her eyes. Fine. Maybe being herself wasn't how to get through to her. The last time she'd gotten Tazmireth to listen to *anything* she said was when she'd threatened to make her a worm.

So, Philippa snapped. "What is *wrong* with you? I have blisters on my feet from walking across the the desert following you, my hands are ribboned from that cavern, and I still have a splitting headache from healing that leg of yours that you can now so easily walk on—"

Tazmireth slapped a hand over her mouth, silencing her. Her onyx eyes narrowed into slits, and she shook her head once. The message was clear. Slowly, she let go of her face, and exhaled sharply. Taz raised her hands, and dropped them in a sign of defeat.

"I'm sorry," Philippa said, rubbing her head. Taz slowly raised an open palm again, to which Philippa retreated. "Okay, okay. You don't like apologies, is that it?"

A nod.

"Are we good now?"

Taz shrugged. That was good enough for Philippa. She didn't expect she'd get much more out of the warrior.

Philippa turned to enter the tent again, just to see, as she had with all the others thus far. She looked over her shoulder at Taz, who unsurprisingly was too close for comfort. "You know, I could tell you weren't going to leave me in that cavern, either. So maybe we're becoming friends."

As she lifted the flap, she caught a glimpse of a man laying on a table while a tall, elderly woman raised a spike to his flesh. His arms were tied down. Bile rose into Philippa's throat as she careened backwards, wanting to be anywhere away from that tent. Is that what they planned to do to her? Was she next in line? Maybe that's why Taz didn't want her opening it in the first place.

Her legs started to run before she even had the thought. Sand flew up behind her, her feet barely touching the ground. Tazmireth yelled what was distinctly a foul word and tore off after Philippa. The world flew by in a stream of colors, yellow, crimson, mauve, as tents were nothing more than obstacles. She'd run faster than this before. She could escape again.

Fear had grabbed her heart, but the thrumming in her mind didn't warn her. Maybe because she wasn't going to die, but she was certainly going to be tortured.

She couldn't lay on that table. She wouldn't. She had seen what leather straps and metal tipped instruments could do to a body, and it wasn't worth going home for. So, she ran.

Sprinting across the Wahanar encampment, in a useless attempt to escape. She had no idea where she was after entering the doorway they had created. Sweat ran in bullets down her back as she pivoted around a cooking pot stoked over a fire. There was no plan, no hope.

Flashes in her mind kept her legs moving.

A knife being held to delicate skin that had been pallored from smoke intake. A blade dripping in the blackest of ink. A back split open. Words that couldn't be taken back were whispered. The person on the table wasn't screaming. How were they not screaming?

Because you might have heard, a different voice whispered in her head.

Stop, stop, stop!

Her hands caught the worst of her fall. Sand and grit filled the cuts in her palms. Her chest was a wild thing, breathing inconsistently, and her mind was not her own. Whose memories were those?

Or had she blocked them out, trying to protect her little self inside of her?

Somewhere, deep in her mind, a door was opened. One that she didn't know where it led to.

Tazmireth was in front of her. Strong hands hauled her up by the shoulders. She didn't remember walking. Maybe she was being carried, she wasn't sure.

Placed in the shade, a cool wash of a cloth was pressed against her forehead. Tazmireth's concerned gaze flitted across her vision, and words were exchanged. Taz gently grabbed her face, turning it to face her. Disappointment rested on her face, an emotion she had hardly seen the warrior wear since meeting her.

Taz raised her other hand, and used two fingers to mimic running. She then pointed to Philippa's chest, and then to a nearby Nazheris that was asleep next to a bush for shade. The next time she ran, it wouldn't be Taz chasing after her.

"You run fast," Heru's voice cut through her hazy thoughts, "surprised you didn't try that sooner. Or maybe you wanted to see where our people reside, little rat."

She dug her nails into her palms, steeling herself. "What happens now?"

Taz slunk behind her cousin. Heru smiled, her face wholly shaded, turning her into a smokey visage of herself. "Now, you meet the chief. He decides what to do with you."

CHAPTER NINE ✦

Even if Philippa wasn't being led there against her will, she knew this is where she would find the chief of the Wahanar. The central tent was made up of yellow, purples, reds, and browns. It possessed many rooms, and was guarded by two hulking men with tattoos that spiraled up their legs and arms.

Without needing to stoop under the rolled up tent flap, she took in the adornments of the huge home.

Intricately woven rugs were scattered about, layered comfortably with dozens pillows in corners or resting areas. The tent seemed to stretch backwards for miles, and at the center, was a large, carved seat. Censers filled with fire lit the entire room, casting strict shadows onto the fabric walls.

In that beautifully carved seat sat a man that was so tall, it explained why the tent needed to have ceilings supported by cut down trees.

He was shaved bald, like Heru, with two large golden earrings that opened up the lobes of his ears and elongated them. Philippa thought he looked like a reverse elf.

His chest was bare, hulking in size, covered in such intricate tattoos that Philippa couldn't make them out from one another. They seemed to slither over his skin with his deep breaths, coming to life as he sat up straighter at the sight of her.

Heru put one fist to her chest, the other to her abdomen, her elbows straight out. Taz mimicked the motion.

Philippa shyly bowed her head instead.

When the chief moved, it was with great purpose. Leaning forward to observe over Heru and Taz, his dark gaze drank Philippa in. If Philippa were to write about him, she knew what word she would use: imposing.

"*Atun*," Heru began by way of greeting.

The chief held up a massive fist. "Speak in the common language. Our guest should know what we say."

The word *guest* seemed to be strained, as if he didn't quite know the right translation for it. Or maybe, because she was a prisoner. Flashes of the old woman running a tool against the man's back in the tent made her shiver despite the heat.

"Father," Heru adjusted, and Philippa's eyes went wide, "it is with great honor that I bring you the Scribe that Tazmireth hunted in Levanta. Your prize, my chief." Heru held out her hands, as if to present Philippa. When Philippa didn't move forward along the red carpet, Taz gently shoved her forward.

Chewing on the inside of her cheek, Philippa moved towards the chief. Her bare toes ran along the rug's thick stitching nervously. She met his gaze, trying to hold her head up high. He moved to stand, but considered her height deeply before making the choice. Was he nervous that he would scare her?

If he was, he was right. Philippa shuddered in the shadow of Heru's father - Taz's uncle - barely able to find his face as he stepped in front of her. This is where it began, she realized. The torture. The endless tasks she would be forced to perform. It's what made some of the scribes at the end of the war escape to Soffer; they would not be claimed as prizes to be used at someone else's whim.

"I am Olekashan, leader of the Wahanar, He Who Is Seated By The Flame!" His deep voice, thickly accented, boomed through the tent. The fire in the censers shuddered with the vacuum of his words.

Philippa fell to a knee, unsure of what else to do. Besides, it kept her from trembling. Taz snorted behind her. Philippa expected a slap, or a kick, *something* to tell her she was doing this wrong. Her eyes flicked up, looking through her dark lashes, she only saw the chief's feet moving uncomfortably, as if he didn't know what to do, either.

"Stand up little rat," Heru hissed.

She obeyed, her knees wobbling. His fist struck fast. Philippa grimaced, readying for the blow, but it never came. Instead, his palm pinched either side of her face, holding her in place to look at him. The only pain that came was when her feet began to lift off the ground so he could study her closely to his own face.

"You now know my name," he was inches from her, but his voice was not any quieter. Philippa wondered when the last time he'd brushed had been. "Now, we are almost friends."

He dropped her with an unceremonious *thud* on the compact sand floor. Taz rolled her hands at her, urging her to reciprocate.

Philippa rubbed her backside, and sighed as she looked up at the huge man. They were all the same with their greetings, weren't they?

"I am… Philippa Aporo. The uhm, the scribe. Of Levanta. Or Soffer. But you knew that, I think."

Olekashan's thick eyebrows became a hard line. He extended his hand, grabbing hers, and moved it to his face. Philippa awkwardly grabbed his cheek, his skin rough and weathered beneath her fingers. She reluctantly used two hands, since one couldn't fit the magnitude of his skull.

"Again. More… More…" He used his hands to gesture to his chest like he was building up something inside himself, then gestured to her. He sought for the word but settled for, "more *oomph*."

Her ears twitched. Maybe this was the torture. "My name is Philippa Aporo, and I am the scribe you sent for, Olekashan." She didn't think her voice was all that much stronger, but it must have sufficed, because he smiled as if she'd just given him a handful of gold.

But then his smile faded. "You cannot pronounce it. Call me Ole—"

"It annoys you less?" Philippa cut him off.

He laughed once, a deep, hearty sound, before tousling her hair. Except, he didn't know his strength with her, and her brain scrambled in her skull. "She knows much! I like this one! The last we captured was not funny. He is too serious."

Philippa's mouth fell open. "There's more of me? Where, where is he?"

Olekashan waved his hand, as if it was unimportant. "The prisoner's tent. You won't stay there. You will stay here, in my home. Herunavira and Tazmireth will keep you safe."

Herunavira leaned forward, whispering, "the prisoner is not your kind. He just reads a lot."

Her heart sank. She really was alone.

"You are likely wondering why you have been brought here, Philippa Aporo," Ole began, waving them along. Heru jabbed Philippa in the shoulder, urging her to follow. Tazmireth hung her head as she followed. "I would like to hear your guesses."

Philippa tucked a stray hair behind her ear, staring at his massive back as he wove through the fabric rooms of the tent. It felt a lot bigger on the inside than even the outside had suggested. Maybe it was a form of magic, like their glass portal they made to transport them to some unknown part of the desert. She'd heard of other types of magics, apart from her own and the fire she'd seen the Wahanar produce, but watching his shoulders with such delicate tattoos, she knew Scribe magic was intertwined with them all. Maybe the Wahanar and other peoples of the desert had wielded flames before scribes were common, but the ink on their bodies suggested they needed ink to further use their gifts. Spatial magic was rare, if it existed at all. But being inside the luminous silks and cloth, she believed it.

Her ears lowered as she pondered Ole's request. "I've seen what happens to scribes when they are found."

Olekashan glanced over his shoulder, pausing at a closed room in the tent. He knelt down, only now at her height. With a gentle amount of pressure, he squeezed her shoulder in his massive fist, his eyes gentling.

"We know a great deal about being taken from, Philippa Aporo. I am sorry you were in Soffer when Nazheris was. She speaks ill of what happened there. I do not wish to use you. Our laws forbid it." He spoke with conviction, the weight of his hand growing as he continued. "But, as a father, I must use the magic our laws swore off in the ancient times."

When his eyes found his daughter, Philippa felt her own heart clench. There was so much that was unsaid there, stories she would never hear. The ache for her own parents suddenly overwhelmed her, wishing it was *her* father looking at her with such loss and reverence. Heru only looked down, avoiding her father's gaze. Ole seemed hurt, but hid it well as he lifted the hand from her shoulder.

The small hope she'd had when he said he didn't want to use her faded into nothingness when she saw the certainty in his eyes. He was doing this.

"If your laws forbid it, why am I here?"

"Because," he said, pushing his hand through the layers of fabric that separated the room, "my family is more important to me than laws."

A scene all too familiar awaited Philippa inside.

The room was darker than others, only one censer burning, with candles scattered about with countless texts sprawled about on stone tables. Three medicine workers were poring over the slabs, before scuttling back to the flat, white stone that was raised above the others, a small form covered in blankets laying motionless atop it. Crystals that resembled the ones from the glass portal jutted out of the stone, and Philippa immediately knew that she should not touch anything.

An older woman with beads draped over her face from a leather strap serving as a circlet eyed Philippa as she looked up from the body, gasping and dropping her mortar and pestle. It bounced off of the stone resting table, landing with a thick slosh onto the sandy floors. With a wave of her hands, the other two medicine workers hurriedly left the tent through a flap Philippa didn't notice before.

The woman stared at her, her gray eyes sharp and hawkish. Heru's mother, without a doubt.

A slew of words Philippa didn't understand came from Herunavira's mother, which Ole silenced with a hand. Tazmireth remained at the entrance of the room as the fabric entombed them, the sound somehow being kept to this room only. *Magic.*

Philippa followed Ole, rounding the table, Heru hot on her heels. The chief's wife watched her, waiting to strike. Incense burned in the corner of the room, the smell of peppermint filling the air. A soft reprieve from the dryness of the Wahanar homelands.

Toying with Morgana's locket, Philippa felt her heart bursting in her chest with each step she took. She could picture Elodie perfectly, laying so similarly to the body she was approaching. Her breath caught in her throat.

A boy, no older than sixteen, lay on the table. He was skinny, but not from a poor diet, but rather having been stagnant for a long, long time. There were muscles that should have been thicker, had been at one time, were withering away.

Tears welled in her eyes. She couldn't look at Ole. "I cannot fix the dead."

"You insult me by bringing this wretch here!" Herunavira's mother screeched.

Philippa's head snapped up in time to avoid the grasp of the chief's wife. She retreated behind Heru, who was frozen, staring at the boy. *Her brother?*

"The boy is not dead," Ole explained, ignoring his wife's comment, "he is asleep. We haven't woken him in… Many days."

"Was he sick before?" Philippa asked, peeking over Heru's shoulder.

"You see? She knows *nothing*!" Ole's wife screeched.

"She is a scribe of Soffer. The best of their kind. I will not have you questioning me." The warning in his voice was clear, enough to echo in the sound protected room. "She will perform the healing."

"You bring a *vashir* into our home! An unclean! You think she knows more than I about healing the boy?"

Ole went to put a hand on his wife's shoulder, which she swiftly avoided, clutching her shawl closer around her. He sighed, closing his eyes. "She does not know medicine like you, Dagna, no one does. But she has more power than you. She can heal him without medicine."

His words made Dagna press her thin mouth pressing into a hard, thin line. Philippa felt the bitterness of his words with her. She didn't want to be a rift between this family, and didn't want to be in this tent with the expectation that she could heal this boy.

"Fine. Go against the laws. The *Tanvirok* is in three weeks. See what they think when they hear you brought a *vashir* into our home! You will be exiled with the finest scrutiny, Olekashan. This girl was not raised in the ways of her people. She would have been a *child.*"

"I'm twenty-two. I'm not a child," Philippa said, surprised at the evenness of her voice.

Dagna only sneered, sparks appearing between her clenched teeth.

"That said," she continued, feeling their gazes on her, "I have never healed someone who has been asleep for so long. I barely understand what I can do. I don't know if I can help you. I think… I think I should go home. Your laws prevent this, and… I don't know what I'm doing."

That seemed to satisfy Dagna. Ole, on the other hand, looked disappointingly at Herunavira. As if she'd brought him fool's gold.

"Liar."

All eyes whipped to Tazmireth. She stood at the entrance of the room, arms folded and expression sure.

Dagna sneered at her niece, and Philippa thought if the woman set her jaw any tighter, her teeth would crack.

Heru shook her head at her cousin, waving her hand. But Taz didn't seem phased, ignoring her cousin's command for the second time since Philippa had known her.

Taz sauntered over, and glared at Heru for an explanation. The wordless exchange between the two of them read fairly clearly: Tazmireth thought Heru owed her this much.

Sighing, Herunavira recounted the experience of the scorpions in great detail. How they'd fallen fifty feet down, Tazmireth clinging to Philippa to save their catch, breaking an artery on the way down. That, in an effort to save the scribe, Taz had taken a scorpion's daggertail through her kneecap. Philippa wished she'd saved the part about the tendons and blood, but Heru missed no such details. While Ole listened with rapt attention, Dagna's disgust grew with each part of the story.

"I ordered the scribe to heal Tazmireth," Heru continued. "And so she healed her."

"You used a scribe on her, against her will?" Dagna blanched.

Heru nodded.

"I don't believe my daughter would do such a thing."

Tazmireth didn't miss a beat. She cleared her throat, and hiked up part of her layers of fabric to reveal a scar that Philippa didn't know was there. A jagged, ugly thing, almost the shape of an exploding spider web around her knee and a line across her thigh.

"Stars above, amazing," Ole whispered.

The awe was short lived.

Dagna's fingers were around Taz's throat in an instant. Olekashan's hand went to a dagger she hadn't known was there, and Heru stood motionless, caught between her respect for her mother and the love for her cousin.

Only, Tazmireth didn't fight. She met Philippa's gaze, her eyes dark and unyielding. Pity filled them, sorrow creasing her face as she let Dagna throttle her. Moments ago, Philippa wanted to free Tazmireth from Dagna's grasp, but now she understood that what Taz did earned her no favors. She had condemned her to service for Ole.

But the guilt in Tazmireth's eyes was driving Philippa to insanity.

"You have no right to kill her here," Ole warned, "Tazmireth acted on orders. So did the scribe."

Dagna only drew Taz closer to her sneering mouth, her beads swatting the warrior in the face. Taz's lips were turning purple, her eyes bulging. Hatred seethed out of Dagna, before she dropped her.

Taz hit the rug below, gasping for air, but she did not rise. Dagna's rage was palpable, little sparks falling from her tattooed mouth.

"I remove you from the rank of *Ruhvann* underneath Herunavira. You are *vashir,* and you disgust me." Dagna then drew a blade from underneath her shawl, and sliced it across Tazmireth's face.

Philippa cried out, covering her mouth and squeezing her eyes shut.

Dagna muttered something about being unclean again, and Philippa heard her leave. The tent had fallen silent for a moment. She opened her eyes slowly and wished she hadn't.

Tazmireth was cradling herself on the ground, her forehead pressed against the rug, as if she'd melted. Her back wracked with quiet sobs, shoulders shaking with each breath. Olekashan did not look at her. Herunavira was stunned into silence. The boy's body between them all was the only one who reacted, groaning wordlessly.

Philippa's skin was on fire, every hair standing on edge. What did Taz give up for her on the *chance* that she could heal this boy? Why did it feel like she was stolen to help them, but that the one person who had been kind to her, was paying all of the prices?

Tazmireth made a sound that Philippa didn't think could come from her. A deep, heavy weeping that filled the tent. A cry that strangled her throat.

Herunavira was on her knees in an instant, going to lift her cousin by the shoulders. Tazmireth wretched backwards like it hurt to be touched. Hot, ugly tears streamed down her face, mingling with the blood dripping from just underneath her eye.

Heru moved to touch her again, but Taz shoved her back with so much force that Herunavira hit the resting table. Taz jabbed an angry finger in Heru's face, words spilling out of her like fire, as actual flames lit up her tattooed palm.

Her wild gestures were enough to make Philippa cry. She couldn't understand the words, but she saw how Taz madly waved between Heru, herself, and Philippa, and the message was clear enough.

You did this to me. I did this for you. Get away from me.

Tazmireth backhanded the blood pouring from her face and slunk away, not daring to glance back at the small group of them left in the tent.

When Philippa urged herself out of paralysis, she looked to the chief and nearly jumped out of her skin.

Ole watched her intently. She couldn't run. They would catch her again. But maybe Dagna was convincing enough to let her be taken home?

No. Dagna wouldn't send her home. She'd send her head on a spike back to Levanta to warn them not to send another Scribe to her home. She was *vashir,* unclean, and Tazmireth paid the price for it.

"What say you, Philippa Aporo?" Ole asked, his voice thin.

Philippa looked down at the boy. Then, to Heru, still on her knees.

Finally, her gaze landed on the chief, desperate to save his family. She knew the feeling.

The only way she had a chance of keeping her promise to Raff, was if she healed this boy. She took in the severity of the concern on Olekashan's face, this massive man of myth, who had *asked* her for help.

Philippa exhaled, stretching her fingers to quiet their anxious buzzing.

"Call me Pip."

CHAPTER TEN ✧

Philippa was permitted to sleep in a guarded portion of the tent that night by herself. Every time she closed her eyes, she felt phantom hands wrapping around her throat or a dagger slicing her face. The little sleep she got was riddled with nightmares of ink being driven into an unwilling back, hands clawing to get away. She saw her father most of all.

In the morning, she was escorted to the boy's healing room, who she'd come to understand was called Panu, which was, of course, the shortened version of his name. One day she'd learn how to pronounce all of them.

His was the least challenging thus far - Panukirah - which they hadn't given her a translation for yet like the rest of them. Though Philippa could pronounce it, even the healers affectionately seemed to call him strictly Panu, so that is what she tried to do, too.

Inside his healing room, everything was as it had been the night before. She looked at the Wahanar who'd escorted her across the tent, an older man who never quite looked her in the eye, and cautiously decided that she could look through whatever she wanted in the room.

Most of the stone tablets were written in Wahatan, and she'd had to simply cast it aside when she couldn't understand it. The boy slept quietly in the room all hours of the day, never waking to medicine workers refilling the incense or if Philippa came to look at him for clues.

He looked rather sad, she thought, for supposedly being asleep.

Humming to herself, she made a stack of information with a few words she could understand, and a stack that she couldn't begin to decipher. The medicine workers, loyal to Dagna, ignored her faithfully, even when she tried to ask questions.

Olekashan hadn't seemed to mind that she wanted the entire three weeks before their *Tanvirok,* which she'd come to understand was a meeting between all the tribe's leaders. These Wahanar were one of three major groups of the natives of Sapria.

The chief had been the most talkative and understanding since she'd arrived the day before, though he was hardly around. He had other things to attend to, as any leader would, but she could tell the condition of his son was weighing on him. How could it not? The boy was supposed to be having fun with his friends, or… Well, whatever Wahanar youth did other than wrestle; a pair of them had nearly taken out a tent pole earlier in the day when they were roughhousing in the common area.

Philippa glanced down at Panu, noting his strong nose and dark strip of hair down the center of his head. He looked very much like Heru.

Herunavira had not been back since the exchange with Dagna. Her package had been delivered, and she was now free to be hands off from Philippa.

As she rifled through old, delicate parchment, Philippa wondered why Heru had been so eager to use her abilities if they disgusted her so much. She'd been willing to let her die, thankfully Taz wasn't, if it meant saving her cousin. But Heru wasn't willing to tell her own mother that she'd ordered a scribe to heal Tazmireth. Families, Philippa knew, were complicated. Her own included. Maybe that was enough of an explanation.

She checked the dial they kept on the floor of the tent, which used mirrors to reflect the sun outside to tell the time. Morgana would be bringing in the day's catch right about then. Raff would either be with Elodie, or at the storyteller's shop where a weathered old man would spin tales of far away places. Stars, Raff loved those fairy tales.

A hum of dismay snapped her from her thoughts.

Taz was standing across from her, arms crossed. A pink, thin line was livid against her cheek. She gestured to Philippa and the stone notes, as if she knew that she was slacking off.

"I'm allowed to take breaks, your uncle said so himself."

Taz lifted an eyebrow.

"Well, I don't exactly know *what* I'm doing. No one has left ink in this stuffy room, I haven't eaten since… Well, I don't know when. Before we arrived. And, to be perfectly honest with you, Taz, I'm a little jumpy about being tortured, so if you wouldn't mind *not* sneaking up on me, that would be great."

Taz rolled her eyes and tore one of the rare papers Philippa had been able to find from her hand. She skimmed the words, and slowly, her expression was filled with confusion. Medical jargon, likely.

"Who watches me when you're not here, anyway?" Philippa asked.

The warrior made her fingers into two horns on her forehead, and Philippa smacked her lips in response. Of course, Nazheris. The one she'd met when they first abducted Philippa had been constantly easing around the chief's tents. Somehow, Philippa could tell it was the same one. The others she had seen were less respectful of her space than the first she had met.

At least now she could readily understand Tazmireth. They were getting fairly good at the whole silent communication tactic.

Tazmireth disappeared past the tent flaps for a few minutes, and returned with a wooden bowl filled with dried meat that sat in a bowl of stew. Philippa graciously accepted, shoveling the portions into her mouth. The food wasn't seasoned like in Levanta, with salt and herbs, but rather filled with spices and peppers that tingled on her tongue. It was *delicious.*

She licked her fingers, thanking Taz with a nod, who just smiled as she ate.

But it was clear Tazmireth's mind was elsewhere.

"I didn't see you sleeping anywhere in Ole's tent last night," Philippa said slowly, trying not to tread too far. Taz wasn't one for soft conversations. "I thought you lived here. Ole said you'd protect me."

Tazmireth took the bowl from her hands and stirred the contents with her finger. Philippa decided she would *not* be sharing food with her again. Taz pursed her lips, then shook her head as she lowered her gaze. She didn't sleep there anymore, then. Not since she'd been demoted by Dagna.

"I know you don't like apologies," Philippa began, and Taz leveled a look at her that could crush mountains. She quickly pivoted her thoughts. "So, I won't give you one."

Taz looked impressed.

"Help me figure all this out. I don't know what I'm doing."

Taz gestured to her leg, starting to pull up the skirt she was wearing that day, when Philippa quickly stopped her. She had seen far too much of that woman already.

"Healing you wasn't the same as this. You were hurt and…" The words caught in her throat. Philippa stared at the swirling stew, picturing her mind making the same motion. "You were hurt, and I couldn't let you die. I wanted nothing more than to help you. Because you're my friend."

After their brief time together, it was hard to grasp that she felt this way, but she did. Maybe something about Taz's rough edges and big heart made her think of her sister.

Philippa pointedly ignored the tears welling up in Tazmireth's eyes. She'd shut Philippa out again if she dug too deeply into her emotions. Though Ole seemed rather free with his, Taz wasn't the chief, or his daughter. She had to operate on different terms.

Taz nodded in agreement. The scar on her cheek *had* to burn with the tear that escaped her eye. Without thinking, Philippa wiped it away, and Taz caught her hand, squeezing her wrist.

"You're not weak," Philippa whispered. "Not to me. You're allowed to be in pain."

In an instant, Tazmireth pulled her forward and into her arms, embracing her. Philippa did her best to ignore the shudder of the warrior's shoulders that she hadn't even let her cousin comfort. Her strong, muscled arms reminded her of hugging her sister. Tears welled up in her own eyes, and she didn't fight them from spilling. She had to be strong now. She'd gotten Tazmireth ousted and hurt, and she made a promise to heal Panu. Both things she held close to her heart, and as Tazmireth pulled away, she knew what mattered more to her.

They couldn't communicate with one another like they could with their own people, but in that moment, they became each other's people.

"Now," Philippa said, halfheartedly chuckling and wiping her own tears away, "you tell your chief that if I'm going to heal Panu, I need a guard, and that the only Wahanar I trust is you."

CHAPTER ELEVEN ✧

Philippa was no healer. Of that, she had been made very aware, since her frequent visits from Dagna were often filled with more threats than anything else. The chief's wife had taken every opportunity to inform Philippa that she was not only a master of medicine, but poison as well.

Olekashan had ordered Dagna to stop entering Panu's part of their home, which she was all too eager to do. The venom in the older woman's eyes spoke nothing of motherly love for Panu.

At least the chief had granted Philippa the courtesy of having Tazmireth on hand at all times. Though the warrior had been stripped of her rank of being Herunavira's right hand soldier, Taz still could find purpose in protecting Philippa. The Wahanar woman took it a bit too seriously.

Philippa sifted through the old documents as she chewed on the inside of her lip, thinking back to the evening before when Tazmireth had pleaded her case to Heru and Ole. The way she'd looked at her superiors was not full of hate or loathing, but earnestness. Maybe it was because Tazmireth had seen Philippa's power, had felt the good it could do, or maybe it was just to scramble for some semblance of belonging again after her aunt had removed her. Whatever the reason, Philippa had watched the tall warrior humble herself before her family - her leaders - and plead her case.

And they listened.

Herunavira hadn't answered Tazmireth's request, only turned away and remained in silence. Olekashan had smiled, giving his niece a squeeze on her shoulder and nodding. That was enough for her.

But having Tazmireth around also gave Philippa angst. She would surely report to Ole and Dagna that Philippa was *failing.*

She'd tried to tell them on the first day that this was different than when she had healed Taz, but they still seemed so hopeful. Ole, at least.

But focusing on why her using mud and dye to write on the boy hadn't worked like it had with others gave her more purpose beyond her self loathing. Philippa's mind had been fairly quiet, giving her peace the past two days of working with Panu, the voice only warning her when Dagna was around.

You've almost forgotten that you've killed someone, haven't you?

Her head snapped up.

She had to get this done. Had to get home.

But what would be waiting for her there, in Levanta? Stars, had Morgana been ousted for harboring a scribe? Morgana had never presented any signs of magic, even as a child. It had irked their father to no end, but the gift was no certainty when having children.

How badly Philippa wanted the pit in her stomach to fall away, to speak to her sister. Morgana *should* have been the one born with scribe magic. She would know how to harness it, when to wield it and when to refrain. She was always better at that, Philippa thought. Yet, there was no way to get in touch with her. None.

Unless… No.

There was no ink to write to her sister. Besides, she hadn't practiced the magic of transporting a written letter since she was a child.

That hasn't stopped you recently, has it?

She covered her ears. That new sarcasm to the voice was growing tiresome.

Philippa closed her eyes and breathed. She took in the waxiness of the burning candles, the minty refreshment of incense burning nearby.

Do this for Morgana, her mind whispered, *for Raff. For your family.*

Her eyes fluttered open. She turned to Panukirah, who still lay fast asleep on his raised table, never speaking, never giving her clues as to what had happened to him. Gently, Philippa laid a hand on his forehead. He was warm, but not feverish, betraying no signs of what was actually ailing him.

Tazmireth cleared her throat and shrugged her shoulders.

"I don't know what's wrong," Philippa replied, voice soft. "Is there any more dye in here? I tried writing on him earlier with it, but…"

There was no need to finish her sentence. Tazmireth nodded with a tight lipped smile, feigning encouragement, but they both knew that all of Philippa's earlier attempts had done nothing for the boy.

Philippa's warrior friend disappeared behind a tent flap for a moment, and returned with a leather pouch that had been stained purple on the bottom. Tazmireth tossed it to Philippa, who barely caught it, nearly sending its contents onto the sandy floor below. She glowered at the Wahanar, but Tazmireth was already back in a chair by the doorway, closing her eyes to rest.

Philippa rolled her eyes, about to open the pouch, when a snore tore through the tent. Inside the sound barrier of the room, she startled, heart jumping into her throat.

Woodenly, Philippa turned around, and all of the air whooshed out of her. That slimy Nazheris was slumbering just by the sundial, nostrils flaring with its velvety, guttural snoring. Those creatures were going to be the death of her, she just knew it.

Back to the boy, she reminded herself.

She took the pouch to the desk, and dipped her fingers into the water bowl they'd provided for her. With shaking hands, she pressed a fingertip into the chalky dye inside the leather pouch, coating her index with as much dye as possible. Gingerly, she approached Panu's still form and tried to steady herself for the magic about to leave her. Once he was awake, she could go home.

Morgana. Raff.

She wanted them more than anything in the world.

Indigo smeared Panukirah's forehead as she swiped her finger across it. The first time she'd tried, she had used the dye to ask his body to heal, which had led nowhere. If he wasn't sick, and this was some other oddity happening to him, she would have to try a different tactic.

Awaken, she wrote.

The room remained silent. Her body felt the same, sunburnt and tired, but not exhausted. Nothing had come out of her. She rewetted her fingers and wrote again, this time over his heart.

There.

A tingling.

Philippa closed her eyes.

A sharp, sizzling sensation on her hand.

No, her wrist.

Sizzling.

Like…

"Fire!" Philippa reeled backwards, knocking into the table, sending vials and pouches flying down.

Tazmireth was up in an instant, and crouching over where Philippa had fallen.

The fire licked at her wrist, at her fingers, at her palm, but it wasn't eating at her flesh. Philippa stared in horror as a white-hot flame danced over her skin, encircling her hand like layered bracelets and rings to adorn her ruddy appendage.

"Is this you?" Tazmireth's common tongue startled her even more, but the warrior's dark eyes were fixated on Philippa's flaming hand in sheer terror. Taz thought this was her scribe magic, imitating the Wahanar's. Despite having an affection for Philippa, she could tell that her magic frightened her friend.

Philippa's mouth was so dry that no words came out when she tried to speak. Eventually, she shook her head, and Tazmireth eyed her more carefully. Then, the Wahanar's eyes lit up as she slowly turned back towards the table.

Standing over Panu's body was the Nazheris. Her flame was strong between her jagged horns, but her orb-like eyes were sadly turned down to Panu.

Tazmireth turned back to Philippa and her expression nearly scared Philippa out of her skin. Taz was smiling like a wild hyena, wide and hungry, all teeth.

The warrior spat out so many words in her own language that Philippa couldn't begin to keep up. Then, Tazmireth was pulling Philippa to her feet, completely ignoring that her hand was still very much *encased in fire.*

Taz broke into a run, dragging Philippa who was still staring at her palm in bewilderment. Through and through the tent rooms they went, each time startling caretakers or extended family members that Taz paid no mind to. In one room, they'd stumbled upon the privy, which was really just a big hole in the sand, but Tazmireth marched in there anyway, angering a Wahanar man that Philippa understood to be a respected elder among the people.

Philippa awkwardly waved at him and kept her eyes downcast.

Taz didn't stop dragging her until they were outside of the tent, and she whipped around with a crazed look in her eye until she spotted the chief. Philippa's wrist ached, feeling like it had been pulled out of its joint, but she was so fixated on the fire around her hand that was now cooling to a deep orange that she barely even noticed when Tazmireth had started telling Ole what was going on.

"Is this true?" Olekashan's voice broke Philippa out from her bewilderment.

She blinked at him. Held up her hand. "Help."

Beside him, Dagna sneered, her eyes locked on Philippa's smoldering hand.

Philippa winced as Ole reached out his massive hand, but it was surprisingly soft as he took her by the flaming wrist and turned her hand over in his palm. He looked to Tazmireth and asked, "Nazheris did this?"

Swallowing hard, Philippa couldn't help but picture the smoldering bodies in Soffer with those creatures harrowing screeches echoing in the night.

Tazmireth nodded.

Ole turned to his wife briefly, who clicked her tongue and waved her hand away. Olekashan, however, seemed in pure amazement. "Do you know what this means, Little Pip?"

She didn't say what she was thinking, and thankfully, he continued on his own.

The chief smiled. "Panu's magic still lives. It breathes. From him, to Nazheris, to you."

Her ears twitched. Philippa didn't understand what any of that meant. "Does that mean he'll wake up?"

Dagna cackled and stood, pushing her husband aside to get a better look at Philippa's hand. The healer woman's grip was not like her husbands, she was all nails and pressure, until she clasped her large hand over the flame and completely snuffed it out. Though it hurt, Philippa was grateful that the fire was gone.

"She asks *us* if he will wake. What do you think of your scribe now, Olekashan, He Who Sits By The Stupid?" Dagna asked, turning sharply so that her beads smacked Philippa in the face.

Other Wahanar had started to gather, no doubt having seen Tazmireth parade Philippa around like a madwoman. Philippa grimaced, sure that Ole was embarrassed of his wife speaking to him in such a way in front of their people.

But when she looked at him again, he just seemed disappointed. Then, a mask quickly fell into place, a placated smile replacing how he truly felt as he took in Philippa.

"You are small, Little Pip, but you are strong. Nazheris and Panu are very close. She had watched him since he was a small child. They are like siblings. His flame connected to hers." The chief then gingerly took Philippa's hand and raised it for the crowd to see, effectively hoisting her up off the ground by her arm. She whirled her free hand, trying for balance, but it was no use. Her cheeks rushed with heat as she let herself dangle from the chief's grip.

"Listen well, brothers! Sisters! Children! The scribe has news! Dear Panukirah lives! His magic is strong! Soon, we will celebrate!" His voice thundered over the sandy courtyard, all the way to the prisoner's tent, the structure's flaps blowing open as if in response to his declaration. Inside, Philippa saw a glimpse of a dark form hovered over a low table, in chains, scribbling madly against a piece of parchment, and there was a glint of sunlight off of something glass-like inside.

So *that's* where they were keeping him. She hadn't seen any sign of the other prisoner since she'd arrived, although she hadn't really left Ole's tent.

Strong outcries ripped her from her intrigue, as some of the Wahanar lit their flames in excitement over the news. Some of them seemed like they were happy to hear about Panu, but they glowered at her like she was a snake in the grass.

Philippa tossed and turned in her blankets, unable to get comfortable in the darkened room. The fabric walls rippled around her as the wind howled outside, mimicking every monster her mind could conjure.

Sighing, she sat up and pressed her palms to her face.

She was none the wiser about the flame that had touched her hand, or how to wake Panu. Something was utterly *wrong* about the sleep he was in, and nobody had an explanation for her. Everyone she'd asked, and really, those who'd been willing to speak to a *vashir,* had said that Panu had suffered no accidents, or that anyone would wish him any harm.

He was well loved, evidently very gifted in his powers at such a young age.

They may not wish him any harm, but they were certainly willing to just let him sleep forever, because even those who had answered her did it with disgust written all over their faces.

She groaned, stretching her back and wiggling her toes on the woven rug. Three days already in the Wahanar camp, and she had no answers. When she tried to scribe or alter Panu, it felt like she was pressing her mind up against a wall. A sheer amount of *nothingness* that was forcing her magic to stay in her body.

Philippa tried to recall everything her father had taught her about their magic, sure that she was missing something. But between his lessons and the teachings of the instructors back in Soffer, she could not think of anything that she'd been doing *wrong.* There were surely things about her magic she simply didn't understand, like why she could work her magic without ink sometimes, but what she *did* know was that Panu should have at least reacted to what she'd been doing.

Elodie eventually had. Despite what it cost.

Her head snapped up. Maybe *that* was it. Lucille had wanted so badly to heal her child, that she was willing to give her life. Maybe Philippa didn't want it enough. Maybe if one of Panu's family members—

No.

A dullness settled on Philippa's shoulders as she pictured a white sheet covering Elodie's mother. She would not ask someone to do that ever again.

There had to be answers elsewhere.

Blindly feeling around her small sleeping quarters, Philippa sought the few pieces of parchment she'd stolen from Panu's healing room. She'd been trying to piece together some of the language of the people, in case it could yield anything about what had happened to Panu.

When she found the stray pieces of parchment, she strained her eyes in the dark to read some of the swirling, harsh script of the Wahanar. There were some words she could decipher based on their spoken language, but nothing major of note.

Groaning, she set the papers down and pictured the boy's face in her mind. So harsh, like Herunavira's, but there was a kindness to his features that betrayed his nature even in his sleep. Something so unlike the rest of the little family Philippa had been thrust into the midst of.

Her hand absentmindedly went to the locket around her neck. She touched the cool metal, letting it bite her flesh, and then walked her hand methodically over her shoulder to her shoulder blade, where she always seemed to ache when she was over stressed.

Like the Wahanar, she had dark lines about herself, too. Morgana had a nearly matching mark on her shoulder, but they didn't talk about it. Even in Soffer, when things were peaceful, it didn't mean things were always *right.*

It's what drove her half brother to be outcast. To leave. Philippa wondered if the historians and fanatics in Soffer had inked his shoulder, too.

Pushing the dredge of memories away, Philippa popped open the locket. Morgana had been wearing it when they escaped Soffer, and had never taken it off since.

Tears pricked Philippa's eyes as she peered inside, her eyes finally adjusting to the darkness to look at their little family portrait inside. Morgana always talked about how she should replace the art inside, get a piece done of their little family of three. But Philippa couldn't imagine taking out the drawing of her mother's face.

The softness of her mother's mouth, the downward curve of her nose. Philippa took a finger and ran down the bridge of her own nose, the sensation unsatisfactory in comparison to when her mother would trace it for her.

A deep sob welled up in her chest, and she didn't bother choking it back. It was like she'd been collecting stones all of her life and swallowing them, letting them settle in her chest so that one day she might wade back into the ocean that saved her and sink to the bottom. The heaviness in her chest threatened to come all the way up now, to consume her in tears and let the reprieve of crying ease her soul.

Just when she was on the edge of letting it all go, Philippa swallowed it back down.

She needed that weight, that heaviness, that *guilt*. It was all she had known, all she could be. She had failed so, so very much, and she didn't deserve to let herself rid the weight of it now. That heavy, thick sludge of worthlessness kept her going.

She had to prove to others that she wasn't that *thing*, that concave mass of failure and emptiness and *waste*, and only then would some of that weight go away. She had failed her mother, failed her sister and her nephew, so she had to *earn* feeling light.

But it was all okay.

Her fingers were trembling, but it was all okay.

If she could just help this family, help *her* family, it would be worth it.

Then she would feel that soft relief of worthiness seep into her bones, like she'd always pictured.

Philippa curled in on herself, staring at her mother's face in the locket. She was being cynical, she knew, cradling herself like a child, when she should be working on saving Panu. She wouldn't wish the way she was feeling on her worst enemy. But…

It was different, with herself.

She knew it wasn't healthy, wasn't right, but it was her.

Once she helped Ole and his family, she could go home and be free of this weight.

Were you free of it when you were back in Levanta, wanting more?

Her mind's voice was soft, curling like fine smelling smoke around her skull. Luring her to a conclusion she wasn't ready to face: that she had, and would, always amount to nothing. That her desire for adventure wasn't enough when it actually came and called her out of Levanta, and nothing would ever *be* enough because how could the cycle of needing to help others ever solve *anything?*

Stars, she was driving herself mad.

Worthless, worthless, worthless…

She wanted to grit her teeth. To slam the locket shut. To scream into the night.

But none of that fight was inside her tonight.

No, tonight she was not the scribe, the *vashir,* a sister, or an aunt. Tonight she was Philippa Aporo, the version of her soul that she kept to herself, because it was too hard to show others.

Tonight, she sat in a catatonic silence, too paralyzed to move, clutching the locket like an artery to stop the bleeding.

So she bled. Bled into the dark air of the tent, where she would continue to fail tomorrow, because even if she healed the boy, her worth was only determined by what she could accomplish, and like a condemned clock, it always reset after the task was done.

That night, Philippa Aporo did not sleep. Did not dream. Did not think.

She let emptiness and thoughtlessness consume her into the wane hours of the morning, when she would paint on a smile and mask her thoughts with an eager attitude.

No, that night she was simply herself; someone who she did not think deserved any magic, any connection, any reprieve.

Because she was a failure. Always had been. Always would be.

For what use was the mightiest magic when its vessel was so worthless?

CHAPTER TWELVE ✧

On the fourth day, after failing once more to gain any ground with Panu, Philippa peeked out of the healing room.

Footsteps padded against the sand in nearby rooms, separated only by fabric and evidently no sound barriers. Voices were hushed, but she could hear light laughter and even some bickering.

It was odd, Philippa thought, that the leader of a people welcomed all who wanted into his home. Olekashan must've had great trust in all of his people to allow that, but then again, it only seemed odd because the rulers Philippa had heard about were strictly cruel and greedy. Chief Ole did not seem either of those things. His daughter, surely, but the past few days, he seemed more concerned with giving Philippa room to work with Panu undisturbed than anything else.

Philippa ducked back into Panu's room, effectively cutting off all sound from outside. Her ears twitched at the sudden vacuum of air, and she had to clamp her hands over them to stop the incessant reaction.

Her eyes locked on the bag of dye.

With a sigh, she dipped her fingers inside after wetting them and once again pressed her hand to Panu's body. The Nazheris, ever present, snored in the corner. Philippa shuddered at the memory of the creature's flame twirling around her hand, about how unnatural it felt.

Pushing the thought away, she began to write an entire sentence over Panukirah's body.

Let me understand

Expecting nothing to happen, she stood idly at his side, but when her hand fell away, something *lurched* inside her mind. She slapped a hand to her forehead, dizziness overwhelming her.

Darkness and fire and sparks and *nothing,* a deep well of inky blackness cascaded in her vision, a sensation that was distinctly not hers.

Her hearing faded out, as if she'd been placed in a room opposite the one she was really in. She stumbled, and flung her hands to the side to catch herself, feeling bottles cascade under her palms as they tumbled down. When they hit the sand below, it sounded like she was underwater, and that's when she froze.

Raising a shaking hand, she snapped her fingers, right next to her ear. Again, it was like the sound came from a dream, a waterlogged room next door.

Blindly, she felt her way back to Panu's table, knowing the coolness of the stone intimately now. As awkward as it felt, she reached out, and found the bulge of his shoulder, traveling up to find his ear. She snapped again.

Her head wrenched sideways as an explosion of sound burst in her eardrum.

Ringing ensued, effectively deafening her.

Then she was sure.

She was seeing and hearing in *Panu's* mind. Which meant he was alive, but his hearing was distorted, and the sensation of being locked in the darkness was making her bones itch. She had the urge to rip her skin off, to pry her way out, to burn the shell that was trapping her in isolation.

It was so *lonely.*

Lonely enough that her real throat tightened, her own eyes wetting. She was about to swipe off the dye she'd used, to see if it would allow her to come back to her own senses, but as she blindly hovered a hand over where she'd remembered writing, the sensation changed. Though still in darkness, a flash of fire sparked in the corners of her vision, like distant fireworks exploding in the night sky.

Panu wasn't just alive, he was fighting.

Philippa drew her hand away, and the sensation worsened. Walls of flames, a pillar of fire, clawing around her eyes, trying to grab her.

He knew she was there.

The organ in her chest began to beat wildly.

He was afraid.

Softly, she replaced her hand on his shoulder, and the light flames dulled to a low roar, back to pinpricks. After snapping into his ear like an idiot, she knew he could hear clearly if she was close enough. Somehow, her magic had connected them. Maybe he could offer answers.

Bending down in the darkness, Philippa put her mouth near his head. "Can you tell me what's happened to you? Your family is worried sick."

Nothing changed. The little sparks continued to pop, but she heard her voice through his ears, and despite hearing her, Panu gave no clues as to what was going on.

Philippa sighed, the sound pooling in her own mind from the boy's senses. She patted his shoulder.

"I'm sorry. I don't know what to do. I'm going to cut this connection now, if I can."

When she finished speaking, the flames began to fizzle and boil up the center of her dark vision.

"I'll still be here. Even when you can't hear me, I'll be around," Philippa assured him. "To figure this out, I need to be able to see. You're going to be alright. Now that I know you can hear us, I'll send your family to you, alright? They can speak to you even when you can't respond."

She waited a few moments, but when he didn't make any kind of protest, she swiped her arm across the still wet dye. Color and shapes began to reform before her eyes. Blinking away what felt like vertigo, Philippa steadied herself on the edge of his stone slab until she could see straight again.

It may not have yielded what she'd hoped - answers - but now she knew that her magic wasn't denying her. It was trying to connect, to push outward and into Panu, but simply trying to wake him was like trying to hold back the ocean. Something was cutting her off, locking her out.

Her fingers curled into her palms. Stars, she needed him to *wake up*. Part of her felt like that whole ordeal was a product of her imagination, especially since she'd never heard of that kind of reaction from using scribe magic.

Philippa was about to chalk it all up to her mind playing tricks on her, when she stopped and stared at Panukirah.

His eyes were still closed, but he was smiling.

***

Philippa swore under her breath.

Ahead of her, she was facing another wall of red fabric. The chief's pavilion was more maze than home, and she'd really only memorized the route from her sleeping quarters to Panu's healing room. She had the strongest urge to throw her arms to the sides, but then she would've dropped the slew of supplies she'd brought from Panu's room; the leather pouch of dye, a fragile parchment of medical terms in the Wahanar language, and a nearly empty pouch of water.

She was trying to find chief Olekashan to tell him of her discovery, but every hallway led to a dead end or to other healer's quarters rooms, of which the healers inside glared at her.

About to give up, Philippa turned to retrace her steps, when she heard voices. She clutched her items closer, peering around the corner of fabric walls, trying to find the origin of the sound. Two distinct voices, both women, and one made Philippa smile.

It was Tazmireth's voice, speaking in Wahanar.

The only, as Philippa wandered closer, made her blood curdle. Heru's voice sounded *livid.*

The chief's daughter wasn't screaming, but Heru's voice couldn't be classified as *quiet* either.

Taz's voice shot back a cool, collected response, which only earned a bark from Heru. Philippa slowed her steps when she could start to make out some of the Wahanar words she knew already, and peeked around a rippling woven wall.

She dropped everything in her arms. Thankfully, they landed without any noise comparable to the raised voices of the two cousins before her.

But Heru was in Tazmireth's face, a dark blade drawn, gesturing wildly between Taz and the air.

Philippa would've said something, but Taz looked rather bored, staring her cousin down like an overtired parent might sate their child's ramblings.

Whatever was being talked about, was one hundred percent *none* of Philippa's business. Which meant she was deeply and unchangeably intrigued. After her odd results with connecting to Panu, she was feeling gutsy, and she gathered the dye pouch and other fallen items into a neat line on the sandy floor.

Hiding behind the fabric, the cousins' argument still hot, Philippa skipped wetting her fingers and dove straight into the dye pouch. Her eyes darted between the materials, unsure of how to do this, when she finally bit her cheek and just *acted.*

Faster, faster, faster...

She swiped the chalky dye across the medical parchment as quickly as she could, hoping the dusty writing would simply grant her a temporary response.

On the parchment, she wrote: *let me understand, let me hear*

Then, she dusted the rest of the dye onto her ears.

Philippa's fingers suddenly felt heavy, as if detached from her body. The price of the alteration had been paid with her energy, and she quietly sat back on her haunches as tiredness trickled into her consciousness.

"My father is a fool! We should have never brought that unclean woman here. She cannot wake Panu, no matter how hard she tries."

It took a solid ten seconds before Philippa realized that she was hearing two versions of the same words at once.

She blinked and rubbed her ears. It had been Heru's voice. Herunavira was still rambling and ranting, so Philippa covered one ear, and the common language version of Heru's voice deafened. When she covered her other ear, the Wahanar words were garbled.

Philippa covered her mouth as an excited laugh bubbled forward. She bit her lip, reminding herself what she was there for.

Taz's voice responded coolly, "It has only been four days."

"*Four!* She healed you in a night! I don't trust her. Maybe she wants something from us. The scribes ran over our people in the past, what would stop them from wanting to use us now?" Heru's voice was strained, tight. Philippa didn't know what Heru had meant by the scribes of old harming the Wahanar, but based on what Philippa knew of her own people's history, she didn't put it past the old scribes.

"Little Philippa Aporo does not *want* anything other than to go home. She is a good person." Tazmireth said, and Philippa could picture the warrior's easy smile as she dissuaded her cousin.

Heru smacked her lips. "You only say that because she saved your life. I should never have asked her to heal you. Then father would have no reason to trust that she had any power."

Philippa peeked around the corner, and her heart dropped.

Tazmireth's arms were at her sides, but now she crossed them, covering her heart. Shielding herself. "So you wish you had never saved my life."

Heru's hawk tattoo distorted her face as she blanched. But then she set her brow bone into a tight, harsh line, her mouth hard. "I owed you a life debt."

Nodding with pursed lips, Taz stepped back, putting distance between herself and her cousin. "Then it is paid. Do not keep trying to convince uncle to get rid of the scribe. She's here to help. *You* of all people should want her to succeed."

That, of all things, seemed to sting Herunavira. "I may do whatever I please. Panu does not need to be tainted by that woman's magic."

With an icy calm, Tazmireth took back the space she'd initially put between them. She stood over Heru, their noses almost touching. "If you try anything, I will stop you."

Herunavira set her jaw and bared her teeth. "What has happened to you? You are scared of scribe magic. As children you *wet yourself* when we were told stories. You used to be my Heart Guard, my *ruvahn*. You would choose that unclean woman, a *stranger*, over me?"

Taz nodded, just a fraction. "I fear her magic. I do not fear her."

Heru scowled. "Answer my question, cousin."

Half hiding behind the curtain, Philippa was holding her breath. She didn't realize how far the division of her presence had spread, certainly not between the cousins that had seemed so strong together.

Tazmireth pointed to the new scar on her cheek. "You did not stop your mother. I spoke up for you, for the scribe, so that Panu may be healed. You would have stood by and said nothing, and Dagna would have exiled him into the desert to rot, because she sees him as weak. Do you know what I think, cousin? I think the weak one in this camp is you. You who would not speak up for the one who should matter most to you, little Panu. You ask if I would choose the scribe over you? I choose who my heart says. As you reminded me, I am no longer your Heart Guard. You let that happen, too. So my heart follows someone good. Someone who I think is trying to do well. Tell me cousin, do either of those things sound like I speak of you?"

It was hard to tell when Herunavira's expression shifted from gutted to bloodthirsty. Whenever the change happened, her body tensed and sprang into action. Heru shoved her palm underneath Tazmireth's jaw, shoving her head backwards.

Taz held her ground, snapping her jaw like a shark at Heru's hand.

Philippa gaped, her body locked in place, unsure of whether to call for help or let this play out. But the way the cousins fought each other, it was clear that this was not the first time.

After exchanging a few blows, they both stood apart, both bleeding from their faces, at a stand still. Philippa exhaled, her shoulders drooping with relief.

Then Heru flashed her blade and charged.

CHAPTER THIRTEEN ✧

Philippa yelled for Heru to stop, but it was too late.

The warrior princess charged Tazmireth, blade aiming low, for the gut, when Philippa felt a rush of air that sent her careening to the ground.

Both of the cousins froze as the Nazheris barreled forward.

Its sinewy wings were spread wide, with long strides like a war horse on the charge. The flame between its horns grew taller, hotter, burning white, and as it lowered its head, it aimed right for Herunavira.

In the span of seconds, Tazmireth stepped in front of the Nazheris, blocking its path. The dragon-like creature dug its claws into the sand, trying to stop.

The Nazheris was about to run straight into Tazmireth, when Taz opened up her arms, wrapped them around the writhing body of the beast. With a grunt, Tazmireth leaned into the motion of the Nazheris, toppling it over, and landing atop the monster with a thud.

Heru stood where she was *supposed* to be flattened, and Philippa thought she would be looking in bewilderment at her cousin, but she was doing something much, much worse.

Herunavira's black eyes were fixed straight on Philippa. The warrior's chest was heaving from exertion, her lip bloodied. Running a hand over the stubble of hair starting to sprout from her head, Herunavira composed herself, muttering in her own language under her breath.

Philippa touched her ears, the dye having worn off in effect, and leaving her in the dark about what Heru was whispering about now. Fear thrummed between her ribs as she watched Heru slowly cool off her bloodlust. Black eyes darting between Philippa and Tazmireth, Heru cleared her throat and stalked out of the tent room.

Limbs like jelly, Philippa sank back onto the ground. She was sure that Heru was going to scream at her for sneaking around, at the very least spit in her direction.

Tazmireth clambered off of the Nazheris, dusting off her hands, and patting the creature on the snout. It hooted - yes, hooted - playfully, before lowering its head and slinking off past Philippa to return to Panu's side.

When Taz looked at her, Philippa realized that she wasn't out of the woods yet. Tazmireth walked over, grabbed Philippa's shoulders, but then bent to pick up her fallen items.

Taz met Philippa's green eyes and shrugged. "Training," the warrior offered in the common tongue.

Philippa blinked.

Taz and Heru had no way of knowing that she just understood every word that was just said, but hearing Tazmireth lie to her face about it made Philippa's cheeks burn. The woman before her had just defended her honor, on a rather shaky basis, and denounced her belief in her cousin all in one go. It was enough to make Philippa want to cry, but then she'd have to explain to Taz what she'd really done.

Instead, she plastered on a smile, and told her friend what she'd discovered with Panu.

CHAPTER FOURTEEN ✦

Olekashan listened to Philippa with rapt attention, not caring that others were close enough to hear, seeing as they were seated around an afternoon fire.

Philippa was sweltering, but the Wahanar children kept feeding the fire sticks and dead brush from the dunes, letting the flames dance in their hands and throwing sparks at each other playfully. Ole only ever broke eye contact with her when he turned to smile at the children, before ushering them to continue to play without him.

When Philippa was done explaining, Olekashan's eyes were as wide as saucers, his mouth open in a hopeful smile. "Unclean magic my *krund*! Wonderful news, Little Pip. You are close to waking Panu, then?"

Her heart sank. "I… I can't."

The Wahanar gathered around the fire all exchanged glances with each other, before their gazes fell sharply to their chief, who had become very still.

His massive muscles shuddered as he exhaled. "Tell me why."

Philippa's mouth clammed up. How could she tell this man that his son may never wake, because she simply *couldn't* heal him? Her magic was not strong enough to push through whatever was happening to the boy.

Warmth enveloped her shoulder. Taz squeezed Philippa's arm, before nodding encouragingly at Ole.

With a shaking breath, she did her best to explain. "Something about Panu is keeping me out. The fact that I was able to alter him at all means that my magic is working, but… I don't think I'm strong enough to break through with him."

Olekashan nodded thoughtfully, resting his head in his hand. He tapped his bare feet against the sand as he closed his eyes, his mouth moving like he was processing all of his options. The Wahanar around the fire lost their patience and began to disperse.

As the last of them left, Ole cracked open an eye and smirked.

He looked at Philippa. "So if you had a way to have more power, you could heal him?"

Don't lie, don't lie, don't lie.

She didn't want to, but he was looking at her with such hopefulness that it was crushing her to not give him anything to count on. "I think so."

That seemed to be enough for the chief, who clapped his hands together and stood up. "I will see to it. But you seem tired. Are any of my people being too harsh with you, Little Pip? I know they do not believe like I do, but they should not be treating you badly."

Philippa shook her hands in the air. "No, no, it's not that."

"Then what tires you so?" Olekashan asked, tilting his head.

That was a question that would take years to explain, and Philippa didn't have that kind of time. She pushed down the feeling of stones in her chest and smiled up at the chief as sweetly as she could manage. "Nothing, Ole. I'm well."

His elongated earlobes bobbed as he nodded thoughtfully. He then turned to Tazmireth, who looked far more worse for wear than Philippa did. "You have protected her well, Tazmireth. A *ruvahn* you may no longer be, but a *hannir* you remain."

Tazmireth blinked and shook her head like she'd been struck. Slowly, she bowed her head to her uncle and murmured her thanks.

Philippa didn't know what a *hannir* was, but it was certainly a lofty compliment to make the warrior blush.

The chief turned his attention back to Philippa. "Come. Leave Tazmireth to rest. You also need to take your mind away from all of this."

Tazmireth nodded immediately, sensing her dismissal, and left Philippa with Olekashan.

Philippa's brows knit together, her lips pursing. "You don't want me to keep trying with Panu?"

Ole gently put a hand to her back and began to lead her further into the camp. "In Wahatan, we have a saying. In your language, it goes something like, *"when the horse is dead, do not continue to slap it."*

Her mouth quirked as she bit back a laugh, not wanting to offend him for his command of the common language.

He didn't seem to care and simply ushered her into a small tent that was filled with racks and chests, displaying tools of all sorts. Olekashan knelt, opened a chest, and rifled through its contents. He threw scythes and shovels over his shoulder like they were toys, a big child sifting through his toy box to find a favorite item.

"It means you need a break. Trying the same over and over will get you nowhere. I will ponder on this for both of us. But for now," Ole rose, a sheathed blade in his hands, "we take your mind off of the slapping of the dead horse."

Philippa's ears lowered and she crinkled her nose in disgust at the weapon. "Sorry, chief Ole. I am not going to spar with you with that thing."

He looked at it, his eyes full of hurt, the weapon still extended in his hand to her. With a free hand, he gestured to it, asking, "What is wrong with this thing? It was forged from the fires of my grandmother's great fiery passion for my grandfather."

Her throat burned with the sense that she could vomit at any time. "Now I'm really not going to touch it."

The chief rolled his eyes and grabbed her palm roughly, shoving the blade into her grasp. "We do not spar with weapons."

Philippa gagged and held the weapon with two fingers by the hilt, the blade surprisingly lightweight, and she let the sheath fall to the ground unceremoniously. "Then what am I doing with your grandparents' passion sword?"

Olekashan grinned like a mischievous imp. "We are going hunting."

Being thrown across a sand dune was certainly not what Philippa had imagined happening that afternoon, but plans often change.

She landed against a thick pile of sand with such force that she saw stars, her vision only clearing just in time to see the giant crustacean rattling towards her with visceral, angry clicking. Its cream colored shell vibrated as it launched into the air, fully intending to squash her.

Rolling out of the shadow, Philippa was launched into the air from the weight of the giant crab landing on the dune where she'd previously just been.

Thankfully, as she turned around, hair plastered to her sunkissed face, it appeared that the giant creature had stunned itself like she had when it had thrown her there.

Her heart was pounding in her ears as she painstakingly reached for the sword that the chief had strapped to her back, but her arms were like noodles. Even when she gasped for air, her heartbeat did not quiet. Philippa pressed a hand to her chest, and while her heart was, in fact, fighting for its life, it didn't explain the thunderous pounding in her ears.

And then Ole charged past her, battle axe raised and alight with fire, as he threw himself through the air towards the crab.

Midway through his descent through the air, he called out to her, "your mind is off of Panu, yes?"

Sand began to dip underneath her body, rattling with what she knew to be the tell-tale sign of another ginormous crustacean about to burst from the ground.

Ask me how I know, she grumbled internally, rolling out of the way of the next crab to burst from the sand.

She scanned the dunescape for Ole, before her jaw dropped open. He had landed on the crab, gripped both sides of the shell around its shadowy maw, and was *pulling* it apart with his bare hands. Cartilage cracked and creaked under the chief's iron grip.

Look out, look out, look out

Philippa ducked. The claw of the second crab creature flew so close over her head that she felt the air draft.

Keeping the small sword an arm's length away, she ran through the sand, feet sinking, to try and escape the giant creature.

Ole crowed with a victorious laugh behind her.

At least *he* was having fun.

Philippa whirled around, breathing in hot, dry air. The giant crustacean was still scuttling towards her at great speed, snapping its larger claws at her, the smaller ones chittering to a beat that was making her teeth ache. She didn't picture herself as a violent person, but as she threw a glance at the chief, her shoulders sank.

Olekashan sat atop the cracked shell of his slain beast. He wiggled his fingers at her, before making an ushering movement towards her.

She began to back up, her pace quickening as the shelled beast worked its way across the sand. Maybe if she let it get close enough, her guardian would come and get her out of the cursed desert. No wonder the Wahanar were frightened to be exiled; death by the desert didn't just mean heat, it meant creatures that were supposed to be the size of your foot coming out in hordes, towering like giants.

Sunlight reflected harshly off of its armored back.

Philippa had never stabbed anything before. She even closed her eyes when Shanti would remove the heads off of the fish back in Levanta.

But she had killed someone before.

On accident, she reminded herself, *it was to save a life.*

Could she kill something now, to save her own?

Did she have to?

Her feet slowed, drawing to a sloppy stop, her legs bowing under the tension of the afternoon hunt.

Olekashan sat up, watching her earnestly. His muscles tensed, like he was ready to jump into action.

The beast continued to hurl its way towards her. Philippa took a breath in. She brought the sword up above her head, sheathing it onto her back. Her leg outstretched, and she stuck her toe into the sand, writing a single word.

She squeezed her eyes shut just as the crustacean closed the distance…

and stopped just before her.

The ground stopped quaking. She peeled open her eyes, jaw falling open. The crab stood before her, eye stalks swaying from side to side, its massive pincers dancing above her head. But it stopped. Just like she'd written it to do.

Philippa let out a startled, wistful laugh. She'd only seen this done once, in the last moments of her mother's life, and she wasn't sure it would work for her now.

Ole hooted from atop his slain crab, jumping up and down, sending sparks into the air.

She couldn't help but smile, resting her hands on her knees, swallowing huge gulps of air as she stood in the shade of the creature. It shouldn't have been possible. Up until now, Philippa had needed substance to write with, and the only person she'd seen use etching or mimicry of a silvertongue was her mother. But maybe her own ability to scribe with items other than ink meant that she didn't have to limit herself to those, either.

The crab shuddered. She looked up, taking in its quaking legs, the way its eyes seemed to be unfocused. Her brows knit together, and she peered around the giant creature's body to lock eyes with Ole, who had stopped cheering, and was now staring straight past her.

All the hair on her arms stood up. Philippa looked back to the crab as it danced nervously, and saw something in its eye stalks. Light glinted in the crab's black eyes, causing its pupils to dilate randomly. It grumbled like it was confused.

Slowly, Philippa began to turn around. Her eyes were on the ground, and as she looked, another shadow was cascading across the ground to hers.

Long and lanky, distorted by what looked like a furry growth in the shadow.

Her eyes flicked up.

In a nearby white barked tree, crouched a masked figure with something metallic in their hands, shifting it in the daylight to blind the crab. Philippa looked down at where she'd written in the sand, and saw that the crab had destroyed her single command. Her magic didn't stop the beast from running her over or snapping her spine. This person did.

When she looked up again, the figure was gone.

Which meant the crab could see.

And it snapped right over her head.

Philippa threw herself to the ground, hearing Olekashan yell her name, and the crab scuttled over her, completely blotting out the sun.

Then, in a flash of feathery black, the figure appeared again. There was the sound of metal scraping, a sword being drawn, and the stranger struck the crab straight through the shell. They stabbed it again and again, until the protective layer completely cracked open, causing thick purple blood to drench over them both.

It was so gelatinous that as the stranger stabbed the creature through its unprotected hide, Philippa couldn't breathe. The salty, hot purple blood filled her nose, her mouth, and coated her eyes.

Breathe.

She needed to *breathe.*

The creature gave one last pitiful cry as it began to fall towards her. Leather swiped across her mouth, freeing her airway, and as she gasped, arms wrapped around her like she was being embraced by death.

She would never quite find the words for the sensation that happened next, and being blinded by the crab's blood certainly didn't help. It felt like she was thrown backwards, through the earth, but spat out on the hot, dry sand.

Wheezing, Philippa scooped the indigo substance from her eyes and snorted to get the excess out of her nose.

Stars, she reeked.

Ole appeared above her, whole body alight with fire, looking concerned. He knelt before her and grabbed her shoulders, looking every inch of her over.

"Are you alright?" He asked.

Philippa was still trying to drag down fresh air, but she nodded. She was more than okay - she just had *proof.* She'd seen him. Her. Them. Whoever they were.

She wasn't sure in Levanta, but this time she just *knew.* That was no Wahanar that jumped in to save her, and no one could disappear that fast. No one, except her guardian. Maybe she wasn't so alone after all.

"How is your brain?" Olekashan asked, sitting beside her as he began to wipe the blood off of her back in sheets.

Philippa winced and pulled away. The gesture was overly parental, and she wasn't sure how she felt about that.

Ole didn't notice her apprehensions, and simply continued to slough off the grime from her. She deflated, giving in.

"My brain?" She asked.

He hummed. "Your thoughts. Are they no longer slapping the horse?"

Philippa chuckled and eased against his touch. "I suppose I was not thinking about Panu while I was running for my life. So, if that was your goal, then good job."

"It was part of my intention, yes."

She toyed with a lock of her stained hair, watching the blood congeal and drip off in massive clumps. "Why did you bring me out here?"

"Didn't you have fun, Little Pip?"

She shrugged. "In a way. But, *why?*"

Olekashan took her hair into his massive fists and wrung it out like a wet towel. "Your mind was clouded. Like a fire in the rain. Thick and muddled. You needed a clear fire inside you."

Philippa chewed on her lip and gently took her hair back so she could face him fully. "But why do you care?"

At that, the chief's shoulders drooped. His mouth was a hard line as he looked away from her, as if *he* was the sheepish one. "I have a daughter who was once your age. She had a clouded mind about herself. Now, she will not let me be the light in her smoke. She… does not listen to the ramblings of an old man. In my wish to save my family, I suppose that… When I look at you, Little Pip, I see little Heru."

The emotion in his voice could cut someone's soul in half. Philippa saw the way he looked away, how his fingers fiddled with the sand to keep his mind busy while he spoke.

He may have been a chief, but Ole didn't seem the type to put responsibilities over his family.

Philippa thought of herself in the previous nights, baring herself as just Philippa Aporo. Worthless.

The way Ole was sitting, the curve of his expression, the weight of his chest, she could see how he saw himself. Goose flesh covered her arms despite the heat, her cheeks flushing. He was not Olekashan, chief of the Wahanar. He was Olekashan, a father who felt like he was losing his family. He was alone, but he was trying.

Unable to see him in such obvious discomfort, she cleared her throat. "I don't think I'm very much like the little fireball she must've been."

He chuckled. "No, no fire. But strong willed. Powerful, and unsure. Like you."

She sat up straighter, feeling like she'd been flayed open.

Olekashan shook his head and ran a hand over his brow. "My greatest wish is to save my family, Little Pip. I would cast aside tradition for that. You want to know why I brought you out here?" She nodded. "It is because I believe in you. My family has been broken for some time. But now, with Panu being *so* broken, maybe it can save us. If not… I will let it go. I will let them be on their own paths. But I must have hope. Forget tradition and *vashir,* I must simply be me. A father who loves his family. So you see, I do not like to see you feeling broken. I cannot stand it. I must believe in something. You are all I have left to believe in. So if I could help you, my thinking is…"

He searched for the word in the common tongue, gesturing vaguely with his hands, but he seemed unable to express himself. Philippa reached out and wrapped her hands around his fingers, stilling him.

She wasn't sure if that was appropriate to so casually touch a chief, but he just stared at her with big, wet eyes. Much had happened between him and his family, she could tell, and there were things she would never know about them. But she was here now, and she wanted to help.

"My family is broken, too," she whispered. "Thank you for wanting to help me. I know what you were thinking. But you're wrong, Ole."

He startled, almost pulled his meaty hands away from hers. She squeezed him tighter.

"You're wrong to think that by helping me, I will want to help you," she inhaled sharply, her breath quaking, "I would help you anyway, Ole. I see the man you are. Your heart is big and full, and you love your family. Do you know how precious it is to find someone who would do anything for their family? That's *beautiful.* Thank you for wanting to cheer me up… and keeping me safe here."

The chief's chest expanded with a great, strong breath that racked his bones as he exhaled. Slowly, and gently, he tightened his grip on her hands in thanks. "You speak like you know of someone who is that precious."

She smiled. "My sister and her son. He's only small, but he tried to take on Taz and Heru on my behalf… and, I suppose, my parents. My mother was fiercely protective. My father would've done anything to keep us alive, even if it wasn't the right thing."

Ole ruffled her hair as he stood and shook his head. "It is a funny thing you call me beautiful for doing anything for my family."

Philippa tried to flatten her hair to no avail, and stood to follow him. "How so?"

The chief of the Wahanar smiled at her, teeth bright like starlight and eyes dark as the depths of the sea. "Because clearly you are here for your family, and here you are, in my desert, willing to do anything for *my* family. I wonder, Little Pip, which is more beautiful?"

When her mouth opened to respond, he pushed her jaw shut, winking at her like a father inviting his child in on a secret, and he stalked off to gather the crab bodies.

Streaks of orange and the brightest yellow filled the room, inky blackness trying to blot out the waves of light.

Philippa pressed her hand closer against Panu's forehead as she connected with him once more, trying to understand. In her mind, she asked if Olekashan had come to see him. In response, her vision filled with swirls of fire, dancing around like fireflies. A sense of joy filled her chest, and comfort.

She smiled at the boy's obvious elatement that Ole had listened to Philippa when she had told the chief that Panu could still hear them. Next, Philippa asked if Panu's sister had come to see him.

Within the dark scape of his imaginative mindscape that swarmed her vision, a gray cloud like ash fell down from what would've been the sky, if there was any sense of direction in his mind's eye. Confusion.

Philippa chewed on her lip. Maybe Heru was so set on scribes being unclean that she didn't bother to come see her brother.

Parting ways with Panu's mind - and promising to speak to him again soon - Philippa wiped her writing from his skin. True vision began to come back in particles of color and shape, until the room was clearly in focus once more.

The tent flap suddenly opened, and Taz, who'd been sleeping on a chair in the corner, startled awake with a smirk.

Herunavira had finally returned. After almost eight days of Philippa not seeing her, she looked refreshed. Her head had been freshly shaven, and she'd lost the armored top in exchange for a tight band around her chest and shoulder, leaving little to the imagination of her toned body.

Philippa inclined her head. Heru nodded back at her, rounding the stone in which Panu rested.

Olekashan had taken Philippa on hunts almost every other night in efforts to balance her work with Panukirah. Something about her time with the chief gave her the courage to speak with renewed strength when Heru looked disapprovingly at Panu's still form.

"Your brother still hasn't woken," Philippa said. "But your people still feed him and give him something to drink at all hours of the day."

The warrior was quiet for a long time. Then, she said, "I miss him."

Philippa was about to remind Herunavira that if she only took the time to speak to Panu, it might give her some comfort, but she did not get the chance. As if her brief admission cost Herunavira greatly, she snapped her eyes up to Philippa and narrowed them. "Our chief is done waiting on you. If you are still here when the *Tanvirok* happens, you at least have to fit in. They cannot question you."

Though Heru spoke with confidence, Philippa saw her mouth twitch, the angry feathering of her jaw. Whatever this was, this was not her idea. She was a messenger today.

Taz squeezed Philippa's shoulder, which did not go unnoticed by Heru, who said, "come with me now. You will not be asked a second time."

While Olekashan had been kind enough to take Philippa out for breaks, it typically had been at night. After a week inside the tent, only lit by firelight and the dusting of sun that came through on the dial, sunlight blinded her. White flecks filled her vision as she carefully tread after Heru, who dutifully did not slow down to wait for her.

"What's going on?" Philippa asked Tazmireth.

Her friend was guiding her by the wrist. Taz squeezed it once. Philippa didn't want to know yet, then. In their week of working together, they'd developed a simple 'yes' or 'no' system. Either nodding, or a squeeze or two on the wrist to indicate an answer. Philippa had come to understand that Taz did know the common language of Sapria, but was bound by her honor to keep as true to her culture as possible.

Yes, even more than Heru at times. It's why Tazmireth wouldn't lie to Dagna, or even just simply omit the truth about being healed by Philippa, and why she had readied herself to be stripped of her rank. Evidently, in an old text of the Wahanar, speaking any language other than their native one was considered sin. There was an antimony, however, that if a situation presented itself, speaking another language was acceptable.

Most Wahanar greeted her in the common tongue, and Ole seemed rather comfortable in letting her understand what they were talking about. Despite having become friends, Philippa wouldn't ask Tazmireth to abandon her morals. That's *why* they were friends.

The clamor of the Wahanar made her ache for home. Families played, hunted, cooked, and laughed together. A father wrestled with his teenage daughter, and the mother gently tousled with their young child. She felt herself smiling. Maybe the heaviness in her chest wasn't such a bad thing.

She slammed into Heru's back. The warrior woman's shoulders tensed, but she did not speak. Philippa looked past her and felt her legs tense. A phantom hand crawled up her spine, clutching her throat. An ugly, unwelcome amount of fear danced lit her nerves on fire.

Two huge boles propped up the front of the pavilion, red fabric cascading over the sides and shading a rug outside. She had seen this tent on her first day. The torture chamber.

Heru ripped open the doorway, and did not wait for her to follow. Tazmireth's grip on Philippa tightened.

Philippa thought about taking off again. Scenes of a back being torn to shreds in efforts to tattoo it plagued her mind even now when she looked at the table inside. Though the memory hadn't been her own, it was visceral and burned like she was reliving it herself. Her green eyes fell to Tazmireth's newly healed scar. The story that she would not laugh while telling to her friends, like she did with the one on her chest. It was a scar of shame, and one she'd earned because of Philippa.

Never again.

She walked inside.

Beside Olekashan was the elderly woman Philippa had seen doing the tattooing on her first day. The Wahanar tattooist was willowy, not quite as tall as the rest of them, with long, knobby fingers that were turned black by ink. Both of their eyes flashed to meet Philippa's, understanding passing over the chief's face. The table was waiting.

"With *Tanvirok* fast approaching, we cannot risk the other elders seeing someone not a part of our people," Heru explained, her voice thick and steady. She wanted no part of this.

"I know I haven't been able to heal Panu. Maybe if I had access to ink, I could try something more than just researching—"

Ole held up a hand and the tent fell silent.

"You will." His voice was firm. "You misunderstand, Little Pip. You will have ink. You need to have as much time as you can to heal Panu. But the other elders must see you as Wahanar."

Philippa's breath hitched at Ole's words, the weight of them pressing down on her. She took in the room, the incense burning, the elder with a needle in her hands. Ole's skin, decorated in intricate black designs, Heru's face marked in a hawk, and Tazmireth's palm hidden in ink.

Tattoo her. Make her one of them. A ritual meant for warriors, for those who belonged. But she didn't. She was an outsider, a scribe, a secret held together by ink and fear.

Understanding settled first, cold and stark. She had seen so many tattooed marks before, symbols of allegiance, of identity. She knew what it meant. The Wahanar didn't do things halfway. If they marked her, she would be one of them, bound by their laws, their expectations. This wasn't just about healing Panu anymore. It was about *changing* her to fit their needs.

Then came the dread, slow and creeping, curling around her spine like smoke. What if the ink didn't just stain her skin, but *claimed* her? What if it sank deeper, into the very magic she wielded? Would she still be herself when the needle lifted? Or would she be something new, something rewritten? These were the horror stories told to the children in Soffer. The ghastly memories felt like they were changing who was being tattooed, morphing them into a creature of design… losing who was once underneath.

Her fingers twitched at her sides. She should refuse. She should run. But the eyes of the Wahanar were on her, their faces unreadable, except that of Ole. A father, willing to break all of his laws for his family. Deep down, a terrible truth whispered:

There is no going back.

"Say yes, Little Pip," Ole urged. "For my family. For yours."

Somewhere deep inside, Philippa Aporo knew that she should feel used. That he had gained her trust and affection, playing on her love for her family in order to serve his own purposes. But something else completely shrouded out that cynicism, and it was the inexplicable trust she had in Ole. He had not lied to her yet. Had not struck her, ordered her around. All of this was because he loved his children, and would do anything for them - whether or not it was the *right* thing.

She met his gaze, seeing her reflection in his dark, flinty eyes. Within them, she also saw pieces of her father.

Philippa swallowed her fear. "For family."

CHAPTER FIFTEEN

Philippa laid on her back, her hand stretched out on the smooth stone, fingers trembling despite her attempts to still them. Inkwells sat nearby, their surfaces reflecting the low, flickering firelight. It wasn't quite the ink of the apothecary, not diluted, but not the kind one would simply write with either. No, this was homemade and thick, meant to penetrate into the flesh. The tent smelled of oil and something sharp - something metallic and earthy, like blood and dye mixed together.

Ole, massive as he was, knelt beside her. His usual lopsided grin was absent, replaced by something steadier and unreadable. Tazmireth sat at Philippa's head, her presence solid and unmoving. Philippa tried to focus on them, imagining Taz's hands lost in her mess of wavy hair as roots of an ancient tree, keeping her moored. She worked to focus on the warmth of their hands as they adjusted her arm, but her mind kept drifting to Herunavira's departure, how she'd left in a huff, scoffing at Philippa's hesitation before disappearing into the night.

Coward, she had muttered under her breath, as if Philippa had any choice in the matter.

"Breathe," Taz murmured in Wahatan. Philippa didn't understand the word, but the intent was clear in the way Taz placed a firm hand on her chest, pressing enough to remind her to let go of the tension.

Ole exhaled through his nose, a poor attempt at a laugh. "My niece is right. You will only make it worse if you fight it."

Philippa swallowed hard. "That's not reassuring."

Ole turned her palm upward, running his thumb along the skin there as if mapping out the design. "You're lucky." he said, his voice softer now. "Most have to earn this through war or sacrifice. You—"

"Am just trying to save someone," Philippa finished, her voice tight.

Taz spoke again, low and weighted. A string of words in Wahatan, the cadence rich and unshaken. It was more words than Philippa had ever heard her speak, in any language. Philippa only caught one word: *vasharan.*

Ole hesitated, then translated, though something in his pause made her think he was choosing his words carefully. "She says… that it is still a kind of sacrifice."

Philippa swallowed, but before she could speak, Tazmireth reached down and smoothed her fingers over Philippa's brow. More Wahatan words followed, murmured like a prayer.

Ole sighed. "And that you are braver than you know."

Philippa almost laughed. Almost.

But then the elder dipped the needle into ink, and all that was left was the weight of the moment before the pain.

The ink was cool against Philippa's skin as the needle pressed into her flesh, embedding the dark liquid in winding patterns that felt almost alive. She'd only gotten one choice: where the tattoo would go. If she had to be marked, she wanted to be marked like her friend. Her palm was the clear choice. Instead of a harsh, thick covering of her flesh like Taz's, the design began at the base of her wrist, circling outward in delicate rings like ripples of water, each one broken by sharp, deliberate lines that branched towards her fingers like veins of power. Small dots marked the intersections where the lines met, following the natural curves of her bones and joints, as if mapping the pathways beneath her skin.

On the palm side, the pattern was softer, but no less intricate; a swirling sunburst of lines radiating from the center of her hand, curling towards her fingertips in a dance of precision. The ink settled deep into the creases of her palm, merging with the folds of her skin, as if it had always been part of her. When the final stroke was finished, Philippa flexed her fingers, watching as the circles and sharp angles shifted with her movements. The tattoo felt like more than just ink; it was a map, a binding, a key. And the power beneath her skin hummed in response. A strange warmth pulsed beneath the surface, spreading outward like a slow burning ember.

"It will help you channel the power," the elderly woman said, her voice reverent. "Right now, your power is raw and unfocused. This will guide it, direct it, so you do not burn through yourself before the work is done."

Philippa glanced up sharply. "Burn through myself?"

The elder met her gaze without flinching. "You are a conduit, Philippa Aporo. Ink is not just a tool for you - it is a part of you. It wells beneath your skin, like fire does ours. It can take a physical design to bring it out of us. Without balance, without direction, it will take as much as it gives."

She swallowed, flexing her hand again. The ink gleamed, dark and sure, everything she was not. She felt the hum of something settling into place, an ancient rhythm aligning with her heartbeat. For the first time, she wondered if power had always been meant to be written into her skin.

"This will help me channel?"

The elder nodded. "Take Tazmireth with you. She will keep it clean. It will itch." With that, the elder disappeared into another fold of the tent.

Ole stood, towering over her as she sat up. "Welcome to our family, Little Pip. We will have to think of a new name for you, as a Wahanar. The *Tanvirok* will worry less if you sound like you are one of us, too."

She stared at her hand, the new tattoo hot and angry. "Thank you."

Ole looked confused.

"For giving me more time. To heal your son."

"You are very strange, Little Pip. You thank others for choices you do not make."

CHAPTER SIXTEEN

She was running out of time. Though now, as less prisoner and more Wahanar, she could travel about their homelands more freely. It only allowed her mind to wander farther.

There was a week and a half left to do this. Heal Panu, hopefully get to go home, and find out what to do from there.

Levanta is not your home anymore, her mind whispered. She stopped in her tracks. Dagna was watching her from afar, having stopped grinding herbs into medicine to shoot daggers in her direction.

"Move, Kelthari!" A gruff voice said from behind.

Philippa scooted out of the Wahanar's way, and though his tone was unkind, she had come to understand he didn't mean to be. Her ears twitched. She'd just understood him in Wahatan! Granted, it had been her Wahatan name, which Tazmireth had deemed her with a laugh. Kelthari meant "silent fire". A little on the nose, but she didn't mind.

Finally, she was getting somewhere. She had been able to read a bit more of the parchments they'd left for her in Panu's tent, given Tazmireth's help. Not enough to heal the boy, and she'd tried using her new tattoo with a small amount of ink Tazmireth had snuck away for her to write on the boy's body. Nothing had changed.

It felt like pushing her mind against a wall, as if her power was there, under the surface, trying to transfer into Panu but something stronger was blocking her. There was only one place left in the Wahanar region that she hadn't gone to look for answers.

Philippa had been avoiding the prisoner's tent since she arrived. The

Wahanar spoke little of him, only calling him *ohrika,* a trespasser. But Philippa had heard whispers that he was from Aresef, where the Great Libraries stood. A researcher, which meant he potentially had access to the most powerful place in the world. In the days past, she had only caught shadowy glimpses of him, but he never ventured out of his tent. They didn't even have guards outside.

A very good prisoner, indeed.

If he was from Aresef, and truly was a researcher, then he may have even been inside the Great Libraries' inner sanctum! Not even the king and his new queen could be given access to that place, not without a scribe able to break the wards first. And none had been stupid enough to return to the Great Libraries since the war and what happened in Soffer.

Philippa shook her head, clearing her thoughts as she walked towards the tent, her tattooed palm flexing. They were right about the ink making her feel like a conduit. Now, when she swiped her fingers across Panu's skin to connect their minds, it took such small amounts of dye that she wondered if she needed any at all.

She held up her hand, turning it over in the sunlight. Maybe the ink embedded in her skin acted like a constant inkwell, something to draw upon and give life to her magic.

Focus, she thought.

The trespassing researcher had been caught, somehow near the borders despite not having a glass portal, apparently walking about like a stray shadow. The Wahanar should have killed him by their standards, but given his career, he was a man who knew how to read the histories they had long lost. Ole had explained that, during the Scribe Wars and the king's reign, much of their way of life had been ripped from them in the form of their history.

So, instead of killing the man, they used him.

The first time she saw him, he was hunched over a low table, hands bound with woven fibers, but still turning pages with careful precision. The dim lantern caught the indigo streaks in his dark braids, the soft angles of his face. His clothes were torn, but he held himself like someone who knew his worth.

The entrance of the prisoner's tent had been bound up, letting the hot sun fill the tent. Sand and dust drifted through the air, marring his appearance, but this close, she was nearly in awe. Seeing this man from afar did not do him justice.

Stop thinking that! Philippa chastised herself. *But he is rather handsome...* She lingered too long at the entrance.

"Are you here to gawk, or to help?" His voice was rough, but not unkind. Philippa stiffened, but stepped closer into the shade of the open tent.

"Help? You didn't strike me as someone who would want that." Unsure of why she spoke so harshly, she rubbed her palm and felt herself blush.

Something flickered across his face as he looked up - surprise, maybe. Her breath caught. His eyes were of the finest golden color, irises that could buy a castle. He studied her for a little longer before exhaling. "I don't suppose you have a knife?"

She wrinkled her nose at such a direct request, but couldn't hold the expression because the way he said it made it sound like he was asking for tea at a restaurant.

Focus!

"I don't think they'd appreciate me cutting you free." she said, eyeing his wrists.

"Ah, well. Worth asking." He shifted, the ropes tightening against his skin. She wanted to cut him loose. His golden eyes flicked up to hers, sharp and searching. "You're not Wahatan."

Her tattooed hand covered in loose silken wraps burned. It wasn't a question, but she answered anyway. "Not by birth."

His gaze flickered past her, to the open tent flap where the clamor of the Wahanar filled the air beyond. "You've gotten rather comfortable here," he nodded at her tattoo peeking out.

Philippa frowned. "They've given me a place."

"For now." He tilted his head slightly, watching her. "But you must know that won't last. Not forever. Eventually, they'll decide you've given them all you can, and you'll just be another outsider. An intruder in their lands."

"Aren't you just a little ray of sunshine?" She swallowed hard. She wanted to tell him that he was wrong, that in their own way, they had welcomed her… but deep down, she knew the truth. There was a heaviness in her chest anytime she started to feel like she belonged here. Like this was home. Her real home had a sharp tongue and a son. Despite that, she was perturbed that he had been observing her from his tent, and that he'd gathered as much as he had. A researcher for sure, then.

"Which is why," he continued, tilting his chin towards the scrolls scattered across the table, "it wouldn't hurt to have a contingency plan." He held her gaze. "Their laws are older than they know. Maybe older than *your* kind."

She knew he didn't mean that she was an elf.

"A contingency plan," she repeated. "If you were planning on running away, I would think that you'd have done it by now. So if you're offering me an escape route, excuse me if I'm not exactly excited to join whatever it is you're planning."

The researcher lit up at her retort. "A fine scholar always questions things. You're already on the right track."

Philippa waved her hands in the air to clear it. "Okay, okay, slow down. What is happening right now?"

She felt like her cheeks were on fire.

"You came to me for help, because the boy won't wake. Am I wrong?"

Her ears twitched. "You would be… somewhere within reason."

When he closed his eyes to give her a triumphant smile, there was a pang of worry in her chest that he wouldn't open them again and she'd forever lose the sight of his golden irises.

What am I thinking?

"What is going on here is that I live to understand. You live to presumably get out of here, after you heal the boy. Scribes aren't exactly popular around Sapria, so once you're done here, you'll need to find a safe place to hide. I came here to research the Wahanar, and I've already succeeded at that."

"You were captured," Philippa interjected, crossing her arms.

He didn't miss a beat. "My point is, I learned how to find them, and I can find a way out. Unless you just came over here to make friends, I'm guessing you would like one of two things. Perhaps both."

"And what would those be?"

"To use their own writings to find a way to heal that boy, or to use my knowledge to escape when things inevitably go astray." He punctuated the end of his sentence by dropping a heavy stack of parchment onto his low table and resting his cheek atop his bound hands.

Philippa hesitated. She'd come to this tent out of curiosity, not trust, but the Wahanar had never mentioned that their texts could help her before. She was against the clock to heal Panu. If she didn't, more than just her head was under the knife. Raff and Morgana needed her to come home. If the scholar was right, if their own laws and ancient texts could hold answers, she needed to know.

She stepped forward, lowering herself to the mat across from him. "Show me what you know."

A slow, knowing smile crossed his face. "I thought you'd never ask," he extended a hand to her. "My name is Shem."

Philippa moved without thinking, ignoring his hand and grasping his chin to make him look her in the eye. "My name is Kelthari."

Shem eyed her incredulously. Realizing what she'd done, heat rose to her cheeks as she released him. "You are… very at home here, as your name suggests."

Her ears lowered with embarrassment, and she quickly took a scroll to examine. "Philippa. My name is Philippa Aporo."

"Good to make your acquaintance, Miss Aporo." he said, settling back onto his cushion. "Let's get to work."

She knew that he was only here to learn for himself. Why else would someone seek out the Wahanar by themselves? Once he was done researching, he'd find a way out and escape.

But she was sitting in that tent for Panu, for Tazmireth, for her family. She'd learn the language, learn the customs, whatever she needed to in order to save everyone that she could.

CHAPTER SEVENTEEN ✦

She'd spent four days with Shem just learning how to translate the Wahatan language, much to Tazmireth's dismay, who seemed to have a strong aversion to the man.

Philippa hadn't minded him so much, after spending the time with him. She marveled at his intellect. Shem had been there for weeks before she'd arrived, and after pleading his case before Dagna of all people, convinced them to let him read their scrolls in exchange for his life.

Not much had lent itself to Panu's condition. Much of the laws and beliefs of the Wahanar people, unsurprisingly, did not survive on parchment due to their nature. One thing they did find, however, was that Wahanar believed the strong were meant to survive. Anyone with an ailment that could not be dealt with by medicine was not treated at all.

Though they harnessed magic themselves, scribe magic was strictly forbidden amongst the people. Philippa had never heard of a Wahanar possessing scribe magic anyway.

Philippa and Shem sat cross legged in his tent, a single lantern between them as they poured over a brittle, ancient text.

"That word doesn't mean 'exile', it means 'separation by necessity,'" Philippa insisted, jabbing a finger at the faded ink.

Shem sighed, leaning back on his hands. "You're splitting hairs."

"No, I'm not." she said, her voice firm. "If the Wahanar law doesn't condemn people like us explicitly and outright, there's a way to appeal to them."

And give me more time, she thought.

Shem watched her for a moment before nodding. "You… are right. But convincing them is another thing entirely. I can't find anything to wake someone from such a deep sleep."

There was a glimmer of admiration in his expression. He wasn't just humoring her, he respected her mind, her thoughts. She buried her nose in the scroll to hide the blush on her cheeks.

But Shem was already deep in thought, as he tended to be, rambling out loud when he was on the precipice of a discovery. She could've listened to him piece things together for hours. Which she had.

"Maybe we're missing something. If the copied law we have found says that those who aren't strong are to be left aside, and anyone practicing Scribe magic should be *separated by necessity,* why is it necessary? Why the prejudice from people who understand it better than most?"

Philippa made a noncommittal noise. "Because they were here before scribes. Before Aresef claimed the whole continent of tread under its rule."

"When did your people become, well, a people?"

She thought a long time before answering. In her mind, she could hear her mother's voice as she explained their history. Then, a second voice, her father's. They'd both described the scribe's history very differently. As she grew up, she realized both could be true at the same time.

"Until the Scribe Wars, there were no *people.* Scribes operated freely. They had no laws," Philippa said, running a hand through her hair. "But then they split into two factions. One set of scribes agreed to abandon their practices, their cultures, in the name of peace. They fled to another continent just across the Shifting Sea to live their own lives, away from where they could hurt people."

"Soffer," Shem offered, clearly well read on the subject.

Philippa nodded. "The other faction… they wanted control. Peace by means of an iron fist."

"How could they do that? Wouldn't they have to rewrite *every* living story?"

She shook her head. "Just enough to manipulate people into believing that they were the only way to co-exist peacefully. Then, the new king came into power when he was very young. He outlawed all forms of scribe magic. The peaceful scribes ran. The others made creatures to defend the kind. But creatures can be rewritten into monsters, and not all scribes wanted to run or rule. They took a deal brokered by the king. Scribes create monsters. Monsters kill scribes. The king rules forever."

Shem clicked his tongue and shook his head. Absentmindedly, he pulled his dark braids up into a loose bun, one tendril falling back into his face.

"What? You don't believe in monsters?"

His eyes flashed, and he set his scroll aside to meet her darkening gaze. "Monsters are one of the only things I believe in," he paused, as if he'd said too much. "Our king brokered a deal with scribes. Who's to say he hasn't been manipulated?"

She gawked at him claiming the king as his own. No one in Levanta dared speak it out of superstition. No one wanted to be owned. Out here, though, in the wilds, things were different. Here in the tent, there was just Shem and Philippa.

"My mother said he wasn't. That he captured scribes and forced them to work under jurisdiction of the royal family. Those who didn't obey had their books burnt."

Shem folded his scroll. "An awful way to go, really."

She nodded in agreement. It was one of the only ways to ensure a scribe was killed. If no one could open their sealed tome, they couldn't be brought back. It was a rare, almost dangerous ability to have that much scribe magic to undo a death sentence.

"I can't blame him, the king," she admitted softly. "He was trying to protect his people. His family."

Shem thought about that for a long moment. "I'm surprised someone of your background can say that, Miss Aporo."

A sad smile found its way to her lips as she stretched, rolling her shoulders to ease the tension. "My father wrote monsters into existence to protect us. He did what he thought he had to. Just because ideas are different, doesn't make them inherently evil."

"Some people are simply evil, Philippa. It's an unfortunate truth they cannot escape. Alters or not, we all still have a choice. The king despises choices."

"You know him so well, do you?" She teased. He caught her attempt at fishing. Shem waved a hand, ignoring the comment.

"And what of these monsters your father created? Do *you* know where they are now?"

She studied him. "One is with you everywhere you go, Shem Tetra."

Unease settled on his face. Shem's broad shoulders tensed, his fingers wrinkling the closed scroll in his hands.

She pointed out the Wahanar's home center, where a Nazheris carried a child on its back. There was still no way for her to get used to seeing them out in the open, interacting with people as if it was no big deal. But the Wahanar looked past what Nazheris had been written to be, and they'd looked past Philippa's inability, too. At least a small number of them believed in her to heal Panu, or to find out what could be done for him. That meant something, didn't it?

Shem sighed. "Another example of the intensity of our situation. Your father's people made a creature that was inherently made for destruction, for evil, and yet, here Nazheris is. She's found a home. But our rulers do not *create* anything. Like any monarch, they see something shiny and must have it. A crow to a coin. Your father, it seems, believed in something bigger than himself. His methods were extreme, but his love for you was his motivation. The king believes in nothing but control. He married a woman from Diamond Forge, for star's sake. An enemy he swore off until it became convenient for him. That, I would define, as a form of evil."

Resting her chin in her palm, she stared at her other hand, getting lost in the designs on her skin. She'd once believed that the Wahanar could only be cruel. Brutes. Her mother without a doubt thought that the creation of Nazheris and other creatures was evil.

Philippa traced the design of her tattoo into the sand, sighing. Politics were not for the faint of heart. Everything had become so complicated.

Her own people were outcast for using their power against the common person, meaning that really, some of their punishment was deserved Of course not to the extent that the king had taken it to, but if someone meddled with *her* life book, she certainly would not have taken it lightly. The king used their power to fight back against them, imprisoning some of her own, if not worse. What she was doing was illegal, and against the beliefs of the Wahanar, but not against the beliefs of a desperate father. What did being good or evil really entail, anyway? There was no map. No guide. Only one's own conscience.

"It is a violent, harsh world out there. We have to adapt," Shem said by way of regaining her attention.

Philippa shook her head and gently took the scroll from his hands so she could examine it herself. "I know the world is violent, and unkind. But in a ruthless world, I choose to try and be gentle. How much more is something worth, if it's rare?"

For the first time in several days, she'd stumped him. Shem's eyes were downcast, flitting between the sand and his own hands, as if he was piecing something together. When something finally clicked, he looked up at her with a dazzling smile.

"So, you're saying you're a rare commodity, Miss Aporo?"

Her skin heated. "I just want to be useful. Help people. Whoever they are. I need to go check on Panu."

His bound hands seemed to reach for her, but stopped just short of making contact. Taking the scroll with her, which she was sure had *no* medical explanation for what was going on, she gripped it like it held all the answers. Because she needed *something* to make sense, and the thudding in her chest most certainly did *not*.

"Let me know if you find anything out about the chief's grandson," Shem called quietly, as if not to disturb anyone in the late hour of the day, "I'll keep looking for more answers here."

Her head whipped around. She was going to correct him, that Panu was Ole's son. But then it all fell into place.

Dagna's lack of motherly nature towards him, yet she had it for Heru. Ole never once called Panu his son, but his family. The way that Heru was willing to break the law, despite it being like poison to her.

Panukirah was not Olekashan's son, but Herunavira's.

Philippa picked up her speed to the tent. If Herunavira was the mother, then she *had* to figure this out. Otherwise, there was no way Heru would let her out of their lands alive.

Tazmireth handed Philippa a jar of salve that was almost empty. Philippa nodded in thanks and removed the cork before slathering her tattooed hand with the substance. Whatever it was, it didn't smell like the aloeweed they used in Levanta for burns, but it certainly helped with the itching.

The two women walked in relative silence towards the chief's pavilion. Wahanar families went about their days around them, seemingly oblivious to their presence, but Philippa could feel the weight of their disinterest.

Ever since Tazmireth had been formally assigned to Philippa, there had been stares. But now that they walked around like friends, there was utter disgust. Most of the people showed it by simply ignoring them while others curled their lips or turned their noses up as they passed. Philippa didn't know how Taz appeared so unbothered, so collected. The warrior woman simply chewed on a bit of dried meat, her hands tucked lazily into the folds of her skirts.

Ears twitching, Philippa wondered if she was just bad luck to be around. Her mother would certainly agree.

She almost stopped in her tracks at the thought. Why would she think something like that?

Maybe the sun was getting to her. She needed to rest before she tried to connect with Panu again.

The day was burning away into dusk, hazy shadows dancing over the sand. Torches were lit with the snap of fingers and lanterns were hung from tent poles to illuminate the camp. As Philippa and Taz rounded a corner, there was a shriek followed by what sounded like air hitting a wall.

Then, a ball of light came straight at them.

Philippa ducked just as heat and a burst of air flew over her head. Tazmireth laughed, pounding her on the back.

Sweat ran down her neck as she looked up, and instantly relief flooded her veins. It was just a group of Wahanar children playing around a circle of torches, and one of them had gotten a little too excited about winning, the child's small hand still smoking.

A little boy tackled the cheater and began to try to smash his face into the sand.

Philippa gaped, but Taz just rolled her eyes and sauntered over to the group of young ones, barking something in Wahatan that had each and every child standing at attention. Curiously, Philippa walked over.

Taz was shaking her head at the children, disappointment plain on her face. In Wahatan, Tazmireth told them that cheating did not make them winners. But Philippa saw the smirk that Taz was trying to hold back and decided to join in.

"Oh, yes," Philippa said sagely. "You won't win like that."

One of the children cocked his head at her, a mess of tangled black hair falling into his eyes. He looked between Taz and Philippa, as if wondering if he should acknowledge the scribe's presence. Taz gave a nod of approval.

"She also said we would win if we beat *you*," the boy said with a playful snarl.

Philippa's blood went cold. Slowly, she turned to Tazmireth, who only smiled innocently. Stars, that woman was infuriating.

She was about to decline, but when she looked at the children before her, she saved. They all looked up at her with curious, expectant eyes, and she couldn't help but think of her nephew. With a sigh, she took a knee and met the boy's stare.

"Alright. How do we play?"

The game was fairly simple once she worked out what they were trying to tell her. One child would take a turn being "the light" while the others were "shadows" that were trying to avoid being caught in the light's path. If you were caught, you had to become a light too and try to capture more shadows.

Tazmireth slunk away to grab fabrics. She draped them along poles and beams to create a semi sheltered area for their shadows to dance around on, giving them more room to play.

The first boy she'd spoken to - called Benni - announced that he would be the light first. All the children took their places, spread out between the fabrics and torches, letting their shadows elongate on the ground or the makeshift walls. Philippa crouched eagerly beside two little girls, wholly sure that somehow this would get her singed.

Taz shoved Philippa in the shoulder, falling into a ready stance next to her.

It began without warning. Benni's tongue was stuck out of the side of his mouth as he concentrated on pulling a bit of fire from a torch and onto his hand. Unable to fully conjure a flame on his own, he watched with awe as his palm lit up, before turning mischievously to his friends.

In Wahatan, Benni warned, "your shadows better run!"

Then, he launched the smallest fireball that Philippa had ever seen into a shadow. Chaos ensued, the children running in circles and darting around each other to avoid becoming lights. Tazmireth dodged right along with them, even grabbing a child by the leg to make their shadow fall into the path of Benni's small firelight.

The little girl protested, but just as quickly began to chase other shadows with Benni.

Philippa was just trying not to step on any of the kids, since some of them were as young as three. Benni himself couldn't have been older than five or six. None of them seemed to care that there was a size difference, though, tackling and shoving each other to try and make them lose the game.

After the first round, Tazmireth stood triumphant, her shadow the only one remaining. Philippa was breathing heavily from all the running around, and began to excuse herself. But a little girl yanked on her arm and waved her back into the circle.

A smile found its way onto her face, and past where they were playing, she caught Shem watching her from the prisoner's tent. He didn't look that interested, if anything a little confused. Chuckling, Philippa nodded at the little girl and joined the game again.

Benni insisted on being the light every time, clearly enjoying the idea of snuffing out his friends.

Except now, he seemed solely focused on taking out Philippa's shadow. She was able to make her shadow dodge a few times, crouching and ducking out of the way, but she could see how set Benni was on getting her out first. After seeing how roughly Tazmireth played with the children, Philippa reminded herself that by nature these kids enjoyed competition. So, with a smirk, she wouldn't just let him win.

She stood completely still, letting her shadow turn to stone behind her on the fabric, and Benni laughed wickedly.

He readied his hand, and threw a small fire-puff at her shadow.

Just as it was about to connect and singe the fabric wall, Philippa swiped her tattooed finger in the air above her shadow. She wasn't sure it would work, but before the fire found its mark, a tiny burst of magic left her body, and her shadow split in two against the fabric.

She laughed and turned to Benni, sure that he would find her trick funny, but the game had gone completely silent.

All the children stared at her, bewildered. Philippa swallowed hard. Stars, why had she done that? So much for connecting with the people, like Taz had clearly intended.

With another swipe of her finger, she let her shadow reform.

Their eyes widened, mouths falling open. Philippa's ears lowered as she winced, watching painfully as they couldn't take their eyes off of her.

Then, with an uproar, they began to cheer.

Benni ran for her, grabbing her tattooed hand. "When I get mine, can I move shadows?"

Other kids flooded her with more of the same.

"Can you teach me?"

"Do it again!"

"Will you move my shadow next round?"

Philippa awkwardly pulled her hands away from the swarm of children, looking to Tazmireth for help. Her friend just smirked and shrugged her shoulders, then gestured to the game area as if to welcome her to try.

So, she did.

Her heart was light for what felt like the first time in days. It was such a simple joy, making the kids' shadows dance out of the way, shortening them or making them disappear altogether, but it felt so *normal.* She didn't know that she needed to laugh or be reminded that she could make a child smile.

Tazmireth didn't take it easy on her, either, and would tackle her to the ground to try and make her a light.

Despite playing with the kids for what felt like hours, it passed all too quickly for Philippa.

"You'll *never* hit my shadow!" Benni declared, taunting the little girl who was now the light.

He was right about that, because in her anger and determination to get Benni, when she launched her little fireball, it smacked him directly in the face. He fell down, eyes squeezed shut, face streaked with smoke.

Tazmireth hushed the other children, forcing them to stop their game to make sure Benni was alright.

And then he began to cry.

It was soft, but Philippa thought he looked utterly defeated. His hands lay limp at his sides as he sat up, shoulders heaving with deep sobs.

Nearby, the parents of the children heard his outcry, and began to gather nearby. Several families came to see what had happened.

Philippa moved without thinking. Taz grabbed her shoulder, wrenching her back, but Philippa shook out of her friend's grip.

Not looking back, she made her way to Benni and sat on the ground next to him. Then, as gently as she could, she picked him up and set him in her lap. The boy didn't fight her, he just cried harder as he melted into her.

Her heart ached. Philippa shushed him soothingly, running a hand through his messy hair, and she pulled away to look at his face.

Hot tears streamed out of his eyes, which were red and irritated from the smoke. Benni's nose was burnt on the end, his cheeks covered in soot and grime.

Philippa reached up with her tattooed palm, but froze before she touched his cheek. She had nothing to write on him with, but now was a better time than any to test her theory.

Simply smudging through the smoke stain on Benni's face, she etched out the word *heal* across his cheek. As softly as she could, she then blew onto his face to try and soothe the burn.

After just a few moments, his cries began to subside. When Benni opened his eyes, they were clear and dark, no longer irritated.

"Are you alright?" she asked.

The boy smiled at her slowly, revealing his newly gap-toothed smile, and he nodded. Benni wrapped his arms around her and squeezed her neck so tightly that she gagged.

"Thanks, Kelthari!" he chimed, and clambered out of her lap to rejoin his friends.

Philippa sighed, letting her shoulders relax.

That is, until she saw the looks on the faces of those who had gathered. Some parents hurriedly grabbed their children and *ran* away from her, while some stared in awe. The rest just grumbled and ordered their kids not to play with her anymore.

Beside them all, Taz was biting her thumb, grimacing. Philippa felt her cheeks grow hot, and she kept her head down as she sprang up, hurriedly walking to rejoin Taz's side.

"You should not have done that," Taz said in Wahatan.

Philippa's eyes shot up to meet her friend's gaze. "He was *hurt.*"

Tazmireth shrugged.

Stars, she was going to rip her hair out. "I know Wahanar value strength, but he is a child. He was hurt. Sometimes the strong thing is doing the *right* thing when no one else will. Have any of them thought of that? Aren't they happy their son isn't burnt to a crisp?"

In response, Tazmireth just crossed her arms and arched a brow. Philippa deflated and closed her eyes. These weren't her ways, but that was exactly the point. She didn't have to agree to stop meddling with how they'd all lived happily for years.

Maybe it was embarrassment or exhaustion, or a bit of both, but Philippa felt her eyes well up. "I'm sorry. I know you are afraid of my magic, Taz.

And that it makes you unclean, Benni now, too. I'm sorry."

There was a long, quiet pause. Philippa didn't meet her friend's gaze, didn't try to make up for what she'd done. Even if she didn't understand why things had to be the way that they were, she could respect them.

Taz's hand came under Philippa's chin. "The children had fun. Today you showed me that your magic can be harmless. For that, you have my thanks. You should not have healed Bennijaduran, but, I would think that he would disagree with me. I do not understand you very well, *hannir,* but I trust you. I like you. Maybe your magic is wrong, but that doesn't mean it cannot be beautiful."

These people were going to be the death of her. Philippa's heart couldn't take the emotional whiplash of Tazmireth's words, and she knew that if she brought attention to how Taz had made her feel, that it would end nowhere.

So, silently, Philippa nodded.

Tazmireth smiled brightly at her. "You understand much Wahatan now. You see? Together we are an odd pair, but we are learning from each other."

Philippa began to reach out to wrap her arm around her friend, but Taz inched backwards.

"Mmm," Taz grumbled. "No. You still embarrassed me in front of my people." There was a lightness to her voice, but Philippa knew that she was only half kidding.

Huffing out a laugh, Philippa rolled her eyes. "You're killing me here."

Tazmireth bared her teeth impishly. "And you will be the death of me. Come along, my nephew awaits your magic powers that do not work on him."

CHAPTER EIGHTEEN ✦

Philippa was alone.

She'd felt that way for some time, but now she was *truly* alone. Tazmireth and Herunavira had been tasked with some kind of mission. They'd left in the middle of the night with only the briefest of explanations from Taz.

In the Wahatan that she had learned, Philippa understood by Taz's warning that they would be going back through the glass portal and use the crystalline room to transport themselves elsewhere. Taz told her not to look into it, not to follow.

Philippa hadn't considered doing so before, but after the warning, she was absolutely eager to find out more.

When she'd asked why, Tazmireth's response was cryptic due to the lack of Philippa's understanding of Wahatan. "The crystals do not see, but they hear."

Herunavira had scowled the entire time as Tazmireth told Philippa that they were leaving, dark eyes roving over her as she studied old scripts with Shem. Heru had been dutifully ignoring Philippa until then, but the way she looked at Philippa made her feel like the warrior thought she was slacking off instead of trying to save her son. *Son.*

Stars, Heru must've only been fifteen when she'd had Panu. Maybe that was why Ole and the rest of the family had omitted the truth, in order to spare Heru's honor. Philippa had heard of the shame that came from some families when their child fell pregnant. After what she'd been reading with Shem, it also seemed like Wahanar pregnancies were very harsh and tumultuous. It made sense why they wouldn't tell her, especially since

Herunavira did not seem the type to share such a private matter.

Or, because Philippa simply didn't need to know. The ink on her hand did not make her one of them, not truly, she reminded herself. Playing with the children had been eye opening enough.

Despite the reprieve of speaking with Shem on the daily, her biggest reprieve had been Ole would take her out on evening hunts with other Wahanar. Most nights, they would return to loud feasts and parties put on by the young ones.

Trudging through sand, Philippa's ears twitched at the unusual quietness as they returned from an unsuccessful hunt. She unstrapped the braces from her torso and silently handed her blade to Olekashan as they stepped back into the camp.

Something was off.

He hadn't seemed dedicated during the hunt, and now, the chief's eyes were roving the encampment like he was waiting to be ambushed. Philippa's brow furrowed, and she tried to meet his gaze. The chief would not look at her.

An unsettling eeriness settled in her stomach.

Olekashan swallowed hard, and began to walk towards the center pavilion.

A crowd had formed near the chieftain's tent, murmurs rippling like wind through grass. Ole had stood up to his full height, abandoning the casual and comfortable slouch he adopted to put Philippa at ease. In one swift step, he became Olekashan, He Who Is Seated By The Flame. It made her skin crawl.

The people parted for him effortlessly, leaving Philippa to push her way through the crowd, barely registering the disapproving glances cast her way.

The air smelled of Philippa and damp earth, thick with something unspoken, something wrong. Philippa's feet felt heavier with each step as she followed the whispers threading through the gathered warriors. Everyone was accounted for, even young Benni, whose mother shoved his hand down when he tried to wave at Philippa. Her blood pumped at a deafening level in her ears as she began to see the outline of Herunavira at the front of the gathered people.

Where was Tazmireth?

Philippa began to push harder through the crowd, not caring if they shoved her back. Where was her friend?

In garbled voices, she began to translate some of the Wahatan she knew, hearing things like *"an outsider"* and *"unclean soul"*. So they'd captured someone then, but why was no one wondering where her friend was?

The way Taz had explained where they were going had been so short, so cryptic - had they gone somewhere dangerous? Did something happen? Was she dead?

Relief flooded through Philippa's veins. Taz stood at the front, her expression unreadable. Beside her, Heru gripped the hilt of a dark blade, gaze storming with fury.

Philippa swallowed her breath, looking around as she sifted through the last of the crowd. Nobody even looked at her, though she wasn't sure why.

Then, she saw it; an iron barred cage, dragged onto the hard packed sand like a trophy.

Inside, a man sat still as a statue, head tilted downward, the sharp curve of an avian mask catching the dim light. His mask was carved into the likeness of a bird that she had seen in fleeting glimpses, in moments she wasn't sure had been real. A shadow lingering at the edges of her life, saving her when she shouldn't have survived. His hands were bound in thick rope, ankles shackled, as if they expected him to sprout wings and fly away. Feathers adorned the crown of his mask, cascading in a heavy headdress that seemed to impossibly frame his back. Grey and white feathers.

Her heart pounded, her mind racing to stitch together every memory - the whispers in her head, the hand that yanked her back from death more times than she could count. This was him. The one who had always been there, just beyond reach. Even when she was sure that he was real, Olekashan had not acknowledged his existence. Up until now, part of her had been assuming he was part of her subconscious, despite the effects she'd seen him make.

He exists.

Her stomach twisted with something like relief, followed by the hollowness of dread. No, he couldn't exist. Especially not here. He had no glass portal to fall through into the crystal catacombs and find his way through the shattered glass into the Wahanar homeland.

She had to be mistaken.

Unless…

Olekashan *had* seen him.

Philippa glanced at the chief, who still was avoiding her gaze. Why did he feel the need to hide this from her? Though her guardian had saved her from the crustacean, Olekashan had no reason to believe that they were friends or that it would bother her to know he was around. Something more was at play, and Philippa was tired of being left in the dark.

"What has he done?" Philippa asked, stepping forward. The question hung in the air like an unwelcome echo. No one bothered answering her.

She shot a glance at Shem, who had crept out of the prisoner's tent. He was doing as he always did: studying.

When she looked back at the cage, the prisoner had raised his head slightly, watching her through the slits of his mask. Something deep in her guts twisted. The thrum in her body suddenly overwhelmed her, a headache forming, and the ink carved into her hand beating with its own rhythm, alive and furious.

Dagna appeared from behind the cage, shoving something into place that jolted the prisoner's body forward.

Ole raised his chin at her, welcoming his wife to speak.

"He is *vashir.* Death, for this one." her voice was cold, unfeeling.

Flames erupted all around as the tattoos of all the Wahanar in attendance burst with red-hot anger, becoming a living, breathing beast above their heads. Philippa shielded her eyes, the brightness overwhelming in the black of night.

Philippa's gaze snapped back to the enclosure, noting the irony that it *did* appear to be a human sized birdcage. Like they *knew* he was coming.

She felt it now, in the way the Wahanar stood just a little farther back than usual, the way that even Ole's fingers twitched as his sides. They feared him.

The Wahanar feared no one.

And yet, they hadn't killed him. Not yet. Dagna had given the order, but other than a fiery response, none had moved on him.

For whatever reason, they assumed that Philippa and the prisoner had something to do with one another. Her fingers tensed. They did, in a way, but even she did not understand why.

In the intense firelight, the prisoner did not move an inch, eyes locked onto hers, she could feel it. There were the feathers, the cacophony in her blood, but part of her was unsure until the whispering in her head flooded her consciousness with full force:

Free him, free him, free him.

Smart woman.

Two voices. One faintly more like her own. The other, one she had grown accustomed to.

"You can't kill him." she said as loudly as she could without yelling. She turned back to Tazmireth, but her friend's silence made her stomach drop. "What happened out there?" She asked, reaching to grab Taz's hand, who looked away sharply. *Vashir.*

This man was going to suffer the fate of someone unclean. Someone like her. What Philippa had turned Taz into.

Ole stepped beside his niece and daughter, lowering his voice. "There will be no explanation, Little Pip. You are Kelthari now. You must listen."

"Then I'll ask *him.*" The words flew out before she knew what she was saying.

She sidestepped around Ole, getting closer to the bars, ignoring the way Heru stiffened in protest. "Who are you?"

"He does not speak any language we know," Dagna said, her long nails clawing at the back of Philippa's arms. "Stupid Kelthari."

His eerie bird mask tilted as he took her in, his arms draped over his knees. Then, softly - so quietly she almost missed it and no one else could hear - he said, "you already know."

Philippa's jaw dropped. In nearly half of her life, she had never heard him speak; she didn't even know that he *could*.

Her savior was real, and they wanted to kill him.

Sharp nails dug into her arms as Dagna latched onto her, throwing her away from the cage. Philippa felt a trickle of blood run down her arm, and the masked man's head finally moved to watch her. How he had found this place, she had no idea. When Ole had taken Philippa hunting, it had been far away from the camp to keep the location safe. Unless somehow this guardian of hers had found a glass portal, but that didn't make sense, either.

The firelight of the Wahanar crackled, casting jagged shadows across the gathered warriors. The cage loomed between her and the stranger she had known her entire life, iron bars black against the embers, and inside, her guardian wasn't moving a muscle. As if chains and the threat of death meant nothing to him.

Herunavira watched Philippa in silence, her sharp gaze unreadable. Around them, the Wahanar whispered amongst themselves. Most nodded in agreement with Heru, who stood at the chieftain's side, his grip white knuckled around a blade Philippa had only ever seen him use while hunting.

"This was your hunt, daughter. Your prize."

Philippa's mouth twitched. "Ole," she whispered, "what is going on? Why won't you tell me anything?"

Olekashan looked around at his people. Philippa followed his gaze and felt the hair on her neck stand up. They looked so *hungry,* so ready for blood.

"Ole," Philippa said more forcefully, "I know you saw him that day on the hunt. He *saved* me. Why bring him in now? What did he do?"

The chief's voice was a low timbre. "You study us, but you do not understand us fully, Little Pip. I brought you, an unclean one, into our home. That was dangerous enough. But for two of you to walk about our camp is foolish. If he came for you once, he would again. I had to send

Herunavira and Tazmireth to fetch him. For the good of my family."

Her tongue felt dry in her mouth, and bitterness coated her throat. Philippa had not forgotten what she was to them, but hearing Ole call her unclean and his wariness of two *vashir* still stung. If anything, it gave her some clarity, and she couldn't stop herself from what she said next.

"Yeah. I keep hearing an awful lot about *family* from you."

Hurt engulfed Olekashan's face. His dark brows tightened, his mouth falling open ever the slightest.

Philippa wished she hadn't said it. She didn't want to hurt him. Reaching out, she tried to touch his arm, but the chief shook his head like he was disappointed in his own child.

At Ole's permission, Heru spoke with venom.

"He is *vashir!*" Herunavira spat, the Wahatan word carrying the weight of something vile. "Unclean. More than that! He serves a twisted power! He does not belong here. He rambled in languages unknown to us about some *purpose.* He found the gate we shattered. Was piecing it together. Death!"

Philippa's hand made its way to toy with her necklace, trying to keep her mouth shut. He'd tried to piece the gate back together. That was where they found him, which meant after he'd saved her from dying, he was still trying to get back to Philippa. She didn't know why, couldn't fathom how this guardian of myth was here before her and not teleporting away like he had all those times before, but she did know that Heru wanted to kill him; and that, Philippa couldn't allow.

Philippa's pulse hammered. "Then why not sentence him to the sands, like all of your other enemies? Why bring him home? Unless, since he is *vashir,* you plan on using him to try and heal Panu as well."

That earned a shift in the air, a tension in the crowd. She struck something.

Heru tilted her head. A test. She scoffed. "You would argue for the life of a man you do not know?"

"I know he's no threat to you from inside a cage," Philippa cast a glance at her guardian, still motionless, save for the slow incline of his head, as if amused by the debate over his life. "I also know I owe you my place here. That I haven't proved myself. But I belong to the Wahanar now." She swallowed and raised her inked hand into the air for all to see. "All of your other people know why. I am of your people now, at your chief's request. That means I deserve to know why you've taken him and why you want him dead." Quietly, she added, "since you chose to take a *vashir* into your home to save your child."

Silence. She'd gone too far.

Herunavira's dark eyes flicked to Ole, and for the first time, Philippa caught hesitation in her posture. She was testing *Philippa,* not the guardian.

"Tell her, Tazmireth. She listens to you," Heru said, waving her hand.

Ole interjected. "The Wahanar people do not give second chances to those who are serving a…" He searched for the word, unable to find it.

Heru raised her voice. "Tell her!"

Taz sighed. She spoke in Wahatan, and Philippa pieced together what she'd said. "Only we know of the portals we make. If he found them… then he was looking for a scribe. He was looking for you, *hannir.*"

Philippa straightened. "So you believe I've betrayed you."

Tazmireth nodded, but Herunavira said nothing. She didn't need to.

Philippa stepped closer to the cage, one hand wrapping around a bar. "I don't ask you to free him. I ask you to let him live so you can understand why he's here. I had no idea he would come for me" her voice softened. "What is one more prisoner to you? What threat is a caged man?"

Her guardian shifted then, ever so slightly, the air heavy with expectation.

"So you finally name your price for your healing of Panukirah." Heru's voice was level. Cold. She hated Philippa. Hated what she was, what she'd done, what she could *do.* Hated that she needed her.

Philippa's skin bristled, her ears twitching. Maybe she could find another way home. Heru was exacting her leadership upon her. She wanted revenge for needing Philippa, for needing to sin. Her life, for another's. Philippa had revealed too much by seeming to care about the man. But he had been saving her for as long as she could remember. She'd thought of him as many things, but immortal was not one of them. A man who would die under the scorch of thousands of flames. She had to repay him. Couldn't help herself. Levanta wasn't her home anymore, anyway.

"That is my price."

Heru's lips pressed together. Philippa hated that she looked impressed with her. Slowly, Herunavira raised her hand into the air.

The murmuring crowd silenced.

Heru spoke, her voice smooth as the wind over the dunes. "If you wish to keep his life, then his fate is tied to yours."

A test. A warning. A trap.

Philippa's breath caught. But she nodded. "I will bear it."

Herunavira watched her for a long, weighted moment. Then, as if nothing happened, she turned, walking away into the firelit night.

She had to heal Panu, and fast. Too many names were being written under her ability to do so.

Philippa exhaled, her grip loosening on the bar, her palm quaking. Inside the cage, her guardian shifted, his mask inclining towards her. "That," he said, "was reckless."

Her eyes flashed, her jaw clenching. "You're welcome."

For the first time, he laughed, a soft, breathy sound that was edged with something she couldn't quite place. And, for the first time, she wondered if she'd just made a mistake.

CHAPTER NINETEEN ✦

Five days left. The *Tanvirok* would not wait.

Philippa skirted the very borders of the Wahanar territory, burying her feet in the sand with each dragging step. Towards the center of the land was a spark, a faint glow of the watch set to keep eyes on her caged guardian. She had a sneaking suspicion he could get out if he wanted to, but if anything, she was still reeling that he was *there.*

Somehow, this complicated so much for her. Too much. She thought of Morgana as she cast her eyes skyward, the stars twinkling overhead like distant watchful eyes. Her sister would tell her that there had not been anyone saving Philippa - that it was all somehow her mind coping with the dire circumstances she found herself in time and again. Even after the run in while hunting with Ole, there had been an other worldliness about her masked savior. Now, there was an undeniable truth that he existed… that he wanted her.

A shiver ran down Philippa's spine. What could someone like that want? Obviously he could track her, and he could infiltrate even the Wahanar lands. It took him days to be caught; Shem had said that they found him as soon as he'd started sneaking about.

She ran her palm over her face, blotting out the stars. Inside her veins, her body thrummed, a whisper in her mind turning sing-song as a wave of dizziness washed over her.

You always wanted more than to rot in Levanta, her mind whispered. No, not her mind, just another voice inside it. The second one that had always been there, had been her contradictions and her conscience since she was small.

It's not like I speak to that little voice, she reasoned with herself.

Didn't you just?

Her eyes snapped open. She looked around, but as far as she could see, no one was there. Stars, what was *wrong* with her?

Philippa rested her head on her arms, drawing her knees close. All of this power inside her veins and it wouldn't work on Panu. What good was scribe magic if it could do nothing useful? The scribes of old, before they ran to Soffer, were said to have untamed magic that could do really anything. Yet she could suck the life from a mother and give it to a child, could split her shadows in two, but couldn't wake someone up. It didn't make any sense to her.

Maybe it had been too long since she'd practiced.

No, she thought, touching her locket. *If that were true, then I wouldn't be able to conjure any magic at all.*

"Poking your nose where it shouldn't belong?"

Philippa startled at the sight of the Wahanar guard, who stood between her and the border of their protected lands. She shouldn't have wandered so far, but she'd needed time by herself to think.

The large man carried an axe, his eyes twinkling with disdain. "Scribes don't belong here. You may be called Kelthari, but you are not one of us."

Softly, Philippa replied, "I know."

That seemed to give him pause, but the way he white knuckled his weapon made her slowly clamber to her feet.

"Are you thinking of running? I'd help you get a head start." Without waiting for a response, he sneered and raised the axe into the air.

Just as before, the magic in her body sang, almost screeched at the threat. Her tattooed fingers tingled. Maybe her magic didn't make sense, but it certainly acted like it was responding to her emotions.

Philippa was frozen, unsure of what to do. If she fought him - if her magic accidentally killed him - there would be no point of return for her.

A voice cut through the tension, cool and collected. "She was doing it for me."

Philippa turned, eyes bright, but her ears drooped slightly. She had been expecting someone else.

Shem spoke smoothly. "I asked her to check the stars for reference to a text."

The Wahanar man studied them both for a moment, eyes darting between the scholar and the scribe as if piecing together a mystery. As if deciding that the work the chief had assigned to Shem and Philippa was more important than his own feelings, the guard lowered his axe. He clucked his tongue, muttered something, and pressed his meaty hand against her shoulder. Forcefully, the Wahanar guard flung Philippa towards Shem, who caught her in hands that felt all too sure, all too comforting.

Get a hold of yourself!

Fear still ablaze in Philippa's chest, she ducked into Shem's tent. Funny, how she now thought of it as *his* and not the prisoner's tent.

Philippa wrung her hands as he stepped back to look her over. "You just lied for me."

Shem shrugged. "I figured you'd do the same."

She wasn't sure if that was true, but as she turned away, she wanted it to be.

———————————————————

She laid her tattooed palm onto Panukirah's head. It had been freshly shaven, except for a thick braid that ran down the center of his head and curled over his shoulder.

Earlier in the day, she'd convinced a medicine worker to bring her the red clay she'd seen them use. She needed this to work. Ink did nothing, and after short trial and error, the clay mixture turned out to be the same. Five days was not enough time to figure this out.

Philippa wiped the clay from her hands and decided to try and just use her tattoo as a conduit for the power like everyone had been telling her.

Using her tattooed palm, she wrote onto his forehead. Nothing changed. So, she moved to his chest. Again, nothing.

Philippa fell onto her seat unceremoniously. "Your tattoos do not grant any kind of power."

Tazmireth stood over a water basin in the corner, rinsing a blade still covered in soap that she'd shaved Panu's head with.

Smirking like a fox, Taz snapped her blackened fingers, welcoming a dancing flame. Philippa stuck her tongue out at her and laid her head onto her arms.

"Maybe you are distracted," Taz suggested in her native language.

Philippa groaned. "Maybe. I don't know what could help."

Her friend set down her blade on a towel, then came to stand on the opposite side of Panu's still form. "I know what helps me refocus."

She shrugged and looked at Tazmireth expectantly. Taz raised her eyebrows suggestively and made a crude gesture with her hands. Philippa gagged and swatted Taz's hands down, nearly falling onto Panu in the process.

"First of all, you're being gross," Philippa said.

Tazmireth licked her teeth. "Nothing gross if you do it right."

She covered her ears and hummed loudly. "*Secondly,* who here would I even proposition that for?" Her friend thought for a moment, then shrugged. Stumped. "Oh, so you will rampart about all that but then give me nothing to work with?"

"Those I have been with would either crush you or your heart would stop."

"Okay, you're not being helpful. Out."

Tazmireth held up her hands and chuckled, before shaking her head. It irked Philippa how pleased she was with herself. But she couldn't help but smile. Taz had become important to her, and it had been awhile since she'd seen her really laugh.

"I will focus, for you," Taz promised. "Your tattoo is not what gives you power. You are a conduit."

"So everyone keeps telling me," Philippa sighed.

Tazmireth flicked Philippa on the forehead.

"Ow!"

"Our fire cannot be called. It is not a dog. It needs room to breathe.

To feed on the space within you. It needs air to *become.* Give your magic the space within yourself to grow. Then call it forth," Tazmireth's hands rose and fell with an intentionally deep breath, "let it fill the chasm within yourself. Then…"

Taz opened her palm, and tiny sparks of fire danced in a circle upon her skin.

Philippa's eyes went wide. Taz was not normally the one to chastise her, but that was the clearest explanation of magic and expressing it that she had ever heard. Nodding thoughtfully, she turned back to Panu's body.

She'd been writing many different versions of things on his body, but none had helped. She closed her eyes, breathing deeply. Tried to quiet her mind. Forced thoughts of all other things from her consciousness - family, friends, desires - and focused on making a space.

Philippa pretended she was wading in the seas of Levanta. Felt the breeze on her skin as the southern winds shook through the lavender fields. A space, all of her own, to let something grow.

She opened her eyes. Looked at Panu. He did not wake, but everywhere she had written *heal,* something had changed.

On his forehead, his hair looked fuller. His chest, where his muscles had begun to thin from lack of use, was full and thick with corded muscle.

Her eyes flicked up to Taz, who looked equally horrified and in awe. Philippa reached over, grabbed her friend's hand. Despite the two women feeling close, Taz still flinched when Philippa touched her after using her power.

Philippa tilted her head, expression softening. "Thank you. I'm sorry this scares you."

Taz clicked her tongue, as if Philippa was being ridiculous. "You do not scare me. But I was told stories about people like you. What they can become. Just do not listen to anyone but *yourself* about how you use this power. Then, maybe I will not be so afraid."

Without another word, Tazmireth slid her hand into Philippa's and squeezed.

CHAPTER TWENTY✧

"Hannir! Hannir!"

Philippa stood up straight. "Are you ever going to tell me what that means?"

Tazmireth came barreling through the tent flaps, and threw Philippa's dinner bowl from her hands. Before Philippa could protest, Taz grabbed her by the hand to pull her along.

"What is going on?" She asked, wrenching free from Tazmireth's grip.

Taz was breathing hard. "Your bird man. They are doing something to him."

"Go, go!" Philippa said without a second of hesitation. She pushed Taz's shoulders, urging her forward.

Bursting out of the chief's pavilion, Tazmireth looked around madly before touching Philippa's shoulder and taking off again. That's when Philippa saw what was happening.

The cage was hoisted above the sand, a fire burning so hot underneath it that smoke nearly blocked out his form inside. Nearby, Dagna and Herunavira stood, watching him with unnatural interest.

"What are they doing?" Philippa shouted as they ran, not caring who heard. Her chest was tight, her fingers tingling.

Save him, save him, save him.

Taz ground her teeth. "My aunt thinks he is *vashir.* She would like to know what lies under his mask."

As if *that* explained anything!

Once they were within earshot, Dagna and Heru caught sight of them.

The chief's wife clapped her hands, and two hulking Wahanar were instantly in Philippa's path, scooping her off of her feet and holding her in the air. The second Wahanar guard tried to touch Taz, but she bit at his finger and he backed away.

Philippa squirmed in the guard's grasp, looking around his bald head to shoot daggers at Dagna. "What is going on?"

The chief's wife pinched the bridge of her nose. "Go and meddle with the boy, *vashir*! This does not concern you!"

Her heart sank. Smoke billowed in the cage, and though her guardian simply held onto the bars and looked out at nothing in particular, Philippa thought she could hear choking. Quiet, subdued, like he was trying to hide it. But he was hurting.

Dagna smiled at her, sparks lighting between her teeth. There was nothing Philippa could say to stop this.

Tazmireth cleared her throat, waving her hand in front of her face to part the smog. "Kelthari, did you not buy this man's life with your own?"

As soon as the words left Taz's mouth, Dagna paled. She looked at her daughter with disgust.

But Herunavira just stared at Philippa with dead eyes.

"I did," Philippa said between coughs, "now tell me what is going on. I'm responsible for him."

Smacking her lips, Dagna indicated with a hand to lower Philippa down. The guard set Philippa on her feet, but did not let go of her arms. Taz's fists shook as she watched, but she didn't intervene.

Dagna dug her nails into Philippa's wrist and pulled her towards the cage. Even from a few feet away, the heat of the fire was nearly unbearable. How he was swathed in black inside the cage, she didn't know. Her guardian didn't so much as move a muscle, except now he seemed to be locked onto what Dagna was doing to her.

"I keep my word," Dagna sneered, "I am not killing him. But I wish to know what kind of *vashir* is under that mask. I will smoke it out of him."

"Breathing all that smoke will *kill* him!" Philippa cried.

Dagna shrugged. "It is not I who makes the killing blow. My promise is kept."

Something simmered inside Philippa's bones, a feeling she'd had only a few times in her life. The first was when she had seen beasts claw at her mother, and the second was when she thought that Morgana and Raff would be harmed on her behalf.

Now, she felt that same bubbling, acrid venom coursing through her veins. There was no reason to punish her guardian. He was just a man who was trying to protect her, and even if she didn't understand *why*, he hadn't done anything wrong. Whatever he was, she did not care, and they. Were. Hurting. Him.

"Stop using your magic to hurt him this instant," Philippa said through clenched teeth. "I tied his life to mine, and I've done nothing to deserve this. Stop." She waved at the fire, at the black smoke beginning to cascade through the camp. In the distance, she heard Ole's booming voice asking what was going on. She ignored it.

Herunavira placed a hand on her mother's shoulder and winced.

Philippa smiled. She was right. They had to stop, because it would kill him and he technically now belonged to her as long as they were in the Wahanar lands.

With a flick of her hand, Heru called the flames back into her own body, leaving only the thick smoke behind.

Dagna scowled at Philippa, digging her long nails in further to her flesh. Philippa turned to walk away, towards the case, but the poisoner held firm, hard enough to draw blood.

That simmering, hot venom inside Philippa reached a boiling point. She whirled on Dagna, magic thrumming in her body to be *let out.* It was like Philippa unknowingly knew what it meant to open herself up to magic like Taz had told her, and a great inky blackness filled it. With the insatiable need to obey the gnawing sensation in herself, Philippa spoke with such unfeeling coldness that she did not recognize her own voice.

"Your word means nothing. You are a lying, unloving, viscous creature who does not care for her family. *I* follow your laws more than you, and I am a *vashir.* What does that make you, Dagna?"

As soon as the words left her lips, Philippa knew they were a mistake.

Gasps resonated beyond them, and Philippa's eyes darted around to see that not only were Tazmireth and Olekashan standing at attention, but nearly twenty others who had gathered to see what was happening. Even little Benni stood in the crowd. He waved.

Awkwardly, Philippa raised her hand to wave back at the child.

Until clawed fingers came straight for her eyes. Philippa's raised hand flew to protect herself, when that untamable power inside of her *cracked* open.

Her tattoos turned red-hot as she caught Dagna's flying hand. Instantly, smoke and the scent of seared flesh filled her nostrils.

Stop hurting us! Her mind cried out, her fingers tightening around Dagna's arm even more.

Dagna cried out, a wretched, pitiful noise. Nearby, a Nazheris prowled forward, lips drawn back to reveal thick dagger-like teeth ready to strip Philippa's skin from her bones.

"*Hannir,* stop!" Taz whispered.

Philippa let go. All the fight in her, all that desire to express her magic faded into a hazy exhaustion.

Dagna curled over her arm, blackened finger marks ruining her skin where Philippa had grabbed her. Shame crept up Philippa's neck, her ears lowering. The Wahanar looked at her one of two ways: in respectful awe, or sheer terror. Benni was still waving.

Olekashan cleared his throat. "Enough spectacle. Our people fight all the time. It is our way. Kelthari was expressing herself as one of us."

"*ONE OF US?*" Dagna looked up from under her beaded face covering, her voice shrill and taut. "She will never be one of us! Look at her, Olekashan! She is poison! She is death!"

Philippa's heart was hammering in her chest, phantom hands curling around her throat. She began to back up, feeling a thousand pounds heavier under the weight from the stares. She wouldn't even look at Tazmireth… Philippa had a feeling she knew the look that would be there.

Unable to stop, her legs woodenly carried her back from the crowd as

Dagna continued to screech. Philippa's back hit the bars, still warm from the fire.

A shadow formed over her head.

Nearly jumping out of her skin, she looked up, and saw that her guardian was standing at the edge of his birdcage, his feet at her shoulders as he slowly swung back and forth in the hanging prison. He fell to a crouch, his bone-white mask covered in soot. Her guardian looked like he was straight out of a storybook with ash falling onto his pristine black clothes and peppering his gray feathers.

The beak of his mask slid partially through the bars, and as she craned her neck to meet his stare, he reached through the bars and offered her his hand. She didn't take it.

He slid it back into the cage. "I like this version of you. You're braver."

Tears pricked her eyes as all the fight left her. "I'm scared."

She wasn't sure why she said it.

As if her words struck him, his head pulled back ever the slightest. She thought for a moment that he would tell her not to be scared, that everything would be alright. But then again, he seemed far too serious for that.

He inclined his masked facade to her again. He was so close that she could smell the salt of the sea on him. He smelt like home. Instead of saying what she'd presumed, his voice lowered into a softness that reminded her of velvet.

All he said was, "I'm here."

The world fell away from her. She didn't know this man, not really. She had bartered her freedom for a stranger, *again.*

What was I thinking?

But she knew what she had been thinking.

Free him, free him, free him, that ever present instructional voice that urged her onward, kept her going when the path did not seem straight.

In those two words, she heard so many more, knew it in her blood despite not knowing him at all: *you don't have to be scared if I'm here.*

She wanted to ask him why, to question everything he'd ever done up until now, but his hands were reaching through the bars and it was as if they were the only two people who mattered. He had answers, she could feel it.

Suddenly, in an unceremonious manner, she realized why he'd reached through his cage at all.

Dagna was suddenly upon her, all rage and snapping teeth, yanking Philippa around by her arms. Olekashan was yelling for his wife to stop, that she had no permission to do this.

Stars, Philippa wished she'd been paying attention instead of soul searching with a man in a bird mask.

"I will no longer tolerate this uncleanness!" Dagna roared, and her hands found Philippa's throat.

Philippa coughed, her head smacking the back of the cage as Dagna kept one hand around her throat. Dagna's other hand shuffled in her layered top, before coming out with a glass vial so small that it was hidden by her fingers. With her teeth, she uncorked it and snarled at Philippa.

"Die badly, witch," Dagna said, voice venomous.

Then, she shoved the poison towards Philippa's mouth.

Philippa tried to conjure her magic again, but shadows formed around her vision, stars blooming like lights between blinks. She thought she heard Dagna yelling at Taz to stay away. Someone yelled for Tazmireth to put her dagger down.

The glass was pressed against Philippa's lips, and it was all she could do to keep her mouth squeezed shut.

The pressure on her throat lessened, and she gasped for air. Philippa coughed and sputtered, colors starting to dapple back into existence.

Dagna slowly pulled the vial away, her other hand hesitating to let go.

"End this, Dagna. For the good of all," Ole's voice was shaking.

Blinking away the haze, Philippa's eyes sharpened as adrenaline flooded her veins. Still hanging onto Philippa's neck, Dagna was gritting her teeth, sparks falling in a waterfall of color.

Under the poisoner's neck was a curved blade so sharp that drew blood just by *touching* the woman's skin.

The person holding it was her guardian.

In one swift movement, Dagna put her hands in the air, stepping back. Philippa's hands flew protectively to her neck. Behind the chief's wife, Heru had wrestled Tazmireth to the ground, twisting her arms behind her back.

"Enough," Ole announced to everyone, "we have fought through our differences. It is our way. This is done."

Philippa cast a glance to her soot-covered savior, to find that the scythe had disappeared and he was sitting idly in his swinging cage once more.

"Four guards around this cage at all times!" Dagna cried out, walking away in a huff. "Only water. No food. It is done."

Immediately, Wahanar moved to fill the space Dagna had ordered, and Heru pushed off of Tazmireth.

Taz shoved her cousin and scoffed, heading straight for Philippa. Ole beat her there, his shadow towering over Philippa.

His lips were pursed, hands on his hips. He looked imposing, but Philippa saw the way his fingers twitched unsurely with the wrapped hem of his skirting. "You fought through a problem like a Wahanar, Little... Kelthari," he corrected, and then whispered, "you spoke true. You fought true. I am not angry with you."

Her heart lurched in her chest. "I... I'm still sorry. That wasn't me. That's not... who I want to be."

Olekashan shrugged and tousled her hair. "Keep trying to save Panu. It is all I ask. Until then, you are one of us, and you must live like us. We fight to speak. Whoever you become, Kelthari, is of no importance to me. Just become you."

Too stunned to speak, she let Ole push her jaw closed and saunter away after his wife and daughter.

I will never understand his capacity to forgive things like this, Philippa thought, *I don't deserve it.*

Her chest was constricted. Maybe that's what made him a good father. Stars, she had to heal Panu, and fast.

Though Ole seemed appeased, that only left one other person, the one she was most frightened to speak to.

Tazmireth was dusting herself off, and awkwardly slowed down when Philippa looked at her. "What, *hannir?*"

"I just did something awful," Philippa whispered, "I'm so sorry. I don't want any of you - mostly you - to be afraid of me."

Taz crossed her arms and looked down her nose at Philippa, distaste written all over her face. Philippa's heart began to feel like it would stop with Taz looking at her like that, but then Tazmireth laughed.

Laughed.

Right then.

I will never understand these people, Philippa thought.

Tazmireth threw an arm around her shoulders and began to usher her away. "You will not be allowed to speak to him again. But between you and me, I am not afraid. Maybe you are making me *vashir,* but my aunt is a *belthezah.* She deserves more than a few burns."

Benni suddenly appeared, running by to catch up with his parents. He pumped his fist at Philippa. "We've all wanted to do that!"

Philippa's brows knit together as she allowed herself to be led away, casting a glance at her guardian who didn't even bother to look in her direction. Turning back to Taz, Philippa asked, "What is a bell...?"

Chuckling darkly, Taz whispered, "you would say it's crude."

———————————————

She was going to lose her mind.

Between not being permitted to speak to her guardian again, and struggling to translate a particularly convoluted passage of Wahanar text, surely madness would descend on her at any moment. Tazmireth had been attempting to check on Philippa's guardian on her behalf, but now the Wahanar had started associating Taz with Philippa; which really just meant they were too angry to let her see the guardian, either. Her head throbbed as she rifled through another piece of nearly scorched parchment.

She ignored it, instead muttering under her breath as she tried to piece together the unfamiliar dialect. Almost two weeks into their collaboration, Shem's amusement was palpable. She could feel his eyes on her, a suppressed smirk playing on his lips, until he finally erupted in laughter.

"*Yes?*" She asked, glaring.

"You've translated that as, 'the great horse that weeps for its own hooves.'"

Blinking, Philippa groaned. "I hate this language."

"No, no, it's beautiful. Really. Very poetic."

She scowled, then against her better judgment, she smiled. Shem kept on watching her, golden eyes searching. She looked up at him, brows knit in question.

"Nothing, I just… It's the first time I've ever seen you relax. It looks good on you."

Relax. The one thing she didn't have time to do.

Philippa rolled her shoulders. "Do you think there's anything in these texts that'll actually help me wake Panu up?"

The scholar put a finger to his chin in thought as he glanced down at his own stack of papers. "I've found a few mentions of their biology which could be useful, but I suspect that you've come across those as well."

She nodded.

"Perhaps we're just missing something about an illness, a genetic defect?" He asked, mostly to himself. "Or maybe we are looking in the wrong places. Maybe the answer is not to wake him yet, but to unite their family another way? That's what you said the chief ultimately wants from you."

Philippa licked her dry lips. "Maybe. What did they want from you, anyway? I got a deal to go home if I make good on what I said I would. What's your deal?"

Shem chuckled. "My *deal*," he said, rolling his eyes, "is that I get to keep my life by translating their older texts."

"Why were you snooping around their lands, anyway? How did you find them?" She'd been wondering about his story since she'd met him, but until now there hadn't been a dull moment to seize the opportunity.

"That is… a longer story."

Philippa set her papers aside and put her chin in her hands. She leaned forward eagerly. "I have time."

He snorted. "You most certainly do not, Miss Aporo."

She shrugged. "Fine, then. I just thought that a scholar and a researcher would like the opportunity to explain what he was learning."

Philippa turned away coyly, hiding her smile. As painfully slow as she could, she parted paper from paper. Her ears twitched as she heard him going back to his own stack, fingers idly digging through papers. Then, he sighed.

"Fine."

She perked up, tossing her stack aside, and sitting at attention once more.

His laugh was warm. Her skin tingled. "Why so eager? I'm nothing more than a stranger to you."

"You don't have to be, though," she said quietly, "you're a stranger who has seen the *world.* Learned languages, seen cultures I've never heard of. I come from an ocean town that exports fish and lavender. The most I've seen is when the Wahanar dragged me through the desert."

"I arrived near the Wahanar lands by accident," he said with obvious embarrassment, "the oldest nation of the continent and I *stumbled* upon it? Absolute nonsense. I had been sent by my colleagues to find them before, but on this particular trip, I was looking for someone specific."

Philippa felt her chest warm as he spoke. "Did you find them?"

Shem smiled. "I found you, which will have to do."

She tucked a stray hair behind her pointed ear. "Colleagues. Trips. Studies. You've seen the world haven't you?"

"In stints," he offered.

"What's been the best thing you've seen?" She asked.

Shem tugged on one of his braided locks. Stars, those *eyes.* Just the way he sat had an air of importance, a wisdom of a life well lived. Philippa wondered if she would ever have that far off, wanderlust look about her like he did.

Before he could answer, Tazmireth appeared in the entrance of the tent. In Wahanar, she said, "Have you discovered anything that will help Panu?"

Shoulders heavy, Philippa shook her head. "Is there anything that we could know to help? Any illnesses Herunavira had growing up? His father?"

Taz stretched her neck and chewed on her lips in thought. "Mm. None. No one sleeps that heavily except you."

Shem's eyebrows hit his hairline as he shot an intrigued look at Philippa, who turned bright red and waved off what he was thinking.

"Is this one any help?" Tazmireth growled, gesturing at Shem.

He narrowed his eyes at the warrior and looked away, burying himself in his texts. In the brief moments that Philippa had seen Shem and Taz interact, this was about as peaceful as it got. Taz didn't mind letting him know how little she cared for him.

"He thinks some of your people's old writings could lead us in a new direction," Philippa said, but quietly added, "unless it's not a natural illness at all."

Smokey eyes flashing, Tazmireth stepped inside and fell into a crouch. She gestured at Philippa to continue. Shem also looked intrigued, his mouth curled to the side.

Ignoring the heat in her stomach, Philippa continued. "Be honest with me, Taz. Has Ole captured a scribe before me?"

Immediately, Taz shook her head *no*.

"Are there any scribes who would want to hurt Ole or your family?"

That took Tazmireth longer to answer.

"Taz...?" Philippa prodded.

Her friend sighed. "It is a complicated answer. If you asked anyone else, they would say all scribes want to hurt us. We do not mix."

Philippa flashed her a smile. "Yet here we are."

Tazmireth began to return her smile in kind, but her face fell when Shem interjected. "So what you're saying is that you have absolutely no clue how the boy fell sick. Did you even bother to tell the scribe - the one you're expecting to heal him - when he fell ill and how?"

Oh, this was bad.

Philippa covered her face, expecting to hear Tazmireth's hand crack across Shem's face. Instead, Taz only answered, "you have me and *hannir* to thank for your hands being free. Speak to us more respectfully."

Shem's golden eyes cooled. "Or you'll bind them again, yes, I'm aware."

There was a metal *twang* as Tazmireth unsheathed a black dagger. "Or I'll remove them."

The air in the tent was thick enough that Philippa wanted to grab Taz's dagger to cut it. Slowly, Shem nodded and dutifully went back to studying.

Tazmireth replaced her blade and looked at Philippa, rolling her eyes and mouthing, "this is who you like?"

Face hot, Philippa shook her head madly at her friend.

In her black palm, Tazmireth lit a tiny flame, one that raced around her hand in circles. Philippa was always mesmerized when she did that, at the casualness of Taz's magic. The way she allowed her flames to take form when she thought was alluring.

With a deep breath, Tazmireth extinguished her fire. "Panu fell sick before you arrived. He is well loved. The perfect Wahanar boy. But… he was a strange child."

"Strange for Wahanar children or all children in general?" Philippa cautiously asked.

Taz caught her meaning and smirked. "For Wahanar children. He would wrestle but always was so concerned with honor. More than even Olekashan. What child speaks of right and wrong? He always had an air about him. Strong. As if he was bigger than all Wahanar before him. I do not know if that was sickness. But it was odd. When he fell asleep, it was the strangest thing.

He asked Herunavira, Olekashan and myself to come watch what he had learned. Panu went into the oasis up to his waist, and told us to be careful. Then, he opened his mouth and a great fire poured out."

Philippa stared, waiting for Tazmireth to continue. When her friend just stared right back, Philippa glanced at Shem, who was scribbling down everything Taz was saying on a piece of parchment with a stray chunk of charcoal.

"What's so odd about that?" Philippa asked.

Tazmireth wrung her hands together, a bead of sweat dripping down her face. "He has no tattoos. We can make fire without them, but… this was different. This was not a flame. This was a waterfall of fire. Like a dragon."

A chill ran over Philippa's arms. "What happened next?"

"He fell. Never to awake again," Taz murmured.

Philippa chewed on the inside of her cheek. Could the expression of his magic been too much? If there was that much fire coming from one person, maybe it overwhelmed his body. But if that were true, wouldn't his body heal and wake up on its own?

He was certainly still alive in his mind, Philippa had felt it herself. The way Taz explained it though made it seem like Panu should not have been able to conjure fire at all.

"Why does Panukirah have no tattoos?" Shem asked, prying Philippa from her thoughts.

Tazmireth waved him off. "It is not important."

"Do you want him to wake or not?" Shem's voice was hard, his eyes not even focused on Tazmireth as he continued to take notes.

"I am done here," Taz growled, "*Hannir,* read as much as you can tonight. We are running out of time."

With that, Tazmireth stomped out of the tent.

Philippa glared at Shem. "You didn't have to antagonize her like that."

"I asked her a question," he countered.

What she'd just thought was so attractive, his nose buried in his studies, suddenly boiled her blood. Philippa snatched the papers from his hands to reveal his shocked expression. He looked half ready to argue, but it must've been written all over her face that he would not win.

Slowly, Shem exhaled. "A researcher asks questions. Even uncomfortable ones."

"And what did you learn from doing that to her?" Philippa crossed her arms.

"That she cares for the boy more than his own mother."

There was a moment where the only sound was the wind over the sands and the ruffling of the tent's fabric. It dawned on Philippa that while Heru had been the one to spare Raff when she thought Tazmireth would punish him for stepping up, that she had no idea what Tazmireth's plan had been that day. While Herunavira admired Raff's courage, Taz likely had seen something else.

She saw a nephew trying to save his aunt.

A lump formed in Philippa's throat. Taz wanted Panu to heal just as badly as Olekashan and had been willing to be made unclean for it. After Philippa was gone, there was no telling what kind of life Taz would live under Dagna's thumb. The Wahanar would not all change their ways, and while Philippa would never ask them to, she *would* ask them to accept Taz once more.

Maybe… maybe Taz would come with her. If this wasn't the life she wanted to live, then perhaps coming with Philippa wouldn't seem so bad to her.

Liar, liar, liar.

Philippa sighed. Taz loved her family too much to leave, even if it meant her detriment. In a perfect world, families would accept one another and allow others to grow into who they were meant to be without fault. But it was not a perfect world, and Philippa knew what it was like to have to hide parts of yourself.

"I'm sorry," Shem's voice pulled her from her thoughts.

She blinked, feeling tears settling on her cheeks. She didn't even know that she'd been crying. Philippa backhanded the wetness away and looked up at Shem.

His brows were drawn in concern, his hand outstretched to touch her shoulder. Philippa forced a smile. "It's not your fault. I'm an easy cry."

The scholar seemed to calculate that and he nodded. "Noted."

CHAPTER TWENTY-ONE ✧

Shem stretched his back against the rug, staring at the ceiling of the tent. "I was supposed to be some great scholar, and I am now reduced to a prisoner who cannot find an answer to a *nap.*"

His voice edged on being delirious. He'd often gotten wistful and stuck in the hypothetical when they worked through the night.

Philippa didn't mind, though. In fact, the warmth in her fingertips as she listened to him ramble through solutions was telling her that she *really* didn't mind. Stars, she could listen to him talk for hours.

Shem was as real as they came. He rarely hid how he felt, and he was goal oriented. She could get used to having someone like that around. No, it did not even bother her when he was melancholic and lost in thought. It was becoming increasingly evident that being a scholar was not part of him, or his career, but who he was at his core. He yearned to understand, to teach, to learn. A smile played on her lips.

Philippa was half asleep beside him. She yawned and murmured, "you're still a researcher. You're still you."

A long silence stretched between them, almost lulling her to sleep, when he asked a question. "What about you? Who were you supposed to be?"

Philippa didn't answer right away. "I don't know. Someone safe, I think."

It sounded rather dull once she said it. But she felt the rug underneath them shift, and even with her eyes closed, she knew he was looking at her.

"Setting aside that we are literally in an antagonistic camp of warriors, you feel rather safe to me."

She pretended to be asleep, to not hear. But something stirred in her heart. Clearly he had chosen to omit the memory of her searing Dagna's flesh with her bare hand. Philippa still couldn't believe that had happened. It had felt like her magic took over her body, like the thrumming inside her was going to scream louder than she ever could. Yet, that isn't what Shem focused on. That glaring, odd, frightening moment where she was anything *but* safe, and he simply overlooked it. Maybe that didn't make him as good of a person as she wanted him to be, or maybe it made him better. There was no way to tell.

She was glad he felt safe around her, that he would describe her so, but if she was already what she was meant to be, what was there left of her to become? Was the only growth she had left that ugly, gnawing sensation she'd had when she fought Dagna?

Maybe she had been around Shem too much. Now *she* was overthinking everything. It hadn't been an entirely long time since knowing him, but still, her guard was falling anytime they tried to solve Panu's case together.

Poor Panu. Philippa had been telling herself that trying to decipher the texts of the Wahanar people with Shem would help him, but at the very same time, this felt selfish. She *liked* Shem's company. Certainly more than she enjoyed the company of Dagna and her followers.

No, she told herself. This would help Panu. There was something odd about the way he slept. Though he rarely moved, his sleep was fitful, as if he were constantly in a nightmare. He often reminded her of how a dog would whimper in its sleep, or its legs would thrash as if chasing something… or being chased. It was no wonder that Ole had called for a scribe when he'd heard of one. Panu had not been poisoned, yet he would not wake, and everyone described him as a dutiful, honor bound young man with nothing to complain about. Someone or something had done this to him.

Morbidly hoping that this had happened to a Wahanar before, Philippa and Shem had dove into the old texts in hopes that it would have *some* answers. Because as Philippa pretended to be fast asleep, there was the unfortunate truth that her magic could not wake up Panu. The thought had come to her days ago, but she couldn't get her mouth to form the words anytime she spoke to Panu's family. Not only would it be admitting that she was worthless to them, but it meant never going home. Dagna would kill her, she was sure of it.

Shem had suggested to Philippa that if the texts didn't give her any leads about Panu's health, that maybe there was a loophole in the laws to ensure that she would get to go home.

The idea left a bitter taste in Philippa's mouth. Panu needed a physician, but they had chosen Philippa, so it seemed that lying in the tent, surrounded by ancient knowledge of a people scorned by all, was to be her fate. Just giving up felt like admitting what she believed about herself was true… and that would break her. Every day, her entire life, she'd been able to fake her worth enough to make it. Making someone smile, helping Raff with his schoolwork, saving Elodie… all of that, just to feel a sense of worth. Just to feed off of the high long enough to wake up again the next day, to try and earn the worthiness all over again.

Shem's voice was modulated as he shifted to his knees. "Besides, you saved your friend in the cage."

Snapping from her thoughts, she opened her eyes to defend her actions, when she saw he was grinning from ear to ear.

"So. You are awake."

Philippa covered her face. "This is all just complicated." Shem nodded dutifully, feigning agreement. Philippa arched her brow. "Oh, you are just having the best time, aren't you?"

"Careful, I'm not feeling very safe," he put his hands up in mock surrender. She chuckled, swatting his arm and rolling to sit up. "How *do* you know that man?"

The very question she'd hoped he would avoid. There was no point in dancing around it. She quickly explained the distinct times she'd been sure that he existed, saving her life, and the times when she'd felt her mind speak, as if being whispered to by another.

"That sounds quite intimate."

She startled, less at the strain in his voice, but that he believed her. "I suppose. But, he and I don't really know each other. Not like we do." She wasn't sure why she added that last part.

Shem studied her, his expression unreadable in the dim glow of the firelight. "Not like we do," he echoed, his voice quieter now, thoughtful.

Philippa swallowed, suddenly aware of the space between them, of how the air had shifted. She hadn't meant to make a distinction, hadn't even realized that she'd felt one until she said it aloud. But it was true, wasn't it? Shem was here, tangible, and a steady soul. She didn't even know the name of her guardian. The masked man intrigued her and he probably had answers to questions she'd carried for some time, but despite him saving her so often, he'd never made the move to be *around* her. To speak with her.

Shem tilted his head. "You trust him."

It wasn't a question.

"I don't know," she admitted. "After seeing him, actually *seeing* him, it felt different. But he's saved my life more than once."

Shem exhaled, rubbing a hand over his jaw, ever calculating. "That doesn't mean he isn't dangerous."

She turned fully towards him, searching his face. "And if I said the same about you?"

His brow twitched, and for the first time she saw a faint scar marring his brown skin. "I wouldn't argue. In dangerous times, we become dangerous things."

She smiled at that, but it was fleeting. Because, if Shem was dangerous, it was different. He was a stranger who owed her nothing, yet chose to at least try and help her. Maybe it was for his own gain. But he'd been honest to her since they'd met. His eyes flashed, reminding her distinctly of Shanti. Not quite human, not quite anything she knew.

She'd known Shanti her entire life, and she'd sold her out. Shem, she'd known for days, and he'd protected her at least once. Valued her. More than she could say for someone she had known since arriving in Levanta.

Shem leaned in slightly. "Just be careful, Miss Aporo. It's admirable you want to be gentle and kind. I've never met a soul quite like you. If you get too close to what you don't understand, they'll rip who you are away from you. There's been too many accounts I've read where it happens to perfectly unassuming, good willed people. I would hate to see that happen to someone I know. You have something special. Don't taint it by wasting it on someone who won't tell you what they want from you."

His voice was so sure, so wispy and full of mirth. He shouldn't care what happened to her, she knew this, but he apparently *did*. Philippa had felt like she was going crazy, conjuring up a feeling about him that was completely one sided. Maybe it was just a fascination with someone so cultured, so well framed and confident in who they were, but she couldn't help it.

Shem had been saying that he didn't want her to get used, to be betrayed by someone she didn't fully understand, but at present, she could only stare at his molten irises.

A strange warmth curled in her chest. The logical thing to do would be to move back. To give him space. But those knowing eyes drew her in, a moth to a flame. He'd seen more of the world than she could ever dream of, had learned languages that were thought to be dead and gone. His mind was a new, ferocious, intriguing thing.

She had no time for distractions, and she hesitated. She wished she had met him anywhere else so she could have the time to explore every corner of his brain, to learn about his soul. Philippa had been with men before, but it was always a youthful, dead end kind of interaction. Around Shem, it felt like the world would open up beneath her feet.

Morgana and Raff flashed through her mind. A scorpion's daggertail covered in her friend's blood bounced around her skull.

Her hand flew to her forehead to clear the unwanted images. It didn't matter what she wanted. She didn't have time to *wish*.

And you're probably making this all up in your head, she told herself.

Philippa nodded once, settling into the mat. "Do any of your stories have anything to help us now?"

Worthless...

She bit her cheek.

Shem hummed thoughtfully and leaned back on his elbows. "Us? No.

Me? Maybe."

"So self serving, for a researcher."

"We are the most selfish kind of people." he said. "Hungry for all the knowledge in the world that we'd spend anything to receive it."

Before she could respond, Tazmireth appeared in the doorway, throwing blankets at them. She spoke rapidly, then excused herself, but Philippa noted that Heru's name was mentioned.

Shem eyed her. "She said there's going to be a storm and that her cousin ordered her to watch the prisoner to make sure he doesn't escape."

Philippa wrung her hands, gathering the blankets awkwardly thrown at them. "Which really means, she expects me to make sure you don't escape."

"A true friend," Shem noted dully, clearly annoyed that Taz had come at all.

Smiling faintly, Philippa laid a blanket over her legs. "Maybe the storm will stop the other tribes of Wahanar from getting here in time for the *Tanvirok.* More time to study. Maybe we can find something to heal Panu and find that backup plan you told me about when we first met, right?"

"There you go again, saving people. You take the first stack," Shem said, and pulled a scroll into his lap to get to work.

CHAPTER TWENTY-TWO ✧

The wind howled outside of the tent, sand slamming against each side, pressing Philippa and Shem closer together. Though it had always felt spacious inside, with the storm blustering so violently, it suddenly felt as if they were in a box. Philippa clutched a scroll to her chest, staring at the fabric walls as they rippled.

Shem laid a blanket over her shoulders. "You're scared," he observed quietly, careful to give her space.

She exhaled sharply. "Not of this."

No, she was scared of failing. Of letting Panu lay in his sleep forever, of Ole losing a grandson, of Heru losing her child, of Taz facing the consequences… of never seeing her family again.

Something shifted in the air between them at her admission, a subtle change in the dynamic that had previously felt so fragile. A flicker of something unreadable crossed his eyes – perhaps surprise, perhaps a different emotion she couldn't quite decipher. He apologized that she was scared, his voice a low murmur that seemed to fill the sudden quiet between them. Yet, despite the seemingly comforting intention, she sensed a reservation in his tone. He was hiding something in his words, a truth carefully veiled beneath the surface of his concern, and the realization sent a shiver down her spine that had nothing to do with fear, and everything to do with a growing unease.

She was continually slapped in the face with the truth that Shem was just as much of a stranger as anyone else here. Then again, so was Tazmireth, and Philippa knew in her heart that she loved her. But something sisterly felt so natural to her. Whatever she felt now, for this handsome researcher, was frightening. Unnerving.

"Do say what you mean." she said quietly.

He waved her off at first, burying his attention in a scroll. His resolve quickly faded, and he planted his chin in the palm of his hand.

His voice was nearly drowned out by the storm. "You are an anomaly to me, Miss Aporo. You fear but you press on, when the threat is very much a reality. It seems to me that you focus solely on being a soft place to land for others, yet you can hardly save yourself. So yes. I am puzzled. I have yet to meet someone like you in all my travels."

"Those things don't worry me." She lied.

"It's what worries me," he quickly said.

Philippa felt her heart lurch into her throat. Her ears twitched against her will. She suddenly felt like the wind had stopped, as if they were alone between pages of a book and no one could read them.

"It worries you because you are unsure of how to describe me in the report you're undoubtedly going to make about this place." she said, meeting his gaze.

Shem stiffened, his hand going to the pocket on his tunic nervously.

She rolled her eyes. "You *must* be making a report on this place. Why else would you have ventured so close? You're a scholar. I know what must worry you. I've seen you write in that notepad that you think is so secret."

"It worries me," he continued, voice uneven and soft, "because if you do all the saving, who ever gets to save you?"

She knew it was true, and couldn't fight that. Maybe that's how she was written. Maybe she could change that now, with what she was learning.

Stop, stop, stop.

She had to focus.

"Then don't worry about me."

He looked taken aback, like she'd struck him. Though they hadn't known each other long, Philippa thought they were becoming something akin to friends. She wanted to be.

"That's like asking you to stop this research and follow me into the desert to find our own way out, Philippa. You're a saver. I'm a worrier. What a pair are we, hmm?" He quirked his lips into a tired smile, one she would have reached out and touched if she could've.

"I'm glad I met you." Philippa said, voice hoarse.

Shem's eyes narrowed. "Why does that sound like you're saying goodbye to me? We only just met."

She nodded, loosely tying her hair back in a braid. She missed the way it was filtered with mauve and purple from eating the fish in Levanta. Since being with the Wahanar for some time now, living off of their meat and stews, it had faded into an earthy, dark brown.

"I can't do this, Shem. I've tried. They gave me a tattoo to be a conduit for my power, and I can't heal Panu. Do you know how many times I've tried to heal him, and it just feels like ramming my head against a wall? They only use ink for tattoos. It's precious to them. When I use it, on a fingertip, wasting it, Panu stays asleep. They put ink into others to create fire, and I can't wake a boy?" She shook her head, pressing her palms against her temples. "You're the smartest person I have ever met in my life, and even you can't help me. I don't even know where to look for their original writings. They can't use paper for everything, it'll scorch eventually. What did they do, write it in stone? They can't carry tablets everywhere, can they? The answers aren't here, and they certainly aren't within me."

Shem's eyes lit up. He grabbed her by the shoulders. "Miss Aporo, you're a genius!"

"Stop, Shem," she waved him off, but found herself unable to pull away. "You don't need to comfort me."

"Listen to yourself. Written in stone. The translations we've been missing. If you're right, we just need to ask, and they could take us to the law. You could have more time! We could get out of here unscathed. Change the price for Panu."

She narrowed her eyes. "What?"

His worn fingertips grasped her tattooed hand, lifting it before her eyes.

He was so warm. "You *are* a conduit. Panu is just a complicated case. A scribe didn't write the Wahanar laws. You can change them!"

She thanked the stars that the wind was covering up the sound of his voice from outside, hiding the plan he was hatching. But he was *brilliant*.

"Because if a scribe didn't alter their laws before, a scribe can alter them now." She'd heard such a law of magic before. It was said that even scribes of lower importance could alter even life books if they hadn't already been tampered with. It took a great deal of power to change an alteration, and as the thought crossed Philippa's mind that she would never achieve such a feat, her mind whispered to her once more.

You lie, you lie, you lie.

Shem clapped his hands together, his smile genuine and excited. "You can do this," he urged. "Ask your friend, the one who doesn't like me."

Philippa leveled a glare at him. "None of them like you."

His smile touched his eyes, crinkling them around the corners like worn paper. "Tazmireth. Your *actual* friend. She can take us to where they wrote their laws. You told me before about having to heal her after the catacomb incident. Who do you think dug those? The Wahanar have claimed these lands for *centuries*. The sands bend to them, making doorways we can't even begin to understand. You could fix this, Philippa. You could save everyone here."

He couldn't have known how closely his words echoed the wishes of Olekashan, of how a chief begged her to save his family.

Her heart pounded in her chest. Shem was so passionate, so alive in this moment, so unfettered by their circumstances. She wanted to be more like him. But the Wahanar thought their laws were sacred. She hadn't even tried to change Taz's mind about her beliefs about being unclean. Philippa adjusted the neckline of her top, feeling like her clothes were trying to cut off her air supply. How could she change their way of *life* if she was unwilling to take away something that hurt her friend?

As if sensing her hesitation, Shem took her hands into his. "Just think about it. We don't have much time. You could get home to your sister sooner than you think."

Morgana. Philippa hated herself for having not thought of her sister's name in several days. But how did Shem know about her?

"I never told you that I had a sister." She pulled her hands away.

He didn't seem as bothered by this as she was. "You told me that you were saved by a phantom guardian who now sits in captivity, rather at ease with being in chains as long as he is near you. You told me the stories of being saved, you mentioned your sister. Do you not remember? You speak of your family often."

She leaned away, thoughts spiraling. Had she forgotten? No. She would've known. When she met Shem, she knew he was from Aresef. He could have been hiding something.

Philippa shook the thoughts away. She was tired, and she *had* spoken about her family before. Superstition would get her nowhere. Just because Shem was from Aresef, it didn't mean that he was hiding *anything.* Growing up, people called the Wahanar brutes because of where they were from and how they lived, and it couldn't have been farther from the truth.

Everything about Shem made sense. He was the one clarity that she'd had here, save for Taz. He was a researcher through and through, and even if she hadn't mentioned Morgana, he could have put together that she was going home for *something* after this.

Shem's eyes widened and he slapped a palm to his forehead. "That sounded like I was calling you stupid. I'm sorry."

She shook her head, chuckling. "It didn't sound like that. I just, I don't know where my mind has been."

"Trying to save everyone."

"Ah, yes. That."

Shem tossed a dark braid over his shoulder. "Just think about it. I believe you could change the laws. You're strong enough."

The wind suddenly howled, thunder and lighting cracking like a whip outside. Philippa lurched, finding herself pressed against his shoulder, only to find him breathing just as heavily as she was.

They both laughed, and she drew her knees up to her chin. He believed in her.

Stop thinking about how he speaks!

"I'll think about it when the storm leaves us." she said under her breath. "But if you know so much about me, tell me about yourself."

Shem shrugged. "I have lived an uninteresting life."

She scoffed. He likely had traveled all over the entire continent in his days, and yet his life was *uninteresting?*

"It's true." he said, stretching his fingers. "I live to learn about others. Gather information. Report it back. Everything I do is to relay more interesting people's lives. My life is that of a bookmark, stuffed between pages. Is the book more interesting, or the marker?"

Philippa let herself giggle. He looked at her incredulously, and she waved her hand at him. "You've described being boring in the most poetic way possible. Don't tell me about your work, tell me about you."

"My work is who I am."

Stars, he was aggravating sometimes. If he couldn't come up with a topic, then she would give him one. So instead, she asked about where he was from, his family, where he grew up.

That question seemed to stump him. The smartest man she'd ever met, and he was lost in the thralls of conversation.

Finally, he conceded. "My earliest memories are of being outside, in nature. I met many different people in my early memories. None liked me very much. After that, I was mostly confined to the courts in Aresef."

"Your parents must be very proud of you."

He ran a finger absently over his chapped lips. Philippa reached into her nearby woven bag, a courtesy of Taz, and handed him a tin of balm that she'd been using to keep her own lips from burning and chapping. Not very close with his parents, then.

"Any siblings?" She asked.

When he chuckled, even *that* was distinguished and manly. She forced her ears to lay flat against her head so they wouldn't betray her blushing.

"That, Miss Aporo, would depend on who you asked."

"Complicated family, dear scholar?"

"Indeed."

Philippa tucked a stray hair behind her ear. She touched her locket, and its metal surface seemed to warm in her touch. "I'm really close with my sister. But our family was not without fault. My father was a harsh man. My mother was stern, but… always kind. I can understand the complicated part, though."

"I would guess as much, seeing as your people were split between two distinctly different beliefs and then slaughtered."

Sometimes he had no salt to his words, and it made her wince. But he was simply being factual. "Right, but I meant my brother."

"Brother."

"I never really knew him. He was quite a bit older than us, but I know that my father was disappointed in him. He was not my mother's son, so she never spoke of him." Philippa's only memory of her brother was hazy, and she wasn't completely sure that it was her own. It felt like it was pieced together with what little she knew about him from her parents and others. He was always described as aloof and obsessive, which is what likely led to him being banished. Well, it was dependent on who you asked whether or not he was banished or he left. "Family is odd."

He hummed in agreement and changed the subject. "I never thanked you, by the way."

She pursed her lips and drew absent patterns on the rug beneath them. "For what?"

"Many things, but specifically for convincing them to undo the bindings on my hands while I'm here."

"Now I *know* I didn't tell you about that."

He leveled a look at her. He was a researcher. Right. He noticed things. She blew out a soft breath and shrugged.

"Now you're free to use them however you like, my dear researcher." That came out wrong. She needed to sleep, and by the look of the creeping darkness underneath the rippling fabric of the tent, it was well past midnight. With the storm, it was hard to tell.

His breath was heavy. "Thank you."

"You don't have to—"

Why is he looking at me like that? But she knew why. She'd been with men before. Knew that look. This felt like more, though, even if she didn't know more of *what.* She'd been partnered with a few men for *months* at a time and hadn't felt anything like this before.

Shem's presence felt like he wasn't after something he couldn't catch. She should tell him to stop, that this was too soon.

But Shem was leaning forward, as if drawn in by something that he didn't fully understand. Philippa, too, felt the invisible bond they'd created, stirring up something that they weren't ready for; because in the back of her mind, she knew who was saving her, even if she'd never seen their face.

Philippa's breath hitched, but before they collided and irrevocably changed their stories forever, the storm surged, sending her backwards and snapping them both out of the moment.

"We should keep reading," she stammered.

Stars, his eyes. She'd hurt him. But she couldn't undo it, not yet.

"Right. Of course," but his fingers lingered near hers just a moment longer than necessary.

CHAPTER TWENTY-THREE ✦

Baking in the sun was the last thing she thought that she would be doing, yet, there she was. Hopelessness was a poisonous sleep in of itself, and she'd felt herself dragging.

No answers had been found between her and someone who had spent his *life* finding them. Panu was going to die, and it would be her fault.

Morgana and Raff would never know what really happened to her. Her guardian would also die, all because of her, for not finding a way out. She doubted that Shem would serve a further purpose once they had their way with her, either.

Sweat ran down her neck as she watched her guardian from atop a small stone watchtower. She'd been trying to figure him out. He appeared without a trace, apparently trying to put together the glass portal himself, which meant he was smart.

Or stupid, Taz had huffed when she'd brought it up to her.

Taz bit into a pomegranate, the red juices flowing down her chin. She smacked Philippa's shoulder, leaning on the raised wall with her elbows to gesture down at the cage.

"Why do I watch him?"

Taz nodded.

"It's a long story. But I think I've known him my whole life. He's saved me before. It wasn't right for me to not try and save him, too."

Tazmireth replied in Wahatan, noting that he had done nothing since arriving but caused trouble. Apparently, he'd escaped the birdcage twice and returned himself as if he'd never left, but the locks had been undone from the inside on multiple occasions. No one had figured out how. He never seemed to move, only resting his arms over his knees, his impenetrable mask never wavering from staring into the distance. Philippa smiled at Taz and shrugged.

Sand ground beneath her bare feet, which had thankfully been healing with the application of lotions that Ole had ordered to be put in her tent every night. Well, it had been moved to Shem's. She'd been there almost every night, trying to find answers.

Shem's request rang in her head.

Her fingers curled on the edge of stone, debris filling the underside of her nails. There was no more time. She had to ask. But bringing this up to Tazmireth felt painful. So far, they had completely respected each other's differences, and they'd gotten along fine that way. If she asked this of Taz, it would be asking her friend to allow her to change a law of their very people. Philippa's stomach ached.

Her tongue felt dry. "Taz, are they going to kill me when the *Tanvirok* arrives if Panu isn't awake?"

Her friend's chewing stopped. She pointed to Philippa's tattoo. She was considered Wahanar. There was no going back. This is what being a part of a people meant.

Taz handed Philippa the fruit, which she accepted.

She'd foregone the idea of not sharing food, as most of the Wahanar shared everything with each other. There was always enough to go around if everyone pooled rations.

Sinking her teeth into the pomegranate, Philippa sucked on the fleshy inside to cool her tongue and soothe her soul. A seed found its way between her teeth, which she worked on with her tongue to distract herself from her next question.

Anxiousness made her heart flutter. If they were going to kill her, they'd exile Taz and Ole, potentially even Heru, for their sacrilege.

"Taz, would you be the one to kill me if they asked?" The words hung between them like an unsheathed blade, sharp with possibility.

Would it earn back your honor? The question echoed in Philippa's mind, heavier than the desert air.

She watched as Tazmireth's fingers drifted, absently, instinctively, to the scar on her cheek. A mark Philippa had gotten placed there. Then the one on her knee, another wound she had forced upon her friend's body. The weight of it pressed down on her ribs, an ache deeper than regret.

For a moment, Taz said nothing, only staring over the camp, steady as ever. Then, as if she had heard Philippa's unspoken thoughts, she rose to her full height. Her shadow stretched long in the midday light, swallowing Philippa in its shelter. The bands of cloth wrapping her chest rose with steady, unshaken breaths, the kind only a soldier carried, the kind that held no fear of death.

"There is more honor in standing by your friends, than there is in standing alone just to be called righteous."

The words, spoken in the rich cadence of Wahatan, struck like a heartbeat against her ribs. Philippa felt tears prickle her eyes, hot and unwanted. Tazmireth would not kill her - not for privilege, not for pride, not even for her own people.

"But this is your home," Philippa whispered, voice tight. "These people are your family. *Heru* is your family."

Without hesitation, Taz lifted a hand, her fingers tracing the ridged scar along her face, then reached down to raise her crimson skirts, revealing the violent knot of flesh at her knee. Finally, she pulled at the fabric of her top, baring the brutal landscape of scars stretching across her breast and collarbone, etched deep, tangled like roots over her heart.

"For my cousin's honor, I would die," Tazmireth grasped Philippa's shoulders, leaning close, her presence fierce and unyielding. "For that of my friend, I would live."

Philippa's breath shuddered, though not from fear. She understood - understood every syllable, not just from the language but from the certainty in Tazmireth's voice. From the way she stood, the way she looked at her, as if she had already made her choice. She understood because she knew Tazmireth's heart.

"I found an old writing of yours that Shem translated for me," Philippa said, her smile wobbling as she fought the tightness in her throat. Taz sneered at the mention of Shem, but she pointedly ignored it. "It said,' *'a sister of the heart is more powerful than the blood of your veins'*," she let out a breath, almost a laugh, unsteady with feeling. "Thank you, for being the sister of my heart."

Taz scoffed, as if uncomfortable with the tenderness between them, but Philippa had already braced herself. She ducked just in time to avoid the swat aimed at her cheek.

Tazmireth narrowed her eyes, clearly displeased with the sentimentality of it all, yet there was no true anger there, only reluctant acceptance. It was a weakness, this affection, but one they both welcomed in their own way.

"And so now you know what *hannir* means." Taz said softly, her eyes crinkling at the corners.

The wind rose around them, pulling at Taz's half shaved ponytail, freeing her black hair until it streamed wild around her like the plume of a volcano before eruption. In the pure sunlight, the vitiligo around Tazmireth's one eye was bright, the lighter gray of the iris sparkling in the golden rays. Philippa watched as her friend touched the unshaded fabric on her clothing, the empty space where the mark of her rank had once been. She was no longer bound to Heru, no longer the blade at her cousin's side.

Then, with slow, deliberate movement, Tazmireth pressed two fingers against the scarred flesh above her own heart, before reaching forward and placing them over Philippa's.

Sisters of heart.

A weight settled onto her where Taz had touched her. Like the ink of a tattoo, it worked its way under her skin. Philippa swallowed hard, biting back the emotion that threatened to overtake her. Tazmireth would scold her for such a display, but the gravity of her friend's situation was excruciating. Philippa's heart could break for her, but at least if Tazmireth was with her and on her side, she could come with her. They could make their own lives.

Morgana was going to *love* her. Well, maybe after she got over the whole kidnapping thing.

CHAPTER TWENTY-FOUR ✧

A medicine worker took a wide step around Philippa, making sure they wouldn't touch her. Philippa had the sneaking suspicion that Dagna had told them not to associate themselves with her, but that they were mostly afraid that Philippa would burn them like she had Dagna. Despite Ole giving the command that Philippa was to be trusted alone with Panu and permitted to wander the Wahanar lands so the *Tanvirok* would not grow suspicious, it was clear that some Wahanar would follow Dagna's lead even before that of their chief.

Philippa's fingers danced over vials of crushed leaves and other ingredients, comparing what they had on hand to the list she'd found of a thick paste that was supposed to fight off fevers that caused unconsciousness. While nothing about Panu screamed fever or illness, it was all she had to offer.

She pointedly tried to ignore the Nazheris slumbering in the corner. It - *she* - hardly left Panu's side. Always watched over him, like a mother cat over a single surviving kitten. She hated to admit it, but listening to the creature breathe was quite soothing. The sound was nearly hypnotic, deep, purposeful breaths reverberating through its craggy rib cage, blowing out through leathery nostrils.

Outside, a bell rang, and she jumped, nearly sending a bottle of murky liquid toppling to the sandy floor. She deftly caught it, and replaced it quietly. What in Istoria could that be?

She peeked towards the sundial set in the floor by the tent flaps. It was noon. Another day half over. Trying to rub the tension from her neck, she walked over to the dial and pushed her head through the heavy fabric to look outside. The fullness of the sun temporarily blinded her, but when she blinked into focus, she could see the center pavilion where the prisoner cages were kept.

Surprisingly, her guardian was not alone there. Shem stood in front of the cage, holding a piece of charcoal and a stone slab, but he was not writing. He was tapping the charcoal to a desperate beat on the tablet, his foot matching the rhythm.

Inside the cage, her guardian was sitting, arms over his knees, looking straight forward. No, more like looking straight *through* Shem. She smiled. Of course Shem wanted to study him.

The Wahanar posted near the cage did not permit her to get too close. Herunavira was suspicious of how he knew that there was a scribe nearby, and chalked it up to that Philippa had hired someone to get her out of their lands. Philippa was just flattered that Heru thought she was smart enough to work that out on her own.

But Shem, it seemed, the Wahanar liked to keep him busy. Keep him learning. There were things that when he presented it to Ole, that even the chief was surprised about. Laws and decrees they had not been able to decipher in a long time.

Her skin prickled.

Most Wahanar couldn't read, could they?

Their laws felt finicky and open to interpretation, and she'd only seen the medicine workers and few others even *bother* to look at stone tablets.

So perhaps they needed a scribe not only for healing Panu, but for understanding. Shem's ability to read kept him from being exiled or executed by the Wahanar who desperately wanted to be left alone.

Shem, currently, looked so frustrated that he wasn't even trying to speak to the masked prisoner. If anything, it looked like she'd interrupted what *had* been an interview or interrogation that had been met with utter silence. She'd have to ask him about it later.

Her guardian didn't seem bothered by Shem, or the oppressive heat of the desert, even in his black clad outfit that made him look like a fallen dragon scale. His feathers shifted in the wind, when suddenly, his skeletal bird mask jerked to the side, and he was staring right at her.

Heart hammering, she slapped the tent opening shut and took a step back, her back meeting something hard.

Philippa turned and nearly screamed.

Dagna stared down at her, hands folded against her stomach, a dagger firmly pressed to her navel.

"You enjoy your time with that man," Dagna sneered.

Philippa did not answer.

That only seemed to make the chief's wife simmer more. "You insult me by making me speak your tongue. *Common tongue* you call it. Tsk. Not common. Intrusive tongue. Unclean tongue. You will respond to me when I stoop to your level."

"I'm sorry." She hoped she wasn't shaking as visibility as she felt like.

Dagna clicked her tongue. "My daughter's child does not wake. You are failing."

Worthless...

She shook her head. Philippa refused to lose her control with Dagna again, even if the magic inside her did begin to coil up like a serpent. "Respectfully, three weeks isn't that much time. You all aren't elven or human, meaning your bodies work differently than mine. One old script I read said that Wahanar babies sometimes implode into balls of fire if you overfeed them."

Dagna raised an eyebrow, slightly.

Philippa waited a moment. No response. She opened her palms, leaning forward. "Other babies don't do that."

The other portion she'd read had essentially compared Wahanar breast milk to nitroglycerin or oil. Motherhood here sounded worse than the average experience.

The chief's wife scoffed and waved her hand, turning away, and thankfully, sheathing her dagger. This close, Philippa could see the tattoos on Dagna's lips and even on her gums when she sneered. Sparks flew from her mouth as she ground her teeth. "You do not know medicine. How could you help? My husband is a *fool.*"

She did not miss how much that sounded like her own mother. Philippa cleared her throat. There was something she had been withholding, because she wasn't sure, but it seemed like it was the only answer.

When Dagna's stormy eyes fell to her, bone necklace rattling, Philippa tried to portray courage. It was not working.

"I think you are looking at this from the wrong angle. Panu is not sick like you think he is."

"If it were my way, the sick would die and the worthy would prevail. That is our way. My husband has forgotten this, so much that he brings a *vashir* into our home," Dagna's long, burly fingers rested on the hilt of her dagger again.

Philippa hurried to continue. "Someone has done this to your grandson."

Dagna whirled on her then, dagger pulled free, pointed it straight at her chin. Philippa backed up, but Dagna curled her large hand into Philippa's hair, bringing her so close that she could feel her fiery breath on her face.

"Do not call him that! He is my daughter's child! He is not mine. It does not matter to me whether he lives or dies. I only try to help because it is my duty to obey the chief and he is blinded by affection for our daughter!"

Tears sprung in Philippa's eyes. She was sure that her hair was tearing away from her scalp. Her throat bobbed against the dagger tip, trying to find her voice. "Why do you hate him so much? He is just a boy."

"Because he is *vashir*! Weak! Unclean! Like you. My daughter was taken advantage of by a man. Used. If it were my choice, she would have taken the bitterroot to rid herself of the child the first time she felt his kicking."

Bile rose in her throat. Suddenly, Philippa did not regret the cold words that she'd thrown at Dagna days earlier. Her magic was curling inside her now, wanting to strike out. How could anyone take advantage of someone as strong as Heru, even when she was a teenager? But looking into Dagna's cold, unfeeling eyes, it clicked.

"Heru was in love with a human man."

Dagna threw her, didn't check to see what shattered as Philippa's back collided with the medicine shelf. Kicked dirt into her eyes when she tried to stand, dug her fingers into Philippa's shoulders and rolled her over to stare down at her, bare foot pressing on her chest.

As the breath fled from her body, she wheezed, eyes bulging staring up at the woman who couldn't even care for her grandson's life.

"Wahanar do not *love* humans. Elves. Others. We love our tribe. What he did to her was *vile*."

Breathless, Philippa whispered, "but did she want to be with him?"

Dagna sneered, eyes piercing slits. "It does not matter. The union would have been *vashir*."

Darkness began to creep in on her vision. Her chest was crackling, and surely she was breaking. Stars, she didn't want to die. Not before she could help.

With the last of her strength, Philippa grabbed Dagna's ankle with her tattooed hand. Squeezed. She had no fire. But there was a smell. Like burnt hair. No. Burnt flesh.

Dagna screeched, removing her foot.

Air rushed into Philippa's lungs. She coughed, and suddenly large hands were at her shoulders. Surely that couldn't have worked. Ole was there. He'd done something.

He picked Philippa up as Dagna swore a string of ugly words at her husband, before limping out of the tent. Olekashan set Philippa in a nearby chair, before kneeling and looking at her.

The chief did not send for another medicine worker. He pulled back Philippa's loose wrap himself, and looked at the deep bruise already forming on her collarbone and sternum from where his wife's foot had sat. With a sigh, he sorted through the mess of medicines scattered about the ground.

When he came back, her vision had sharpened, adrenaline pumping through her. He had salve on his fingers, tenderly applying it to her collarbone and chest. She wrapped a hand around his wrist, tried to push him away. He ignored her, continuing to apply it until the throbbing pain had subsided.

"You don't have to do this. I angered her."

"Yes. But does that mean you deserve pain?"

"Doesn't it?" She rasped.

Ole looked up at her then, eyes wet. Was he crying? He put the tin down. Rested his hands on his thighs as he crouched before her. A chief, taking care of his own prisoner. The irony wasn't lost on her.

Though he obviously disagreed with her, he made no further comment on the matter. "We are nearly out of time, Little Pip. I know you have power. But even I know when the time is up."

He was losing faith in her. Her shoulders sagged.

"What is it you said to upset my wife?"

She shrugged, her nose stinging, and she hoped she wouldn't cry. "I think someone did this to Panu. Maybe someone like me. I don't know why they would. But what made her angry was talking about his father."

Olekashan nodded, taking in her words, mulling them over. " Ah. You found out he is not mine. Heru loved the human man she met. It was her choice to bed him."

His candidness struck her, but curiosity took over. "Dagna forbade them from seeing each other when they found out, then."

His expression was grave. "She poisoned him."

Philippa startled.

"Make no mistake, Little Pip. No one has survived Dagna's poisons. No one."

Her mind was reeling. "And yet Heru doesn't despise her mother?"

Ole shook his head. "She respects her mother. Heru is a daughter of tradition, not of heart. She follows the way. Now. Enough of this. Listen to me now. We have no more time to wait. Dagna is going to try and convince me of another plan tonight. If Panu cannot be healed, I will be forced to listen. To tradition. To her. So do what you must. Save my grandson. Do it quickly. By any means."

⁂

She told Shem that night.

"You're certain that you want to try this?"

Philippa nodded, absently twirling the tassels of the rug around her fingers until they purpled. "It was your idea. We have Taz take us down, I change the law. I get more time to heal Panu, and you get to walk away from this all the smarter for your time with the Wahanar."

His lips pursed into a tight line as he considered that. "Then I would return to Aresef and record everything I found."

"Absolutely *everything*," she smiled, adding, "except the part about their being a fledgling scribe among the Wahanar." It was a subject she'd been dreading bringing up. There was something, some kind of understanding between the two of them, she knew. She wouldn't have been so inclined to be around him if there wasn't. But that didn't mean there was trust. Not both ways.

Shem closed the parchment in his hands and picked up another. Lost in thought, he must have not heard her.

"Shem."

His golden eyes found hers. "Oh. That. I never met a scribe."

She narrowed her eyes, twisting the rug fibers tighter around her fingers. Shem clicked his tongue, and tossed his braids into a loose bun, already moving past the subject.

"Not a single one. The Wahanar kept me rather restricted to a tent, where they had me decipher some of their older laws and writings that even they were confused about. That's the problem with unenchanted paper, you see. It burns. The chief wanted to find a workaround for healing his grandson, because his dear sweet wife is rather *prickly*. But, I was able to gain their trust, slightly, by means of another prisoner, a She-Elf, who was rather intelligent herself."

Philippa watched him carefully, realizing what he was doing. He barely registered her, already rifling through his papers, smoothing out the creases of his tunic as if she were just another conversation to finish.

"A beautiful creature," he added with a smirk. "From a town she did not disclose, as she was rather mysterious."

Her fingers faltered against the fabric. *Beautiful.* A flush burned at her neck before she could stop it, but Shem was already on a roll.

"She was accepted into the Wahanar as one of their own, receiving a tattoo that she carried like a weight around her wrist, believing she didn't deserve it. But I, as an expert researcher, determined it only added to her elusive nature - an enthralling contradiction. For if a She-Elf of unknown origin can become beloved by the Wahanar, what else in this violent world is impossible by way of unwavering kindness? If I were to write anything, it would be this: spending time with someone so set on being gentle in a brutal world taught me more than two months of fighting to understand the Wahanar alone." He smiled brightly at her, his hand fidgeting in his tunic pocket.

Stars, he was good.

Shem reached for her, prying the strings from her fingers before they could turn completely blue. His touch was fleeting, just a gentle pat on her hand before he retreated, a glint in his eyes.

"You'd write all that, but not about a scribe?" she asked.

"I've already written *all of that,* and more," He leaned in close, covering the sides of their faces with his hand as if this were some great secret. "Believe me, Miss Aporo. It would take the queen herself ordering me to out you for that to happen. And seeing as you will be heading off to home, and I to Aresef, we will have no such problems."

The words were heavy in her chest. The promise made her throat tighten and her fingers tingle. He was a good man. She hadn't fully let herself think about what the end of this journey would mean. That they were going their separate ways. That he could move on so easily, already planning his next adventure while she felt like she was standing in the embers of something she was only starting to understand. At the end of this, if they succeeded, she would never see Shem or Taz again.

Shem's fingers stilled as he held two pieces of parchment together. Then, in a flash, he had a piece of charcoal in hand, quickly etching notes that he was obviously too worried to forget. But there was something different about the way he curled over the page, something she recognized from back when he was hiding things from her. Before they trusted each other.

He hesitated, staring at the paper, scratched with fresh pumice. She pretended that she wasn't watching him out of the corner of her eye. Then, too quickly, he folded the page and tucked it beneath his knee.

"Anything interesting?" she asked lightly.

"Nothing useful," he'd replied all too quickly.

Bitterness coated her tongue as Taz came to check on them.

CHAPTER TWENTY-FIVE ✧

The Wahanar fires had burned low, and the sounds of laughter and singing had faded into the hush of the night. Philippa sat near one of the fires, the warmth brushing her face as she traced patterns into the sand with a stick. The scent of roasted meat and charred wood still lingered in the air. Her nose wrinkled when she pictured a giant crustacean being chopped up.

Panu will never get to enjoy this again.

Her head snapped up, and she shot a glare at the birdcage by the chief's pavilion. Was that him, in her mind?

Tazmireth slumped onto the stone seat beside her, silent for a long time. She'd been drinking earlier, a dark ale that made Philippa's toes curl, not enough to dull Tazmireth's sharpness, but enough to let the night seep into her bones. She rolled her shoulders, staring at the sky.

Philippa followed her gaze. The stars were different from the ones in Levanta. Bolder, wilder.

"Have enough to drink?" Philippa asked.

Taz gave a low chuckle, and replied in Wahatan. "Drank enough for both of us."

She smirked, nudging Taz with her elbow. Guilt was already pressing at the edges of her mind. It had started to fill her up the moment that she knew Tazmireth had been drinking.

They lapsed into silence again, a comfortable one. Philippa exhaled, leaning back on her hands. Shem sat a few fire circles away, being pointedly ignored. But he kept glancing at her, waiting for her signal.

"I don't think I'll ever fully understand this place. The Wahanar, the way you live. I feel like I'm always catching up."

Tazmireth considered her words and drank deeply from her clay mug. She replied in a strong accented version of Wahatan. Philippa blinked, utterly lost. Taz's shoulders dropped and she pointed at Shem.

He dutifully came scampering over, unable to hide his enthusiasm. The fire cast blue streaks through his well kept braids, which she had seen him oil from time to time, tightening the coils whenever he had the chance.

Shem translated when Tazmireth repeated herself. "'You don't need to understand everything. Just enough to know where you stand.'"

She frowned, glancing at Taz. "And where do I stand?"

Taz didn't answer right away, shooting daggers at Shem. Instead, she reached down and picked up a small stone, rolling it between her fingers. Her words rolled out with a light drawl that normally wasn't there.

Shem was quick to catch up. "'Do you know why we tattoo ourselves, if not for fire?'"

Philippa shook her head. Whatever her friend had been drinking, Philippa was glad that Shem was there to translate. For the most part, Philippa understood Wahatan conversations, but she also missed a few key words or phrases that she had to go without understanding. Shem's familiarity with their language was a welcome asset.

Shem continued, looking at Philippa as he translated. "'It is not for fear, or for our enemies. It is so we see ourselves clearly before we fight. We see who we are. We remind ourselves, so nothing - fear, anger, doubt - can take that away from us.'" Taz tossed the stone into the fire, watching the sparks jump. "'You are still finding who you are.'"

Shem's translation was so quick that Philippa almost forgot she was hearing two voices at once.

Philippa swallowed. "And you? You already know?"

Taz titled her head, considering. Philippa understood Wahatan enough to piece together what she said next. "I know I am Wahanar. I know I would die for my people. But beyond that?" She exhaled. "We are all still finding something."

She studied her in the firelight. This woman, so steady, so unshaken, felt lost, too.

"I think I'm afraid," she admitted.

Taz turned to her. "Only fools are fearless."

Philippa pursed her lips and took the cup from Tazmireth's hands. She downed a deep swig, letting it burn down the back of her throat. She fought the urge to retch, putting the back of her hand to her mouth. Her vision hazed, liquid courage filling her as the tattoos on her hand wavered into unfiltered squiggles.

"I have to ask you some things that frightens me."

Tazmireth smiled, the idea of danger spurring her on. Philippa had to start with something simple. When planning this conversation, Shem had been clear that it couldn't feel like it was a stranger suddenly talking to Tazmireth or she would never trust them.

"First off, do you just keep bird cages for every person you see?"

Her friend laughed, a thick, hearty sound. She took back her drink and tousled Philippa's hair. Tazmireth spoke quickly, but it was a short explanation. But no translation came.

They turned in unison towards Shem across the fire. He had his eyes focused on the center of their home. On her guardian. There was something faintly there, simmering within him.

Tazmireth snapped her fingers loudly, waving for Shem to translate.

He sighed. "She said they keep cages for little lost sparrows."

"That's it? He wears a bird mask, so he's a sparrow?"

Tazmireth looked a little insulted and hurled her cup across the fire at Shem. He ducked, but it still smacked him in the side of the head. The clay cracked. Philippa covered her mouth, biting back a laugh.

The brown ale coated his cheek, dribbling into his mouth. He was not amused.

"Fine. Have it your way, only because you are Miss Aporo's friend. She said he's from something called a cult of sparrows. That's what they call them. Evidently, they have found many who look like him. I... I have also read up on them." Shem's shoulders tensed, like admitting that he knew what her guardian truly was set him on edge.

"Cult of sparrows?" Philippa asked, digging her toes into the sand warmed by the firelight.

"It's not an exact translation," he huffed.

But if her guardian was part of some cult, then there were many more of him to be found. Maybe it had been several people stepping in to save her life over the years, for whatever reason. Her magic thrummed in her body, a long, resonating beat that made her feet feel heavy. Philippa played with the end of her braid, taking Shem's explanation about her guardian at face value. The masked man wasn't even around, so there wasn't any use in trying to figure out what he was.

Sparrow. At least she had something to call him now.

Listen, listen, listen.

The Wahanar camps exploded into movement, voices rising in exhilaration. Philippa turned as Ole, flanked by Herunavira and Dagna, strode into the heart of the fires, the pulsing center of their people.

"My friends! My family!" Ole's voice thundered across the camp, commanding every ear, every soul. A chorus of cheers erupted in response, a wave of devotion crashing over there. "The *Tanvirok* is upon us! Tomorrow, we welcome our kin, not with steel, not with fire, but with open arms! Let there be no grudges when they plunge into our oasis, for this is a time of unity! Tomorrow, we feast as one!"

The air shimmered with heat, with fervor. Philippa could feel it thumping in her bones. Olekashan lifted his arms higher, his presence swelling.

"Our lands have been torn apart for too long! After tomorrow, the elders of the *Tanvirok* will stand as one! Together, we will reclaim what is rightfully ours! No king. No queen. No rulers in their distant city who think they own us - own our stories!"

His voice cracked like a whip, raw with fury, his body a vessel of unshakable resolve. This was not the man who had once welcomed her into his home for the love of his grandson. That man had vanished. This was a leader who had given up hope in anything but war. Philippa felt it, the cold truth swelling in her gut.

Ole had lost faith in her.

His elongated earlobes swayed as he pumped his fists, his roar met with a frenzy of answering cries. The flames leapt higher, mirroring the fire of his people. This was not a negotiation; it was a war cry. A king, readying his army.

Across the fire, Tazmireth stood unmoving. The only one who had not joined the chorus. Her unreadable expression was locked like a door, one Philippa had to break through. All the hair on her neck stood up.

"After the *Tanvirok* sets the terms, these lands will be *ours*!" Ole bellowed. "No travelers! No thieves! No kings and queens! Only the Wahanar and our people! Will you stand with me brothers?"

Ole's call was met with a deafening response, the men's voices a force unto themselves. Heru joined her father's side.

"Will you stand with me, sisters?" Herunavira called, and the women answered, their voices sharp as blades.

Dagna, the third pillar of power, raised her arms. "Will you stand with me, children?"

The Wahanar's response was absolute. A people ready to carve their future into the sand with blood.

A hand clamped down on Philippa's shoulder, snapping her out of her trance. Shem.

If she didn't act now, it would be too late.

All of the Nazheris in attendance were notably silent while the roar of the Wahanar people continued in their ravenous chanting, echoing Ole's cry of unity before war.

The Wahanar would go to war against the king and queen in Aresef, to reclaim the continent of tread for themselves. Philippa couldn't believe it. It was such a drastic change from when she'd met Olekashan that it was hard to imagine what drew him here.

But then Philippa's eyes settled on the insatiable smile on Dagna's face, and she understood. Maybe this is what Dagna had wanted from the beginning. There was no way to be sure, but by the look on her face, this is exactly what the woman wanted to happen. Her distaste for scribes and other encroaching powers had driven her to violence, and now she would get it on a grander scale.

There was no time to dwell, no time to think of all the lives that would be cost if they did this. This was their choice to make, but Philippa couldn't help but feel that she had a hand in driving them to it. Maybe if Panu had been healed, Ole wouldn't have fallen into desperation. It was clear he blamed the rulers of Sapria for all their troubles, but why Panu? Why take it so personally? It was she who had suggested that someone had done this to Panukirah by means of magic, but it made no sense why a ruler of a continent would seek the book of a child, just to write him out of existence. Panu posed no threat to them.

Her tattooed palm found its way into Tazmireth's hand. Taz turned towards her slowly, disbelief plain on her face. She shook her head, assuming she knew what Philippa was going to say.

"Wait," Philippa urged, taking the opportunity to be drowned out by the yells of the Wahanar. "Your uncle is worried he will be exiled for having me here. That's why he is going to make this bold move, to cover this up. I'm right, aren't I?"

Tazmireth shrugged, but did not take her hand out of Philippa's.

Shem drew closer, ready to interpret.

Taking a deep breath, Philippa noticed the Nazheris slumbering nearby, and brought up the law she and Shem were sure about. Tazmireth bristled, but she listened.

"There has to be something, some precedent. You can't just exile people because it's convenient."

Taz's voice had steeled, the slurring of her words washed away by her urgency. "You think exile is convenient? Our laws were written in stone, not ink. They cannot be changed. We do not even know what they say - we follow the tradition of those who read them to us generations ago."

Shem's eyes widened. He looked fully to Taz, mouth slackened. "You mean literally, don't you? The catacombs!" He quieted his voice, turning to Philippa. "We're right! The translations we've been missing, the details on the law, it's all down there. In stone. Like you said."

Taz stiffened. She yanked on one of Shem's braids, snapping his head back to her. While he rubbed his neck, Taz spoke through grit teeth. "That is not a place for outsiders."

Philippa felt her confidence waver. She didn't want to plead. But she had to. This could mean all of their lives if Ole truly meant to go to war.

"Please, Taz. If the law says those who use a scribe must be exiled, I need to see it. I need to understand it. It could save us. Save your uncle from thinking war is the only option he has. If I have more time for Panu, they could see that a Scribe does not just create destruction."

Her friend hesitated, and finally sighed. "If we do this, you do not tell a soul. If we're caught…"

Taz squeezed Philippa's hand, nodding as she set her face towards the oasis. Philippa followed her gaze and swore under her breath.

The cage was empty.

CHAPTER TWENTY-SIX ✧

The fervor of the *Tanvirok* had taken hold of the people faster than Philippa thought possible. One man's idea became the goal of all in a matter of hours.

Weapons were taken out from storage, families began to tell old war stories to their children. A dark cloud of unease settled over the home of the Wahanar, which pressed down on Philippa's shoulders as she ran after Tazmireth, who led her and Shem towards the oasis.

It had been left in the murky darkness while the Wahanar were ordered to gather at Ole's pavilion for planning. As the Wahanar gathered to prepare, crickets and other small bush life began to slip their sounds into Philippa's ears, the usual rhythm of life having grown dim.

It was deathly quiet outside. The wild stars above were the only ones to bear witness to what they were about to do. Her breath sounded like war drums, every step too loud in the absence of clamor.

Other than the moon, their only light was from Taz's lit palm, guiding them as they sprinted.

Shem, for being someone she assumed spent much more time reading than running, kept up exceptionally. He hadn't even broken a sweat by the time they reached the water's edge.

The water was as still as glass. Completely undisturbed, as if no frogs or wind could touch it. The last time she had been here, she'd been soaked and disoriented, not understanding how they'd traveled through sand and crystal to come out the other side standing on the bank of an oasis, hundreds of miles away.

Tazmireth's palm illuminated her harsh features, made graver by the circumstances.

A spasm was forming between Philippa's ribs. She'd convinced her friend to commit the ultimate sacrilege, and had omitted the fact that she was going to attempt to change her way of life with a flick of her wrist.

Taz asked if they could both swim.

Philippa nodded, pushing down the memory of waves over her head, salt and sand filling her mouth.

Taz wrung her wrist and extinguished her flame. But the world did not darken into the thralls of night.

Philippa's palms felt slick with sweat, and her throat tightened, as if the very air had grown too thick to breathe. Someone was watching them. Closely.

Philippa turned, her jaw already working with an explanation, when she came face to face with the nightmares of her youth. A Nazheris' snout was nearly pressed to her chin, a plume of smoke choking her as it exhaled through its slitted nostrils.

Black domed orbs took her in, surveying the situation. The fire between its horns flickered with anticipation. Waiting. Watching.

One bray from its throat would ruin *everything*.

"Please." Philippa said quietly, and she swore its eyes narrowed, despite not having eyebrows. In that small expression, she recognized its harsh face as one who had been watching her since day one. "You're Panu's friend. I'm doing this for him."

Nazheris tilted her head, inquisitive. Her reptilian lips snarled as she took Philippa in, inhaling deeply as if she could sniff out the lies from the truth. Was she lying? This was not only for Panu. It was for herself, too, but for all of the Wahanar as a whole. No more exiling, no more forced separations just on the account of trying to save your family.

Family.

Philippa lifted a trembling hand. Her tattoos came to rest on the side of Nazheris's face, cradling her cheek.

Her throat stung just from the sensation of hot scales under her skin.

"To save your family."

If Nazheris was swayed, she did not betray it. The slight weight she pressed into Philippa's tattooed palm was her only indication that she'd listened at all.

Tazmireth then stepped closer, pulling Philippa away. Philippa's mouth dropped open. She grabbed Shem's arm, pointing at her friend.

Taz put her forehead against Nazheris's, whispered something, and suddenly, they both froze. No, not frozen, she realized. She leaned forward, Shem equally as interested, and noticed both Nazheris and Taz's mouths were moving.

They were *talking*.

It was amazing. A feat of nature that she'd never considered, never had time to when Herunavira had first told her that Nazheris spoke about their time in Soffer.

Philippa choked out a surprised laugh, turning to Shem, expecting to find him already taking notes on anything he could get his hands on.

Instead, Shem pressed something into Philippa's hand: a folded piece of paper, riddled with a map drawn with careful lines, leading to a place she had never heard of.

"If we get separated, go here." he said, his voice low.

Philippa studied the map, then him. "You'd want me to go without you?"

"I want you to survive."

She clutched the paper tightly. He'd said so much in so little time, but left her more confused. Did he not believe that she could do this?

Tazmireth released Nazheris, taking a tentative step backwards. She nodded at Nazheris.

Then, Taz took Philippa's hand as she led her back to the oasis edge.

The wind tore at her braid, rippling it behind her shoulders. Her reflection was painfully clear. It had been so long since she'd seen herself fully. The Wahanar didn't spend time with mirrors unless they were tattooing.

Her hair was completely drained of all signs of Levanta, save for the very tips which were littered with darker strands in the moonlight. Freckles she'd normally been able to fight off with sun lotions were on full display, her usually ruddy skin tone returned to its fullest, deep russet of that when she was a child.

Absently, she ran a finger along the soft downward curve of her nose. Without the changes of Levanta, of her ever-present smile, she looked like her mother on the day she died.

Ripples in the water broke the call of her memories. Taz was waist deep in the oasis, beckoning her to follow. Philippa cast a glance back at Nazheris, whose back was to them, sitting like a watchtower, aglow in the fire of her horns. Whatever Taz had said to her was clearly convincing enough for her to act like three *vashir* didn't just enter the precious oasis.

The cool, wet sand underneath her feet sent shivers down her spine. Shem was ahead of her, holding out a hand.

His skin was fire compared to the cold of the water. She let him pull her closer through the oasis, before he dropped her hand. Her ears twitched, strangely upset at the absence of his touch.

Tazmireth filled her cheeks with air dramatically, then pointed down at the water.

Philippa filled her lungs and held it. Taz went under.

Philippa plunged down and darkness surrounded her. The moonlight did not pierce the waters of the oasis. Panic flared in her chest, an angry and old feeling of water surrounding her.

Strong hands were suddenly at her cheeks, steadying her. She knew it was Taz without seeing her.

Shem was suddenly beside her, too, and she felt one of his braids touch her shoulder, like a snake in the blackness.

Taz's palm became aglow with the faintest of lights, just enough to see around them. She pointed down, and Philippa followed her into the depths.

It was a sandstone, coral filled paradise. There had been no inclination that the oasis was so deep, or so alive, but the pressure in her ears and temples was telling her that this was real.

Sand plumed in slow motion as Taz's palms hit the bottom, temporarily blinding them all.

Don't panic, don't panic, don't panic.

Shem was at her side. Steady. Real. Safe.

But she needed to breathe, and soon. Knowing how to tread water was significantly different than knowing how to hold your breath for an eternity. Yet, this desert warrior beside her was acting like it was no big deal.

Her throat tightened, begging for air. She fought off a thrash that begged to take over her body.

Philippa *loved* the ocean, but she was also terrified of it. The vastness of a natural force that could not be contained had almost claimed her life before, and despite the oasis not being filled with salty brine or millions of gallons of water, the sensation was all too similar to the first day her guardian's hands had plucked her out of the cold dark.

Tazmireth's palm began to burn brighter, and hotter. Bubbles cascaded around them, warbling Philippa's vision beyond clarity, but the water was getting *hot.* Steam whined in her ears. Heat licked at her face, the white hot glow of her friend's palm turning the oasis into a melting pot.

Philippa needed to breathe. Awe couldn't keep her breath in her chest.

The bubbles that blew out of her mouth were lost in the stream of Tazmireth's power.

Shem had his arms around her in an instant, starting to kick his legs to bring them to the surface. But a dagger of hot water shot past their faces, stopping them. Tazmireth angrily stared at them, her whole body alight with the magma of her hand.

Shem gave Philippa a pleading look, but dove them back down deeper. Stars, was he not losing his grip on reality down there like she was?

Her vision hazed, but she fought to keep her eyes open.

Tazmireth had burned the sand of the oasis bottom into a clear, glass hatch. She flung it open, water beginning to pour through the trapdoor. Taz took Philippa from Shem, shoving her through.

Philippa's body splattered on the frigid surface of the crystal caverns. Two more sounded after her, the rush of water distinctly absent.

Air rushed into her lungs, overwhelming her ribs that crackled with each rise of her chest. Tazmireth was above her suddenly, black hair dripping onto her face. Philippa's chin was squeezed by her friend, which she managed to rattle out a laugh at the gesture.

"I'm alive." Philippa wheezed.

Tazmireth scoffed, gently pushing off of Philippa and pulling her to her feet. Shem stood just a few feet away, clearly still not wanting to be overly close to Taz.

"That was amazing," Philippa said between deep breaths, water threatening to come up from her stomach. She would not let the fear overshadow what her friend had just done for her.

Her heart lurched when Taz nearly hit the crystal floor. Philippa scurried forward, her hands instantly under her friend's armpits, though she had to reach up to do so. Taz pushed her away, holding her head.

"What happened?" Philippa asked urgently. "What did I do wrong?" Guilt pressed against her mind, heavier than the water pressure that had begun to dissipate. She thought of her first time through the glass gate, when she was nothing more than a prisoner to the Wahanar. Remembering how many Wahanar had raised their hands to melt the dune, to form the gate that could fit all of them. An entire traveling party had made that entryway into the Wahanar lands.

Taz had made a trapdoor that had sapped her of her strength, and she'd done it alone. Scribe magic always came at a price. Always. Philippa squeezed her eyes shut, feeling a fool for not putting together that other forms of magic would cost something of the user, too.

For Taz, it was her energy. She'd burned a doorway into the sands of Istoria by herself, all at the whim of *her*.

"I'm sorry."

Shem stepped forward. "We don't have much time. The *Tanvirok* was supposed to come as soon as the sun rose. Where are the laws written? In here, in crystals?"

Philippa let Tazmireth walk away from her, though she wanted nothing more than to let her rest and make sure she hadn't burnt herself out. The words of the elder who had tattooed her echoed in her mind; burning yourself out was a dangerous game to play. Was Taz burnt out? Was she close?

She followed closely, their steps so in sync that it sounded like there were only two pairs of feet slapping against the crystalline floor.

Tazmireth's eyes were downcast, searching through the floors. As they followed, Philippa narrowed her eyes at Shem.

"Don't push her."

"I'm sorry?" He asked, confusion lining his face.

Philippa crossed her arms, rubbing her hands along her skin to fight off the chill. "She's only doing this because she's my friend, because she trusts me. Didn't you see how she made a doorway out of *nothing*? Don't push her to move faster than she can. She's tired."

He looked thoughtfully down at her. Ever consistent, that man. Shem wiped some lasting beads of water from his face, and wrung out a braid. But he said nothing. Philippa burned hotter at that than if he'd retorted against her defense of her friend.

"Nothing to say, researcher?"

Shem bristled. "I'm sorry, are we arguing?"

Philippa whipped her head forward to focus on Taz's back. "I just don't think you appreciate her."

"She's *your* friend," he sounded like the distinction made a difference in what she'd said. "The act of you picking me apart over nothing won't help us where we are going."

She slowed down, letting Taz get ahead of them a fair distance, before she stepped in front of him, digging a finger into his chest. "I *wasn't* picking you apart, but I can gladly do so. I grew up with a sister. You, Shem Tetra, are acting selfish. She just exerted herself for *your* idea because I asked her to, and it means nothing to you. Don't think I'm so blind that I cannot see the only reason you want to see the laws are for your research purposes. You don't care for the people you study, only the information they give you."

Golden eyes flashing, he stepped around her. "I told you that we are a selfish breed."

Her hand was around his in an instant, yanking sharply to make him look at her. "I didn't *have* to take you down here. It could've been me and Taz. Think about *that* while you choose to hide in your selfish cage you surround yourself with. After this, you can go back to your books, your studies, your *Aresef.* But do not for one second think that I would choose you over her. I wouldn't. If she decides you are an outsider and are not allowed in this precious place you desire so badly, I will let her do with you as she sees fit. Understand?"

"You're an outsider too." Shem's words struck where they intended. Philippa had known people who protected themselves by being cruel, by using sharp words to avoid the real conversation. She'd known them, loved them, and lost them, and she wanted to be nothing like them. If this was an argument thcy needed to have, then they'd have it and let it be done with.

Shem was attacking her worth because she was right about him, in some way. She'd rather her honesty sting for awhile than let tension settle between them like a stone.

"Am I?" She held up her tattoo. "Stop pretending to be so lost in your studies that you don't care about anyone else. It's infuriating."

"Maybe I don't care about anyone else," he muttered, "why bring me down here at all, if I burden you so?"

"Because you're my friend now, too."

Philippa saw the moment he put it together. "This is your way of saving me. But is it as simple as we value similar things, and so we are friends?"

The words stung, but she let it pass. "No. Tazmireth and I value completely different things, and I love her. You and I are friends because of circumstances. It can be even simpler than you think."

<hr>

The endeavor of falling into nothingness when Tazmireth had found the right spot was no less stomach-churning than the first time. How she knew what warped, magnified spot in the crystal floor was a doorway was a mystery to Philippa. Her friend knew the cavern like the back of her hand, and gave no warning when she'd stomped on the floor twice to open it up, swallowing them whole.

Instead of appearing soaked to the bone on the other side of an oasis, Philippa's tongue was thick and dry, her skin coated in a fine dust. Ground that had been settled and untouched for the stars knew how long now enveloped her into its cool heart.

There was no sense of light at the depth they were at, but her skin prickled, the eerily familiar sense of danger whispering at her back.

Don't get lost.

"Taz, are there scorpions down here?"

Her friend's palm lit, illuminating her face. Taz grinned at her wildly, which was answer enough.

Philippa shuddered and turned to Shem, who was already taking in the catacombs around them.

Pointedly avoiding conversation with her.

Philippa would deal with that later, she decided. Despite his brashness before, he had been right. They didn't have any time left to spend wondering or worrying. They had to act soon, for all of their sakes.

"Where would the first laws about scribes have been written?" Shem asked.

Tazmireth appeared lost in thought, then turned to the wall to grab a branch with an oil scepter bound to the top. She lit the torch, handing it to Philippa and waved them along. The smell of the torch was *awful.* It was old and heady, leaning into the entire atmosphere of being ancient.

Philippa held the torch higher as the passageway narrowed from an open cavern to a domed hallway, which had been carved out of the deep set stone. Her eyes widened, the fire blocking out some of the detail, but the shadows cast above her head weren't random. They were *words.* All written into stone.

Most Wahanar were tall enough to reach the ceiling if they sat on each other's shoulders or just rocked onto their toes. But to carve all of this? It would've taken ages. By the looks of the room they were in, it had.

Different depths and sentence structure confirmed that there had been several carvers of the law.

"When was the last time you were down here, Taz?" Philippa asked, her voice full of awe.

Tazmireth shrugged her shoulders. "I was a child."

Philippa's ears twitched. "How old are you anyway?"

"Thirty-two."

"Oh."

Taz turned, her brow arched. "What does that mean?"

Smirking, Philippa rolled her shoulders. "Oh, nothing. Just realizing you're about as old as these writings."

A harmless puff of targeted smoke blasted Philippa in the face as Tazmireth gave her a rude hand gesture, chuckling darkly.

Shem was wholly enthralled, eyes glued to every sentence above their heads. Though Philippa didn't know as much as he did, she still tried to pick out words she knew.

When did her people become the villains of the Wahanar? Did these rooms have the answers to things she had lost to time?

Her magic curled inside of her in a distinct, worrisome way. Maybe there was more going on in the caverns than Philippa wanted to believe.

As they descended, sentences flew by, her knees began to ache, and the smell of the earth around them began to settle into something damp and musty.

Wherever they were going, it was a place the crystal caverns couldn't have taken them to, since they were so pressed for time. Either that, or Tazmireth only knew one way into the catacombs. The dark, unsettling thought came to Philippa's mind that perhaps that meant there was only one way out, too.

Philippa took in the tension of her friend's shoulders, the way her muscled back went taut.

That is not a place for outsiders, Taz had said. This place was sacred. Despite the ink marking her skin, the loose trousers she wore, and the lack of unique pigment in her hair, Philippa was not Wahanar. Shem was right. Once this was over, she would go back to being another outsider.

One whose old home was no longer safe.

Morgana's face flashed in her mind.

Philippa had to do this, had to make things right. She'd chosen to expose herself to the world with Elodie, and condemned herself with healing Tazmireth. Neither choice she would make any differently.

If caring is a sin, I'll burn with it, she thought.

Shem's note burned in the slip of her pocket. Maybe she would be condemned for this. For a brief moment, Philippa wanted to turn around and run out of the caverns. She hadn't been honest with her friend about why she wanted to see the old writings, and the thought of Tazmireth never forgiving her was like stab wounds in her abdomen.

Except, Tazmireth probably *would* forgive her. Taz never brought up how Philippa had gotten her removed from her rank or that being her friend made her unclean. As she watched Taz turn her gaze to a flattened wall, eyes searching, Philippa smiled. Maybe they were different, but they loved people they considered their family. For the two women, that was enough.

They'd entered a room that was wide and long, as if it was a throne room. As they crossed the threshold, it felt like walking into another ancient world. The other halls were old, but this room was important from a time indescribable.

Tazmireth had to grow the flames in her hand to reveal a set of stairs, lined by statues carved from long ago. Philippa clutched the torch tighter.

Beginning their descent into the basin, Philippa felt the brush of one of the statue's hands against her shoulder and squirmed away. She nearly careened off the side of the staircase, which best case scenario would've broken some bones at this height.

"Scared of glass?" Shem chuckled from behind her.

Philippa, despite being frustrated with him, found herself nervously laughing along. That is, until they came upon a landing that changed the direction of the stairs, where a statue about her height was placed.

Glass, like Shem had said. Glass statues. With eyes that bore fear and pain. Hands outstretched or clawing at their chests as if they were trying to breathe.

Philippa froze and stared at this one particular statue for a long time. None of them had been the same, reformatted pattern to line the room. Including the one she stared at, they'd all had imperfections. This one had a scar around their ear and cheekbone. The glass was darker, more opaque around the wound, as if it was recent.

Her nostrils stung, her heartbeat racing. She turned slowly, trying to get her legs to *work,* to descend after Taz, but she was frozen.

Tazmireth met her gaze, unwavering. She lifted a hand, pointing at the glass statues. *"Vashir."*

Philippa gagged. Before the bile could rise any further, Shem's hand was at her back and guiding her down the stairs.

She couldn't let this fail.

Taz gestured at a long inscription, carved in jagged symbols. Philippa's breath caught. The word *vashir* appeared a number of times, which she'd come to understand that eventually the word became used in direct reference to scribes, the lowest of uncleanliness.

She took a trembling step forward. The torch revealed distinct letters of the carving, which she couldn't help but touch. Her tattooed fingertip followed the lines, a sense of fear prickling through her. Philippa's ears twitched. Somehow, she knew that whoever had carved this was terrified. Worried that their entire way of life would be destroyed, families torn apart and utterly wrecked, by someone like *her.*

"Shem." His name came out as a plea.

He was at her side in an instant. When he reached out to touch the words with her, Tazmireth slapped him away, muttering the word *outsider* again.

Annoyance flashed across his features, but he schooled himself quickly. "What do you need, Miss Aporo?"

"This. This sentence. Read it, please."

"A scribe's hand changes fate. Those who would wield them or ink shall be cast out—" Shem cut himself off, pushing back a braid from his face. "This is it. That's what needs to be changed, Philippa."

She knew why he'd whispered the last part. If Taz knew what Shem's idea was, what they were planning to do…

He'd given confirmation, but the feeling in her shaking hands would've told her well enough that this is what they were looking for. But how did one change a *law*? Elodie's mother had commanded her daughter to live, and Philippa had begged Taz to heal, because she needed her.

The only reason she was down there, in that dark cavern, away from the world, was because they were out of options. Panu wasn't waking, and Ole's family would suffer the punishment for it. They were going to war to cover up their sins, so they wouldn't be given to the desert to deal with them as it pleased.

Her fear must've been radiating off of her, because Shem's hands were suddenly on her shoulders, his breath hot against her neck. "You can do this, Philippa. You can save everyone."

"I don't know how," she whispered.

Suddenly, she was facing him, his strong hands bracing her as if for battle. "You're Philippa Aporo. You were meant to be safe, to be a savior. This law stands between you and your family. *Move it.*"

At that moment, she'd never seen someone so beautiful. The firelight that danced against his rich, dark skin, the gleam in his endless gold eyes that he believed in her with every fiber of his being. Yes, he needed this to work for himself. But it was more than that. He needed this to work for *her,* for whatever reason.

Taz grumbled something about time.

Philippa broke out of their staring match, and nodded. After letting the torch fall, she lifted her hands, trembling as she prepared herself for what she was about to do. She was going to change history. Betrayal flowed through her like an old friend, her eyes landing on the tattoo of her hand. A gift from people who trusted her to do the right thing.

"*Hannir…*" Taz's voices speaking in the common tongue shattered her. But she had to do this. Taz was too scared of her power to touch her, and she was abusing that.

So she didn't stop. She focused on what she wanted: to have them all walk free of this once it was done. But their words were precious. She felt the memories of those who'd carved this in flames, felt the heat lick her face. They wrote this for a reason. They believed in it more than she believed it needed to change. She pressed her hand to the carving, grabbing a letter as if to slide it over.

Her altering faltered, but the words began to shift before their eyes.

Anyone who exploits a scribe's power shall be punished.

The stone shuddered. Philippa staggered, breathless, as if something in the world had shifted.

Shem caught her shoulders, awe in his voice. "You did it. Miss Aporo, no scribe I've read about has ever rewritten stone without *ink.* You seem to be able to scribe… however you want to."

Tazmireth ripped Philippa free from his grasp, as if he was poisonous. Taz knew it was him who had convinced her to do this. But it had to be done, didn't it?

Her friend held her by the shoulders, but her stormy gaze was on Shem. "You don't know what *you've* done."

"Taz," Philippa's voice was weak, her head spinning. What did this cost her? "You're not speaking in—"

"Wahatan." Taz became as still as stone. She rubbed her temples, and checked her palm as if to make sure the ink was still there.

"Do you feel any different?" Philippa asked, her voice laced with worry.

Tazmireth nodded. When she lifted her head, her onyx eyes were wet. "In my heart," she said in Wahatan, "I know my values. But they are an echo."

An echo.

All the blood pooled in Philippa's feet. She swayed, darkness clawing at her vision. Shem's arms were around her in an instant, keeping her from hitting the ground.

Her friend rubbed her hands together, then touched her arms, as if she didn't feel real. "My sister, what have you done?"

"I told you…" Philippa's words slurred. "If we change the laws, we can save your family. I can figure this out."

Tazmireth looked like she'd seen a ghost.

No.

She looked like she was seeing Philippa for the first time. Philippa pushed Shem's arms off of her, taking a step towards Taz.

"You trust me, right?" Philippa's voice was a whisper.

Tazmireth relit her palm. Her eyes followed the light and shadows on the ceiling of the catacombs. "I was told a story by my uncle," Taz said instead of answering her, "that there would be a time when someone more powerful than I would challenge me. Make me question what I know."

Philippa's fingertips felt like they were on fire. "How did the story end?"

When Tazmireth stepped forward, meeting Philippa's eyes, she knew the answer. "It doesn't matter. I trust you, heart sister. But you have hurt me today."

At that moment, Philippa would've changed it back. She would've done anything to wipe that look off of Tazmireth's face, the hurt, the betrayal, the way her firelight caught her lighter eye and made her look like a phantom. Before she could speak, Tazmireth continued.

She pointed a hand in Shem's face, fist shaking. "You have convinced her of this. This was not her idea."

Shem raised his hands in surrender. "You can't possibly—"

Tazmireth's fire grew, engulfing her palm and trickling up her arm, licking at Shem's face. Spit flew from Taz's mouth as she roared at him. "She would not come up with this! I have not liked you since the day I found you trespassing. You are not Wahanar. *She* is Wahanar. For her, I would die. For her, I would live. I would lie. I would kill. For your choices, I would not speak. I would let the desert take you."

An indescribable emotion passed over Shem's face, but it looked like a cold conviction. "You speak so strongly about someone you have only just met. I know what Miss Aporo is, and I accept that. Do you?"

Taz struck him. Thankfully, she had let her flames die out, but he still went to the ground under the weight of her fist. Her shoulders shook, her teeth clenched. Tazmireth knelt where Shem was trying to shake the dizziness away.

Through grit teeth, she spoke. "You would make her how *you* want her. I see her. I have not known her for long. But I see her heart. For me, that is enough. I would not change her."

Philippa stood by silently, completely unsure of what to do with herself. Tazmireth turned to her and nodded. She would have to make this up to her, but Taz was thankfully still on her side.

As Philippa moved to help Shem up, Tazmireth caught her arm. Brought her head close, her forehead touching Philippa's. "Do not become what others want you to be. They'll make you dangerous, *hannir*. Become who you need to be. Not who they want."

With that, Tazmireth released her, clenching and unclenching her fists as she began to ascend the way they came. Shem was holding his head, already on his feet. He shrugged at Philippa, like it didn't matter. She knew it bothered him.

The world spun, the cost of her magic finally taking her. She allowed herself to fall to her knees, breathing deeply. Tazmireth did not wait.

They had to return to the surface, to see if it worked. But as Shem hoisted her from the earth, the torch flickering out on the ground, all she could see was Taz's hurried stride, and she suddenly knew what this alteration had cost her.

CHAPTER TWENTY-SEVEN ✦

The journey back through the crystal cavern was a blur. Philippa remembered Shem bracing her for the impact of the water. A flashing of light and glass as Tazmireth made the way possible. More than anything, she saw Taz's face. The betrayal there. But this would make things better. For all of them.

Her feverish skin welcomed the iciness of the water in the night, and allowed her to regain some control over her own limbs. Stars, had Shem carried her all that way?

She'd have to thank him.

Philippa crawled on her hands and knees up the bank of the oasis, coughing up water and shaking her head to rid the ringing headache that lingered from the alteration.

She glanced at Shem, who was wringing out his braids, droplets of water splashing into the shallows of the oasis. He gave her a grim smile, inclining his head. For someone so excited to see a scribe use their power, he hadn't seemed phased by it. He certainly wasn't scared of it, not like everyone else had been. Even Taz, her friend, feared the power thrumming in Philippa's blood.

Taz, who now had a sword under her neck.

Wait, what?

Philippa jerked her attention away from Shem, freezing when she saw the curved blade resting just underneath Tazmireth's chin. Her eyes followed up the ornate hilt, beaded with dark stones, to the powerful hand and tattooed arm that was attached to a shaved head that she knew well.

Herunavira spat in the sand, her eyes gleaming with rage. "Oh, Tazmireth, what have you done?"

"She did nothing." Philippa said quickly. It was true. Taz had only been their guide, and they hadn't informed her of anything that they were planning on doing down there.

The Wahanar warrior didn't take her answer for squat, and kept her eyes locked on Taz. "Whatever you have done, I cannot stop the consequences. What this *vashir* has turned you into, I cannot save."

"What are you talking about?" Philippa asked and lifted herself from the water.

Herunavira's eyes narrowed, her jaw set. "The *Tanvirok* is already here. The meeting has begun. And they are most curious about why an honored warrior has been removed from rank, all for the sake of a sleeping child they cannot wake."

As gently as she could, Philippa put her hand on Heru's blade. It didn't budge, even when she applied pressure to lower it from Taz's exposed jugular.

Instead of moving the weapon, she locked eyes with Heru. "We have more time now for Panu. Let them talk. We found a workaround. I promise."

Heru wavered. Her grip loosened on the sword, and she let it fall to her side. Then, her fist collided with Philippa's face.

Stars bloomed in her vision as her head snapped to the side. Philippa fell into the damp sand with a thud, her cheek aching and a copper tang filling her mouth.

Heru was on top of her in an instant. Her thighs held Philippa down as her fists balled into Philippa's wet hair, dragging her head up to meet her eyes.

"Your *promises* mean nothing to me! Panu sleeps, the *Tanvirok* is here, and they *know you are here!* They know what you are, what you have done, and who you have done it to!" Heru's hands left Philippa's hair and found her throat.

It was so fast that Philippa didn't even have time to claw at her neck.

Instantly, air was gone, but more than that, her throat was being crushed. Pain seared through her neck and collarbone from the pressure.

She could barely get the word out. "How?"

Philippa's hands were on Heru's wrists, trying to push her back. Her nails dug in, drawing crimson beads, but Heru did not care, did not sense it. The Wahanar warrior's face was in pure blood rage, the tattooed side of her face suddenly glowing with white hot anger.

Philippa was going to die. She felt the strength leave her fingers, the breath leave her lungs.

So much for that empty cage supposed to be housing her guardian.

Darkness called her.

Your hand, your hand, your hand.

What?

Her palm. Her hand. Her tattoo. The tattoos that made her Wahanar, that meant she answered to their laws. Heru could not kill her.

With a surge of panic, Philippa raised her palm, fingers blue, and pressed it to Heru's face. Though it did little to get her to move, she felt the grip on her neck loosen. A gasp of air found its way down her throat.

Her vision sharpened, her heart hammering in her chest.

A cough overwhelmed her, and though Heru did not get off of her, she let her hands fall to her sides.

Philippa let all the spit and blood in her mouth drip to the dark sand. Her tongue found the gash in her lip from where Heru had struck the side of her face, unsure of how her fist was so big to injure both that and her cheek. Her pulse was drumming against her temples. Risking a glance, she saw why neither Shem or Taz intervened.

More Wahanar, whom she did not recognize, surrounded them with great interest. A woman who wore the jawbone with teeth that were pierced into her jaw looked on with particular scrutiny.

Philippa rubbed her throat and her voice came out as a raspy whisper. "How do they know?"

Heru's chest heaved. "I told them."

Her chest felt like it was cleaved in two. Of course Herunavira told her elders about what happened. Ever the saint to her people, bound by honor and disgusted by the breaking of laws.

For a reason she couldn't explain, Philippa's jaw tightened. Her fingernails dug into her palms, drawing blood. Anger fueled her to stand, to meet Herunavira's dark gaze.

"You speak so much about *faith,* and when it comes to others, you have *none.*"

Even though Heru couldn't kill her yet, she could take advantage of the way Philippa spoke to her. Another fist connected to Philippa's stomach, forcing out all of the breath she'd just regained.

Philippa held her ground, not letting her eyes seek Shem or Taz. If this became bad enough for her, maybe it would be easier on them. She could villainize herself, let them see her as the unclean creature they wanted her to be.

She leveled a glare at Heru, who was barely containing her rage. "No faith, even when it comes to your father saving *your* child."

"Enough of this!" Ole's voice was thunder across the desert. His footsteps pounded against the packed sand, his hand falling to Heru's shoulder to rip her away from Philippa.

Philippa waited for the yelling, for the chastising, the chance to flaunt his feathers in front of his fellow elders. Words never came. His eyes flashed with hurt as he looked at his daughter, recognizing her lack of faith in him. He closed his eyes before regarding Philippa. She stood her ground, though her legs wobbled.

A giant hand took her face gently, turning her from side to side. She had no doubt that bruises were already starting to form around her neck.

Ole sighed and released her. He turned to the gathering *Tanvirok.*

The elder with the jawbone embedded in her face drank him in with reverence. "What happened here is disgusting, Olekashan. Who allowed this outsider to enter our most precious place?"

Philippa didn't breathe as Tazmireth was already about to stand up to identify herself. Taz's hand began to raise, when a flash of firelight made the group of the *Tanvirok* part.

The Nazheris who had agreed to let them go appeared, head raised in indignation. Her mighty claws dug into the sand, a low groan chortling in her scaly throat.

No one questioned the Nazheris, did not ask why, or if it was permitted to do this. The Wahanar that Philippa knew obeyed its right to decide like a law, whereas the faces she didn't recognize looked on in disgust.

It seemed that some Wahanar had been breaking their people's laws for quite some time.

Ole exhaled through his nose and turned to the accusing elder. "Bind their hands. When you're done, bind mine."

There would be no balm for the blisters Philippa earned on this day. Woven fibers bound her wrists around a stone pole that had been erected in the center of the encampment, and the way they'd positioned them left no room for the shade of any tents to give them reprieve. The sun felt hotter than it ever had, turning her skin red and raw in a matter of hours.

Philippa worked her tongue in her mouth, licking against the split in her lip, courtesy of Heru. She was too dehydrated to sweat, her mouth too dry to work up spit.

Her head was bowed, her neck and shoulder tendons feeling as if they were on the verge of snapping. She told herself the small pool of shade from her head on her bare thighs was all she could manage to give herself, not that she couldn't dare meet Shem or Taz's eyes.

The three of them had been bound near one another, in the center of the camp, but Ole had been allowed to be contained in the pavilion for the time being. Silence stretched out through the long hours, and Philippa wished she could cry.

Worthless, worthless, worthless...

I know, I know, I know! Her mind screamed back at the echoing voice.

All of this, because of her; because she couldn't let Elodie die, because she had to save Taz, and because she couldn't heal Panu. All of that power under her skin, and for *what?*

She considered that maybe this was the cost of healing Elodie and outing herself. That by listening to that call in her mind and heart, not silencing that thrumming, the cost was her life and all of those she cared about. It was history repeating itself, she realized, twisting her wrists against one another.

Her father's people let their hubris and inability to let things lie become their extinction.

Soon she would be no more, like them, nothing but bones in the sand.

"Are you feeling sorry for yourself?" Shem's voice cut through her thoughts.

Philippa ignored him.

"You did do it, though. You changed the law. The words changed, and therefore, so did the Wahanar."

"Shem, is this supposed to make me feel better?" She croaked.

His shadow shifted as he rolled his shoulders. "Well, we're supposed to be exiled right now. That was the punishment, to let the desert have its way with the unclean."

She was quiet for a moment, pondering what he was saying. "Now it just says the unclean are to be punished."

Shem smiled at her, his nose peeling from the sun, but his skin glistened with sweat. In that moment, he looked like a bronze statue, carved and glistening in the sunlight.

"This seems like punishment to me." Shem's words weren't encouraging, not at the surface, but his smile never wavered as he spoke. His belief in her, she realized, hadn't either.

Despite everything, she found herself smiling. He was tied a couple feet away from her, in a similar position, but he wiggled his foot towards her and tapped her leg with his toes. She shook her head, resting it on the beam behind her, closing her eyes to the sun.

"Punishment I can take. I deserve this much." Philippa exhaled through her nose, trying to lean into the idea that this would be the worst it got.

But not all of them are guilty.

Her eyes, drawn as if by a magnet, fixated on Taz.

Tazmireth's dark eyes were set dutifully forward, her shoulders straight, knees bent to rest her feet firmly on the ground. Ever the warrior, ever strong.

Philippa ran a thousand sentences through her head, but none seemed worth saying. The quiet that settled was heavier, thicker this time.

When it was broken next, it was not by words, but by the footfalls of many Wahanar as they approached the stakes that they were tied to. Philippa blinked and squinted, their forms a haze in the heat of the day.

Herunavira was at the front, leading the charge. Heru sneered as they turned past Philippa, the *Tanvirok* close in tow behind her. The beating of drums began to ring out in the desert, a heartbeat among the people.

As the group of Wahanar passed, Philippa winced, her nails digging into her palms. On a stone slab supported by several Wahanar lay a dormant body, one she had grown accustomed to seeing day in and day out. Panu still had not awoken, and he was getting skinnier. His eyes were closed and his mouth was set in a grimace, as if he knew what was to come. It was impossible, and yet, Philippa felt her heart hammering and her ears standing at alert. Something was happening. Something bad.

Stay quiet, stay quiet, stay quiet.

She did.

At the back of the stone carrying Panu, was Ole. His hands were bound, as he had requested, and his face was downcast. Streaks in the sand that always marred his face betrayed his recent tears, his mouth a hard line, as if any moment he would cry out in pain… in failure.

They lowered Panu to the ground in the center of the four stakes that were kept for prisoners such as themselves, and Ole was led to be tied to the final pole.

"Shem?" She asked quietly. He would know what this was about. He'd been studying them for months.

His golden eyes flashed in the sun, worry stricken all over his face. "I don't know."

Herunavira's bare feet were in front of her then, and as Philippa looked up, tears shone in the warrior's eyes. Dagna was at her side, unimpressed.

"Tell them. Tell them what they have done, what the cost will be." Dagna's voice was hard. Unwavering. Unmotherly. How awful, Philippa thought, to want a mother's love so desperately only for her to make you her mouthpiece.

"Heru," Philippa began, trying to rise to meet her face to face. Heru's blade was at her chest in an instant, her tattooed face contorting into fury.

"You! You do not speak. Do not use my name as if we are friends!"

In a flash, Heru jerked her blade upwards, catching Philippa's jaw and slicing it with clean precision. She cried out, slumping back down the pole, her hands uselessly wiggling behind her to try and staunch the bleeding. Unable to do so, tears sprung in her eyes, and she looked up at Heru, who was shooting daggers at her.

It was then she noticed the new, dark ink that glistened on Herunavira's skin. The hawk on the side of her face remained, but around her neck were intricate strokes of ink that mimicked claw marks running down her throat and chest, which reminded Philippa of the necklace of bruises she was likely sporting from their last interaction.

The marks that rose and fell with Herunavira's breathing looked an awful lot like the beginnings of the tattoos that Ole wore all over his body.

Philippa's blood ran cold.

Herunavira was chief now.

Dagna saw her put it together and smiled with a venom so potent that Philippa winced under the weight of her stare.

Dagna never wanted to be chief, no, she liked pulling strings from behind a curtain. Instead of a mother, she was a twisted puppeteer, lurking in the shadows. The only "clean" one left in their bloodline anyway, was Heru.

Heru, who now decided with the *Tanvirok* what to do with them. With a wave of her hand, Heru motioned for Dagna to speak. "You tell them."

Her mother looked surprised. "It is your right—"

Heru bared her teeth, fists clenched as she raised the blade to her own mother, who staggered back a step at the outburst. "I am Herunavira, Heart Of Eternal Flame, and I am chief now! Will you listen, or will your tongue be cut with the other *vashir*, mother?"

Oh stars, what was Heru doing? Who had she hurt? None were as loyal to Philippa as to speak out about her treatment. Were they? No, she resolved, they weren't. They couldn't be. Unless…

Philippa's eyes darted to the crowd. "Where's Benni?"

The new chief of the Wahanar did not smile. "Where you put him."

"Oh, stars—" A sob worked its way out of Philippa's throat, raw and ragged, catching in the back of her mouth like a splinter. Her gaze, wide and horrified, was fixed on nothing but the horrific image her mind had conjured. Would Heru truly go so far? Would she allow such a thing to happen to a child, simply to cement her power, to silence any dissent?

Yes.

The answer reverberated through Philippa's mind, a chilling certainty that left her breathless. With Dagna behind Heru, it was not a question of *if* but *when.* Herunavira had shown her true colors many times over. She would not hesitate.

The new chief, driven by the insatiable hunger for control and order among her people, would let her own son rot, if it meant eradicating any perceived threat, any whisper of uncleanness. The mere thought of it, cruel and inescapable, made Philippa shudder.

Philippa, who was caught in the terrifying vortex of Heru's machinations, knew she was paralyzed, unable to act, even as she envisioned the worst. If Herunavira was willing to punish a child for simply allowing Philippa into his heart, there was the chance that Heru had wanted this since the beginning. Perhaps, Philippa thought, Dagna and her daughter had their eyes set on war with the rulers of Sapria for some time, and Olekashan's harboring a scribe was the catalyst they needed to tip the scales with the rest of the *Tanvirok.*

Even if it meant Heru sacrificing her son along the way.

Dagna swallowed and nodded. Her eyes raked over the *Tanvirok,* then settled on Philippa. "The chiefs have laid claim to your punishment, Philippa Aporo of Levanta, Tazmireth, She Whose Fist Is Fire, Shem Tetra of Aresef, and you, Olekashan, He Who Is Seated By The Flame."

The woman strode in a circle around them all, a vulture above a carcass waiting to be stripped bare. Her eyes lingered on her husband, but not with love or care. Detestation.

Philippa's stomach flipped, blood staining her cloth top and bare legs. She prayed Shem's map wasn't visible under the thin garment. They'd stripped them down to their undergarments to let the sun have its way with them, and she'd thought by Shem's assessment that this would've been the worst of it. Not anymore, she realized, not with Heru's anger and resentment burning like wildfire in her heart. She never wanted to make her son Panu unclean with a scribe, but maybe she'd believed in her father's choice, believed in her too, for a time. Now there was nothing but cold calculation in those eyes.

Dagna stopped in front of Philippa and spat at her feet. "They have decided the only punishment that could balance the scales of sin, is *death.*"

Death…?

She had changed the law, how was this possible?

The crowd erupted into a terrifying symphony of screams. The air, thick with the scent of dust and fear, now crackled with fury and unbridled vehemence.

"Justice!"

"Vengeance!"

The cries tore through the stunned silence that had initially fallen, growing louder, more insistent, fueled by a collective, unspoken grievance.

Philippa, caught in the sudden maelstrom, felt her world tilt. Her breath hitched, a frantic bird trapped in her chest, the rough ropes biting into her wrists. Her eyes, wide with disbelief and a burgeoning terror, darted through the surging crowd. All she could discern through the chaos was Shem near her, his usually serene face etched with an expression of profound confusion, mirroring her own bewildered dread. He hung still, a statue amidst the violent upheaval, his gaze fixed on hers, a silent question passing between them: *How do we get out of this?*

The raw emotion emanating from the Wahanar was palpable, a physical force that threatened to consume them all.

"Chief Herunavira," Philippa called over the ruckus that did not die down. Heru met her gaze, sword already lifted. "I am *sorry.* I wanted more time to heal Panu, to help your family."

"You are going to die today, little scribe. I will wash my hands in fire to cleanse myself of your filth, and all you have touched."

"Your law doesn't say you'd kill—"

"Wrong!" Herunavira thundered, sounding quite like her father, who hadn't taken his eyes off of her. "Our laws *used* to say exile was enough. You are not Wahanar, you have no voice here."

A blood frenzy, that's what this was. A thirst that could only be quenched by the death of those who had harmed them. Philippa wasn't one to judge another's beliefs, and all things considered, she felt rather unclean herself, but Taz, Shem, Ole, and certainly Panu had done nothing wrong.

"Speak again, little Pip." Ole's voice was a whisper on the breeze beneath the shouts of the Wahanar.

Philippa craned her neck to see him. She shook her head. "You heard her. I'm not Wahanar. I don't know how to fix this."

"They felt the shift in our laws. Such a long standing command does not easily leave one's blood. They knew one of you was here, and what you were, by the feeling your change made in our hearts. They assume I would tattoo a *vashir,* that you cannot command a flame. But they do not know that."

His words made no sense to her. She was lost, her head spinning as she tried to find Heru who had disappeared into the crowd.

"What did they do when they took your clothes off?" Shem asked, his voice low and tight.

Philippa flinched, a tremor running through her. "I don't think now is the time—"

"The *map,* stars, Aporo." The words were clipped, as if he thought she had purposefully misread his question.

Oh. "It's in my shift."

Shem blew air from his mouth and nodded, resting his head against the pole. His shoulders rolled, as if he was preparing to fight. But there would be no fight, not for them.

"Little Pip!" Ole's voice rose to get her attention. "Your tattoo makes you Wahanar. Do not let them forget it."

Philippa felt her palms drip with sweat. This wouldn't make a difference.

"I am Wahanar." she said, her voice getting lost in the crowd's shouts.

Ole stomped his foot, the sound reverberating through the packed sand. "No! You are not Little Pip to them. You are Kelthari, daughter of the Wahanar by ink. Make them see!"

He couldn't have possibly been asking her to make an alteration somehow, or access the magic in her blood. That all had fallen silent upon their capture. But maybe her words were enough.

Ole chose her to try and save his family, and this was the only way to save hers. She had to try.

Working up strength in her chest, she yelled in a loud voice over the uproar of the chanting for death.

"I am Philippa Aporo, Kelthari, and I am one of the Wahanar!"

The shouting stopped. All eyes shifted to her, specifically that of the Wahanar of the *Tanvirok* who wore the jawbone of an animal on her face.

She was tall and all muscle, but willowy like a tree. She inclined her head to Philippa.

"You are tattooed like a Wahanar, but that does not make you one of us. You dragged a fine chief and a great warrior down with you. What will be enough? Do you wish to die first?"

Philippa felt like her throat closed. "I deserve to speak."

The leader of the *Tanvirok* snorted, the bones rattling around her face. "Fine. Herunavira, cut her free."

Heru hesitated, but when she looked at the elder's face, something inside her hardened. Heru knew what was happening, and when her blade cut through Philippa's binds, sending her shoulders into tremors from the release of pressure, she made sure to step on Philippa's fingers as she left.

Her arms felt like they weighed hundreds of pounds. But Ole was counting on her to be strong.

Shaking, she rose to her feet, legs trembling beneath her.. It took all of her strength to raise her tattooed hand into the air, the dark, intricate symbols twisting around her arm in stark contrast to her skin. Each mark had been intended to be a testament to her power, but it now felt like a brand of shame in a sacred space.

The others who had come with the *Tanvirok,* a group of stern-faced individuals, men and women adorned in woven garb, whispered among themselves as the sight of someone unclean bearing their beloved marks. Their eyes, sharp and accusatory, pierced Philippa, making her feel as though she were a defilement to their very sight. The air crackled with their disapproval, a palpable tension that promised a swift judgment.

The jawbone elder exchanged a dark smile with Heru, her eyes glinting with an unsettling amusement. Heru, who had been a silent observer until now, offered a slight, almost imperceptible nod.

Then, the elder raised her voice, her words cutting through the hushed murmurs, carrying with an authority that commanded instant silence. "You wish to be Wahanar? Then act like Wahanar. Command a flame, and I will not kill you first."

Her voice, though not overtly threatening, held an undeniable weight, a promise of dire consequences should Philippa fail. The challenge hung in the air, a crucible in which Philippa's fate would be forged.

Shem, who had been anxiously quiet beside Philippa, his own face etched with fear, let out a despairing sigh. "We're going to die."

CHAPTER TWENTY-EIGHT ✧

Philippa felt utterly foolish, a pawn in a game that had grown too large for her to play. How could she simply *will* fire into being? She wanted more than anything to survive - for them *all* to survive - but that didn't make fire lurch from her fingertips.

The Wahanar accessed their inherent power through intricate tattoos, but it still simmered in their bodies before then, and it was a power she'd only grazed when she'd, in a desperate bid for survival, *burned* Dagna.

Was she not meant to merely declare fire into existence? A whispered *"ignite!"* and it would appear?

Her ears twitched as the terrifying possibility that it *would* work settled deep into her bones.

Her bare feet burned against the sand, the heat gnawing at her already blistered soles. The elder and Heru decided to give her an hour to produce a flame from her hand, and the longer she failed, the more unbearable the scene became. The chiefs and *Tanvirok* lounged on thick woven rugs in the shade, watching with detached amusement as she floundered.

The cut on her jaw pulsed, packed with sand, a parting gift from Heru's blade. It throbbed in time with her frustration, a painful reminder that she wasn't strong enough, smart enough, powerful enough. Her hand remained outstretched, fingers curled like she could pluck fire straight from the air.

Nothing.

Worthless...

Sweat dripped down her back, soaked her shift to her breasts, plastered her hair to her forehead. She could hear them whispering, the quiet murmurs from the elders, the skeptical looks exchanged between the warriors. She was running out of time, like always.

This was the most humiliating way to die, to stand under the sun and fail, not for lack of effort, but because she didn't understand how to reach the power that she knew had to be there. If she had just been smarter, if she had just prepared more, made better choices…

She squeezed her eyes shut.

Taz.

Taz had once explained that fire resided within the Wahanar's very being, coursing through their veins. It required room to flourish, to consume, and to fully manifest. For this reason, the Wahanar's tattoos were not mere markings, but rather conduits that channeled the inherent power already present within them.

She had been marked too. Not with just fire, but with ink. With words. With stories.

Her whole life, she had been a vessel for something greater whether she wanted to be or not.

She wasn't the source. She was the conduit.

She could almost feel the pinpricks of the needle on her skin as the elder had meticulously carved a pattern into her palm.

Philippa took a slow, shaky breath. Instead of reaching for fire, she let herself become the space it could enter. She imagined the ink on her skin as something more, as an invitation, as an opening. Darkness and sparks whispered through her mind, like when she connected with Panukirah. The mark on her hand burned and whether it was in memory or magic, she couldn't tell.

A flicker. A shift in the air.

Something moved against her palm, warm as breath, restless as a word waiting to be spoken.

Her eyes snapped open.

Encircling her wrist and dancing around her hand, was a string of flame barely redder than the sands around them. It was an infantile thing, she'd seen the children playing with more fire, but this was *alive,* and it licked her skin when she looked at it.

The chiefs and *Tanvirok* were on their feet.

Their eyes were wary and disbelieving.

This was not the flame of the Wahanar, the roaring fire that filled their lungs. No, this was the work of a scribe, of an unclean person who could mimic their power. But it was *something.*

Philippa watched the fire envelop her tattoos, settling into the ink like a glowing work of art. Her body was light, and her breathing was as if wind was channeling through an open breezeway, a path for light and heat to travel through.

Dagna, Herunavira, and the jawbone elder approached like frightened creatures, a Nazheris cocking its head and drawing away. Her heart ached. She was becoming what a monster feared. The flame snuffed out.

For a moment, there was only silence. The Wahanar, who had spent the last hour watching her flounder, now stood frozen, their eyes fixed on her hand where the flame had been. The air itself felt taut, stretched between the disbelief of the elders and the thrum of something ancient stirring within Philippa's skin.

She flexed her fingers. The warmth that lingered in the ink, in the spaces where her magic had touched the real. The moment had felt so effortless, so natural until fear severed it.

She had seen that fear before. In the eyes of those who whispered about scribes, in the wary glances cast toward the unclean, the cursed. She had seen it in Taz, in the way her lip curled at the thought of her power. And now, she saw it again, plain as day, in the faces of the Wahanar.

Heru's face was a flurry of emotions. More than anything after the display, Philippa could tell she only had one thing on her mind: *You can mimic my flame but you can't wake my son?*

Dagna was the first to move, circling her like an animal, her hands twitching at her sides. Heru's fists clenched, her stance shifting as if bracing for battle. The elder who had been so certain of Philippa's failure looked at her as though she had just opened a chasm in the very sand beneath them.

"This is not our fire," the elder rasped at last.

No. It wasn't.

The Wahanar's fire raged, devoured, and consumed. It was a force of will, an inheritance from their ancestors, something written into their very bones. But it was also warmth, light, and creation. A creative consumer that they carried with them.

Philippa's fire had taken the shape of something else. It had settled into her ink, into the marks of a scribe. It had become a part of her story.

A new wave of unease rippled through the crowd, though she saw Ole smiling and Taz was finally meeting her gaze.

She heard murmurs, sharp whispers.

"Not a Wahanar flame."

"Unnatural."

"Trickery."

Panic coiled in her chest, squeezing tight. She had done what they asked. She had called forth fire. Yet, instead of deliverance, there was suspicion. Disgust.

Her heart pounded. "You saw it." she said, her voice hoarse from the dry air. Dagna and Heru stared at her. "You saw the flame."

"A shadow of power," Heru muttered. "Not our power."

Philippa's pulse roared in her ears. She wanted to argue, to demand that they see that this was real, that it had come from her, not some deception. But then she saw the jawbone elder's face harden, her lips thinning into something grim.

She had been given an hour to prove herself, to save them. And she had failed.

A crackling snap rang through the air - Heru's hand and face igniting, flames licking up her to her shoulder in an effortless display of power. Dagna followed suit, the fire in her palm burning hot and hungry. Philippa felt the shift before the words came.

"She is not one of us," Heru declared.

The sentence settled over her like a stone.

The crowd's energy shifted, one idle onlookers now pressing in, closing around her in a way that made her stomach turn.

They weren't impressed. They were deciding how to kill her.

Her feet itched to move, but she stood rooted to the sand. She turned to Tazmireth, who had remained silent all this time, still bound away from the others. Their eyes met.

Help me.

Taz's expression was unreadable, but her hands twitched, fingers curling like they wanted to intervene. But the weight of the Wahanar's judgment was already falling, and Philippa wasn't sure if even Tazmireth's fire could stop it now.

Then, Heru spoke again. "She is unclean!"

Dagna's fire glared brighter. "She is to be executed!"

Feeling as small as a mouse, Philippa felt her knees sway, and she hit the sand. Her breathing came in ragged gulps, her forehead pressed to the ground. Suddenly, the pallor of someone else's skin pressed to her arm.

She turned her head, sand filling her hair, and saw Shem's outstretched foot against her arm. His leg was fully extended, trying to reach her. He mouthed a word.

Map.

The parchment seared against her chest. But even if she ran, she wouldn't make it far.

Dagna carried too many poisons and had too many plans to keep her from running off.

"You all are why we are called *Brutes!*" The jawbone elder yelled. A wave of white hot fire rolled over the entire gathered crowd, causing everyone to duck or turn their tattoos to the flame to save themselves. Philippa felt the wash of heat, somehow so hot she felt a spit of cold air touch her face.

"We asked for flames! She gave us flames! Heru, you are chief now." The woman approached Heru, hands settling on her shoulders. "You must lead with honor."

Confusion danced on Heru's features, contorting her hawk into more of a wave of discontent.

The jawbone elder settled in front of Philippa, taking her arms, and lifting her to her feet. Philippa could feel Ole beaming with pride behind her.

None of this made sense.

This close to the woman, Philippa could see the jawbone had been picked clean and polished before being inserted into the pierced holes in her face. Vulture, indeed.

The elder's amber eyes took her in with great respect, nodding once at her. She wrapped an arm around her shoulder, as if showing her off to the people.

The Vulture preened Philippa's dirty braid with her fingers. "I said you would not be killed first if you produced fire. I will stick to my word."

Relief washed over her for just a moment. Then, the Vulture's knee collided with her stomach, sending all of her air and bile up from her guts.

Philippa collapsed, holding her torso, her ears ringing.

Vulture's eyes turned to Tazmireth. "We will kill her first."

A unified uproar filled the air. Philippa's blurry vision caught Taz's fading pride, replaced by deep despair. Taz's head hung low, dark hair concealing her face, but the soft trembling of her shoulders was undeniable.

The crowd rushed towards Tazmireth, intent on untying and lifting her. It was then that Philippa noticed their tears. Everyone, except the *Tanvirok,* was weeping. Their justice, she realized, was not without pain. How could these people permit such a thing, knowing already the sorrow it caused? Philippa felt her power curling away like a wounded animal, and she longed to claw her way back into the catacombs just to rewrite every law that allowed such hypocrisy.

A fist balled up her hair, lifting her head to face them. Heru's expression was no different than that of the other Wahanar.

"She said she wouldn't kill us." Philippa whispered, her voice barely audible, a fragile thread stretched taut against the looming dread.

Heru spat in her face, and the world narrowed to the acrid vision of her animosity. "She said she would not kill you *first.* My son is going to die for your sins today. You would think a scribe would listen to words more carefully."

Panu had been laid by them, tied down to a cart, as if they were worried he would get up and run away. A Nazheris stood dutifully at the head of the cart, allowing herself to be hitched without a struggle.

Without a doubt, Philippa knew that it was the same Nazheris who had been at Panu's side since the beginning.

The Wahanar had gathered their finest archers, surrounding the execution field. The dunes rolled out into the distance, stretching for the stars knew how far. This would've been where they were sent to walk for an eternity. Philippa's mind was badgering her, and irritatingly, her magic had fallen silent inside of her.

Your friend could be walking out of here now if you hadn't intervened. If you hadn't listened to that man you just met.

Philippa clenched her teeth. Her mind was no longer worth listening to when it spoke like that. Nothing it said had saved her since she left Levanta, not really. A few warnings here and there, but nothing that curbed their fate now.

Would Morgana and Raff ever know what befell her? That her own hubris was the cause of, not just her own death, but that of everyone she'd tried to protect?

A flash of her mother's face sliced through her mind. Then Morgana, older than her, but still so, so young to see their mother die. She hoped that Raff wouldn't know. That he would be able to let it rest and never know the details of what had happened to his family.

The archers of the Wahanar dipped their arrows into a jar that Dagna offered them, coating the arrowheads with a dark, sticky liquid. Poison, in case any of them lost their nerve and tried to run.

Heru, a ghostly figure, moved through the crowd, keenly aware of the *Tanvirok* elders pursuing her. The Vulture elder surveyed the gathering with an almost audacious air of boredom. In stark contrast, Dagna was a picture of rabid joy, all teeth and trembling anticipation.

How could Ole have married someone so ready to murder her own niece?

Philippa looked at him, at the binds on his hands that he could've easily broken, and only saw defeat. He accepted his fate. He had brought this uncleanliness upon his people, and he would pay the price that was named.

She'd heard him muttering to the elders that he would go first, if they allowed it.

"I don't want them to be scared," he'd said while he thought he was out of earshot.

Her heart ached.

Shem had been silent, his eyes constantly roving over everyone who passed. He kept rolling his shoulders and stretching his back, as if he could run away at a moment's notice.

Herunavira's voice cracked over the desert. "Let the cleansing begin."

Air rushed out of someone's lungs as they were shoved forward.

Taz.

Her hair was unbound, wild around her stoic face. The lightened mark on her cheek was burnt from the sun. Evidently, the cream she'd used to keep her vitiligo from spreading was revoked from her for being unclean. The snow white eyelashes on her blue eye looked singed, purple swelling nearly drawing it shut.

Dagna led her to a pedestal they'd erected out of the sand, a glass structure that was far less intricate than their other creations. It gave off the sense that this was solely for function.

Once Tazmireth was atop the pedestal, she was instructed to spread her feet, and to outstretch her inked palm. Taz turned it skyward like an offering.

"For your sins, we remove you from the fire of your ancestors." With the force of a lion, Dagna flashed a curved blade and brought it down through the air.

Philippa couldn't stop herself from retching, even as she saw Taz's jaw working. She'd known it was coming.

Taz let out a muffled scream as her hand hit the glass with a meaty *thump.* Blood strained the pedestal and soaked her wrist where her hand should've been. Dagna reached out with a cloth and tied it tightly around Tazmireth's bleeding arm, that godforsaken smile still on her face.

Philippa churned her feet in the sand from where she was tied, her teeth grinding with ferocity. She willed her magic to bubble up, to appear with such might and ferocity that the ground would shake. It remained quiet, buried as if afraid.

She couldn't let this happen.

Horror lanced through her as she watched Taz simply put her hand and bleeding wrist over her heart and await further punishment.

Summon fire! Philippa begged. Just because Tazmireth's tattoo was gone didn't mean that she couldn't conjure something to release herself. It would be harder, but in the heat of this moment, Philippa knew she could. But Tazmireth was already still as stone, awaiting what would happen next.

Don't move, don't move, don't move, her mind whispered, a tendril of a voice caressing her subconscious.

I am done listening to everything you say!

As they doused Taz in a sticky liquid, Philippa began to try and channel her mind back to when she controlled that small flame. Tried to envision herself as a catacomb that the flame could travel through, being enticed to draw itself out.

Wahanar warriors approached the pedestal with bags of sand they'd gathered. Heru watched with an impassive face.

Ole was crying, a soft, rumbling sound.

Dagna still smiled.

Philippa's heart burned in her chest. Fire was not her magic, but her family was, and if this was the price they were to pay, then she would pay it for them all.

Burn her, cut her into pieces, so be it.

Smoke filled her nostrils, a heaviness that settled in her chest. She coughed, and swore a small plume of grey air left her lips. Shem was watching her, she could feel it, even as she squeezed her eyes shut. Flames coiled inside of her, an angry, consuming thing. It was so unlike the first flicker she had let course through her. This was *alive,* this was ferocious… protective.

The fibers that bound her wrists began to smoke.

Her eyes snapped open, just in time to see them pouring the bags of sand all over Tazmireth. The weight of it all made her lose her balance, her legs bowing. She steadied herself, eyes shut to avoid the grains. Once the downpour ceased, Tazmireth opened her eyes. They instantly found Heru.

The two cousins looked at each other. Taz, who had given up everything for Heru and taken the fall for her a number of times. Herunavira could stop this, if she wanted to. The realization hit Philippa like a ton of bricks. Heru was chief now. She could overrule everything. But her honor mattered more than her cousin, who condemned herself into a sinner to protect her family.

Whatever impassive, saddened mask Heru wore, it wasn't all that lay beneath.

Philippa would kill to read what had gotten her to this point, but there would be no time.

A gust of air flowed through Philippa's mind. Feeding the flames.

"Whatever you're doing, it has to be soon." Shem's voice, to her right. Ole's quiet sobs to her left. Panu's still form behind her.

A group of Wahanar approached the pedestal, and on command, ignited their flames. It roared and scorched the air, reaching into the sky.

When Taz found no comfort in her cousin, she set her gaze to Philippa. The flame Philippa was trying to conjure almost went out entirely. Tears lined her friend's eyes, a mourning and accepting expression that Philippa couldn't dissect.

"What was that oil they put on her?" Philippa hurriedly asked.

Ole took a moment to register her words. "It is of Dagna's creation. It draws the flame only to those it touches. It cannot be rubbed off onto another person. It is like it knows its victims."

A vision like a horror novel racked through her mind. The statues in the catacombs.

On Dagna's command, the Wahanar set their flames to Tazmireth's feet.

She wavered, and for a moment, she actually did try to run. But her feet and ankles were already set against the glass pedestal. Fear tore through Tazmireth as she used her remaining hand to try and pull her leg free from the flames, but it only licked her sand covered arm. When she lifted herself, her forearm came up slower, heavier. It was reflecting the sun, a bleak, dark glass that struck her down to the bone.

And it was *killing* her.

The flames drove higher and higher, eating up to her knees.

Philippa's binds snapped and she was on her feet in seconds. Her tattooed hand was hot and prickling with fire.

No one was fast enough to stop her. The Wahanar archers raised their bows, and those burning Tazmireth faltered, unsure of what to do.

Philippa slipped on the glass, and almost tripped over Taz's fallen hand.

The flames around them stopped, but the arrows did not fly. In an instant, Philippa's arms wrapped around Tazmireth and held her tightly. Taz was shaking uncontrollably, but the sand and oil did not come off her body. Philippa begged it to transfer to herself. If she could take this for her friend, she would. It didn't matter to her that she was likely already too late, that Tazmireth's feet could not be turned back into skin and bone from glass.

"You are only making this last longer for her, *vashir*!" Dagna's voice called out.

Philippa supported Taz's weight as she leaned into her as much as her glass limbs would allow. She turned her head on Taz's chest, fervor burning in her chest.

"You have no love among you!" Philippa screamed, her voice raw. "If you continue this, what do you think the rest of Istoria will see?"

A few Wahanar exchanged glances. She knew she had their attention, because they were looking for Dagna to respond.

Philippa raised her voice, her arms tightening around Taz. "*Brutes*! And I know you are *not*! But you, Dagna, *are.* You did not care if your grandson died, or your niece. You are clawing at the gates of Nyxveil just to get your hands on death!"

Murmurs raced through the people. Even the Wahanar who were doing the burning were only doing so out of being honor bound. This was their life, and now Dagna, through Heru, commanded obedience.

Dagna only smiled. "What I care about is honor. Of which you clearly have none. We remember who stole from us in the first place."

Her last words drew all the Wahanar right back to where they'd started. Their hatred for scribes and the king and queen encroaching on their land would always outweigh anything else.

Philippa met Taz's eyes. Tears streamed down her friend's face.

"I'm sorry. I'm so, so sorry." Philippa's voice was a whisper. "I'm not going to leave you, okay?"

Even if she wanted Philippa to be safe, Taz nodded. She squeezed her arms around Philippa and crushed her into her chest. The uneasiness of Tazmireth's heartbeat made her cry out in anguish.

"Heru?" Dagna's voice was expectant.

Herunavira, the chief of the Wahanar, didn't hide the venom in her words. "Burn them both."

Only, Philippa would turn to ash instead of glass.

She only tightened her grip on Taz, binding them together as closely as she could. Her mind, still open and breezy, rushed with fear and air that engulfed her.

The fire in her hand burned like a star, surrounding her and Tazmireth, shielding them from the flames that dared to eat them both alive. The Wahanar shouted and screamed.

Taz gasped. Philippa's palm was *burning* like it hadn't before. The fire was too much for her. Consuming her. This was not scribe imitation or Wahanar fire, but white hot light.

"Put it out!" Tazmireth screeched.

"No. Not if it saves you." Sweat dripped down her forehead and into her mouth. The salt was keeping her present, as her mind frayed and regathered itself over and over from the strain.

Taz, with her shaking hand, gripped Philippa's wrist. "I am already gone.

Run away. Save my family. Promise me."

Philippa's voice was an echo hollow as she stared into her friend's dimming eyes, and told her something she had no idea how to fulfill. "I promise."

A defeated smile crossed Taz's face. Tears were steaming and evaporating from her cheeks. She shakily squeezed Philippa's face with her hand. "I forgive you."

The starlight went out. With the seconds they had as the fire approached them, they wrapped their arms around each other. The flames did not touch Philippa, and were sucked into the oil that they'd drenched Tazmireth in. She felt the heat, but not the pain that should've cut through her.

She held Taz through the onslaught of flames. Through the cool of air that rushed over them when they were satisfied. Philippa kept her eyes closed and her arms holding her friend until Tazmireth's breaths stopped.

She knew she had to draw away, but couldn't. Much time passed before she felt able to move.

Philippa's breaths were shallow as she drew her head away. Taz's eyes were still open, now crystalline and immortalized. She followed her friend's gaze, which was set in a determined squint, as if she was still looking right at her.

Quick, uneven breaths stirred a cough in her chest. There wasn't even the smell of burnt flesh. It was like Tazmireth had never breathed, never spoke, never moved.

Taking in the stagnant statue was like looking at an embalmed body. Her arm that now lacked a hand was still wrapped around Philippa's back. Tears flowed freely down her cheeks, mingling with the dried blood on her lip. Tazmireth's other hand was outstretched, as if she was still cupping Philippa's face.

Her knees nearly gave out. She placed her chin back into the cooling glass of her friend's hand, pressing their foreheads together.

Sound rushed back to her, the cries of the Wahanar and Shem screaming at her. None of it mattered.

For the first time in her life, she understood something that she never had before. A bitter, coiling snake was burrowing into her chest. Something foreign and yet all natural, a pot waiting to boil over.

This was more than anger, more than the metallic bitterness of injustice rattling inside her body. No, this demanded vengeance and blood.

Her teeth ground against themselves, her very bones aching with anticipation.

A Nazheris brayed. She wondered if it had felt this from other scribes before, the brewing of a storm so great that it would poison her soul.

She'd never understood the stories her parents told her about those who wanted to change *everything* just because they *could.*

But as unkind arms wrapped around her and ropes began to bind her, dragging her away from the hardened corpse, she understood. Whatever it took to change this, she would do it. Tazmireth's life book was somewhere, now closed and bound by death. The map tucked away beneath her wraps burned against her skin. Shem was from Aresef. He could take her to the libraries. Find Tazmireth's book, Panu's while they were at it, and she would fix this.

But first they had to survive.

CHAPTER TWENTY-NINE ✦

The heat from the pyre was unbearable.

Philippa felt the sting of smoke in her eyes, her lungs straining against the thick, acrid air. The Wahanar warriors stood in a half circle around them. Fire flickered in most of their palms, reflecting in the poisoned arrow heads aimed at their her heart.

In the center, of course, was Dagna and Heru. The former was still smiling.

Philippa's throat bobbed. They would not be granted a swift death.

The Wahanar had bothered to rebind her even though they knew she could break free. Except, by the indignation in Herunavira's eyes, maybe they knew she *couldn't.* Her earlier - and temporary - escape was fueled by the need to save Tazmireth.

No matter how much venom was burning inside of her, Philippa couldn't shake the image of Tazmireth's death from her mind. Even with vengeance wanting to simmer out from underneath her skin, grief was a funny thing.

Beside her, Shem stood silent, his jaw clenched, but his eyes kept darting towards Philippa as if willing her to come up with some last second escape. Maybe begging her to free them both and they'd meet up at his predestined location. Philippa didn't even want to look at him anymore. Her body felt boneless, caught between the need to flee and the icy inability to move. It was like she could see herself from an outsider's eyes, the way her hair tousled in the breeze, the firelight glinting in her dull eyes. Nothing would change what was about to happen. She knew she should move or make another scene, attempt anything to stop the impending doom.

But her heart wasn't in it. The chasm she'd opened inside herself for her magic before now felt like it was filled with all the stones she'd imagined swallowing, sinking into an inky black abyss.

Her eyes flicked to the side.

The Nazheris that was yoked to the cart holding Panu stamped its feet. Although its hide offered protection from the flames, it seemed reluctant to witness the executions. Its orb eyes were narrowing and opening in a strange pattern, and when Philippa followed its gaze, it was watching near the empty cage where her guardian had been. There was a Wahanar in a cloak atop one of their few horses, face shadowed by their hood, but the horse's feet seemed to stomp in response.

Ole was muttering what sounded like a prayer, though it was barely audible above the roar of the flames behind them. Panu, ever still, groaned so quietly she thought her mind was playing tricks on her. An innocent boy, murdered by his people.

Because of you, you, you.

"This is retribution," Heru called out. "For the blood spilled. For our stories rewritten. After today, we bend our will to no one!"

Philippa swallowed hard. There was no escape. She had tried to create a space for magic within her mind, to make her body a vessel for power, but nothing stirred inside her. Only the feeling of drowning remained, memories of salty water filling her lungs.

Dagna raised her hand. The archers drew their bows. The fire crackled, poised to consume them all.

And then the world went dark.

Her eyes were open, but blackness, absolute and consuming, swallowed what little light remained. All the torches, braziers, scattered bonfires, and the *sun* that had illuminated the grim execution ground were extinguished in a single, unnatural gust of wind. It wasn't just strong; it was violent, a malevolent force that whipped around Philippa, stealing her breath and sending shivers down her spine. The air grew frigid, tasting of ash and something else, ancient and untamed.

Then, a sensation. Something impossibly soft brushed against her cheek, a delicate touch amidst the chaos. Instinctively, she leaned into it, a flicker of bewildered curiosity piercing through her terror. As the sensation faded, a single, iridescent grey feather drifted down, catching the unseen currents before landing gently at her feet, a stark contrast against the rough, cold earth. It seemed to pulse faintly, almost as if it held a hidden light within its delicate structure, a solitary enigma in the overwhelming darkness.

A sharp clatter rang out as an arrow missed its target. The sun seemed to reappear out of thin air, the veil of blackness gone in an instant.

The warriors whirled, drawing their blades.

A shadow dropped from above.

A glint of steel. A flicker of bird's mask in the dying firelight.

Chaos.

Her guardian landed like a ghost among the warriors, knives flashing. He moved with a terrifying precision, slicing through the Wahanar like water.

They cried out, but he wasn't killing them.

One soldier lunged. A dagger caught his throat before he could blink. Or, he wasn't killing them, until now.

Blasts of fire shot towards the masked man, but he dodged each blooming light as if it were child's play.

Another Wahanar raised his bow. Her guardian was faster, grabbed the shaft and twisted it into the archer's abdomen. Then, in the blink of an eye, her guardian was a shadow that fell through the world.

Philippa gasped as a blade cut through her bindings.

Gloved hands were on her shoulders, shoving her forward. "Run."

She spun, heart pounding. "The others—"

He was already moving, cutting Shem free next, then Ole, and he nodded to the Nazheris, his movements so fluid that the Wahanar warriors barely realized their prisoners had escaped before it was too late. A cloak fell to the ground as he whistled underneath his mask, the horse by the birdcage plowing through the crowd, knocking Heru off of her feet.

A war horn split the air.

More Wahanar would come.

Philippa reached for her guardian's arm, unsure of what to do, but he was already pulling her away from the fire and the falling bodies. Whatever dark smoke he'd used to hide his arrival was choking out anyone who got too close to it.

Suddenly, there was a *thud* in her side, heavy and wrong, like she'd been punched in the torso with a hammer. For a heartbeat, she thought she'd only been knocked off balance, until a simmering fire where she'd been struck began to bloom outward, curling through her ribs, licking down her arm. Each tug of her guardian's grip dragged the arrow inside her, scraping, pulling like a weight embedded in her flesh.

Breath came shallow, panicked, as if the shaft itself stole the air from her lungs. Poisoned.

She tasted iron on her tongue before she realized she was choking on her own cry… and blood.

Her limbs were turning to ice. Her guardian *jerked.*

The edges of the world were swimming, as though ink had spilled across the page of her sight. Dagna's poison would leave no survivors. She knew it, even as her pulse thundered too loud in her ears to think.

Then the second arrow struck.

This one she heard - a wet, ugly sound as it punched into her guardian's back. Fire trailed along the shaft, searing, eating into black cloth.

He grunted, swaying for half a second, then grabbed her before she could fall. As the world spun, she saw Herunavira with her arm poised to fire another arrow.

Her mouth moved before her mind could catch up. "No, you…"

Even half delirious, heat crawling through her veins, she tried to reach for him, her hand scrabbling uselessly against his sleeve. The pain in her own chest didn't matter, not when he staggered beneath the flames. Whirling, he snuffed out the fire with a vial of thick liquid he'd produced from the stars knew where.

He didn't let her speak. Didn't let her collapse.

He pulled her onto his bloodied back, wrapping her arms around his shoulders, which earned her a face full of feathers, and gripped her legs. Then, with a force that shouldn't have been possible for a man just shot through the ribs, he ran.

Disorientation claimed her quickly. She couldn't right herself or think hard enough to wonder where Shem and Ole would go, or if the Nazheris would choose to save Panu.

Herunavira and Dagna weren't going to let them go easily. The Wahanar, once through the dark smog, gave chase.

Arrows whistled through the air, barely missing as her Guardian leapt over burning logs, weaving through the execution ground. Debris littered the Wahanar camp. Had there been a bomb?

Her guardian whistled, and hoof beats tore through the sand.

Philippa's vision swam as he hoisted her up onto his horse, both still moving as quickly as they could. The poison was spreading. Her limbs felt weightless, her pulse slowing, the desert and fire around them blurring into a single, shifting mass.

His body was stiff as a board behind her as the horse took off. His grip on her tightened.

"I've got you," he murmured. "Just stay awake."

She tried. Unconsciousness beckoned her.

She tried again, but the heat and exhaustion and poison were dragging her down, down, down.

Her last bite of sound was the thunder of footsteps.

The last thing she saw was her masked guardian jolting as another arrow buried into his back, and blood spurting over his armored shoulder.

Darkness welcomed her home.

***

Mind in a haze, Philippa felt herself slipping between this world and the next. Words swam in her vision, parchment burning in a plume of smoke and feathers. Pain wretched in her gut.

The arrow.

The arrow meant to kill her and her guardian, her thief in the night, lodged between her ribs. She didn't expect to be able to *feel* the inside of her body so acutely.

Not in this visage of pain and delirium.

She'd been whisked far, far away. Her back pressed against something soft and yielding. Spongy growth reflexed under her twitching fingers. *Moss*.

A whisper of apology licked at her ears. An ambrosial, coppery scent filled her nostrils in the blackness, but the awareness of *someone* above her was a comfort in the abyss. Maybe a greeter at the gates of Nyxveil.

Hands worked across her skin like they had stitched her soul together from the beginning.

Lightning tore through her torso. She was screaming and someone was apologizing. Then, the caress of down. Heat of fire. The burn of metal against flesh.

Somewhere within the pain, her vision swam back to her. The form above her was blurred, outlined in an eerie, shifting light. A dash of grey feathers fell as he collapsed beside her, nestling into the earth as if to fall beneath it.

Then, everything went still.

Time unraveled, slipping through her fingers, lost in an expanse she could not measure. Her eyes saw impossible things; crystals and false sunlight in the darkness, a masked man she had always felt but never known.

Warmth emanated off of his body. She'd expected her guardian would be cold, encased in ice and shielding. But he was alive. Barely. His chest fought to rise.

A poisoned arrow jutted from his shoulder.

Thunder pounded in Philippa's skull, scattering her thoughts, warping reality. Maybe this was all a bad dream. Any moment now, their mother would wake her and Morgana, urging them to start their chores. Or Raff would come bounding into her room, begging her to take him fishing.

A faint smile crossed her face.

Pain speared through her ribs, sharp and unforgiving. The illusion shattered.

She was a pile of broken bones lying in a mossy cavern. Alone, except for the stranger beside her.

Help him, help him, help him.

More time lapsed. Between segments of searing pain, she found herself hovering above him. Her fingers wrapped around the shaft of the arrow and pulled. She wrenched it free. It slid out cleanly, gliding like a knife through butter. But there had been more. *So many more.* Where had they gone?

Her vision danced over his body, and at last, she saw.

They stuck out of his back like spines. He had to be dying. She could do nothing.

Should I want to?

He was still a stranger. Had stolen her away from those whom she had grown to care for. Ole. Panu. Shem.

Shem. His name was a caress on her mind.

Her guardian had saved her from death, but what of them?

Rolling onto her side despite the pain, Philippa crawled over his body and tried to force her eyes to focus. Dried blood sat in scattered splotches around the arrows. How long had they been running? Where was the horse?

Shaking the thoughts from her head, she refocused. No time for questions.

He was on his side, at least, she kept assuming he was a *he.* Arrows decorated his back and shoulders like he was some grotesque, ornate pincushion. Whatever she did now would be too late.

Her heart coiled around itself as Tazmireth's glass face danced through her mind. She would never be able to bury her, or send her off to sea. No honor in what happened to her.

A lump formed in her throat. Her hand closed around the next arrow. One after another, she plucked him free from those hateful spines. Delirious, she imagined she was picking flowers, bundles of lavender, with each awful rip. Her strength was meager, and consciousness was a fleeting thing. But she couldn't lose herself to the poison, not now.

Not when he was here. *Dead.* For her. Another life lost on her account. No doubt her pages were running red right now, wherever her book was.

Her fists trembled as she propped herself above him again.

Death had followed her everywhere. No.

She had led it.

Fate had no hands on what had been done today. This was *her doing.*

More permanent than ink. More final than the tattoo on her hand. More binding than the words etched into her shoulder since childhood.

"For once in your life, Philippa, finish something you started!" Her voice tore from her throat, raw and ragged.

She grasped the final arrow. Her body wobbled, and she had to steady herself, palm flattening against his chest as she wrenched the last shaft free from his chest.

Her breath came in strenuous waves. A dark stain spread beneath her fingers. Her own blood, her own tears.

When did I start crying?

Stars, her body was not her own. Underneath her palm, a thunder bloomed.

Soft.

Steady.

Quiet and resonant, but powerful. Her breath hitched. *His heart.*

Still beating.

Now, she knew why she was crying. His heart had reignited, and she collapsed beside him, accepting fate as the strange twinkling lights blurred above her and threatened to swallow her whole.

There was a shifting beside her. "You're bad for yourself."

The voice sounded distant, but felt close.

The chalk white bird turned to face her like a strange marionette. It was expressionless, but somehow terrified. His hand fell to her neck and her gut told her to flinch, but her mind sang to her to be still.

This isn't real, she knew.

His heart wasn't beating. Neither of them should be alive. Her mind, murky from blood loss and poison, had to be making this up.

Yet, the words he spoke stuck.

"Says the prisoner who got shot for a stranger," she slurred.

The bird-faced mask twitched, unsettlingly animalistic. "I'm only a stranger to you."

His voice was distinct - male, yet unfamiliar.

And yet, she *knew* it.

Sleep called to her, but she fought against it. Just a little longer. Before she left this existence, she had questions.

"You saved me," she murmured. "Today. And before. And before, and before."

His chest rose, slow and shallow. He exhaled, a sound curling inside his mask. He only nodded against the mossy ground.

She studied him in the strange, dim glow. The mask looked like a skeletal form, overgrown with time, abandoned to the elements. *That's how I want to be,* she thought. *Lost to time, untouched by any more horrors.*

"Are we dying?"

His body tensed. "Sleep."

"You sound different than I thought you would."

"You're terrible at following simple directions, you know that?" His voice was smoky and soft. Real.

She smiled weakly. "That's how I ended up here."

"No. You're here because you followed someone else's direction. Someone you barely know. Your choices are not so bad."

"Council from a bird," she murmured. "I really am dying."

Gloved hands slid under her shoulders as he moved her deeper into the shade of the cavern, away from the crystalline glow.

Gentle fingers brushed over her eyelids.

Darkness closed in, but she could still feel him.

Watching. Waiting.

―――――――――――――――――

A warm breeze caressed her skin.

The line between wakefulness and oblivion had become a hazy, unreliable boundary. Her eyes would flicker open, catching glimpses of her surroundings, only for time to dissolve once more.

Yet, this awakening felt distinct.

Her arms were leaden, almost impossible to lift. As she strained to push herself onto her elbows, a sharp pain radiated across her side, a sudden, tearing sensation. She gasped, her hand instinctively flying to her torso, then froze.

Thin fabric covered her, scratchy and unfamiliar. And beneath it, she was as bare as the day she was born.

Philippa yanked the cloth tighter around her. It creased clumsily, clearly meant for something - or someone - larger. Her nose wrinkled. Sweat, old hair… a horse blanket.

Her feet brushed against the mossy floor as she shifted. She listened, ears twitching instinctively, but only the soft trickle of water and an odd twanging sound hinted that she wasn't alone.

She turned slowly and craned her neck.

Real sunlight pierced the ancient, domed ceiling, casting dazzling arcs through the tall, jagged crystals that sprouted from its impossible depths.

It reminded her of the Wahanar caverns, used for long distance passage. But when she looked down, the floor wasn't the familiar, impossible glass. It was stone and packed clay. All tangible, all real. Which meant she could be found.

She needed to leave. Now. Find Shem. He'd be waiting.

If he made it out.

Philippa shook her head as her throat tightened. She could fix this, she had to.

Where were her clothes? Her map? She remembered tucking it into the wrap that was now gone. She hesitated. A faint memory of feathers and a decadent voice like dusk and velvet whispered against her memories. Had that been real?

The ache in her ribs told her yes. Her fingers brushed the twisted skin hear her wound. She'd been shot. She was alive.

So was he, then - whoever *he* was.

Despite herself, her chest stirred. Someone *had* saved her. Maybe always had. She hadn't been wrong, not entirely. But that didn't make him trustworthy.

A stranger who had left her friends to die.

What did that make him? What did that make *her*?

She forced herself upright. Her legs trembled as she followed the sound of trickling water. The stones and moss gave way to a small creek that sliced through the cavern and disappeared into a small crevice. At a quick glance, she knew there wasn't a chance she could fit through it.

She tried to kneel, but her legs gave out, and she collapsed, slamming her knees into the hard rock. A groan escaped her lips as pain shot up her legs, but it was lost as she saw her reflection. Her hands plunged into the water, shattering the image.

Her dark, ash colored hair, now in stringy waves, framed a face where the dried blood had been meticulously cleaned away. Her lip and cheek remained swollen, but the taste of salve hinted at care.

Stars, she needed a bath.

She also needed to find her map, but she had no leads on that, and her body ached for relief.

She began to unwrap the horse blanket from her body when she heard pebbles hit stone. Her eyes snapped up, limbs frozen with the spike of fear that trailed her bare skin.

Thirty paces away, perched on the edge of one of the large stone outcroppings, crouched a man in a bird mask.

This was her first unobstructed view of him, free from bars or the haziness of poison.

From head to toe, he was cloaked in fitted, movable fabric, hidden from both sun and sight. The beak of his mask cast a perfect shadow where she might have expected to see a chin or a jaw. Perhaps he wasn't a man at all, but something else entirely, for she was certain he was dead.

He had a subtle presence, almost as if he could choose to be invisible. She would not have noticed him unless he willed it. He seemed perfectly comfortable in the silence, while she found herself speechless.

The feathers cascading down the back of his mask to hide his hair and neck fluttered in an elegant display as he hopped down, landing on his feet. Her heartbeat crept up to her throat, but it wasn't fear. No, her ears twitched in anticipation and she realized that she was waiting to hear his voice again, even if just to prove to herself that he was real.

He approached her with a dancer's grace, yet his movements held a distinct prowl. He may have saved her, but he clearly didn't trust her.

"You move like you expect me to pull a knife on you." Philippa said, her voice hoarser than she recalled.

He tilted his head, his black boots planted at the opposite edge of the creek, silent as a mouse. Philippa clutched the horse blanket tighter. He hadn't needed to let her hear him.

He crouched, movements precise, and reached a gloved hand into a small, unnoticed pack behind his back.

You should be afraid right now, she told herself. But she wasn't. Not in the slightest.

He pulled a bundle from his pack, and held it in his hands as if he was nervous to show her. This man had nothing to be nervous about. He'd torn through a Wahanar camp like it was nothing, saved her life from a poison arrow, and somehow survived being shot by the same arrows ten times over.

In his hands, wrapped in a belt, was a bundle of clothes. The hollowed, shadowy eyes of the mask bore into her as he inclined his head and swung his arm up. She nodded, and caught the clothes when he tossed them across.

Philippa unbuckled the leather belt, unrolling the tightly bound garments. As the fabric unfurled, revealing the rough hewn stones beneath, a brittle parchment tumbled from its hidden folds. It was Shem's map. Her breath hitched.

Her guardian cleared his throat, and her eyes snapped up. He pointed at the garments.

"Are you asking me if they'll fit?" She asked. More than likely he'd seen her naked - which should've made her skin crawl, but she was more thankful to be alive - so he'd know about what size of clothes she'd need.

"Thank you. Even if they don't, they'll be fine until…"

Until what?

Her throat constricted, mirroring the silence that had fallen between them. He cleared his, a subtle gesture that only amplified the sudden shift. He pointed to the clothes, then to her. He had spoken before; why was his silence so different now?

"You can talk," she said, softer this time, "I'm okay with it."

More than okay. His voice sounded like home. Like forgotten safety.

Feathers ruffled over his shoulder. He pointed at the crystals, and she remembered what Heru and Taz had taught her.

"You're worried they'll hear."

A nod.

"Let me try them on. Then I have questions—" she cut herself off. He had already turned around, and a hidden hood from underneath his feathered mask was pulled over his head, as if to fully shield himself from her.

Philippa couldn't help but chuckle. Quietly, she slid out of the horse blanket and gathered the clothes. As she pulled the tunic over her head, she got half lost, and realized there was only one sleeve. It was a dark material, one she'd never choose for herself.

Once dressed, she looked at herself in the water.

The tunic was asymmetrical, its fabric draping in flowing layers around her thighs. A single sleeve clung to her left arm, fitted like a second skin, while the right shoulder remained bare, exposing the sharp lines of her collarbone, but hiding the words on her left shoulder. Twin belts of weathered leather cinched the garment at her waist, with buckles of bronze clasping them together. She slipped snug pants underneath the tunic, which allowed for ease of movement, but their sheen caught the flickers of crystal. When she looked from herself to her guardian, she realized the material he wore was the same. All that was left were simple black boots, which Philippa turned her nose up at.

"Am I really going to need…?"

"Yes." His first word was sharp and indignant.

She frowned and slid them on, hating the feeling of her bare feet confined to leather prisons.

Then she took out Shem's map. The lines were faded and smudged, but legible.

But this cavern was nowhere on his map. The rest of the terrain she didn't recognize. It had started from the Wahanar camp, but she was supposed to have traveled through the desert and into a nearby canyon until she reached what appeared to be a coastal forest.

She looked up, and found her guardian already looking at her. "Thank you. For saving me."

"Don't ever thank me for that." Sharp. Annoyed.

Philippa toyed with the belt on her tunic. She needed to ask for his help, despite everything she'd done. Whoever and whatever he was, he could get her out of this cavern. But she needed him to talk to her first.

"So, your people like wearing dark colors?"

Nothing.

"Are you here to help me?" She asked.

He cocked his head to the side, as if debating. "You're going back home."

She noted how he didn't say where she was going. Did the crystals really listen that much? How much could a crystal say, anyway?

"I can't do that yet." Philippa fidgeted with her map. Even without a proper face, annoyance radiated off of him. "I need to get here. To find… them."

"No."

Her skin crawled. "Why save me? Why come back? Why care?"

"I can't explain everything to you."

"Because I won't understand?" She took a step forward, attempting to close the gap. "I know I don't understand what's going on. Believe me, after my day yesterday, I am *frightfully* aware. But please, please, do not tell me what I can't do. I need to find them. Find *him.* If you won't help me, just point me in the right direction. I'm flailing here."

She continued to close the gap, but when he didn't react, her ugly boot slipped on the side of the creek. Her breath rushed out, and a blazing pain shot through the burned wound in her side. She fell into the water, bashing her elbow on a rock so hard that jitters went all the way up to her jaw.

Embarrassed, she looked up at him, his mask impassable.

"No quips?" she asked through clenched teeth.

He dropped to one knee, a gloved hand outstretched not to assist her, but to seize the map she held.

"Hey—!" She scrambled up the bank after him, slipping again. He spun as she lunged, and she crashed into the rock wall. Philippa caught herself in time to avoid slamming her head into the stone. Anger bloomed in her chest.

He was *smiling* under that mask. She could feel it.

"You'll not find me to be very *quippy*." he said.

Then, without ceremony, he tucked the map into one of the straps on his chest. Hidden. Gone.

She closed her eyes and craned her neck back, trying to release the tension in her body. "I can't believe I just tried to chase my guardian for a piece of paper."

At the word *guardian* he inclined his head, and the warm sound of a chuckle filled the inside of his mask. "I can't believe you just drenched brand new clothes."

By the look of the clothes, they most certainly were *not* new. So, he could lie to her. That was good to know.

She leveled a glare at him. "Who's not quippy, again?"

His usual indifference slid back into place. "I'll get you out of here. That's the extent of what I promise."

"Let me guess." she said, rolling her shoulders. "On the condition that I don't ask anymore questions?"

He strode towards her until they stood toe to toe. If his intention was to intimidate, it failed; he wasn't significantly taller than her, and in their solitude, nothing about him radiated danger. If anything, he appeared immensely irritated. His response shocked her.

Philippa anticipated a response that would assert his dominance, but he simply stated, "I don't mind your questions. But we really do need to go."

A bit stunned, her voice came out a squeak. "I want my map back."

"Maybe." He replied, voice even.

He walked to the cavern wall where the light was brightest, shining on his bone-like mask. In the pure light, she noticed flecks of gold peeking out between his feathers. So he *did* have real hair. Blonde. Strange, for this far into Sapria.

He placed his hands on the stones, testing various spots with his weight, effortlessly pulling himself up each time. She wondered why he didn't continue climbing until he looked her way.

"How's your climbing?" He asked.

Philippa blushed. "Can't we do your… falling into the ground thing?" When he didn't respond, she rolled her eyes. "Oh, please, I know you can."

His body tensed. He took her in, head to toe. "You'll throw up."

A little offended, she trudged to his side in her heavy boots. "I would climb better without these horrible things."

The beak of his mask nearly knocked into her as he turned sharply. The intent was clear: *stop complaining.*

"You seriously don't have any conditions for me, guardian?"

"You read too many love stories. I have no conditions or expectations for you. I have a job to do." He grabbed her wrists and placed them on the rocks, then dropped under her feet to boost her up with ease.

"That's not what I - I mean, I like to read," she muttered, already breathing harder, her side aching with each stretch.

"I know." he said. He was beside her, reaching for the next hold.

Philippa's feet awkwardly found a place to balance, and she relied on her arms to balance her weight. "You know a lot about me, guardian."

He sighed, hooked his legs around a mossy branch, and flipped backward. In one fluid motion, he grabbed her beneath the arms, hoisting her up like a child so she could reach the branch.

"Here's a condition," he said, righting himself beside her, "stop calling me that. That's not who I am."

"Then who are you?"

Her worthless boot slipped on the moss, and she fell. Her side screamed as she slammed into a jutting stone. Stars bloomed in her vision. By the time the world steadied, he was already standing above her on the outcropping, tapping his foot in clear annoyance.

He didn't offer to help, but as she climbed back up, he checked the back of his wrist. That rat didn't even *wear* a time piece, Philippa realized as she scowled.

She clambered to her feet and met his expressionless stare.

"Take the blasted boots off." he said, a lilt in his voice despite his annoyed posture.

CHAPTER THIRTY ✧

She planted her hands on the flat, warm outcropping. With a sizzling ache in her side, she weaseled her torso up as far as she could.

The climb had taken them into a crevice so narrow that both her chest and back were blocked in by jagged rock and dirt. At least, without the boots, she could get a grip on the footholds below. Her toes wiggled, debris and slivers working their way under the nails.

Unable to turn her head, she could only hear the steady, strong breaths of the man beside her. Unlike her own shallow gasps, his breathing was even and pooled within his mask, creating the faintest of sounds, a rhythmic whisper that filled the oppressive silence of the space.

He'd been helping her climb for what felt like hours. Though she doubted she still needed his physical assistance, her mind was a torment. She imagined the clicking of pincers or the sting of venom with every slip or misplaced foothold. In her darkest moments, she heard Tazmireth's scream and saw her face, twisted and decaying, before her eyes.

Philippa pushed her forehead against her wrists. Her heart was a wild thing in her chest, on the verge of explosion.

Just the *thought* of Tazmireth believing in Philippa made her stomach churn and her eyes unfocused.

She bit her lip until it bled, tasting the copper. Her fingernails scraped against the stone, grounding herself.

I need that map.

Her promise to Taz, to help her family, hinged on finding Shem. The thought of his knowledgeable smile and keen eyes was a welcome change from Taz's face, which haunted her mind. Yet, when she found him, it would not be for comfort or friendship.

No, in the silence her guardian demanded after she pressed on and on about the map, she'd hatched a plan. If the world demanded that she slay mighty dragons and shake the earth, she would. Even if that quake was saving a sleeping boy. She'd kept these thoughts to herself, despite the ache of wanting to ask her masked man beside her for help. The longer he'd ignored her questions, the more she realized that she was on her own.

For whatever reason, he'd saved her, and for that she was grateful. But not once had he stated his intentions.

And he thinks he's sending me to Levanta? Fat chance.

He would have to drag her kicking and screaming. Which he probably would try.

She sucked in her stomach, and the smooth fabric of her clothes glided through the crevice and into an open plateau of space. A gloved hand was already outstretched.

She paused halfway up, pulling her aching arm back. "I still want my map."

Above her, he was crouched like some carved creature of the stone itself, head tilted down toward her, unreliable behind the mask.

"You don't need it." he said quietly. "You'll follow me anyway."

She exhaled, chest tight. "You don't know that."

"I do."

There was a beat, quiet except for their breath and the faint dripping of water from the ceiling above.

"I don't follow people I don't trust." she said, fingers curling around the rock. "But I follow maps."

He didn't move, but she could feel him calculating. "Why try and save that boy?"

Her eyebrows shot up, but she supposed she shouldn't be surprised that he knew about Panu and her being a scribe. But there was another question hidden in his words: *do you really think you're powerful enough?*

"I'm the only one who can save that boy, save Tazmireth and my family.

It's the right thing to do."

Something about her answer seemed to both irritate and satisfy him. "You have an inferiority complex."

"No, I—"

"You would rewrite the dead because you failed. If that is not inferiority, what is it?" His voice was cold.

His words landed with their intended impact. Philippa froze, her next move uncertain. His hand was definitely not an option.

"I can climb on my own." she said, not meeting his gaze.

Finally, he stood. True to his earlier word, he offered no quips, and stalked away to ascend in silence.

With a groan, she dragged herself over the ledge and onto solid ground, her lungs burning, finally reaching the top. She had expected a blind stare or an outstretched hand, but there was nothing. At first, she was glad, because it meant he had listened to her.

Then, she clenched her jaw and squeezed her eyes shut at the notion that he did in fact leave her. When she cracked open an eye, there was the notable absence of his breathing, the way the air shifted around him when he looked at her. No, there was nothing but her god forsaken boots with the laces looped with an irritating precision… and the map. Unfolded and smoothed flat with little stones at the corners, like it had been studied.

She glanced around, heart still pounding. No movement. No voice. No shadow.

But she felt *something,* like the brush of a hand at her spine. The undeniable sense of eyes on her, just out of reach. Of course he hadn't really left.

Reluctantly, she slipped her boots back on and folded the map carefully, trying to not her fingers tremble.

"You're not subtle," she muttered under her breath, then louder, just in case, "but thank you."

No reply. Only the faint shift of wind through the cavern mouth, like a breath exhaled.

Good. That was good. She had the sinking feeling that if this was going to work that she would need him to return.

Because Shem wouldn't go along easily with what she had in mind. He wouldn't want to help her, surely, not after everything… especially not if he knew the extent of what she meant to do. But he would take her to Aresef. One way or another, he would lead her to the place where the life stories were kept.

It was the only way to save everyone. Even there, she could fix the law she broke for the Wahanar if she found the right tome. Her wrongs would be righted, and as far as she was concerned, she was the only scribe left to do it.

Philippa inhaled deeply, closing her eyes and listening to the lack of sound in the cavern.

Outside, the shadows of thin trees laced the ground, a warm breeze inviting her to walk amongst it.

In Aresef, she could fix this. Fix everything she'd done. The list was growing, Elodie's mother, the Wahanar law, Panu's sleep, Ole's exile. Fix everyone's story.

Even if it meant the king and queen would mark her with fire and hunt her like a beast.

Tazmireth.

Clutching the brittle map, she stood at a decision's edge. The faded symbols, a path into the unknown. Her heart hammered, destiny's whisper now a roar. Her dangerous path, shrouded in legend, felt certain, conviction burning away doubt.

With a breath of pine and earth, she began her quest: to find Shem. The ancient forest held its breath. Sunlight dappled, guiding or misleading her. Every sound amplified, a symphony of comfort and unease. Her journey had just begun; true trials lay ahead.

CHAPTER THIRTY-ONE ✧

The land unfolded in harsh contrasts; sun bleached sand that shimmered like molten glass under the midday light, broken only by the sudden patches of tangled green that rose like mirages from the dust. This was no ordinary desert; it pulsed with the tension of two biomes locked in a quiet war. Trees with thick, knotted roots burst from dunes, their bark dark as burned wood, their leaves waxy and broad to trap every drop of rare moisture. The air hung heavy with the scent of sap and sun scorched herbs.

Philippa pushed through it all; thorns dragging at her sleeve, sand crumbling underfoot, insects buzzing in sultry clouds. The boots thumped rhythmically at her back, the strings cutting into her shoulder where she'd tied them. The landscape was not unlike Levanta, except the air here was thicker, heavier, and there was no reprieve from passing sea breezes.

The forested oasis had no clear path, only dry riverbeds and stone markers carved with symbols she couldn't yet read. Parched wind tangled her hair, and the heat clung to her bones like a second skin, but she kept going. Somewhere in this strange crossroad of life and desolation, Shem had marked a place. Philippa could only hope that he was still waiting there.

The shadows shifted oddly here. Even the trees seemed to lean closer, listening. Watching. It was hard not to assume that the poison was still affecting her mind. At times, she felt so lost and addled that she sat down, listening to the breeze. Wiggling her fingers against her knees to make sure she could still feel them. No one was supposed to be able to survive

Dagna's poison. Yet, here she was. Had her guardian somehow had an antidote? It didn't seem likely.

Unease filtered through her each time she thought she heard him coming. He obviously wanted her alive, but for what, she could not say for sure. How else would he have the perfect antivenom for whatever concoction Dagna had made, had known what path to take to get her out...

When he'd been found, it was said that he was looking for a scribe. But she had known he existed her entire life. He was not a phantom out to get her head. He was something else. Something she didn't know what to name.

Absently, she pulled up her tunic and looked at where the arrow had pierced between her ribs. The veins around it were protruded and angry, but not discolored, as if from poisoning. It had been burned shut. No stitches for her. When she rolled her shoulder, she could feel it tugging, worrying it would come undone. It never did.

She forced herself to stand, to continue. When she was still for too long she could see Morgana in the trees, see Tazmireth turning to glass and hear Raff screaming.

She passed flowering cacti the size of shrines, and knobby shrubs that bled red when bruised. Vines laced the lower trunks, curled like sleeping serpents.

Ahead of her, in the wavering lines of heat, she thought she saw the first bite of stone that didn't fit in. The place Shem had marked.

She flew across the ground, blood rushing in her ears. The map flitted in the wind, loose in her grip as she tore towards the rocky structure, only to realize it was larger than she thought.

Quiet, quiet, quiet.

She stopped.

Caution was necessary, she reminded herself. Shem may have come and left, and others were following her. If the Wahanar found out where they were to meet before she did, then this was all for nothing.

In between the gnarled trees, the stone pile marked the crumbling ruins of a place she had never been, but she recognized. An old scribe sanctuary, one like her father had described, long buried beneath layers of sand and encroaching forest, nearly lost to time.

It was hidden in a sunken hollow, where the tree roots gripped the stone in desperate fingers. Pillars carved with forgotten runes rose around her from the ground, half swallowed by moss and sand.

Her bones ached and her body thrummed in such a powerful way that she nearly doubled over. Something was alive here, but she couldn't determine what. The power of the scribes of old, before the wars, was immeasurable. Who was to say that the current rulers of Sapria had completely expunged the remnants of their magic?

Half crouched, Philippa spun in a small circle to fully take in the sanctuary. At its center lay an obsidian plinth etched with faded silver script, early scribe language, the kind only those raised in the libraries would recognize. The libraries that were being rebuilt in Soffer by the time her people were exterminated.

She remembered those places. Full of life and history, the smell of fresh ink that seemed to envelop the entire building.

Her fingers outstretched towards the plinth, and her body thrummed again. This was not a place for someone like her, she thought, someone raised outside of the true culture of the scribes.

No.

She bawled her fists at her sides. That is what her father would've said, not her mother, and certainly it is what the rulers of Sapria would be telling her. Those who pummeled and pillaged, raped and scavenged her home for any sign of their magic.

Philippa squeezed her eyes shut, a tremor running through her as the bile of vengeance threatened to rise. She'd never considered herself a vengeful person before, not in the slightest. The idea of harboring such dark emotions felt foreign, an insidious poison she couldn't allow to consume her now. The path she was on, the path of retribution, felt like a descent into a shadowed abyss from which there might be no return.

She knew there had to be other ways, gentler solutions to mend what was broken, to heal the gaping wound without inflicting further damage.

The thought of breaking someone else, even those who had wronged her, felt like a betrayal of the person she aspired to be. There had to be a way to find peace, to restore balance, without succumbing to the very darkness that had caused her so much pain. Her jaw tightened, a silent vow forming in her mind: she would find that way, even if it meant forging a new path entirely.

Everything surrounding the scribes and her people had led to destruction, to agony. But she still couldn't reconcile the hatred towards everyone with scribe magic.

That curling, insidious power surge within her was screeching to be let free, to be *used.* Philippa shook her head to try and rid the bottled up headache pressing against her eyes. She just needed to focus on helping who she could, who she'd hurt. The bigger problems of the world were not hers to fix, even if all of the history she'd been told seemed to be staring at her in the face and asking for retribution.

When she opened her eyes, she was facing the plinth, nearly touching it. She hadn't remembered walking towards it. When she drew her hand away, the dark, prowling power inside of her quieted.

But *this,* this is what was alive, and it called to her.

Her eyes raked over it, and as she studied it, it dawned on her that this was not a sanctuary of just healing or record keeping. It was a site of binding, where ancient scribes once sealed stories that could not be rewritten - cursed histories, twisted beings, and powerful truths too dangerous to let live.

She worked her jaw. Her father's people, then. Taking sanctuary in a place they'd hoped the rulers of Sapria would not find so they could continue their works. She'd never seen her father be slain, and an almost hopeful part of her wondered if he had been here himself. It was ludicrous, everything here was ancient, but Philippa couldn't help but wonder. A binding site seemed like the exact place her father would go for hiding.

A flash of skin being forcefully inked upon seared through her mind, almost sending Philippa to her knees. She spat as if bitterness had coated her tongue just by being near such a horrible place.

Amongst her mother's people, binding was considered a sinful and awful practice. Even in Sapria, Philippa had heard whispers and wicked stories about those who had been bound.

She turned away from the obsidian stone, not wanting to read anymore. But it seemed to be newer than the rest of the forgotten place, less growth and vegetation around its dark presence.

Or maybe other life refuses to touch it.

A crumbling wall drew her attention. It was shadowed, half caved in, perhaps where a secondary entrance used to be. On it was painted a mural of a stylized city of crystal towers and lava lit caverns: *Diamond Forge*, read above it in the old language, the lost stronghold of a rival power; once allied with the scribes before the royal betrayal. In more recent etchings scrawled over the art with sharp, angry precision were symbols Philippa had never seen before.

They were most certainly newer than the sanctuary itself, but they had an ancient simplicity about them that felt unseemly to look at. The most recurring symbols were eyes with open pages for pupils and feathers pierced by nails.

And one phrase repeated in the common language, over and over, in blood colored ink: *The Queen steals stories to rewrite the world.*

Philippa pushed aside a curtain of hanging moss, the air shifting cooler as she stepped into the hollow. She spotted movement near a crumbled archway. At first, just the glint of something metallic. Then a figure rose from a crouch, dusting sand from his knees.

His tunic had been torn, and one of his braided locks had been half burnt off. But she'd recognize his square shoulders, the way he carried himself with importance.

"Shem." Her voice broke around the word.

He startled, turning to see where her voice had come from. He didn't smile, not quite, but the tension in his shoulders eased as their eyes met.

"I was beginning to wonder if you'd make it." His voice was low, more tired than she remembered.

"I had help," she said. She hesitated, then added, "he left me the map."

His brow lifted, but he didn't push. Instead, he nodded toward the stone steps beside him. "You should sit. Last time I saw you, you were getting shot at. And kidnapped."

She didn't sit. "You made it out. Ole and Panu?"

He gave a short nod. "Alive. A little burnt. They escaped with the Nazheris who let us into the oasis. It's a complicated beast, I think, but she's kept them safe so far. They're waiting east, near the salt flats."

Relief surged through Philippa, sharp and sudden, as she closed her eyes. Guilt immediately followed; she hadn't gone back, hadn't been able to search for them.

"I should've—"

"No." Shem's voice cut gently across hers. "You survived. We all did what we had to."

Their eyes met as she opened hers, a silent tension crackling between them. It wasn't anger, but the weight of unspoken words since their encounter in the Wahanar camp. They were strangers, their focus solely on survival.

If that were wholly true, she thought, *I wouldn't be holding a map with Shem's handwriting all over it.*

He took a step closer, but didn't reach for her.

"You look different." he said. "Stronger, maybe. Tired, too."

"Ah, ever the observer," she muttered, and he actually huffed a laugh.

Their eyes met for a breath too long. Philippa looked away first, her gaze drifting to the broken wall where the ancient mural glinted faintly. "What is this place, really?"

She wondered if he knew where he'd marked, if he really understood it. Shem was a researcher, a clinical observer. She assumed that emotional stakes didn't quite matter to him as much as the next person.

"Old," Shem said, stepping beside her. "My studies of the lay of the land, before I was apprehended, always left this space underdeveloped. On common maps, that usually means it is somewhere the public isn't meant to go; by proxy of the Wahanar camp, I eventually came to the conclusion it was an ancient scribe structure. I hadn't the faintest idea that it would be a binding site. Before the wars, anyway, and certainly before our queen ever ruled here."

There was no reason then to pin him as ignorant on her people, then.

She traced a feathered carving on the wall. "And what's this Diamond Forge doing on the mural, with the new carvings?"

Despite the purpling underneath his eyes, he smiled at her. "Oh, how I would love to have the time to find that out."

They stood in silence for a moment, shoulder to shoulder. She could feel his presence, steady and warm, and something in her chest ached. Grief, maybe. Or the wish for things to be easier between them. Unburdened by circumstances.

"The carvings," Shem began, already entranced by what he was piecing together, "are a new addition, you say? Well, you'd be right. There's an unsavory group of individuals who like to frequent these sights, as if they could harness scribe magic again. Your friend told you about them. The cult. Their carvings are hard to explain, though. They don't have any meaning, ancient or present, that anyone I know in Aresef could decipher."

"The feathers are certainly a bit on the nose." she said quietly.

Shem's golden eyes flashed. "Let's see. A bird man appears in a secret Wahanar camp, guarded by a portal only they can make, speaks not a word, steals you, but then leaves you a map to find your way back to your party? I'd say, just like these carvings, that makes no sense whatsoever."

Philippa gave him a tight smile. "I'd have to agree."

"And, he buys you new clothes, evidently," he muttered. Philippa looked down at herself, and before she could respond, Shem was already onto the next thought. "The people who carve these nonsensical pictures and try to practice illegal scribe works are, in fact, called the Cult of Sparrows. After all this, I'd wager that your bird man friend is one of them. Which begs the question, for me, are you too?"

There was no accusation in his voice, though there should've been. Philippa's knowledge on the scribe cult was minimal, and whether or not they had scribe magic, evidently they were very dedicated. Tazmireth had mentioned that the Wahanar called him a Sparrow simply because of the cult's name, but this was the first she'd heard about them being a magic seeking people. The idea that a cult member had been watching her since she arrived in Sapria was more than concerning. But she would have to consider that later, because the way Shem was staring at her, crouched in the shade of the ruins, waiting for an answer, was leaving her weak in the knees.

"No. He wanted me to go back to my home. Away from all of this."

Shem nodded. "Likely a good solution. I can draw you up another map if you help me define the landscape—"

"I came here to find the books," she said, her voice even, "I think I can rewrite what's been broken… What I broke. But if I do, it won't be the end of it. I'll fix what I should have never touched, never looked at, but they'll come for me."

There was no resignation in his demeanor, no trace of disbelief. He smiled at her like a prince in one of her romance novels would look at a princess, his eyes alight with a fire that intrigued her. Shem didn't flinch. "Then I'll help you run."

Philippa turned toward him, surprised. Shem's voice was steady, but there was something under it, a shadow of hesitation. He was standing close now, too close for someone who still claimed they were operating only out of survival, but she didn't step away.

"You believe in this?" She asked. "In me?"

He held her gaze for a long time. "I believe you'll try. Even when it's stupid. Even when it's impossible."

Her breath caught, unsure whether it was a compliment or a warning. She studied his face, looking for cracks, signs of resistance, but he just looked tired. Real. Maybe even relieved.

"I don't want to run." she said. "I can't. There's something in Aresef, in the libraries. I know it's illegal for me to go—"

"Technically, it's illegal for you to exist, but there's moral complications there that I won't get into."

"*Shem.*"

He cleared his throat. "I can't turn off who I am, but, proceed."

"The king and queen are clearly interested in it too, at least in protecting the books, evidenced by their massacre of the scribes. But, besides Panu's book, I think I can fix things. Maybe even fix what the old scribes broke."

"There is danger in what you're saying, Philippa Aporo, even treason. What you want would be to rewrite the world," Shem said, voice quiet. "You want to save it."

She nodded, but a heat stirred in her stomach. "I want to give people their lives back. I want to stop others from stealing them before they ever begin."

"Do you really think you're so powerful already, Miss Aporo? The only way to take away the possibility of altering others' stories would be to wipe scribe magic clean. Even the royal family wasn't capable of that, and they committed genocide, if you didn't recall."

Her blood boiled. She lifted a tattooed hand, nearly shoving it in his face. He stepped back. "I was there, *if you don't recall.* Why so eager to help me, then, if you're unsure? You told me you believe in me, and then you try to dissuade me. Which is it, Shem? You can't have it both ways. I know I'm asking for a lot, but I'm *asking.*"

Shem looked away, jaw tight. "The libraries aren't what you think. There are inner sanctums, and there's a reason why they were sealed. Researchers and royalty cannot enter. You go there, Philippa, and you'll draw fire from every corner of the realm. Even the monsters written into hiding will come for you."

"I'm already being hunted," she whispered.

His hand twitched. She thought he might reach for her, but he turned his back, breaking their fleeting connection and walked toward an old archway.

His tall, lean figure became a silhouette against the blinding sun and the ruin. His tunic slipped, revealing a glimpse of skin and a fleeting flash of what looked like an inky tattoo. She blinked and it was gone. The sun lit dust motes dancing in the air. For a long moment, only silence filled the space between them.

"The queen will be watching Aresef closely," he said at last. "She's always wanted a scribe who could open the sanctum. The moment you touch that gate, she'll know."

Philippa's heart skipped. "You've spoken to her."

It wasn't a question.

Shem didn't answer right away. He rested his hand on a half buried obelisk, head low. "Researchers only work in the libraries through permits made by Queen Aura. Her signature is the only kind of magic for scholars. I used to believe in the order they claimed to bring. When you are made to be controlled, your bias is that of an ant under a hovering boot. After all, you are only grateful the boot hasn't dropped. But that's not protection. It's ownership. This woman, Miss Aporo, is obsessive. Why do you think we need her to sign off on our pursuit of knowledge? She wants the libraries and life books to herself, not to save everyone as they claim, but to rule everything with a closed fist."

It dawned on Philippa then that Shem had spoken with the wife of the man who'd ordered her mother's head to rot on a beach. It wasn't Shem's fault, she knew. He would've been a child then just like her. But knowing that he had been so close to *all of it*, had been on the inside for his entire adult life, sent shivers across her skin.

All the more reason that she needed him more than ever. The queen would never let her follow one of her researchers inside and simply take books to attempt to alter them, and surely wouldn't let her near a sanctum to relieve all of Istoria from being controlled.

"Then help me stop her long enough for me to do what I need to do."

He looked back, and for the first time, she saw real pain in his eyes. "If I take you to Aresef, I won't be able to protect you."

"You think I need protecting?"

"I think you don't know what it'll cost you yet."

Philippa stepped closer, her voice steadier than she felt. "I'm tired of hiding. I was given this power for a reason. My entire life, since leaving Soffer, there has been this *calling* inside me that I cannot quiet. It gets louder around you, around mention of scribes and freedom and destiny, and I cannot silence it now. This power was never meant for war. But I've seen what happens when stories are stolen, I am seeing it now, and I fear that Panu is only asleep because someone wants him to be. I *have* to go. I have to try."

Silence stretched between them. At last, Shem nodded once, slowly.

"If you're set on this," he said, "we need Olekashan's help. I can take you to where he's hiding, but that won't mean he'll want to help you."

She felt the fragile thread between them. Trust. Woven not from promises, but from shared danger, from wounds neither had words for yet. And beneath it all, that quiet, echoing pull toward something more than survival.

CHAPTER THIRTY-TWO ✧

The walk to the salt flats was a tense one, the sky lightening to daybreak above them. Wind whispered through the bones of the woods, brushing dry leaves over Philippa's feet, each rustle a stark reminder of the unspoken weight between her and Shem. He had said little since agreeing to leave at dawn, his usual easy chatter replaced by a quiet that was not cold or distant, but rather a profound, expectant silence. It was the quiet of a shared burden, of two souls bracing for a journey into the unknown, each stride closer to the vast, shimmering expanse that lay ahead. The air grew cooler, carrying the faint, briny scent of the flats, a scent that hinted at both desolation and the raw, untamed beauty of the world.

"I know going to Aresef won't just cost me," Philippa finally said, breaking the silence.

Shem didn't look at her. "No."

"You'll lose whatever protection you have, your place as a scholar. The queen will know one of her own people has betrayed her." She was only guessing, but by the rigidity of his shoulders, she knew her suspicions were true.

He laughed, but there was no humor in it. "It's only a matter of time before she finds me out anyway."

Philippa cocked her head, silent for a long moment. "What are you saying?"

Shem looked at her sideways, his voice as warm as a dead body. "Because I've already been betraying her."

"Okay, we're going to be very honest here for a second, *stranger*," she said pointedly, but he smiled at her anyway, "explain to me why a highly esteemed scholar of Aresef would betray his queen, and then help the very kind of person that she would despise."

"Highly esteemed?" His eyes twinkled in the morning light.

Philippa groaned and rolled her eyes. "Shem. Why?"

He met her gaze directly, his voice firm and certain, a deep conviction resonating within him. "Because knowledge doesn't belong to tyrants. Neither do people."

A sudden understanding bloomed within her. She'd only ever heard him speak with such unwavering conviction when discussing undeniable facts or research, never before about matters of the heart or the human spirit. Her ears flattened against her head as she blushed, realizing that she hadn't considered someone from Aresef could have seen as much suffering as she had. The way he spoke, the way he clenched his jaw when he finished, she knew that look.

There was more to his story than he was willing to admit. Shame made her heart beat irregularly, knowing that just like the Wahanar, she'd prejudged Shem, too.

He still hadn't answered her question, though.

As sly as foxes, two dimples she hadn't noticed before formed around his mouth. "So surprised, Miss Aporo?"

"It's just that... you spoke with such conviction about her. You *claim* her when you speak. I just assumed that you believed in the rulers of Sapria," Philippa said. "In the order they keep."

"I did. Until I realized order was just the word the queen used for silence." He strode past Philippa, his sandals scratching the surface of the salt flats that had begun to appear over the last day's journey. His gaze, once earnest and brimming with the hopeful zeal of a true believer, was now shadowed by disillusionment, the kind that only comes from witnessing the decay of cherished ideals. "She hoards the stories. She locks away the truths that could free this world." His voice, though a whisper against the vast, empty expanse, held a resonant power, a low thrum of conviction that cut through the silence.

Philippa had to speed up to keep pace with him, but she didn't speak, not as he seemed lost in the story he was telling her.

He gestured vaguely towards the distant, shimmering haze that marked the edge of the queen's dominion, a kingdom built on carefully curated narratives and censored histories. "I was taught to think that those books were dangerous. Forbidden for a reason. Propaganda, they called them, full of seditious whispers and forgotten magic." A bitter laugh escaped him, a sound as dry as the salt beneath their feet. "But they're not. They're just… unfinished. Fragments of what was, glimpses of what could be, if only we were brave enough to piece them together." His eyes, once bright with youthful naivety, now held a deep, troubled understanding. "I think she's afraid of what people might remember. Afraid of the echoes of a past she's tried so desperately to bury, a past that could ignite a revolution with a single spark of truth."

Philippa had something hot and electric thrumming in her ribs. "You owe me nothing, but there's more you're not telling me. One does not so easily betray their ruler for a stranger they met. I'm glad you are taking me, I need you, but you believe in me for what? For research purposes? Would you please just tell me more than you have already?"

"Leave it alone, Miss Aporo. I'm but a selfish scholar in pursuit of knowledge about scribes. Does that satisfy you?" Shem tossed a braided lock over his shoulder and continued to walk away from her.

Philippa's ears were burning, her mind trying desperately to process everything she'd just been told. He may have been a scholar from Aresef, but he was *more* than that. Someone or something had hurt him, had disillusioned him from his blind service to the rulers.

After spending *weeks* trying to figure out what the Wahanar weren't telling her, all the secrets they kept paired with their lofty expectations of her, Philippa was done dancing around questions.

She sped up and latched onto his arm. Her green eyes definitely met his golden ones, her jaw set firmly. "No, that does not satisfy me. But you know what can." In the briefest of moments, his eyes sparkled with something unsaid, and she panicked, letting go of him. Averting her eyes,

Philippa clenched her fists to continue. "Why believe in me? I know you're curious. It's part of who you are. But just tell me, *please.* I can't keep checking to see if someone is going to stab me in the back. Why can't you tell me the reason that you're doing all of this with me?"

He paused, facing the horizon. "You don't know what they wrote me for."

Her breath caught. "Wrote…you?"

He glanced at her, eyes like fools' gold in the birthing light, almost smiling. "You already guessed, didn't you?"

The realization felt like a new stone settling in her chest. She was embarrassed to admit that she *had* wondered if something was… off, about him. Somewhere deep down, she'd known it the moment they'd begun working together that something was different. The way that he watched her not like a stranger, but like someone afraid of what he might become around her.

Shem had a steadiness about him that allured her, but now when she saw the tension crinkling around his eyes at his admission, she remembered how quick he was to redact any information about a scribe being among the Wahanar. How quickly he'd chosen to protect her.

If someone had written him, he knew what it was like to be a strange outcast, just like her. And… if he was written, then he very well could be afraid of her.

The truth of it felt heavy on her tongue. "I would never use my magic on you, Shem. Please know that. I don't judge people for choices they didn't get to make."

He chuckled like she'd just made the funniest crack at a tea party. "I was designed for diplomacy. For peace. A scholar meant to soothe the nobility. Designed to be loyal, soft spoken, obedient. You once asked me about my childhood memories? My earliest inklings aren't memories at all. The first sentence in my book was not a cry, but a command." His voice thinned. "*Serve the crown.*"

Philippa stepped closer. "Then every choice you've made since…?"

"Is rebellion." he said. "Quiet, maybe. Slow. But rebellion all the same.

By me having a choice, my thoughts are known, my choices are *mine.*"

They stood there, bound not by shared blood or even trust, but by a quiet understanding of what it meant to live half written. To have your story coiled in someone else's hand.

"I will lose everything I have ever known." Shem said.

Philippa reached out. Not to touch, but to offer stillness. "But you'll go anyway."

"To gain everything I have never had. So you ask how I can believe in you, Philippa Aporo, as you are new in your ability and we are practically strangers. I can believe in you because I am the product of scribes who were half the power you have shown at their best, and none of them cared an ounce of what you do."

Their eyes locked in the dimming light, and this time, there was nothing but truth between them.

"So the little one lives." Ole's voice cut through the silence like a blade.

Philippa turned, her hands trembling before she even realized it. She hadn't been this nervous when she had met him, as Olekashan, leader of the Wahanar; but now he was simply Ole, a grandfather whose world had been razed because of her. And it showed.

The lines under his eyes were nearly blackened, and his gait was heavy, as if he now felt the weight of all of those muscles packed onto his body. When they had first met, he had been hopeful. Now, he had every reason to hate her, to kill her.

Coming up alongside him was the Nazheris, who betrayed no signs of exhaustion. Behind them, the crunch of the salt flats under wooden wheels drew Philippa's eyes past both figures to the prone form of young Panu, resting in a cart. His face was pale, still. He seemed grieved, Philippa thought.

"One would have thought," Ole continued, his voice haunting, "that the Nyxveil had welcomed you into its embrace."

Even Shem took a slight step back. "Now, Olekashan, you and I have become acquainted on this journey to the salt flats. Let's not make any rash decisions. Miss Aporo here has a plan."

Ole's onyx eyes searched her. His lips pursed, as if he found nothing of note. "Our laws are not your doing. Exile is our way. But my grandson is dying now. I cannot blame you fully, little one. I called for you. You only answered."

Philippa swallowed the lump in her throat. "I answered you, Ole. I want to make good on my word."

With a profound shake of his massive head, Ole, a man whose very presence usually commanded the space around him, sat heavily on a jagged rock. It seemed to groan beneath his weight, just as he himself seemed to buckle under an unseen burden. He buried his face in his colossal hands, a gesture of profound despair that made him appear impossibly small, a mere speck against the vast, indifferent landscape. The guilt that enveloped him was a palpable thing, clinging to him like a thick, grimy soot. Philippa, who had never witnessed such a powerful figure reduced to such a state of vulnerability, felt a pang of something akin to pity, mixed with a chilling understanding of the gravity of the situation. Philippa's heart ached for him. If someone put Raff to sleep… the thought sickened her.

Her voice felt so very small. "Shem is going to take us to Aresef. To the life books. There, I can help Panu."

Ole peered through his fingers, voice thick with accusation. "You worry the tribes will not let you through our lands again to go home. You worry for your life."

She did. But she needed him to be on board with this. If she could heal Panu, then it meant she could fix everything. Without that motivation, she felt as though she'd shatter just like glass. The weight buckled her. Tazmireth's dying face flashed before her, and she crumbled to her knees.

Her eyes welled up, and she crept towards Ole, gripping his large fists in her hands. He sharply drew a breath, clearly startled.

"I happen to care a great deal about Panu."

Ole's voice sharpened incredulously. "You have not met him."

Philippa lifted her eyes to meet his gaze. Such a broken, saddened man. Raised by the fires only to be burnt by them. But she *had* met Panu, in a way, inside his foggy mind. What she'd seen reminded her a great deal of her own nephew, someone who wanted his family to be happy.

Worthless, worthless, worthless...

"I have met *you*. I care for you." Philippa's voice was raw. Ole could barely hide his shock as she continued. "And your grandson reminds me of someone I love dearly. Someone I would go to the ends of Istoria for. Panu deserves that. But I need your help."

He pulled his hands away, and she felt the hope drain from her, knowing she'd lost him. He sought action, not words. As Philippa almost crumpled, Ole's thick fingers cradled her face, gently lifting her gaze to his.

"You have a heart that is too big for your body," he murmured, casting a glance at Shem before fixing his gaze on her, "I want my family back. I will go with you. But you must tell me the whole truth, little one. This could kill us all."

She realized she could tell him. She'd already told Shem the plan, but would that make him a conspirator? All she truly needed was Olekashan's strength to gain entry to, and perhaps exit from, the libraries. Words carved in stone, condemning her kind as unclean and sinful, flickered in her mind. Philippa drew a shaky breath.

"I can't explain it, but we were all meant to be here. I can feel it. Even this," she lifted her tattooed hand, which he grimaced at, "I wouldn't be able to do what I need to without it. Your laws say my people are unclean. But they are not. What they choose to do with their power is unclean. If after I heal Panu, if I could reach further into the libraries in Aresef... maybe this power wouldn't be needed anymore."

His eyes narrowed with something between understanding and warning. "All I want is my grandson. My family. Beyond that, I do not care."

"I won't make you help me past that. But I need you up to that point."

Ole rose, towering over her. "No more promises between us, little one. I do not care for them anymore. But I have seen your power shine like a star when your heart was breaking. I'd like to see what happens when you get angry."

Philippa pushed herself to her feet, looking at both Shem and Ole. "This isn't about revenge."

Ole's gaze darkened like midnight waters. "Maybe not for you. Not yet."

CHAPTER THIRTY-THREE ✧

"Panu never did such a thing," Ole explained, walking solemnly beside Philippa. "Heru, many times."

She gaped. "She survived?"

Ole shrugged. "Obviously. She hunts us now."

Philippa waved her hands to clear the air. "No, I mean… your babies can implode, but they just… are fine? Shem, are you hearing this?"

Up ahead, Shem grimaced and tightened a bandage on his arm. "I had the displeasure when I was first captured of being kept with the children before I was moved to the prisoner's tent. Many a Wahanar baby would scream itself silly before bursting into flames. By the stars, you would not imagine the smell."

Ole thumped a fist on his chest, the sound thick and harsh. "You speak like it is odd! Talk about something else, if you do not understand it."

Philippa cast a sideways glance to the unconscious boy on the cart. "So… Panu was not a very normal child for the Wahanar."

The former chief shrugged and rubbed his chin thoughtfully. "Maybe it is because he is half blooded."

"There aren't very many mixed families then, in your culture?" Philippa asked.

Olekashan shook his head. "Marrying from other tribes happens at times. But never outside of our own kind. Not since the wars. Wahanar became distrustful of anyone who was too different."

Though she knew nothing about him, Philippa wondered what Heru's lover must have been like. Brave, and maybe a little stupid for getting involved with someone who he likely knew he could not be with. But no one ever really got to choose who they loved, Philippa thought, and her eyes flicked to Shem.

She could *feel* the blush creep up on her face. Philippa bit the inside of her cheek and shook her head.

He's not a piece of meat, stop looking at him like that! It's only been a few weeks!

Shem's disembodied voice informed them that it would take a week to arrive in Aresef if they hurried. By the looks of Panu, they would have to try and cut that time in half.

The salt flats dissolved into a parched tropic forest, which began to grow more dense as the first two days came and went. When she'd asked if he would need a map, he'd only smiled at her. On the first day, they'd spotted a caravan of travelers heading from a smaller city towards the salt flats. Shem had bartered with them to get three waterskins and a bundle of food that would last them until they reached where the caravan had come from.

"What did you have that they wanted?" Philippa had asked.

Shem handed her a full waterskin. "Information."

He explained that the caravan had never traveled that far beyond their city, and he outlined a route for them that would cut their journey in half if they followed it. Stars, she could get used to having someone around like that. Someone knowledgeable with a soft smile, all curves and no hard edges.

They made good time through the forest, the air thickening with each mile. Sweat clung to their necks and soaked the fabric on Philippa's arm. She decided that she hated sleeves, if not for the way the material awkwardly melted to her body, but the odor it gave her underarm.

Suddenly, the whirring of insects and the trickle of air through the trees ceased. The Nazheris' cart was the only noise aside from their breathing. Nothing soon became of it, but afterwards, even Ole moved quieter and closer than usual, one hand constantly hovering near the hidden dagger at his hip.

It was on the third night that Shem stopped abruptly and raised a hand.

"We're not alone."

The fire Ole had just started was crackling faintly behind them. Philippa followed his gaze. The underbrush trembled, not with the rustling of wind, but a strange rhythm that was measured and stalking.

Philippa felt her head begin to pound. Ole and Shem were speaking, but they sounded far away. The thrumming in her body became a wild thing, barging around in her skull, in her tattooed fingertips, in her chest. It felt strangely like she had at the obelisk, around a power that felt too great for one person to hold.

Ole drew his weapon. "It walks like a beast, but too clean. Too certain."

Then the forest exploded.

From the ancient woods, a titan emerged from the twilight gloom, its monstrous form eclipsing the gnarled trees. It stood a colossal twelve feet, each stride crushing the forest floor, snapping boughs like kindling. Its hide was a mosaic of gleaming, silver scales, each plate catching the fading light like a shard of a shattered moon. And upon its neck, a face of pure terror and disbelief: Philippa's face.

A twisted visage. Cold. Unfeeling.

It moved like her, spoke in her voice.

"I am what you could be."

Shem lunged first, slicing low. She didn't even know he carried a weapon. His blade met air. The thing blinked behind him, back arched, limbs warping until it suddenly bore Ole's bulk, Shem's grace, and a flickering echo of Philippa's ink across its arm.

It was not just copying them.

It's studying us.

Panu, though asleep, cried out weakly from the cart, and Ole roared, rushing the beast. It caught his fist with its own, and the ground shook from the blow. The fight churned into chaos - Shem trying to flank it, Ole keeping it occupied - but Philippa could see it learning faster than she could adapt.

Stars, why couldn't she move? It was like the creature being near her stunned her feet into place.

She lifted her hand, inky tendrils of fire sparking from her fingertips, and tried to write, but words fled her mind. Nothing came but static and fear.

The creature lunged, straight for her.

Time slowed. Her body was leaden. The mirror-face grew closer, its hand outstretched to crush her throat.

Then a shadow passed between them. A blur of feathers and ink.

He landed like falling dust, one knee down, mask glinting in the firelight. He didn't speak. He simply raised his arm and threw a dagger.

The monstrous beast screeched, its massive frame stumbling as the glowing rune, etched deep within its spine, was struck.

The masked figure, having precisely aimed for the mystical mark rather than the chest, vanished beneath the earth as swiftly as they had appeared.

Philippa's head was on fire, pounding from within. The closer the mirror beast got, the more she felt as though she were alive and dead at the same time. A great nothingness in the form of a splitting headache, pain so pure it was numbing.

A small reprieve came as the beast fumbled its warbling arms behind its back, trying to pry the dagger free. The blade wasn't killing it, but it was disoriented. In pain.

"Philippa!" Shem's voice cried out. "Back away from there! It'll kill you!"

Ole's onyx blade only enraged the beast, which roared and headbutted him, sending his body skidding across the forest floor. The very ground trembled violently as the monstrous creature moaned and crooned, knocking Philippa to her knees. The monster, a warbling heap of scales and muscle, had stunned itself into a temporary stupor.

The rune, the rune, the rune.

Her bones ached with the need for relief. The pain had to stop.

Philippa dragged herself to the rune, her breath ragged. The symbol on it pulsed like a heartbeat, written in the same old ink script that she had seen in the sanctuary ruins.

She reached for it.

The beast roared, but it was too late. Her body was moving without her even thinking about what to do. She clambered onto its back. When her hand closed around the rune, the surfaces of its skin encased her, flashing images that could only come from the horrors of her mind. Her body was thrashed between its silvery platters of carapaced surfaces, being tossed from one nightmare to another.

CRASH! She saw Morgana's head being taken off by a curved blade.

THUD! Her teeth rattled in her skull as she saw grimy hands reaching for her clothes, her breasts, her heart.

CRACK! Tazmireth's glass eyes sounded like screeching metal as they roughly turned in their frozen sockets to plead for help.

"Philippa!" Shem yelled. The beast couldn't reach her, on its back, so it reared up, raising its now claw-like hand up to Shem. Shem wouldn't just hit the ground like Ole- that kind of a hit would kill him.

The monster's reflection showed her everything that *could* be.

SMACK! Shem lay still, a broken pile of bones in a courtyard running red with blood.

She gripped the rune so harshly that her palms split open. The ink on her hand blazed. Without even trying, she rewrote the rune. The words from her lips became etched onto the glass protrusion.

"You are not a weapon. You are not owned. You are free."

A howl rang through the forest, high, strange, and shattered. The mirror beast convulsed, its features collapsing inward like glass under pressure, and then it was gone. Nothing left but dust and ash.

Philippa collapsed to her knees, panting. The ink on her hand was blistering her skin. The price was high, she could feel it rumbling in her bones.

Beside her, on the ground, lay the rune, now completely dull. Philippa grabbed it, slipping it into her pocket. She didn't know why, but leaving it felt wrong. Like leaving the body of an innocent animal she just slaughtered. Did it really need to die?

Ole approached, blood trickling down his brow. "What did you do?"

Shem looked pale. "You rewrote it," he whispered. "No book. No ink. Just… will."

Philippa looked toward the trees. Her guardian Sparrow was long gone, as always. But something about the way he'd known *exactly* where to strike told her this wasn't the first time he'd seen a creature like that. He was following her, she'd known that he would, but that likely meant he'd been killing whatever had been hot on their trails this entire time.

She turned back to the others, ignoring their wonder and disbelief. "Ole, do the Wahanar keep creatures like that?"

He shook his head. "Only Nazheris. That thing was not written during the Scribe Wars."

"If the Wahanar didn't send it, then someone knows we're coming," Shem said, his eyes unfocused. "Your people spoke of war on the king and queen, Ole. What are the odds they would barter a common enemy with the rulers of Sapria to get what they want?"

Both of their eyes landed on Philippa, still crumpled on the ground.

Ole swore under his breath. "We must move."

Philippa clenched her ink-burned hand to her chest.

———

They didn't stop until dawn. They just slowed to a staggered walk, led by Ole, who insisted they push until the trees thinned and the ground had more moisture.

Shem had been giving directions from the back, but had dutifully kept pace beside Philippa. He hadn't asked if her hand was hurting, but he did offer a strip of cloth from the pack he'd gotten from the caravan.

By the time they set out again near a rocky stream, the air had shifted. Not just from the creature's death, but from the unspoken questions pressing on them all. Philippa sat apart from the others, winding fresh cloth over her palm where the ink had blistered. Shem approached, settling beside her without a word.

"I saw your face go white," she murmured, not looking at him. "When I rewrote the rune."

"It's not supposed to be possible," Shem said quietly. "Not without a book. Not with ink from the air." He was looking at her like she was a wounded animal.

A sob suddenly built up in her throat. She covered her mouth, burying her forehead against her knees.

"Oh, stars, Shem, I killed it! I killed it! And her, I killed her," her voice was strained, her throat felt like jagged glass.

She was certain he would see her as a monster. The very act she had sworn never to commit against him, he had witnessed, and it had filled him with fear. His terror mirrored Tazmireth's justifiable dread of her, but now he understood the consequences of being close to her. How could she, who had committed these very sins, dare to ask for help in a mission to atone for them?

Rather than the expected chill of solitude, a profound warmth enveloped her. It emanated from his skin, a radiating heat as he drew her close, an arm encircling her shoulders, pulling her against his side. Philippa didn't fight it.

Shem's voice was soft, his words drifting against the top of her head. "You are not what killed Tazmireth. She chose to help. As for the monster, Miss Aporo, you saved us. If it's any consolation, I have a very dreadful feeling that the creature does not really lie in Nyxveil."

Philippa blinked away the unwanted tears sitting in her eyes. She didn't deserve the comfort, and certainly didn't deserve the way his gentle eyes met hers. With a shiver, she realized that, in part, he was trying to distract her in order to get her pointed in the right direction again. They had to move forward. Breath rattling against her rib cage, she nodded and wiped her nose.

Philippa chewed on her cheek. "You knew what it was, didn't you?"

He hesitated, then nodded once. "Mirror-Touched, or Visages. That's what we called them. I've never seen one in the wild. They're... not supposed to leave the royal reach."

She raised an eyebrow. Silence stretched between them. Then she said, "That thing was written?"

He nodded reluctantly, clearly a bit hurt by her choice of the word *thing*.

"By someone who knew me. Someone who knew how to get close. It's like it knew..."

Shem leaned in closer, examining her expression, as if he could read her thoughts. "Knew what, Miss Aporo?"

"Knew what I'm afraid of. What's in my head." The flashes of her own face in the Visage's body still haunted her.

"They're called scribes," Shem said dryly. "You'd know something about that."

Philippa gave a soft, humorless laugh. "So the queen has scribes working for her."

Shem didn't answer.

Even though they were her words, Philippa felt a creeping tendril of dread snake up her back."She's not one herself, is she?" Philippa pressed. "She's not like me?"

"No." he said too quickly. "She's nothing like you."

"But someone in her court is."

A long pause. Then: "Yes."

That one word hit her harder than she expected. "So she's using scribes to build her monsters. Her servants. Her scholars. Her whole empire."

Shem didn't deny it. A foreign queen sat on a throne that had slaughtered her people for using their magic, and she wanted it for what? For her guard? To punish others?

Philippa shifted toward him, her voice lowering. "And if she has someone like that, we don't stand a chance unless we have someone too."

"You mean *you*," Shem said. "You're the strongest scribe I've ever seen."

She shook her head. "Not strong enough. Not for what we are trying to do." She hesitated, then added, "That's why I think our Sparrow friend was written."

Shem stiffened.

"He showed up at the exact moment that thing was going to kill me. And he knew how to stop it. That wasn't chance. That was… design."

"Or obsession," Shem muttered.

She ignored him. "What if a scribe wrote him to protect another scribe? Maybe even me. Maybe he's one of us and he just doesn't know it."

"That's dangerous thinking."

"It's *possible* thinking." she said sharply. "And if he is one of us… we could use his help. Someone's been training him. He's been through this before, you saw him, he knew what that thing was. That's more than we had to go off of! He knew how to kill it."

Shem rubbed his jaw, his eyes dark. "You're not thinking about all the possibilities. What if the scribe cult was successful and created someone like him to drag you away from your goals? Even if *they* didn't write him, what if he was written to kill you when you're no longer useful?"

She held her tongue for a moment.

Part of her felt ready to scream that it was just nice to feel that she had usefulness, value, even to those she would never agree with. He didn't need to know that despite the odds stacked against her, all this failure looming up to overshadow her, that it was oddly appealing to think that even for a brief moment she could actually mean something to somebody.

Her breaking point was simmering up inside her again. That coiling, instinctual unease that whispered in her mind anytime she gave it room. The thought that nobody really needed her, and when they did, when someone *really* needed her to step up, she failed. She failed in ways that got mothers beheaded and friends turned to glass. Failed in ways that ripped sisters apart and let families tumble into the ocean as separate stones to drown, never to be pieced back together.

Worthless…

She shook her head. Warded off the evil thoughts.

Philippa met his gaze. "If that's true, then I'll rewrite him to free him. Let him choose to help."

He looked away, clicking his tongue. "It's not that simple. I thought you were against using your power to fit your needs."

All of the fight left her. Philippa let her shoulders drop, and realized he still had his arm securely around her. Wiggling out of his warmth, Philippa grabbed his hand. He had a good point, but she could stop her magic from using her instead of the other way around, couldn't she? Her grip tightened around his fingers. "But Shem… If this Sparrow *was* written, that means there could be more like him. People who were made, who never got a choice. Just like the people the queen uses. Just like you. Wouldn't it be better that they were freed? They wouldn't have to serve *anyone.* He may not be a written person, but if he is, wouldn't you want him to be able to make his own choices?"

That stopped him. She could see it in the way his throat worked when he swallowed. She couldn't rewrite someone for her own gain, but to free them? That she could do.

"We could save them." she said, her voice stronger.

Shem didn't speak for a long time. Then, softly, he said, "you always hope for too much."

"Someone has to."

He finally nodded, the faintest motion. "Just don't trust him blindly."

"I won't."

"But if you're right…" He sighed, staring into the stream. He released her hand to rest his chin in his palm. "We'll need him. Whatever happened to wanting to just help Panu and go home hmm?"

Philippa smiled, toying with the specks of grass between her toes. "I met some people that made me want to listen to a part of myself I've tried to keep quiet. What about you? You didn't have to agree to come. You and your quiet rebellion seemed to be going alright as it was."

Shem brushed a braided lock over his shoulder and leaned back on his elbows, so they were eye level with one another. "My thirst for knowledge cannot be quenched."

The part of her that had been rushing with some kind of anticipation quieted down. She made a noncommittal sound, and was about to turn away, when he cleared his throat.

"I'd very much like to learn all I can about you, Miss Aporo." His voice was quiet, laced with something she couldn't quite name.

It dawned on her that they were very much alone. Ole had gone off to scout the area for a campsite, and the Nazheris typically followed him with Panu in tow.

Philippa's fingers stilled in the grass. She didn't look at him right away. The way he'd always said her name was different now; *Miss Aporo,* like it was a secret title he wanted to memorize, made her stomach twist.

She met his eyes again. The quiet flicker in them was more than curiosity. It was a search. For what, she wasn't sure.

"You want to learn about me?" She asked softly.

He nodded. "In a selfish, scholarly way, of course."

"Of course." She was breathless.

"You're the most dangerous person I've ever met. And the most hopeful. I don't know how both can live in one heart."

She gave a dry laugh, but it caught in her throat. "I don't either."

Their eyes lingered. She should have looked away. Should have made some clever remark to keep the edge off, but the silence between them was warm now, not heavy. Shem's gaze dropped to her mouth. Barely, but it did.

"You shouldn't look at me like that." she whispered, not moving.

"Like what?"

"Like I'm someone safe to get close to."

He didn't answer. Just reached a hand forward, slowly, giving her every chance to pull away. He brushed his fingers lightly along her jaw, and something inside her buckled.

"Maybe I like danger." he said. And then, with maddening gentleness, he kissed her.

Electricity shot through her limbs at the surprise of it all. It was too soon, too fast, but she didn't want it to stop, either. Maybe it was a distraction, a way to keep her mind off of the horrors of what had happened and what was to come. Philippa felt like she should break apart from him, declare that they couldn't be this close this soon, but the way his mouth moved against hers was simply too comforting to stop.

It wasn't urgent. It was slow, exploratory, like he *meant* it. Like he *meant* her. Her hands curled into the grass, unsure what to hold onto. When they parted, just barely, their foreheads stayed together.

Philippa's breath trembled. "This doesn't change anything about what I said."

"It could," he murmured.

She shook her head. "We're still walking into fire."

Shem's thumb traced the edge of her jaw. "Then let me burn beside you."

Philippa let her eyes flutter shut, just for a moment. His lips were gracing hers again. The warmth of his breath against her skin, the feel of his hand still cupping her face. It all felt too gentle for the world they were in. Too *good.* But she didn't pull away.

Shem drew back just long enough to look at her again, as if checking whether he'd imagined her softness. His hand slid to the back of her neck, thumb brushing over the place where her pulse danced like wings beneath the skin.

"I'm not sorry," he said, voice low, "I thought I would be."

Philippa blinked at him. "For kissing me?"

"For wishing." Shem's voice was so soft, so alluring, that Philippa knew if she was standing she would've fallen over. "Usually the truth isn't as good as you expect it to be. Yet, here we are, Miss Aporo. A mess you've made me."

Her lips were parted, but the words that came out weren't the ones she expected. "I thought I was the only one left in this world who still wanted anything."

It wasn't exactly true. Others had wants. But she'd been *wishing* for this.

He smiled, slow and even. "You're not."

She leaned into him then, forehead against his collarbone, her fingers curling into the loose fabric of his shirt like they could root her to something real. They stayed that way in the fading light, tucked in the hush between trees, where no monsters had names and no scribes ruled over fate.

Just for a while, there was only breath. Skin. Hope.

And when she finally pulled back, his hand fell away like he was reluctant to let go. But he did, and so did she.

Philippa sat back, her breath catching. The few inches between them allowed thought, and fear, to return.

Shem let his gaze linger on her face like he was trying to memorize it. Then, with a quiet exhale, he leaned away and began tightening a lock of his hair, something to busy his hands.

"You should try and get some sleep. I'll take the first watch until Ole returns." he said, though his voice lacked conviction.

Philippa nodded, but didn't move. Her toes were still half buried in the grass, still warm from where their legs had brushed. Shem continued to tighten his locks, and she watched the way his fingers moved. Quick, deft, like he'd done it a hundred times just to keep himself from reaching.

She looked away. "We'll need to move fast in the morning. Panu is weaker by the day."

"We will," he said, "and you'll need your strength if we're walking into a city run by people who think your kind should be bartered for."

She flinched, not at the truth of his words, but at their quiet fierceness.

Philippa's voice was softer than she intended it to be as she leveled her eyes at him. "I'm not afraid."

Shem's eyes danced as he truly looked at her, and Philippa felt like she was a mural on display with the way his golden irises drank in her every move. "No, and it's my professional opinion that what you just said is part of our problem."

"We're really going through with this." she said, shaking her head with a smile.

He leaned in close, his voice a low rumble she felt rather than heard. "And if I have anything to say about it, you'll make it through."

Philippa swallowed, then stood, brushing grass from her pants. "You're not the only one who wants that."

Shem watched her a moment longer before rising, his gaze lingering on her silhouette against the fading twilight. They gathered their meager belongings in silence, the only sound the rustle of their clothes in the breeze. As they walked back to the campfire's flickering glow, side by side yet separated by an unspoken chasm, each step resonated with the echo of a question neither was ready to ask.

Yet.

CHAPTER THIRTY-FOUR ✧

One would've thought being threatened with the flames of the Wahanar was torture, but the real malevolence was trying to forget the way Shem's lips felt on hers. Even as the terrain shifted and Panu grew skinnier still, she couldn't fight off the tingling sensation that would cross her lips from time to time.

Shem had taken up scouting at night with Ole kept watch, the theory being that Philippa would rest enough to garner enough energy to heal Panu once in Aresef. But she hardly slept. When she did manage to close her eyes, Tazmireth's glossy face would come running at her with the speed of a monster, but before Philippa could defend herself in the dream, Taz would shatter under Philippa's touch. More than once she dreamt of Taz's face plastered on a Visage, the queen haunting her via controllable monsters.

They're not all monsters, Philippa reminded herself. She couldn't lump those who were written into one category. The Nazheris was written, and she had a conscience and loyalty and wishes. Shem admitted to having been written, and he was the farthest thing from a monster that she'd ever met.

Philippa still couldn't wrap her mind around that.

In a twisted way, she could understand writing the Nazheris and the Visage: creatures to do others bidding, to intimidate. Shem's origins puzzled her. He was kind, intelligent, and a little bit socially awkward at times, but he was *human.*

Why write a man at all?

The only reasons she could come up with sickened her. What he'd told her of Queen Aura led her to believe that she was a foreign queen bent on control, both afraid and enamored by the power of the scribes that came before her. Evidently, according to Shem, the books she locked away for herself were all some form of history novels. Things she wanted others to forget. Maybe she and the king decided that they didn't want others, like the Cult of Sparrows that Shem described, to get their hands on how scribes harnessed magic?

But did life stories or history books detail the methods of creation, destruction, altering?

Philippa had never seen a life book on the continent of Sapria. In Soffer, the babies born there all had life books that appeared in their homes. Life books appeared when a baby was born, though they contained rather intimate details of the birth and conception as well. They also contained genealogies at the start of the books, as it was scribe custom to keep family books together. All of those baby books were naught but ash by now. Philippa's fists clenched. What did Queen Aura think to garner from the books, from keeping those who were written around her?

Philippa had half a mind to ask Shem if he had ever seen his life book, or if he remembered *when* he was written into existence. Had he always served in Aura's court, or before? How new of a creation was he?

She shook her head. Shem had gone off scouting, nervously toying with his tunic pocket. Those were no such questions he would answer now, in front of Ole, who may judge him for what he was. Ole, whose grief was written all over his face.

The chief crouched near the edge of a crumbling stone pillar, one hand resting on his knee, the other gripping the leather strap of his water skin. The old ruin they'd found for shelter leaned drunkenly over a slope of cracked marble and dust choked grass. The sun dipped low, casting long fingers of burnt gold across the plains. He hadn't spoken much since the attack, and even now he kept his gaze fixed outward.

Philippa approached slowly, wary of disturbing him. "I could try and connect to him again." she said quietly, glancing at Panu, who lay bundled in the shade of a nearby stone. The Nazheris watched over him dutifully, the flame between its horns flickering in the breeze.

"I know." Ole murmured. His voice was hoarse from a silence that hadn't been restful. "I have seen you at night. You still try to wake him, even when we think you are sleeping. I thought by now he would have opened his eyes."

She sat beside him, knees brushing the brittle grass, but left space between them. "I think he can feel us. Feel *you.* There is no poison in his system. I've tried writing it out. Someone has altered him this way, for a reason I can't begin to think of."

"I'm the one who was supposed to protect him." Ole's voice cracked. "And now he is slipping further away, and we're gambling on a city of enemies to save him."

Philippa didn't know what to say. Her throat tightened.

Ole finally looked at her. "You know what I keep thinking about?" He asked, eyes shadowed. "That man. That mask. The one who took you out from our camp and survived Dagna's poisoned arrows. That kind of man…" His voice trailed off, hardening. "Maybe we need him."

She blinked. "You *want* him around?"

"If he is what I and the scholar think he is, then yes."

"He technically *kidnapped* me." Philippa countered. "Wait, you two talked about this?"

"He saved you, little one."

She couldn't argue with that, she agreed, but she didn't know after what Shem theorized if they should bring him around. "He dragged me through a portal while I was bleeding."

Ole stood. "And still, you are here. Alive. You saw what my people did to Tazmireth. What Heru ordered. What would have happened if he hadn't turned up?"

Philippa's mouth opened, closed. She looked away, teeth clenched. Worry soured her gut. "You think he'll just help us again?"

"I think he already is," Ole's voice was sharp with grief. "Much of this is my fault. I would like the solution to be much of mine, too. If your solution, little one, is to get in and out of Aresef with my grandson's book, then we need someone like him."

Philippa felt a strange swell of pride in her chest. If Olekashan believed that her little Sparrow friend could help them, then maybe she was right. This great wall of a man agreed with her, and so far, he'd been a guiding force through all of this. Ole didn't have all the answers, but as far as Philippa was concerned, he was doing his very best to be good, and that was enough for her.

Shem stepped out of the shadows of the ruin, arms folded. "We should rethink that."

Philippa turned, startled. She hadn't heard him approach.

Shem's face was unreadable. "You don't know what he is. What he's capable of."

"You don't either, do you, scholar?" Ole shot back. "You only guess. But Dagna's poison did not kill him. The Wahanar cannot catch him. He slipped through our fingers like air."

Philippa bit the inside of her cheek, trying to ground herself. "You didn't seem so against it earlier."

"That was in a moment of weakness. He's not trustworthy," Shem growled, a sound she very much didn't like. "You think he saved Miss Aporo because he's noble? Something is binding him to her. Whatever he does, it's not for free."

A moment of weakness? She thought.

Worthless, worthless, worthless...

Philippa stood, that dark coil inside herself tightening. "If that's true, maybe we should use that. We're going to face worse things than Visages in Aresef."

Shem's jaw feathered. "You'd turn to someone like that? Someone who only seems concerned with keeping you alive for his means?"

She shouldn't have expected the kiss to change his disposition about things at all, and yet, his words stung. Something was pulling her to Shem, drawing them together, but he was ever less pragmatic than she. A moment of weakness. If her kiss had made him agree with her, then he'd never agreed with her at all.

"He might be a scribe." Philippa said quietly.

That made both men pause. Shem had heard her theory before, but he exchanged a wary glance with Olekashan, as if seeing if the chief agreed.

She looked between them. "If he is… maybe he knows how to better go about this than we do. And if he doesn't, then maybe he's like you, Shem. Someone who… didn't ask to be what he is."

She chose her words carefully, as to keep it between them, but Shem didn't reply. His silence was enough of an answer.

Philippa pressed on. "We're all misfits here. If he is too, we already have common ground.This is bigger than us. Bigger than healing Panu, than getting back to my family, than fixing the law that I broke for the Wahanar. Bigger than being told what you are, Shem. If we get him to appear again, maybe this is easier for all of us. Shem, you can lead us into Aresef, I believe that."

She reached out, touched his arm. Though he didn't pull away, she could feel his tension trembling through his body. Shem was used to being the smartest, the most respected mind in the room. Maybe he felt threatened by her wanting someone else around. Whatever the case, she didn't have time to argue about it again.

Her voice hardened."But you're not a warrior. You defended us against the Visage. But that thing would have killed all of us."

Shem opened his mouth.

Philippa cut him off. "It would've. Ole's right. We need the cultist."

Ole stared into the distance, his shoulders hunched. "If nothing else, all I wish is to see Panu smile again. To return him to my daughter, so she might bring him back into the fold."

A quiet fell over then, heavy with sorrow and half swallowed truths.

Philippa sighed, brushing the hair from her eyes. "We press on. But if he shows up again, I say we don't let him run off this time."

Neither man agreed, but neither argued further. Ole only nodded and drank from his waterskin, heading off to rejoin Panu to continue the journey. Philippa moved to follow him, when Shem caught her arm with surprising roughness.

He leaned close, whispering. "You can always stop. Go back home to Morgana. There's ways around the Wahanar lands."

She tried to wrench free, but he held her firmly. "You know where I stand. I'm going to fix this, even if it kills me."

Shem's face was then right next to hers, his teeth barred in a way that made her skin crawl. "Which very well might happen at this rate. I know the libraries, even have access to a few that were opened. But when the queen finds out about a scribe in Aresef, and she will, there is no telling what she'll want from you. What she'll do to you."

Her eyes searched his. The golden color had turned molten, and staring at him this way, it felt like she was looking at someone completely different. There was an anger there, a rebellious spirit that simmered underneath the surface. He was scared, she realized. Scared to lead her into the lion's den of Aresef, where her kind would surely be put to death on the spot. Scared of what bringing her into the libraries might do to whatever small rebellion he was conjuring.

Frightened or not, her bones sang with disharmony.

Something inside her shifted.

She leaned in close, letting their lips touch. Shem's grip on her dissolved, completely caught off guard. As soon as his fingers weren't digging into her skin, she gripped his hand as tightly as he'd held her, drawing a shocked whimper from him.

Philippa drew back, and there was nothing but determination on her face. "Just because our lips have touched, it does *not* give you access to handle the rest of me."

With that, she threw his hand away from herself.

Shem looked like she'd slapped him right across the face. "Philippa, I'm sorry. I don't think you realize what someone from the Cult of Sparrows is capable of, and I don't want him running around—"

Philippa held up a hand and was surprised to see that it silenced him. "I liked it better when you called me *Miss Aporo*. Let's go back to that, since it seems you can't handle anything more than that right now."

Her words stung, she could tell, but she didn't like this side of him. There were more important things to do than worry over whether or not a man *liked* her or not.

They both turned, Shem going to call after her, but they were met with a wall of muscle.

Ole's eyes were wider than saucers, his mouth quirked up in a smirk. "I knew from the moment I met her that I liked her."

Shem whipped his head around to retort. Philippa beat him to it. "Boy dying, being hunted, no time to talk. Let's go."

Ole's clapping emitted a mighty *crack* as he followed her, his laughter genuine and well missed. He quickly caught her stride - one of his steps was about four of hers - the Nazheris falling into line with them.

His large hand found her back, his pat sending her careening forward. He didn't seem to notice. Ole leaned down and whispered rather loudly, "I see why Tazmireth liked you so much. You are fiery with a big heart."

Philippa smiled despite herself. "She called me the sister of her heart."

Her smile faded. Shem broodily stalked past them, picking up his pace to lead the way in determined silence. Philippa felt her throat tighten, her limbs grow heavy. The tattoo on her hand seemed to burn, as it so often did when she thought of Taz, and the words marred into her shoulder too cried out.

She cradled her inked hand to her chest to avoid crying. "How do you speak of her so easily?"

Ole gave her a sideways glance. His gaze shifted to Panu in the cart as he spoke to her. "Tazmireth paid the price of her sins. Of her beliefs. She is gone and I cannot save her. But I am fond of her memory. Panu is here and not, so I grieve for him now. I cannot change the fate of those lost to the grave. But we all give something to our loved ones when we die."

Philippa bit her lip and thought about that for a long time. When she spoke, she found her voice stronger than she expected. "Taz gave me hope. Friendship. Even in my home, I can't say that I had either."

His smile was a bright contrast to the dark lines in his face. "She gave me strength."

"You, in need of strength?"

He nodded gravely as if suggesting that he too saw the irony. "Strength to believe differently. I knew bringing you would make me unclean. Make Panu unclean. Did you know, when you arrived, when I saw how angry my wife had become, I was going to send you back. It was Tazmireth who came to me that first night and pleaded your case. She said, this woman has honor. She has power. She did not like your kind when she was sent to find you. Yet, she loved you the most out of all of us. I was ready to throw away my beliefs because my grandson needed help. Hah! If only I knew better then. Tazmireth changed *my* mind. Because you changed hers."

Philippa felt herself welling up, clenching her fists over and over to let her nails bite into her palms. The pain gave her focus. She could not think of what to say.

His thick voice was near fatherly in emotion when he continued. "I still thought you would make us all *vashir*. Only, knowing you, growing fond of you, being disappointed in you, I still do not think you are unclean. You are as you should be."

"I don't know, Ole, there is a lot you could hold against me."

The chief smirked. "There is. I am mostly, at this moment, holding against you that you did not tell me you were bedding with my other prisoner."

Philippa's cheeks flushed, and she saw Shem tense ahead of them. "We are not!" she lowered her voice. "*Bedding* together. And we're not your prisoners anymore. We're friends, aren't we?"

"Hmm. You should bed him. He looks like he could use the experience." Ole's voice was far too loud, and Shem was far too decent to turn around, but Philippa swore she could see horns of anger stemming from his head.

"That's not very nice, Ole."

"I am being honest. Honesty makes us friends." he said cheerfully. "Truly, bed the man. He is too stuck in facts and research. In Wahanar lands, we encourage this. Men are called to serve our women. Did you know that our women can only become pregnant if their heartflame aligns with their man? I do not think your heartflame aligns with the scholar, but there is no reason not to try."

"I don't want a *baby!*" she hissed, feeling her ears turn hot and red as they lowered in embarrassment.

Ole shrugged. "I give you my blessing. Bed my prisoner to see if it realigns you both. Although you may not enjoy it. One could say he has a flame so far up his *krund* that he could benefit from—"

Shem whirled around, a blue braided lock whipping in front of his face. He threw his hands up at his sides, exasperation written all over his face.

"I am suddenly very drawn to the idea of someone joining us. *Miss Aporo,* could you please call your friend to our aid? Please?"

Philippa stifled a laugh. Ole flat out cackled.

"Are you serious?" She tried to keep her voice even.

Shem nodded, a dark flush high on his cheekbones. "I am setting aside my personal beliefs for this. Please spare me my pride. If this continues, I just may end up being the danger you two face in Aresef. At which, we are almost upon."

She narrowed her eyes at Ole, as if to ask, *was this your plan the whole time?* Ole only rubbed his bald head and whistled to avoid answering.

"Alright, fine. We're all in agreement." She noted. "Only… I can't exactly summon my guardian."

"Oh, how adorable, you have a name for the savage cult member who has followed you around since you were ten."

"He's guarded me." She countered.

Ole leaned on Panu's cart, nearly toppling it and the Nazheris. "Shem of Aresef, you claim to be well read but you are quite dull. Little Pip is from a small town so I cannot hold it against her."

"Hey…" Philippa started.

Ole groaned. "One daughter trades me in for death and in return I must parent two adults. Terrific. Your bird man showed up when you were facing execution. He did again with the—" Ole waved his hands around, clearly not knowing how to translate *Visage* from Wahatan, "tried to flay you. Endanger yourself and he will appear. Simple."

"I… can't say I disagree." Shem offered quietly.

Philippa spun on a heel. "Of course you'd agree to it after an argument."

Shem's golden eyes flashed. "Well, if it's as you say, that we need him and he will let no harm come to you, then really, I'm just finally following someone else's idea. Isn't that what you were saying you preferred, when I suggested you go home to save your own skin?"

Ole let out a low whistle. "You bicker like bed sharers before battle. Call me when the blades come out, I am going to get Panu some drink."

CHAPTER THIRTY-FIVE ✧

Ole stood in the middle of a ruined square they'd happened upon, sweat running in rivulets down his temples. He turned to Shem, a low flame flickering in his palm.

A rush of heat blurred past the side of her head, burning the stone behind her. Philippa turned her nose up at the smell of burnt hair, but so far, that had been the worst of it.

"Maybe we should take a break." Philippa offered, licking her fingers and pinching a singed strand of hair. Her sparrow friend hadn't made any sign of appearing, and her usual thrumming of magic was eerily silent. She only felt a tickle in her fingertips when Ole would launch another fireball from his fists, and even then, it was so faint she thought she was making it up.

"I won't actually hit you." Ole snapped.

"Well, he won't come unless her life is in *actual* danger, will he?" Shem said, arms crossed tightly over his chest. "That's what we've learned, haven't we?"

Philippa stood off to the side and awkwardly rubbed her arms, eyes on the horizon. The air smelt of ash and juniper. Nearby, the Nazheris stood watchfully over Panu, its flame casting haggard shadows over the young man's face. Before they could enter the inner city of Aresef, they had to travel into Kamath. Another two days of journeying before they reached the libraries, and then there was the task of getting *in*.

As much as she hated to admit it, she was just *tired*. Philippa drew in a deep breath, trying to revitalize her urgency. It only half worked. "We don't have time for this."

They didn't.

That night, as Ole threw another fireball close, but never too close, Philippa didn't even flinch. She sat on the edge of a broken step, hands curled into the sand and grass beside her. Olekashan was too kind of a soul to actually try and hurt her, even if all of their lives depended on it. Philippa, in between bursts of hot air being flung in her direction, let her mind wander. Ole, of all people, had every right to *want* to burn her to a crisp. Yet, he seemed like he'd rather let them all fail than condemn her for their sake. Even though she deserved it.

Philippa rubbed her eyes that were dry from the smoke. "He won't show."

Ole, exhausted, simply sat down with an unceremonious *thump* on the ground. His dark eyes settled onto his grandson, his shoulders deflating.

Shem stepped up beside her, quietly. "You sound disappointed."

"I'm angry," she bit out, "and scared. And tired. And maybe a little bit disappointed."

A beat passed between them.

Shem shifted. "I meant what I said before. I don't trust him. But I trust you." When she glared at him, he held up his hands defensively. "I know, I know. I'm going back and forth on this. Call me a broken record, but I can't help but feel uneasy when I don't have all the facts."

Philippa furrowed her brow. "What's a record?"

At that, he seemed confused, and ignored it altogether as he pressed on. "I believe you missed the part where I was attempting to make peace by saying I still trust you."

She huffed, shaking her head. Despite how her body reacted when he was around - those traitorous shivers and hollowing of her belly - there were parts of him she didn't understand. But she could try. "Are you sure about that, especially after this insanity?"

He offered a tight, crooked smile. "Especially after all this."

"You confuse me," she said softly, the air between them taut, "I need some air."

She knew it wouldn't make sense to him, that was plain by the puzzlement on his face, but she couldn't sit still. She'd come from a town where she *worked,* where she provided, and sitting still watching the sky waiting for someone who might never come felt all too much like every forsaken night of her childhood.

So, she climbed. The ruins stretched upward like fingers reaching for the stars, and she followed them until she stood atop the highest wall, the wind tangling her hair and the lush dessert spread wide below. Thankfully, Shem hadn't followed her.

She closed her eyes, as she had so often avoided recently, and let everything come crashing back to her. The familiar thrum in her body returned, a vibrant, pulsing rhythm, like a second heart beating within her.

Please, she thought, *you've pulled me so far along and now I'm to fail? Please, let me save Panu. Let me fix this.*

In her mind's eye, she saw glass eyes dripping with impossible tears. Staring at her. Coaxing her.

The edge of the crumbling tower was so close. So enticing.

Worthless, worthless, worthless...

Nobody needed her. They just thought they did. The world would be better off without Philippa Aporo, of that she was sure. Maybe without her, mother and Morgana could've run faster. She had hesitated when her mother told them they had to leave. Had let fear consume her. Or, if she had practiced harder, like her father wanted, she could've slain the beast where he stood, as much as the thought churned her stomach.

Without her, Morgana could've been raising Raff *anywhere* she wanted. They wouldn't have had to stay in Levanta to hide Philippa's powers.

Scribes themselves just seemed to be such a problem. She couldn't even bring herself to cry. Nothingness just felt right. Natural. Like she belonged in the void. The heavy stones she collected inside herself pulled her downward. Her toes wiggled on the cool stone. The world would last longer with one less scribe to interfere or not meet expectations. This, she could be useful in; ridding the world of one more tormentor.

Worthless, worthless, worthless...

In this act of selfishness, she could give the world back the magic she stole, that lived in her body.

Just a step. Just a moment. She could be free of it all.

"Really?" The voice came lazy and sharp from behind her. "After all of that drama with the fire chief, this is how you coax me out?"

Philippa whipped around, her heels brushing the edge of the spire.

He was leaning against a broken column, arms folded, his bird mask slightly crooked as if he'd put it on in a rush. His voice was familiar and impossible.

"You." she breathed.

He tipped his head, feathers falling over his black-clad shoulders. "Isn't that obvious?"

She stared, her heart hammering against her ribs. "You… you're here."

"As much as I hate to admit it, I do like to make an entrance. Though usually not in response to a very *bad* attempt at suicide. Stars, you've grown to be quite dramatic."

She blinked at him. "I wasn't—"

"You weren't going to jump," he finished for her, "you were just 'thinking about ledges in an *abstract* way."

She stared at him, words caught behind her teeth.

"Also, the chief's fireball idea? Amateur. I'm insulted."

"You came." she said again.

He uncrossed his arms, a calculated movement. "You're in danger."

"I wasn't in… real danger."

He stepped closer, gaze unreadable behind the mask. A morbid part of her wondered if he had eyes underneath. "You were thinking about it."

Silence stretched between them. The thrumming in her body was singing now, alight and overwhelming and distracting. "You're *really* here?"

He cocked his head. "One of the most powerful people alive and you're having to convince yourself that someone who is speaking to you is real."

Her magic coiled inside her then, a bitterness snaking its way up her throat. She was ready to scream at him that she'd seen people speaking to her every time she closed her eyes and they were *never* there. They never came back. She blinked away the hot tears that threatened to fall.

Then Philippa exhaled - half laugh, half breathless disbelief - and she nearly backed over the edge. "Shem is going to hate this."

"Oh, I look forward to it," he said, and then his voice became quiet and cutting, "why?"

"Why what?"

"Why summon me." he said. "Why risk yourself. I have other things to do."

His tone was sharper now, no longer holding a hint of playfulness. The kind of sharp that cut deeper when it came quietly. It struck her that she really never had pictured him doing anything else other than following her.

Philippa drew a breath. "Because we're going into Aresef. Panu is dying. I don't know what's waiting for us there and I need..." She hesitated, then lifted her chin. "I need you."

That clearly wasn't what he wanted to hear. He turned his mask away. 'You don't know what you need."

"Sparrow, please—"

He looked back at her, head cocking slightly. "What did you just call me?"

She stilled and repeated herself, more softly this time. She felt so stupid. He didn't enjoy being called a guardian, and by revealing that she believed that he was part of a cult of all things, he most certainly didn't sound inclined to help her.

His body went rigid. Even the mask didn't hide it.

"I don't know what else to call you." She admitted.

His black leather gloves crackled as he clenched his fists, the snark drained from his voice, leaving it hollow. "You shouldn't be here. I told you to go home."

Her green eyes narrowed to slits. "*You* left me the map. I can't go home until I fix what I've broken... and maybe more than that. You don't get to choose for me."

He stood his ground, then recoiled, his voice like tempered steel. "I am not your guardian, Philippa. Your beloved scholar hasn't told you everything. I am not part of your traveling circus. You don't know what to call me? Call me Nothing. Call me by no name you can conjure. *Don't call for me.*"

With that, he vanished, dissolving into the floor like smoke carried on the wind. Philippa gasped.

"No, wait!" She'd ruined her one chance to get him to help. Her hands dug into her hair, and she spun around to pace, to put some movement to her anguish, when the crumbling edge gave way. There was a sharp jolt in her chest, the sickening weightlessness of a fall. Her arms flailed, scrabbling at the air, and the world spun.

Strong hands caught her wrist, burning against her skin. She slammed into the side of the wall, breath whooshing out of her, and looked up. It was no surprise who lurked over the edge, mask askew, arm outstretched. He hauled her back to the solid floor.

"Stars," he muttered, "you really don't make this easy."

Her arms shook underneath her. While he was captive, she'd make him listen. "Will you *please* just hear me out about this? You owe me some answers. Why keep saving me if you hate this so much? You accuse me of naivety, when you're nothing but a wraith in the wind. I *know* that you know me."

The sound of his breath pooled inside his mask. Her Sparrow removed his arms from her and scuttled away from her. After a long moment of sitting, staring at her, his body shaking for a reason Philippa didn't know, he moved. He lifted his body off the floor of the spire with his arms and flipped his legs behind him, stretching into a crawl. His mask filled all of her vision as he closed the gap, like a predator evaluating prey that wouldn't scare.

"You're right about one thing. I *do* hate this. I hate this with every fiber of my being, and yet here I am, encircled to save you from destruction no matter what else I might like to be doing. You want answers? Fine. This is *not* care, Philippa Aporo of Soffer, this is *slavery.* Ask away, so your servant might answer, if it troubles you."

If he wasn't going to make this easy, then neither was she. Philippa had grown up with a sister, and she knew exactly how to annoy someone into talking. She shoved her face into his, her nose touching his mask. He didn't move a muscle. "Stop being so cryptic. Leave, if I *trouble you so.* You don't have to come save me anymore. Disappear and never come back."

The words were acidic in her mouth. She didn't want him to leave, but she was so consumed in her anger, in grief, in self loathing. His cryptic nature wasn't bringing out the best in her, and she had no energy to fight it.

A dagger appeared in his hand, a metallic whisper against leather. Pure terror, untamed and raw, seized her, a sensation she hadn't known in his presence until now.

Feral. He was feral.

Everything Shem had warned her about was true, and now he was done with her. Tears pricked her eyes. She hadn't even found out what he was using her for. But she wasn't going to die like this.

Her body sang *be still, be still, be still,* but as he raised his dagger, she could do nothing of the sort. Her fist collided with the underside of his mask, finding the strong bone of his jaw, but he didn't so much as make a noise. But while his head was turned, she brought her knees up into his chest and scrambled backwards.

Philippa sprang to her feet, prepared to run, to scream, but he stayed there, frozen. Like a statue lost in time. The only sign he was alive at all was the gentle rise and fall of his chest, followed by the sheathing of his dagger. But he really *looked* ready to stab her before… Maybe he wanted to, but that shakiness of when he'd drawn it…

Philippa had seen him kill. There was a grace to him, even as he'd slaughtered Wahanar like they were flowers in need of deadheading.

A strange sensation trailed across her skin as a frightening realization dawned on her. "You… *can't* hurt me, can you?"

He rolled to his feet effortlessly. "Unfortunately."

A crisp rustle came from the edge of the ruined archway, dried vines snapping under delicate steps. "I leave you alone for one moment," Shem's voice, dry and unmistakably annoyed, "and you start knife dancing on a rooftop." His wind-tossed braids framed his face with sharp, assessing eyes darted between Sparrow and Philippa. His hand, not threatening but not at ease, rested on the hilt of a blade Philippa hadn't known he possessed until the Visage.

Sparrow didn't seem phased. He tilted his masked head at Shem with a kind of theatrical bemusement. "Oh, it speaks. The guard dog returns."

Philippa's breath caught. "Hey."

But Shem was already walking forward, placing himself a step in front of her, gaze never leaving Sparrow. "This is the part where you vanish again, yes? Before or after the next threat as always?"

"No threat." Sparrow said, voice smooth. "I'm just lamenting on how hard it is to stay away when your friend here insists on throwing herself off ruins for attention."

Philippa shoved Shem's shoulder, stepping back beside him. "I didn't do it for attention. I thought… never mind."

Shem glanced down at her, his features tightening with worry. "You didn't tell me it was that bad. You said you needed air."

She wanted to admit *I didn't know until it was,* but instead she just locked eyes on Sparrow's mask. "I just needed to get him here."

"And did he help?" Shem asked coolly.

She hesitated, then gave the smallest shake of her head.

"I didn't come to help." Sparrow replied, and though he was only about her height, he suddenly appeared just as tall as Shem. "I came because I had to."

Shem moved closer to Philippa again, this time gently. "Then you're not needed. Go. You said it yourself. You hate this."

Philippa shot him a glare. He'd been watching for a lot longer than she'd thought.

Sparrow stared at them, long and unreadable, then bowed mockingly. "Try not to fall to your death again, Philippa. Some of us are trying to keep our schedule light."

With that, the shadows seemed to reach for him. But before he disappeared entirely, he gave her a lingering glance, and there was something almost human behind the mask. Then was gone.

Shem exhaled. "I hate that he wears your name like a badge. As if it gives him the right."

Philippa was quiet for a moment, then whispered, "You were right. About the cult of Sparrows. It surprised him when I called him one."

They stood there in silence, the breeze teasing his hair, the broken edges of the ruins glowing faintly in the low sun. Finally, Shem offered his arm. "Let's get off this rooftop before someone else gets any big ideas."

She huffed a laugh, but took it. "Deal. But he's not gone."

His arm tensed around hers. "Did he say what he wanted?"

"No. But he can't hurt me."

"That's lovely thinking, Miss Aporo, but…"

She stopped their descent down the spire. "No, as in, he *can't*. Something is stopping him."

He faltered, as if he was stumbling over his own thoughts. Now that Philippa knew her not-guardian couldn't hurt her, she was one step closer to proving one of two things: he had power like her, or he had been written into existence like Shem. Neither option put her at ease.

Shem and Philippa paused on their descent of the spire, her eyes boring into his as he stood thoughtfully. There was always something about him, she thought, that was wondering. A part of him that seemed always so lost in putting pieces of something together that she knew it must've been consuming him. With a mind like that, she didn't know how he ever found peace. It was a mind not much unlike her own.

"I only know the history about scribes, Miss Aporo, but that does sound eerily similar to something I'm not sure we should touch."

Her skin prickled. "Silvertongues?"

Shem tossed a braid over his shoulder and pursed his lips. "Maybe. You said yourself that your mother and father were not of the same beliefs. That they were of two different peoples. If this man apparently *cannot* harm you, but keeps showing up moments before your demise, of which group does that sound like to you?"

"My father's people," she said without hesitation, "the hungry ones."

She already picked up the slight difference in his breathing, in the way he held himself, as if something shifted into place for him. "We should tell Ole. And, if you're comfortable… you should tell us more about your father's people. It wouldn't surprise me if others survived the massacre in Soffer."

Philippa stopped him before he could walk away, her fingers drifting into his. He froze at that, all of the thinking and processing coming to a halt. "I'm sorry for the other day. We're friends, aren't we?" A nod. "I shouldn't have snapped at you like that. This just all became so much bigger than I would've guessed, and… I'm sorry. You don't have to ask me if I'm comfortable all the time. And you don't have to call me Miss Aporo."

A weight lifted off her shoulders, even if he didn't accept her apology. Shem hadn't treated her immensely differently since the argument, but then again, she guessed that wasn't in his nature. He wore his frustration plainly, but if anything he seemed more hurt that it had happened at all.

It had been a long time since she'd kissed anyone. Shem had consumed her thoughts anytime there was a quiet moment, and he'd filled in the gaps of space between planning and worrying. The last kiss she'd had before Shem hadn't been particularly memorable, not in a good way, at least.

She shivered at the mere thought of her last courter's lips on hers, the way his hands had dug into her wrists and made her feel small in a breakable way.

Shem's smile lit up his face, with a hint of bemusement on his lips. He leaned closer, all the hair on her neck standing up as his lips hovered just above her ear. "What if I enjoy calling you *Miss Aporo?*"

Philippa's ears twitched. She could feel the blush creeping up her cheeks as he gently touched her locket, which had somehow survived all of this time.

"It's not an argument I'd care to have again." she said by way of settling it.

But Shem's hand encircled her waist, drawing her closer. Her breath caught, mingling with his, the scent of him earthy like cedar.

"You seem rather content with marching yourself into the city that would put your head on a spike," he murmured, "why is that?"

She couldn't help but stare into his golden eyes. "Because I can fix what I've broken."

"And entering the inner sanctum is, what? To prove to yourself that even though you haven't practiced magic since you were a child, that you simply *can?*" His eyes were expectant, searching her face, but Philippa tried to remain impassive. She trusted him, wanted him, but her plan for the inner sanctum was for her alone. Maybe soon she could share it with him, but… Not yet.

He could see that she didn't have an answer she was willing to share. Shem groaned inwardly, then pressed his forehead against hers. "I am getting all too attached to this *friendship* to have you walking into your suicide without knowing why."

Her hands pressed against his chest, both to put some distance between them and to steady herself against his heartbeat. "My father always taught us that our power was a gift, and that it was our right, our fate to use it as we saw fit. My mother taught us that if we had the opportunity to help something bigger than ourselves, then it was our obligation to do so. To be a bigger person. I don't know why I could heal the girl in Levanta, or why I could conjure fire for Dagna, or why I could rewrite a rune that I had never seen before. But I do know that I *can, which* means I *should.*"

"Hmm. A hard way to live."

"There is life, there is hardship." She whispered, feeling his chin come to rest on her head. She welcomed the embrace, trying to ground herself in this moment, trying to piece it all together. Why would a foreign queen order the massacre of scribes, just to want them for herself? Where did Sparrow fit into all of this? Why *did* her power reawaken with such force, and such an ability to harness it? Altering and scribe magic always came at a price, most of it physical, but Philippa couldn't help but wonder what the price at the end of this would be.

Shem gently stroked her back, sending tingles down her spine. "Those were some pretty heavy lessons to teach you in the short amount of time that she had to raise you. When did these lessons all start, Miss Aporo? What father shoves the idea of power mongering down his children's throats, and what mother finds the time in between to put the weight of the world on her children's shoulders?"

"I don't remember when they started," her voice was light, strained, "but they made sense when they decapitated my mother on the beaches of Soffer."

Her chest felt leaden. Shem tensed around her. "I'm sorry you ever had to see those things. But if that's why you're wanting into Aresef, Philippa, to bring them back, or to alter what's been done, I don't think that's the way to go about this."

She pulled back, meeting his gaze. "I am *not* going into Aresef for vengeance. I'm fixing Panu. My parents are long turned to bones. Altering life stories to that extent was taught to us as sacrilege."

He put his hands up in a sign of surrender. "Alright, I believe that. But you were willing to commit sacrilege for your friend. Tazmireth. What cost, do you think, would come from trying to piece someone's soul back together?"

"Do you only comfort me to belittle me?" She asked.

Shem's eyes widened. "Absolutely not. I'm worried."

"About losing your quiet rebellion and your place." She countered.

He sighed, exasperated. "We've been over that. This is the same argument. Can I not be worried for your safety? Can I not wonder what your plan exactly is if you can open the inner sanctum of Aresef's libraries?"

Philippa ran a hand through her hair and chewed on the inside of her cheek. "All of my life, Shem Tetra, I have been helpless. Helpless to do anything because of inability, the law, or my own stupidity. Yet what I want, to roam, to live freely, comes at a cost that demands I not be so helpless. I have been worth so, so very little. My parents died to save me, when I did nothing. My sister has watched over me since then, because I was too headstrong and helpless as a child that they entrusted me to her. Then, for the stars know why, a cult has had someone keep an eye on me since the massacre of my people to keep me alive. I am indebted everywhere I go, to all, for all have suffered so I may live. How is that fair? When I come close to helping, oh so close, death springs up like lavender in the fields of Jorta. How can I be so important, for some reason, and yet so *worthless?*" Her voice cracked. Her bones ached. All of these thoughts and ramblings had been floating around in her head since her mother's head was separated from her shoulders.

No matter what thrumming, calling, or voice whispered in her head, there was always the same constant. One she had never shared with anyone.

Worthless, worthless, worthless.

"How many lives am I worth, even still that I may not understand why?" Tears sprang up into her eyes. He watched her like a cat watches a baby, wholly unsure of what to do. The romantic thing would've been to kiss her again, to pull her close. The friendly thing to do would've been just as fine, she thought, to grab her shoulders and shake some sense into her. But it seemed that Shem, written as he was or sheltered as he was by being in his books, could only observe her at that moment. His hand fiddled with uncertainty deep in his pocket, as if he was fidgeting to keep himself busy.

He let her cry, let the tears splash onto the dusty stone floor of the spire. The time passed quickly, and she covered her face with her hands to hide her sniveling nose.

Then, at the moment she could breathe again, Shem spoke. "I can only tell you one thing with certainty. Where you're going, what you're planning to do, you will be worth more than all of Istoria, Miss Aporo. I believe that."

<hr>

The screaming began as soon as they descended the last set of stairs. *Duck, duck, duck.*

Philippa's ears twitched, and she threw all of her weight against Shem as the first of the fireballs blasted into the stairs. She rolled to her side, the stairs not only singed but very much on fire.

Her eyes followed the yells, and landed on Ole who was viscously protecting Panu from two other Wahanar who were driving everything they had at the two of them. The Nazheris brayed frantically.

Run! Philippa begged in her mind. Why wouldn't it get Panu out of there so Ole could fight?

Then, she saw it. A dart between its two front legs, lodged in the bony protrusions of its chest. Dagna and Heru's scouts had finally caught up to them.

"Shem, get that dart out of the Nazheris and get Panu out of here!"

"What about—"

She was already moving. Fear thrummed in her like a war drum, guiding her steps as the shorter of the two Wahanar turned to face her. Philippa's feet thundered across the stone ground, her footsteps echoing through crumbling broken archways as she made a break right towards the scout. The woman seemed surprised that Philippa wasn't running away, but the emotion only crossed her face for a second before it turned to fury.

Philippa was breathing deeply, trying to let herself become a tunnel for magic, like Taz had taught her. The only way to do this was to fight them with their own fire.

But then, as her fingertips tingled and her tattoo felt like it was a breathing creature, Taz's face flashed in her mind. All sensation of fire magic fell way into the dark abyss inside of her. The Wahanar scout noticed without missing a beat, and instead of conjuring fire, they pulled a reed chute from their hip and put it to their lips.

Philippa's branded scar on her shoulder ached in response, remembering the point of metal and the dosage of poison large enough to kill a horse.

You are still a scribe! She yelled in her mind and lifted her hand anyway, flame or no flame. She could stop Visage, she could stop a poison dart. At least, that's what she was telling herself. Wait. Visage.

The rune, heavy in her pocket.

"Don't you fire another dart!" Philippa yelled, skidding to a stop a few yards from the scout.

The Wahanar woman snickered. In Wahatan, she asked why, though her lips were still faintly pressed against the chute, her voice whistling through it.

Philippa brandished her tattooed hand, yanking the sleeve up for all to see. Ole grunted as he wrestled a large Wahanar man to the ground, both men's fists were balls of fire. She didn't see Shem.

"You were at the *Tanvirok* meeting! You know what I can do!" Philippa yelled, breathless.

The Wahanar woman lifted her lip in disgust. *"Vashir,"* unclean, "the hand of a sinner. Conjuring the light of a star, with the power of an ant."

Philippa bit down on her cheek, trying to keep memories of Tazmireth at bay. She took the insult on the chin, and kept her tattooed palm raised, all the while her free hand dug around in the folds of her pocket. Her fingers brushed something sharp, so deadly that just by grabbing it, her finger sliced open.

"What do you want?" Philippa called out loudly.

Voice like ice, the Wahanar hunter called out, "Herunavira demands a blood price on your heads. You most of all."

"Let's talk about this." Philippa said, her voice uneasy. She tried to remember exactly what she'd thought when she unwritten the rune from the Visage, and her stomach grew heavy with guilt. She didn't want to do this, not to the Wahanar, and not to the creature.

The Wahanar scout spat, and tossed a fireball at Ole that knocked him off of her companion. Ole scrambled to his feet, his fists already up, but when he saw the standoff, he slowly sidestepped his way to stand by her. Philippa risked a glance to where he'd been, and the cart with Panu and Shem was gone.

She let out a shaking breath.

"Then talk. Your heads are next." The male scout sneered.

Philippa's hand closed around the rune and she closed her eyes. *I'm so sorry,* she whispered in her mind. She unveiled the rune, the blackened glass dead in the darkness of night. "You are a weapon. You are mine. Fight."

Philippa let the rune fall as the Wahanar scouts laughed incredulously.

She let it sink towards the ground as she put her insignificant arm around Ole's barrel of a stomach to turn for him to run with her. She allowed it to shatter on the ground as the Wahatan scout blew into their dart chute.

A great burst of sound crashed through the forested ruins. Wind knocked Philippa and Ole off of their feet, sending them flying across the scape.

Guilt flooded her chest, drowning out even the pain of hitting the ground with such force that her teeth rattled. Ole's giant hands hauled her up, as her vision swam. Her head was hanging upside down over his arm.

The dart had simply glanced off of the mirrored surface of the creature. Both Wahatan scouts' mouths dropped in shock and awe, before utter terror set in.

The Visage reborn looked almost beautiful from behind, Philippa thought. Only warbling plates of light and reflections. Harmless, unlike when she stood face to face with it. She remembered her own reflection, warped and horrid, beckoning her with a strange resemblance that rang with an uneasy sense of what *could* be.

The creature had no real mouth, she could see that now, but she could tell that it was speaking to them like it had to her. They covered their ears.

The man had vapid tears leaking out of his eyes, mouth still agape. He looked that way even as the Visage sliced through his abdomen and spilled half of him onto the grass. Ole was already running.

Warbling, the creature mirrored the Wahanar woman, grabbed her reed chute with a glinting appendage, and filled her to the brim with poison darts. She didn't die as fast as the man. She had enough time to cry out desperately, to beg through sobs, before she was drowned out into the night as Ole's long strides carried her through the darkness.

"What do you think they saw?" Philippa asked in her stupor.

Ole's ragged breaths sounded like distant wing beats. "It shows you what you most fear."

Philippa still was sure that it was her face they saw.

CHAPTER THIRTY-SIX

She was getting better at protecting herself, which was a relief, if only a small one. Watching someone so stubbornly kind face danger after danger had grown painful for Sparrow to endure.

There weren't a lot of purely good people left out there, but she certainly seemed like she was trying. It was one of her more infuriating traits. Whether it was her easy trust, or her belief that everything deserved a *chance* at being good. That kind of mentality would get her killed, if not for him. The thought made him smirk.

With a harsh tug, he bound a strap of cloth around his bleeding forearm. He didn't know why he still did that. It would heal on its own eventually. A gash was nothing that could stop someone like him.

Silent as a mouse, he slid on his belly along a branch as he waited for the Wahanar chief to appear with her limp body. That woman had an infuriating ability to collect concussions. She did know that would damage her brain, right?

You know she doesn't care, he sighed and laid his bare cheek against the branch. Bark pressed into his skin. If only she knew that there had been an entire pack of Wahanar waiting for them, and that if he hadn't stepped in, they would've been overwhelmed. He didn't much enjoy killing, not anymore, but it was a small sacrifice he could make on her behalf, even if it irritated him. Philippa Aporo only seemed to care for others. To the outside eye, she would look completely selfless. But he knew better. He knew her intimately, probably better than she knew herself. The perks of being a shadow meant that you could see what was coming and had hindsight at the same time.

No, she was not selfless, he thought. If she were selfless, she would have gone to the Wahanar camp and admitted she couldn't heal the chief's grandson and been sent on her way home. She wouldn't be here, traveling with a band of misfits, ambling through the wilderness to try and pry her way into a place her own people were forbidden from. She wouldn't be marked by the ink of the Wahanar, pomping her power around like she knew how to use it. Her abilities were pure luck at this point, that and good breeding. That's all she was to him, this Philippa Aporo; a well bred scribe who'd made his existence hellish.

He rolled onto his back and let his arms hang loosely over the sides of the branch supporting him. He hadn't been getting much sleep chasing after her across the continent. His mask loomed over him, hooked over a higher limb, staring at him with emotionless eyes.

"I do feel that way." He grumbled.

The mask only peered down at him. Judgingly.

"Well, how else would you describe her, oh wise mask?"

Silence followed, but the feathers of the mask ruffled in the wind, the longest tendrils able to almost tickle his nose. The stupid decoration had a point though, if inanimate objects could, in fact, make a point: he didn't think of her only as an obstacle for him to overcome.

He pitied her, in a way. They were both slaving towards something bigger than themselves. It could've been delayed if only she'd gone back to Levanta, like he'd told her.

As much as he wanted to hate her for everything that she was, it would be like hating a part of himself. A man may grow weary of running, but that doesn't mean he'd harbor resentment against his legs if a beast was chasing him.

And a beast chases us, he thought. A quiet blight that crept across the land, soon to infect them all.

He felt that he was already ridden with the plague, malformed and strange of mind. At least, he reasoned, that he could still identify that talking to a bird mask and hiding in the trees was strange. It was when he forgot that any of this was abnormal that there would be a problem. Despite the thrumming in his body that drove him half to insanity, he could acknowledge a higher story at play. Magic was a funny thing. For some, it gave them calls towards greatness, like Philippa. Others, a desire for power or an insatiable greed to control others.

For him, it made his back itch and his skin crawl. It made his muscles tense and his mind wander into other's spaces that were not his. One space in particular.

He heard them coming. With the ease of a serpent, he rose to a crouch on the branch. The mask fit perfectly in his long, thin fingers. He stared into it, considering leaving it off for a while longer. But as soon as her voice, distant as it was, tickled his ears, he settled it into place.

His head throbbed. It always did when the inscribed words on the inside of his mask sealed him away.

The Wahanar chief was no longer carrying her. Their pace had slowed from exhaustion. Sweat soaked through her dark tunic and he sneered when he saw that she was still barefoot. Stars above, she begged for adventure away from the sea and yet she still walked around like she was home. He would never understand that. The way she couldn't let go of things.

Letting go was all he had ever known.

Her hair was plastered to her head, and they slowed just a few paces underneath his perch.

There was blood on the back of her neck. The Visage had hurt her, despite it being somewhat under her control. He rolled his eyes and crept along the massive branch on all fours, a panther in the night. She wasn't even powerful enough to fully control a monster that scribes had *created* and yet she thought she could enter Aresef and unwrite the alteration to the chief's grandson?

He clicked his tongue, the sound hidden in the beak of his mask. But despite himself, he was staring at her.

Taking in the way her shoulders were set, her chin high. The firm line of her mouth, the way her hands trembled but her strides were strong.

She could've taken the beast fully under her control, he realized. She just didn't want to. Something inside her hated the idea of others being owned, being controlled. Oh, how she'd despise him, then.

Philippa Aporo was the product of good genetics, sure, but her heart made her strong. He'd seen it dozens of times, for as long as he could remember. Her heart let her transfer the will of a mother into the dying lungs of a girl, let her leave her family to save them, allowed her the strength to try and repair an entire race of people who didn't want help. But it was that same heart who got that little girl's mother killed, and who got Tazmireth turned into glass instead of flesh and bone.

Tazmireth. It was the only name he really bothered to remember. He knew the chief's name, and the insolent little scholar who thought he knew everything, but Tazmireth rang in Philippa's head constantly, and so it rattled around in his.

He liked Tazmireth. She was strong and kind, and she protected Philippa. It was a shame that everyone Philippa loved had to die.

From the treeline, the faint glow of a tired flame appeared. The Nazheris walked alongside the scholar, dragging the unconscious boy.

The scholar got around too quickly, he thought. Not that it mattered. Philippa liked him, for reasons he couldn't understand, and she trusted him enough to keep him around. He'd have to follow up on that. But he was kind enough, and seemed to care enough to stay with her, so that gave Sparrow some leeway to do other things other than keep her from dying.

There was a restraint about the scholar when he reached out to grab Philippa's hand, like he was afraid that he would frighten her. Interesting.

But she took his hand into hers and squeezed it. Far less interesting.

They conferred with one another. It would only take another few hours before they left the forest and reached the edge of Kamath. From there, Aresef was only a short journey. Aresef was the center palm that spread into rays of smaller towns before civilization became more wild with the terrain.

Sparrow watched as they all turned to follow the scholar, the chief walking a fair distance behind the group, his head swiveling.

Sliding to a lower branch, he let himself hang from his arms, a dozen feet in the air, dangling like bait as he watched her walk away.

Go home, go home, go home, he thought. Begged. But Levanta wasn't her home. Her home had been taken, like his.

To his surprise, as he thought this, she slowed down without the others noticing. Her ears twitched. She was listening. Seeing if she could hear *him,* he realized.

She was growing more aware of his presence, like he was hers. He didn't know what that meant.

Philippa threw a glance over her shoulder. Lit only by the moon, her green eyes were like two pieces of rune glass, sparkling with an eeriness that only a woman could possess. She could see him, but he just hung there, unsure of what to do with himself. If she tried to get him to follow along with her little group, he'd lose his mind, surely. She drove him to insanity trying to do 'good' when all she caused was chaos.

As he readied himself for her onslaught of words, she smiled.

What in Istoria was *that* about?

Then, she raised her palm and wiggled her fingers at him. Was she… waving at him? He cocked his head to the side - something she so often made him do - which seemed to make her grin widen. How could she smile at a time like this?

Philippa pointed two of her fingers at her eyes, and then at him. He scoffed. As if she was watching *him.*

Instead of trying to bargain with him again, she chewed on the inside of her cheek and turned to follow her party once more. It irked him that she knew that he would be following her.

He dropped silently to the ground and did just that.

With a sigh, he bawled his fists and closed his eyes, letting gravity and magic take him. The world spun, his stomach churning, and when he opened his eyes, he was inside the caverns again. After only a moment of searching, he saw her reflections in the crystalline wall and began to walk alongside her. Following this way at least gave him time to rest, if he needed it. After removing his glove, he let his thin, pale fingers glide along the crystals over her form. Let them dance by her shoulder, by her arm, as if he were walking alongside her, able to pull her out of harm's way in a heartbeat. But keeping up at a distance would soon be a thought of the past.

Once they got close enough to Aresef, there would be enough people trying to kill her that he wouldn't be able to leave her side.

CHAPTER THIRTY-SEVEN ✧

In their hasty escape, no one in Philippa's traveling party had remembered to look over Panu's cart. After all, a beast so great and nearly dragon-like seemed unkillable. That's what Philippa thought, right up until the Nazheris staggered with a sound that was more vibration than groan, a high, mournful tremor that thrummed in the air.

Philippa's ears pricked up and she turned just in time to see the creature pitifully wheezing as its knees buckled. Panu's cart rolled to a stop, covering half of the Nazheris' body despite the yoke that kept the two connected.

"Ole!" Philippa was already moving, her knees skimming gravel as she slid to the creature's side.

The Nazheris lay curled on herself, massive ribbed chest heaving, one clawed limb twitching against the ground. The dart stuck out between scaled muscle, pulsing faintly. Its blood oozed around it, dark and thick; not red, but black like tar, like rot, like the ink etched into Philippa's skin.

"Dagna's poison," Ole muttered, arriving at her side, eyes blown wide. Philippa waited for more explanation, but none came.

For one heartbeat, she didn't move.

She wanted to reach out and heal the Nazheris, she really did, but she couldn't help but picture all the death she'd seen them cause when she was a child: the way their horns skewered innocent children just because their parents bore illegal magic, or the hot breath it used to bubble and boil people's skin clean off. Back then, they had only been beasts with bone scaled hides with eyes like furnace glass, monsters written by scribes only

330

to be the very cause of their destruction.

Philippa had grown up fearing the shape that now was sprawled before her, ribs hitching in shallow gasps. Wings that hadn't been used in a long time half covering the wound, as if to keep up appearances of strength and brutality. It should have terrified her.

But it didn't.

It looked… wrong like this. Wrong to see something so powerful brought low. Wrong to see it twitching helplessly, blood oozing around the dart.

"Miss Aporo…" Shem's voice warned, but she ignored him. He may have seen the way her body went taut and remembered what she'd seen these creatures do, but she couldn't let herself give into fear. Not when the Nazheris was watching her.

Just *watching*, all of those two black eyes locked on her like she was the only thing left in the world. There was no hate in that gaze. No threat. In the eyes of the monster that she should've been happy to see die, Philippa saw herself. Afraid and unsure, but asking to be saved.

Philippa's hand hovered just above the wound. She swallowed hard. She'd seen what these things could do, what they *had* done, long ago, in her village. But this one… she'd seen it wrap its body around Panu like a shield. Not from command, or magic, but from choice.

It had *wanted* to protect him. Maybe even loved him. The Wahanar of Ole's tribe regarded them as equals. Even now, Olekashan hung his head, eyes pinched in a grimace as he stood over the Nazheris, sure that he was about to watch it die.

You can do this, Philippa told herself, *just talk yourself through it.*

She could feel it now, in her bones: a thrum in the air, a pulse of old magic twisted wrong and heavy in the creature's blood. Her father's people had written this being into existence cruelly and carelessly. But somewhere along the way, the Nazheris - *she* - had chosen her own meaning.

And Philippa couldn't let her die.

With trembling fingers, she broke the dart off near the skin. The Nazheris flinched, and a low, guttural sound rumbled from her chest.

"Hold her," Philippa said. "Shem, give me your waterskin."

Ole hesitated as Shem handed her the waterskin, of which she quickly poured onto the red dirt below, mixing it into her palm. She closed her eyes and opened that pit inside of her, becoming a tunnel for something more. Once the fingertips of her tattooed hand were covered in the mud, Ole knelt beside her.

"The poison, Little Pip… Nazheris, she is not like your Sparrow." he said. His voice was soft, and he laid his massive hand on the Nazheris' head to steady her.

"I have to." she said. Olekashan studied her face and nodded, but he seemed almost hurt. Philippa glanced at his unconscious grandson and understood why. But she could only save the Nazheris in the moment, and so it would be.

Her other hand braced against the Nazheris' flank which was hot, wet, slick with tar blood. Then, slowly, she began to trace her fingers just above the wound.

Inside her chest, she felt like she was falling, and like a breeze was stirring within her as she focused wholly on what she wanted to happen.

Words began to appear underneath her fingertips, a phrase asking for binding of poison, and to heal, and a third phrase as the mud ran out, coming from somewhere deep inside herself. It was a selfish wish. A selfish writing.

She couldn't let her die. Why? Because her heart couldn't take another soul dripping in blood because of her.

Philippa sank back onto her haunches, waiting. Nothing happened. The Nazheris' breathing was still ragged, still thick with phlegm.

Shem's hand found her shoulder. She leaned her head onto his thigh as he gently squeezed her.

Ole grumbled. "Worth trying. Scribe magic is not exact."

He began to turn away, as if he couldn't bear to watch her die.

A flash blinded them all suddenly. Philippa blinked, raising her arm over her eyes, and gasped. The words on the Nazheris' body flared with a golden, almost white light, and then sank, and along with it the blood stopped running.

The Nazheris shifted, chest rising slower now. Easier. Her breath came in low, thick pulls. She blinked again, but it was like sleep was taking her.

Philippa sat back, heart pounding, hands shaking.

"She's going to live," she whispered.

The Nazheris reached out with one massive clawed foot - hand, whichever it was - and pressed it gently, almost reverently, against Philippa's chest.

Something broke open in Philippa, just for a moment. For so long, she had been afraid, and had been wary. Had looked the other way when a Nazheris entered tents or crept up alongside her. A Nazheris represented everything that she was supposed to fear, a living testament that her power made her a worthy head to hang on a wall.

But Philippa saved her.

Her breath came in shuddering waves as the claw rested against her chest, the snag of its razor sharp edge tickling against her flesh. Philippa's hand shook tremendously as she raised it, but tentatively, she placed her hand over the top of the Nazheris' claw. It was smoother than she expected it to be, warm as if from an internal fire. Philippa's fingers relaxed around the claw, her head sagging, and she absently began to stroke the mighty creature's foot.

"I'll never be able to forget what they wrote you to be." she said softly. "But I can see who you chose to be and… I'm glad you're here. Are you alright?"

The last time Philippa had spoken to this Nazheris, it had been when she tried to beg it to allow Tazmireth to let her see the laws. If the Nazheris blamed her for Taz's death, for everything that was happening, it didn't show.

The Nazheris blinked once. An awareness flooded Philippa's mind like a fog, clouding out every conscious thought. Philippa saw smoke and fire dancing across her vision, a beating of a heart that wasn't her own.

Olekashan and Shem faded away from reality. Philippa was seeing the world through someone else's eyes, and she saw atrocities that made her lips curl into a snarl like that of a creature so foul that she'd once feared them without thought. She saw inks pressing into animal's hides, experimenting on them, morphing them into the perfect vehicle of destruction. Philippa felt like her own ribs were expanding and clamoring to fit a chest cavity that filled with fire, a raging white hot pain that tingled throughout her entire body. Then, in this connection between her and the Nazheris, she saw her malformed reflection, half herself and half Nazheris, staring at the waves of an ocean crashing on an all too familiar beach.

In the memory of the Nazheris, Philippa heard shouts of terror, and through its eyes, her head snapped up as its long neck swayed to find the source of the noise.

Whether in the shared memory or in reality, Philippa gasped. She saw her father. He was glowering at the Nazheris, his face coated in blood and grime, green eyes shining like two liquid emeralds. He cursed the beast's name, but did not engage it. He was screaming something to another nearby man about a boy. A boy who he needed, but for what, she did not know.

The Nazheris' memory pulsed with agony as its eyes locked on a young boy being dragged by another scribe with Philippa's father. The boy's eyes were open, but he didn't seem conscious, even as his head lolled to the side. Philippa had never seen this before.

Then, with a bray, the Nazheris made a decision. It did not wait for its sisters, did not bother to try and convince them to follow. With great, agonizing effort, it *severed* the connection between itself and whatever laws had written it into existence. It would not kill anymore scribes just because someone wrote it to be so.

With an icy plunge, the Nazheris threw herself into the ocean. For a moment, she let the waves carry her, even splashing at the flame between her horns, not caring if she lived or died. Philippa's heart ached, knowing how many times she had wished the waves would've just stayed over her own head. But then she saw something through the Nazheris' memory that made her freeze.

In the Nazheris' mind, she saw a hazy outline of a small boat. It was thrashing in the sea, but it was steadily heading away from Soffer. The

Nazheris whipped her head around when there were the screams of children, and Philippa did not close her eyes even though she knew what was coming. She had heard that scream wrench from her own throat on that day, right as a sword separated her mother's head from her shoulders. A rage so pure that Philippa felt her fingertips tingle in reality passed through the Nazheris in the memory. Its gaze shifted to Philippa and Morgana in the little boat. Something stirred within it then, something that scared it. For it was only the second time in its existence it had ever made a choice for itself.

The first, had been to delve into the ocean rather than kill anyone else. The second was to *live.*

But the waves in the memory were too strong. The Nazheris struggled, salty brine rushing down its throat. Its wings opened frantically, splashing in the ocean, trying to get back to shore.

Then, like a phantom, a human like figure appeared in the warbling sea. Golden curls that fanned out in the waves, but it was gone in an instant.

A wave pushed the Nazheris back to the shores of Soffer, where she lay for hours in turmoil. Beside her lay a prone figure, the boy that her father had been asking for. Philippa could not make him out perfectly in the memory, but he had a smattering of light freckles and he seemed all too pale. The Nazheris pitied him, and scooped him up into her wings. Then, she looked out to the sea where young Philippa and Morgana had been floating to safety, and made her third decision.

Nazheris wrapped the unconscious boy up in the safety of her wings, and waded back into the ocean. She would follow the boat. Ensure the girls made it away from Soffer, and get the boy off the isle before any more harm could come to him.

Philippa's hands were reaching for the memory, for anything to hold onto, but somehow, the connection was severed just as quickly as it had been made.

Soft outlines of trees began to fade back into her vision. Philippa blinked several times and realized she still felt Shem's hand on her shoulder, and Ole was still watching in awe. No significant time had passed, and she wasn't exactly sure how she connected to the Nazheris like she had with Panu. When she'd done it with the boy, it had been a distinct scribing command. But this…

Her eyes met the Nazheris' black ones, and her throat welled up.

Philippa understood, somehow, the weight of the decision that had been made. In the Nazheris' eyes, this hadn't been as simple as choosing to save her life, but it was a choice *of* her. The Nazheris had chosen Philippa, too, in a way that transcended simple selection. It was an act of profound faith, a declaration of unwavering belief in her unique ability. How terribly arrogant of her to have assumed that the Nazheris, a creature the Wahanar renowned for their meticulous discernment and unyielding loyalty, would ever even consider approaching her if they were not already fully invested in Philippa, in the profound conviction that she could heal Panu. Their very presence was a testament to their absolute certainty, a silent, yet powerful, affirmation of her destined role.

Both Ole and Taz had told her that the Nazheris had become part of their family. When they left Soffer, chose to become more for themselves, they needed a new purpose. For this Nazheris, her purpose was protecting Panu. Everything she did was for him, to keep him safe. For a creature that could never have a child of her own, she surely put the ferocity of motherhood into her act of overlooking the boy.

It was more than that, though. Thanks to the memory, Philippa now understood that before Panu, there had been herself. There had been Morgana. There had been a scribe boy on the beach.

Philippa's mouth worked, trying to form words, but no sound came out. The Nazheris' black eye looked up at her in a conspiring way, despite it nearly falling asleep. All Philippa could do was touch her chest where the Nazheris' claw had been. Her heart was steady, Morgana's locket cool against her flesh.

Beside her, Ole was wiping a tear away, not trying to hide it.

"This Nazheris," Ole explained, petting its head, "she has taken care of Panu since he was small. Thank you, Little Pip. For saving part of my family."

The sky had darkened, and clouds clung to the stars like breath on glass.

Philippa sat in the hush that followed pain, her mud stained fingers resting on her knees. Across from her, the Nazheris lay curled, breathing deeper now. Healing.

The others had pulled back to give her space, though she could feel Ole's eyes on her from the treeline. They'd removed Panu from the cart so Olekashan could lay him in the grass and give the Nazheris time away from the cart. Shem had disappeared up the slope with a blade in hand, scouting. But Philippa stayed.

Because the Nazheris hadn't moved. She was simply *there*, watching. If she made no move to get away from her, then Philippa was determined to honor her request. Their sparking connection hadn't happened again, but there was something about the way the Nazheris was looking at her, like she could see *into* Philippa.

Philippa met her gaze, trying not to flinch at the heat and intensity of her colorless eyes. One blinked. Then another.

A soft huff of breath, steam curling from wide nostrils. Then the Nazheris lowered her head to the earth. Philippa stilled. This creature didn't need to submit to her, or to give her leeway. No, this was trust.

Philippa didn't have much experience with animals, but then again, maybe Nazheris weren't so animalistic in comparison to people after all. She didn't need a book or a study to decipher this. The knowledge slipped into her mind like ink into parchment: slow, deep, permanent. A name, not made of letters but of feeling: *ancient stone, fire warmed scales, the sound of claws scratching earth to stand beside someone you love.*

It was not a name Philippa had ever heard, but she *knew* it. Knew it the way a scholar knows his studies.

She reached out, palm up. "Vaelith," she whispered.

As if the name was a command, the Nazheris rose on strong limbs and stepped closer, towering over her. A beat passed. Then another. Then Vaelith bent her head and pressed her brow gently to Philippa's.

Philippa closed her eyes, breathing in the smoky, husky scent of the creature before her. This wasn't human affection like anything she'd ever known, it was older than books and kings, a creature made of unmaking and unwriting itself. A concept with life breathed into it by those old enough to be bones by now.

And in that moment, Philippa wasn't a girl haunted by her parent's makings and stories. She was just a woman, experiencing something completely ethereal and new by every standard in the world.

Vaelith pulled back, and something more passed unspoken between them, more understanding. The fight ahead would not be easy, and a fight it would be indeed. The pages unwritten would not be kind.

But Vaelith believed in her. And maybe, just maybe, Philippa could believe in herself, too.

Vaelith's dark eyes regarded her with something that Philippa's elven mind couldn't quite describe. But when Philippa stared back, all she saw was herself.

Her ears twitched, and she looked over her shoulder as Shem came treading back into view. He spoke quietly to Ole, who only nodded as he stared at his grandson's sunken cheeks. Shem gave him a tight lipped once over, before walking to where she sat. Vaelith had retreated into a ball, curled in on herself like a house cat.

Philippa gave Shem a light smile, though it didn't reach her eyes. His hand was nervously tucked into his pocket.

"You never seem to stop surprising me," Shem said with dimpled cheeks that made her heart flutter. "Healing a Nazheris? Why, Miss Aporo, you're extraordinary."

Philippa chewed on her cheek and put her chin to her knee to hide her blush. "You just want another kiss with all of those compliments."

Shem settled beside her, his eyes wide and his lips twitching. "Where does one get the boldness to say things like that? You leave me speechless, Miss Aporo."

She chuckled and shrugged. "When you have a sister, you know how to get under people's skin. It's a survival tactic."

"Ah," he said, nodding enthusiastically, "I see you're very well practiced.

But I wouldn't say no, if what you said before was an offer."

Her ears titled downward as she blushed and gave him a tight lipped smile. "Who is good at getting under whose skin, again?"

Shem's laugh was like firelight on a cold night, and it spread warmth throughout Philippa's limbs. "How do you feel, though? I can only imagine the strength it takes to expel energy into another creature's body."

Philippa didn't answer right away. She took stock of how she felt. Drained, sure, but much of that was from whatever connection she and Vaelith had created. Seeing what happened to Soffer from someone else's perspective… from someone who had been on the *other side,* was harrowing. It made Philippa want to crawl into a hole and never come out again. But seeing the way that Vaelith had been disturbed, the way her heart ached when she had seen all the destruction… It was like the antivenom to the paralyzing effect those memories had on Philippa.

Even someone who had done such horrible, disgusting things, could choose to be different. The gift of choice was offered to all, and in a strange way, it gave Philippa hope for herself. Maybe after all of this, if she couldn't hang onto who she was, like Taz had wanted her to, then maybe who she would choose to be would be better than who she was now.

Slowly, she shrugged. "I'm tired. But I wouldn't have made any other choice. She needed me."

"Ever our savior." he said warmly.

She shook her head and tucked her hair behind her ears. "You're still right, though. Believing in me won't necessarily get us into the inner sanctum, or even heal Panu. I don't know what happened to his story, but it's different from anything I've seen. So far, what I've been able to do with my power hasn't been against something scribed to *keep* a scribe out. It feels like if someone tampered with Panukirah's book, it was meant to be permanent."

Shem's golden eyes focused on her, his pupils wide and his entire expression so beautiful that Philippa wanted to fall over dead. "Would you like a researcher's perspective?"

A breathy laugh escaped her lips. "Ah, I think that's always what I get from you, Shem."

He narrowed his eyes provocatively, which made her cheeks warm, but he thankfully refrained from mentioning anything on the subject. "An orphaned scribe from a town of immigrants, making ink from dirt to heal a creature of myth? I'd say you have a fair shot at getting into that library."

Her fingers walked across the grass to squeeze his hand. "*We* have a fair shot. We're in this together now. I've been thinking, Shem, about after all of this. You wouldn't have to go back to serving the courts, if you didn't want to. You could explore when you want, research what you want, all of that. You wouldn't have to be what they wrote you to be."

Heat radiated from his palm, and sliding his other hand from his pocket, he gently pushed back a tendril of her hair. She liked seeing him this close, taking in the curves of his face, the way his indigo locks set off his golden eyes. Surely someone so ethereal had to be written, not born, because who could really exist in such symmetry and perfection?

And he *was* beautiful. Beautiful in a way that almost hurt to look at. The intelligence behind those eyes was his, though. He had hungered for knowledge, though he'd been written to be polite and studious, his mind never quieted. Philippa let her shoulders relax, simply taking him in.

"What is it that you're planning on doing in that inner sanctum, Miss Aporo? The whole truth, if you please."

Her tattooed fingertips danced over his, before pulling away to rub her shoulder. That spot never seemed to quiet when she spoke of magic.

"I've told you what I know, Shem. The rest I will figure out when I'm there. I think… I think I am just quite tired of others writing everyone else's endings."

His eyes seemed to flash at that, and the way his jaw worked made her think that he was once again putting pieces of a bigger puzzle together. "What of those who had written beginnings?"

The haunting note in his voice made her shiver. Philippa shook her head fervently. "You're living proof that creation can be beautiful," as she spoke, Vaelith huffed with jealousy behind her, "I'm walking a fine line here. I may have magic able to heal, to release a monster already written onto rune glass, but to free magic altogether?"

Shem waited, staring at her, waiting for more, but she was at a loss for words. Philippa felt like she'd already revealed too much of her plan. At that, he nodded, and Philippa thought he shot Vaelith a rather unsavory glance before standing up. He offered Philippa his hand, and when she was pulled to her feet, he didn't let go.

"We should set out. An hour or two, and we'll enter Kamath."

"Let's hurry. But, Shem—" Philippa grabbed his arm, drawing him closer. "Think about what I said. About after."

He laid his hand atop hers, his eyes dark like molten gold. "There is still a very real possibility we get caught and all of this is for naught."

She could smell him this close, the air of their journey mingled with spices and mint. "Then, if there's an after."

Shem's jaw set, a muscle feathering as he considered. This was a lot for him, she knew. He was going against everything he'd been written to do, and what they were hoping to accomplish was quite *impolite* by the standards he'd been created to follow. He cradled her neck, and rested his forehead against hers.

"If there's an after," he promised.

CHAPTER THIRTY-EIGHT ✦

Kamath took her breath away.

The hill dropped away in a slow, curving descent, and beyond it lay the city. It sprawled like a painted ribbon across the valley floor. Even from this height, Philippa could see the way it moved: not in motion, but in intent. The city stretched in a sinuous, deliberate line, its outer edge tapering like the elegant finger of a hand pointing inward, toward something greater; toward Aresef.

Tall spires rose like chiming bells in the misty dawn, each with slate or copper rooftops that caught the morning light in burnished streaks. The buildings were stacked and terraced into the rising edges of the valley walls, layered like the pages of a story someone had forgotten to finish. Tiny garden plots spilled over balconies, bursting with lavender and mint and the golden leaves that Philippa had only read about, their color bright even in the dim fog. Wind chimes swayed in the breeze, carrying a sound so delicate that it felt like the city was humming to itself.

Steam curled from bathhouses and bakeries alike, the smell of yeast and anise threading up the slope where they stood. Glass walled structures glittered like dew at the heart of each district, refracting the morning into shifting mosaics of rose and pearl. Archways of sandstone and white veined marble cradled long avenues where horse drawn carts and early risers moved together in a lazy morning rhythm.

Philippa's mouth parted. It was unlike anything she had ever seen in Levanta, or even in the richer merchant towns along the coast that often brought their own goods. This city hadn't grown over time, slowly and naturally, it had been designed. It was a story written into the land.

And still, she thought, this was only a finger. The real hand, the mind and heart of the growing empire, waited deeper in. Aresef would rise like a god beyond this. But even now, Philippa looked at this place as if she were seeing the world open for the first time.

"It's beautiful," she whispered.

Below, bells began to chime the hour, and the sound rolled up the hillside like an invitation. It was almost enough to forget why she'd come. Almost.

"Beauty is often deceiving."

They all spun to face the voice that cut across the hill, but only Philippa looked up. She didn't need the voice in her head to tell her that he would be perched, as always.

Sparrow lazily leaned against the trunk of the tree, one of his black boots tapping quietly on the thick branch. The feathers cascading down his shoulders and back had changed color, and were now a stark ivory color, almost melting into his mask. Philippa smiled at the thought of him hand stitching new feathers into his own mask, a vain little thing that made her shoulders fall a little.

"Are you here to scorn her again?" Shem asked, arms folded. "We haven't the time for games. You seem to know everything, so then you must know the hurry we're in. If you'll excuse us, keep a fair distance while we head into the city."

Without another word, Shem turned to descend the hillside. He took all of ten steps before there was a rustle of leaves and Sparrow simply *appeared* right in front of him, as if sprouting from the ground. Shem swore and stumbled backwards, his hand finding the blade under his tunic.

The mask only tilted in response.

Sparrow inclined his head, as if to speak to Shem, but then he deftly stepped around him and approached Philippa. "As soon as you step foot into Kamath, you'll all be arrested or killed."

"I can escort them just fine, thank you," Shem interjected, voice wane. He looked rather cross, with his eyebrows knit together and his shoulders up. Philippa thought he looked like one of her teachers back in Soffer when they got irritated at her for talking. "No need to fear being arrested."

Sparrow laughed once, a sharp, unfeeling sound. "Look at the lot of you and tell me you won't raise any sort of suspicions."

Philippa covered her chest with her arms, and looked down at her bare feet. None of them had bathed in days, save for rinsing off in rivers and dousing themselves with waterskins. Actually, now that she thought about it, she hadn't seen Ole bathe at all. Which, at present, became increasingly more prominent as she breathed deeply and had to crinkle her nose. On top of that, there was the issue of Vaelith...

"She knows you're coming. They both do."

Philippa's gaze shot up to meet Sparrow's. She didn't have to ask who he meant. Her skin prickled and her bones sang in fear.

"I know I can't change this one's mind," Sparrow gestured to her, and put his hands on his hips as he leaned to one side, taking them all in. "So you'll need clothes and disguises. And the Nazheris needs to stay behind. As does the corpse."

Ole finally spoke. "No. My boy stays. Little Pip can protect us."

The confidence he had in her warmed her heart, but she had a feeling that Sparrow knew more of what awaited them than he was letting on. He always spoke of danger and turning back, but maybe now with understanding he couldn't stop her, he would actually come along. She needed him for this.

An odd thing, to need a stranger that you felt you knew so well. Maybe he felt the same way.

"Listen, big guy, you need to trust me on this. Vaelith and your grandson are going to draw too much attention to yourselves. The queen already sent a Visage and the stars know what else to hunt you down. She has assassins. Men, women and children she's paid to hide in dark corners of every street of every city. A toddler could slit the boy's throat as you walk through town and you'd never know."

"I do not take orders from a strange man who breaks into my home, my tribe—" Ole's hands were already smoldering, his expression severe.

"Wait, wait!" Philippa stepped in front of both Ole and Shem, her head cocked to the side, staring at Sparrow. How did *he* know Vaelith's name? She'd only discovered that herself. She was sure that Vaelith hadn't met this man in some other time, some other journey, and entrusted him with that precious knowledge? The knowledge he'd just spilled like it was worthless ale. Vaelith hadn't, had she?

Philippa's breath was caught in her throat. She stared at Sparrow, unsure of what to say, if she should draw attention to it, when he seemingly realized what he'd done. He only looked down, for once not staring straight at them like an obstacle he needed to overcome. In knowing Vaelith's name, there was something he was not supposed to betray that he had.

Was he… inside her head? Listening? A scribe meant to spy on her every thought?

"Are you how Queen Aura knew where to send the Visage?" Her accusation was laced with pure ice. Stars, had she endangered everyone out of her own stupidity? She let out a bitter laugh, wondering how she ever thought she was smart or powerful enough to fix any of this.

At her accusation, Shem's blade came free and he adopted the same stance he'd fought the Visage with. Ole's hands were pure flames now, and Vaelith snarled with black spit pooling out of her lips. But when Philippa glanced at Vaelith, the Nazheris seemed more upset at the situation than ready to pounce on Sparrow. It reminded Philippa of an exasperated mother trying to get her two children to stop quarreling.

Sparrow sighed, like this was *such* an inconvenience. "I am not."

"Stop hiding what you know. Who you are. Please." She hated how her voice broke. Hated how weak she was sounding. Normally, she wouldn't care to cry, to expel the emotion, but now it would feel like she was incapable of holding her ground.

He slowly put his hands up, as if in surrender. "Queen Aura has scribes. An amount I do not know. The Visage found you because somehow, she has a way to track you. It is not perfect, otherwise, many of you would be dead. A scribe can send a beast on a trail, if they wish."

Philippa took a step forward. "How do you know all of this?"

Shem answered for him. "Because he is of the Cult of Sparrows.

Practicers and zealots of their own ambition. He doesn't respect what your people were, Philippa. They study and practice to become abusers. Hungry like jackals and never satisfied. I tried to warn you. He cannot be trusted any longer. He's going to get you killed."

She ran her hands through her hair. There was no time for this. Panu had stopped accepting water a day ago from Ole. In two more days, he would be nothing but a sleeping, lifeless husk for Ole to mourn all alone. Maybe the queen knew she was coming, but why would the queen care about one little scribe from Soffer? Her mind drifted to the obelisk at the binding site. The words the cult left there, *the Queen collects stories...*

Queen Aura would know that they could just kill her. If she truly had scribes of her own, like Sparrow was saying, then there was no point anyway. But she had to try.

There was a crack in the air. Philippa startled as Shem's head snapped to the side, Sparrow's hand still in a fist. Shem stumbled, but did not fall. Still, Sparrow was faster, and jumped onto the taller man, weaseling over his back like a spider and flipping Shem onto his stomach, the dust plumed up around them like smoke.

Ole raised his hand to release a spit of fire, but hesitated. Maybe he couldn't see through the settling dust, or maybe he saw what Philippa saw. Sparrow had a boot to Shem's chest, leaning over him like a predator.

"It is because of this 'cult' that I know all this. And it is due to the very same group that I know you are an *abomination.*" Though Sparrow's voice was quiet, it was like white hot venom in the air. Philippa remembered the gas they poured over her home as a child, the way it stung their eyes and throats. His presence tasted very much like that now.

If the words hurt Shem, he didn't show it. He just stared at Sparrow, unmoving. But as Philippa stared, partially clinging to Ole, she saw murder in those precious golden eyes.

Sparrow removed his boot from Shem to allow him to roll out. Shem stood and dusted himself off. There was clearly no point in retaliating.

"If you're trying to convince us to let you come, calling him that is *not* the place to start," Philippa said, and was surprised at the anger in her voice. Ole grunted in agreement.

Sparrow muttered something to himself, muffled by the mask, but it sounded something like *why do I even try*, before he rolled his neck and looked back at them. "You're *all* abominations. The lot of you are a traveling circus of broken stories."

He pointed at Ole and Panu before continuing. "You betrayed your beliefs on a whim, knowing it would earn you exile, and you don't seem particularly upset that two of your people were slaughtered by this woman you follow without question. That doesn't sound like a fearless Wahanar leader to me. No, to me, it sounds like a coward with too much heart for those who do not give a *thought* about you."

Philippa saw Ole tense, and the mountain of a man deflated. How could words hurt so much, Philippa thought for only a moment, because she *knew*. She knew how much words could hurt. What damage they could do, scribed or not.

Worthless, worthless, worthless...

Sparrow whirled on Shem. "I don't even know *what* you are, but you are not natural. Tell me, how does it feel to be born of words and dark intentions, rather than of the love of parents you will never have? It must be horrid to live in the absence of affection, to seek it from a woman you barely know, because for the first time you were looked at like a *human*." Sparrow laughed, a bitter, brokenhearted sound. "That is not love, dear scholar, that is obsession with the ideal that you could *have* something for once."

She wanted him to stop, to be silenced, but they all stood there like dumbfounded children being scolded by their parents.

When he turned on her, she almost let her shaking legs give out. He knew all of this because of her. She knew that somehow, in her heart.

"And you," Sparrow's voice hardened, "orphan of a people marked for death. Trying so desperately to make something of herself, because you must have this power for a reason right? Because it wouldn't be enough to be blessed with power but not be able to do any good with it. That your only value is measured by how much you can do for others. Otherwise, you're worth nothing. Abominations. The lot of you. So do not act as if any of you are better than me, a cultist assassin covered in so much blood that my pages must be *red* with it. If I wanted her dead, she'd be dead."

Now the tears came without question. Emptiness surrounded them in swaths. She turned her head to look over at the city, the hollow feeling sucking any beauty that had once been there. What were any of them, really, other than empty pages waiting to be filled and sealed?

With a quivering lip, she looked at Sparrow, whose chest rose unevenly. "How did you get to be so heartless?"

"No." Ole said sternly, seemingly the only word he'd spoken the entire time. "Not heartless. He speaks from it."

Shem seemed about to argue with him, but Ole strode across the plateau and towered over Sparrow. The chief's wide shoulders completely hid Sparrow from her view. It was like a giant looking at a human child.

Is that how she looked next to him?

The former chief of the Wahanar then knelt, still much taller than Sparrow, but the gesture was there. "You speak of us like we mean nothing. Your heart hurts. You try to break us down beneath you, so we will listen."

Sparrow pointed at Shem. "He started this."

Ole sighed and swatted Sparrow's hand away. "We are not so easy to topple, bird. Maybe we are weak because we do not follow the path we should. But maybe we are strong together because we understand what it means to be alone. To want more," he glanced at Panu, asleep and groaning, "you are no different than us. You say you are coming? Make proof to her." He pointed at Philippa. "I follow because she is strong. Even if we fail, she has hope. Not many can say they follow hope and goodness. Can you?"

Sparrow was silent for a long time. She wondered what he was thinking, what he could be looking like under that mask. Then, she nearly gasped as he knelt before Ole, settling into the grass like a phantom of shadow and feathers.

"I follow her." Was his only answer.

Somehow, that seemed enough for the Wahanar chief. He nodded and rose, looking over his shoulder at them with a new determination.

To Sparrow, he said, "what is your name? If you are to help, we must be on the way to friends."

Feathers cascading, he looked up at Ole, but she felt like his eyes were on her. "Sparrow is just fine."

"Rise, Sparrow. Help us. I will not lose my family today." Ole's voice thundered like a command, and in an instant, Sparrow was on his feet.

He never apologized, but perhaps he didn't need to. Ole was right. Everything Sparrow had said was true, and out of a place of anger and hurt. It didn't make it right, but it helped her reconcile with the idea of him coming along at all. She couldn't believe that she wanted him to come initially, without knowing that someone so vile lurked underneath the mask. She knew him as selfless, perhaps even generous, soft and slumbering beside her in a cave.

On top of that, she couldn't believe he knelt before Ole, or obeyed his command. Maybe he knew a chief when he saw one.

She looked to Shem, whose fists were clenching and unclenching, his jaw set so firmly she thought he could crack a tooth. He didn't argue about Sparrow coming along. There was no point. They couldn't stop him if they wanted to.

Sparrow approached Panu's cart, Vaelith snorting at him. He stopped in his tracks. "We cannot take the boy into the city."

Ole only nodded. "I will stay with him."

"No, we'll need your muscle." Sparrow commented, half to himself. Philippa could only watch him in earnest, still shocked and reeling. "I can transport him. Put him somewhere safe. The Nazheris can come with him."

He seemed rather careful not to call Vaelith by her name again.

"Where?" Ole demanded.

"Your crystal passageways are not privy only to you," Sparrow explained curtly, "I'll hide him there. When we're done, I'll pull him out."

Ole considered this, and no one spoke. This was wholly his decision. He ran a hand over Panu's head, his huge chest releasing with a sigh. "If you die, we cannot find him."

She could hear Sparrow's smirk in his voice. "That won't happen."

Olekashan bent and pressed a kiss to his grandson's forehead. Then, he nodded at Vaelith, who no doubt would shred anyone who got too close to Panu.

Sparrow sliced through the straps of the yoke holding Vaelith to the cart. At Ole's permission, Sparrow jumped up into the cart with Panu, staring down at the boy like he was some foreign object. Vaelith clambered up into the cart with them, staring at Sparrow expectantly.

He put a gloved hand on Panu's chest, and reached up to Vaelith, who hissed at him. He glared at her and hissed right back. Stars, where in Istoria was this man from?

His mask lifted to nod at Ole, before he whispered, and a dark shadow enveloped them. Then, they were gone, as if never there before.

In an instant, Shem was speaking. "How do you know he didn't just murder him? What if *he's* a scribe working for Queen Aura? Chief Ole, this is absolute madness!"

"I will hear none of it. He is no scribe. That is a man who is powerless." Ole sounded firm, but Philippa certainly wouldn't describe Sparrow as *powerless*. "He does not work for the foreign queen. He only follows Little Pip."

"How can we be sure?" Shem asked.

"Because I'm already back." Sparrow's voice cut through the field, and there he simply was, yet again. In his arms were stacks of clothes, and notably, boots. Philippa pursed her lips. He approached slowly, then set the garments on the ground. "You'll have to blend in. Play traveling merchants. Out of towners who are down on their luck and came to the nearest city after being robbed. I would have joined you all sooner, but it was hard to find clothes that would fit the chief."

Then, he pulled a heavy looking sack from his back, tied with a red ribbon, and tossed it in Ole's direction. Ole caught it, eyes questioning.

"Sands from the Wahanar lands. So you can look in on him, should you worry."

Ole nodded in thanks, notably silent and eyes glossy.

Shem dug through the clothes, handing Philippa her respective garments. His golden eyes narrowed as he jerked his chin in Sparrow's direction. "You're so concerned with us looking out of place, and you think dressing like *that* won't draw attention?"

Sparrow clasped his hands behind his back. "Assassins travel quite frequently through populated areas."

"The mask," Philippa said quickly, voice tight, "the queen surely wouldn't ignore a cultist in her cities."

Sparrow regarded her for a long moment. Philippa saw his foot tapping against the ground, the way his fingers twitched restlessly at his sides.

With a reserved sigh, he reached up behind his head. A small leather strap became visible as it was undone, and he whispered a word she didn't understand. Then, gloved palms braced against the face of his mask, it fell into his hands.

Sparrow shook out his golden locks, looking around and blinking as if his eyes needed to adjust to the light.

Philippa's jaw dropped. Ole even made a noise.

Shem dragged a hand over his face. "Oh great. That's *much* more subtle."

CHAPTER THIRTY-NINE ✦

While her feet were the least of their problems, Philippa was consumed by the itch of the sandals digging into her heels. Even the band separating her big toe from the rest of them was driving her half mad. Why even separate the toes, anyway? All it did was make her feet sweat against the leather.

The rest of her outfit felt equally as ridiculous. She'd worn wraps and skirts before, but never one like this. Instead of being short and allowing her to wade into the ocean, this skirt would drag her into the tempests and drown her. It was high in the front, exposing her lower thighs and knees, while nearly dragging on the ground in the back. Her hand was firmly pressed to her breasts to keep the corset from coming undone. It was a god awful color of brown, almost matching her skin, and she felt naked walking into the streets bustling with people.

I need pants, she thought. If they needed to run, the skirt would trip her. *Or, I'll just cut off the train.*

Pointedly, she could feel Sparrow's eyes digging into the back of her skull. He still didn't walk alongside them, but at this point, she was certain he could hear or ascertain at least *some* of her thoughts.

Beside her, Ole grunted and toyed with his tunic.

"Uncomfortable?" She asked, sidestepping her way through the crowd.

He nodded. "I will never understand why others *want* cloth to stick to their sweat. Better to be shirtless or naked than to be confined this way."

Philippa grinned and gestured to her corset top. "Tell me about it."

As they swam their way through the sea of bodies, Philippa chewed on the inside of her cheek. Reasonably, she knew that they were complaining about small inconveniences to avoid lingering on the more gruesome thoughts. Ole, no doubt, was hoping that his grandson was alright. He had the bag of sand tied to his thigh, and his meaty hand rested atop it.

There was no mistaking that he wasn't fully human. Wahanar were simply too large to confuse with anything else, and with the additions of his tattoos that could not be fully covered, well, they got a few stares. But Sparrow had made the story clear to them: they were a traveling party that had recently been robbed and would be making their way through town performing to earn back their wages.

Evidently, this satisfied the few people who'd asked questions, and even more surprising was that she learned of other Wahanar who had similar circumstances when they were exiled. Not that any more would get the chance, now. Exile was a thing of the past. Execution was the way to go, now.

Murderer, murderer, murderer...

She wrapped her arms around her torso. Soon. Soon she would remedy that.

Shem took the lead of the group, wading through Kamath with ease, as if he'd been there a hundred times. Which, in all likelihood, he had. Philippa wondered every time he glanced at a building or nodded to someone if they were part of his 'quiet rebellion' he was so fond of, or if certain storefronts were meeting places for their secretive discussions. He didn't mention any of this, though, and rather acutely kept an eye on Sparrow anytime he glanced to see if they were keeping up.

Sparrow, who at this point, Philippa was focusing on the discomfort of her clothes to avoid thinking of.

Stars, how could she have missed it? As soon as he'd taken his mask off, she'd realized what it was.

Lavender.

She stopped in her tracks. The scent was so vibrant, so fresh. Ole wandered on ahead without her, but she didn't notice.

Slowly spinning in a circle, her eyes floated through and over the heads of people, inhaling deeply, trying to pinpoint where it was coming from.

There, across the street, in an open window storefront.

A pie lay on the sill, a kindly old woman selling her baked goods to some children. And there, beside her, a pot of lavender tea boiling over a fire. Hanging above the woman's head were fresh bundles, tied with a purple and yellow ribbon.

Philippa's feet moved beneath her without hesitation. At once, she was waiting in line, barely patient enough to stand still. When it came to be her turn, the old woman was turned around, taking a new sheet of sweets from the pastry chef inside. Philippa reached up, and pulled a single bundle down. She raised it to her nose, inhaling deeply. There was the earthy, herby scent of lavender, but the hint of salt that only came from the sea. The hint of breeze from fields full of purpling flowers, of sourdough rising on front porches.

This was Levanta's lavender. Their greatest export to the other merchants that passed through. Only Levanta's was so large, so fragrant.

Philippa hadn't realized she'd closed her eyes, but when she opened them, the woman was smiling fondly at her.

She smiled back.

"It's from a small town, barely within the reach of His and Her Majesty." The elderly woman explained, and Philippa saw even her clothes were dyed purple. "I'm rather fond of it, too."

Philippa felt tears prick her eyes, despite her smile. This woman had no idea what memories and fondness this scent carried.

"How do you get your hands on it, out here?" Philippa asked, her voice tight.

The woman gently took the bundle from Philippa's hands, turning it over and examining it. She missed the weight of the bundle in her palm.

"I have a relative there. Another old bitty like myself. I always get the largest shipments. I send my son to purchase it for me, each month. It's eight coppers, my dear."

Philippa's mouth tightened. She had no money.

Suddenly, Shem was at her side. "Unfortunately, we don't have time to pick them out, Miss Aporo."

"Right." she said.

The woman nodded, and quietly replaced the bundle on its hook. But her eyes never left Philippa's. They were almost… amber. A shade of yellow, perhaps.

Then, the woman poured some of the lavender tea into the mug. "Here, dear. On the house. Refreshment for the road."

Philippa looked to Shem, who only shrugged. Smiling in thanks, Philippa raised the mug to her lips. Then it shattered on the cobblestones below.

The woman scoffed, and Philippa took a wide step back.

Sparrow knelt, picking up the pieces of the mug, and tossing them back onto the sill. "Free? In this town?" It was all he said. Shem and Philippa's mouths were agape. She began to apologize when the woman simply took her pastry sheet and tea pot and slammed the window shut.

She whirled on him. "Do you have to be so rude?"

He cocked his head to the side. "Nothing is free in this life. And, you might take more care to look *where* you're accepting goods from this time."

At that, he sauntered off, heading towards Ole whose brow was drawn, clearly upset to be waiting on them. Shem just shook his head and grabbed her wrist, dragging her back across the busy street. She glanced over her shoulder and felt her stomach drop. It was an apothecary, not a bakery.

She wiggled out of Shem's grasp, and fell into step alongside Sparrow. Though he still wore the black cloth that covered the bottom half of his face, and his hood was drawn, she could see the tension in his eyes. The eyes she had been pointedly trying to not think about by focusing on her discomforts.

"An apothecary. So the tea was…"

"Poisoned." he said.

Her toes curled on the edges of her sandals. "I'm sorry. It just… reminded me of home."

Home, and people.

Sparrow curtly nodded. "Just making sure you don't die."

"About that," she began, changing the subject, "I don't know how I feel about you saving my life and leaving others behind."

He chuckled, though it was a dry, humorless sound. "It's a cruel world."

She stepped in front of him. He ran right into her, glaring. She met his gaze defiantly. "And we are allowed to be gentle."

At that, she stormed off after Shem, weaving through people to keep up. She tried not to focus on the pointed ears that she knew lurked under Sparrow's hood, or the eyes so green that it could only mean one thing: he was born in Soffer, too.

They had gathered in a bar that smelt like sweat and other bodily fluids. Philippa's ears twitched as she tried to ignore the clearly over exaggerated moaning coming from one of the rooms upstairs. Bar and brothel, it seemed. A co-venture that she only saw one head of, which was a heavyset human man behind the bar with two beautiful girls in his arms. Both of which didn't hide their displeasure. In a sad way, Philippa thought, their fierce expressions only made them more attractive. A rather unpleasant combination for them, she thought.

Ole was also at the bar, using some of the coins that Sparrow gave them to order food. Philippa didn't imagine from the look of the bartender that it would be edible.

Shem's fingers were drumming on the table, his back pressed firmly into the booth. His golden eyes were watching Sparrow, who was not sitting with them. He lurked in a corner, at a lone table nearby, eyes closed. Asleep.

Or, so it seemed. Every now and again he would crack an eye open. Always observing.

She turned back to Shem. "Alright. Tell me more about the cult."

Shem seemed to fall back into his body, blinking rapidly. "What a way to start a dinner date."

Philippa's ears lowered ever the slightest as she blushed. Before she could respond, Shem was already onto the next. He leaned on his arms, drawing close. Though the clamor of the crowded room was enough to conceal what he had to say, he whispered.

"The Cult of Sparrows is after something. Their leader is a murmur in the wind. No one finds them unless they *want* to be found. You saw their carvings and paintings at the ancient scribe site. They're zealots. Obsessed with their catch." Shem's eyes darted to Sparrow, who didn't seem to notice. "If they get what they're after, we can only assume they'd use it to rule. Scribes were often dissected into two sects, as you well know."

She nodded thoughtfully, wincing as a drunk man glanced at them as he passed. For a moment, her skin prickled. Anyone here could be a spy for the king and queen. Or, at least willing to sell a scribe for the reward. It didn't matter if they agreed with the law or not. In a town like this, money was money.

It dawned on Philippa at that moment, that since entering Kamath, the population had one thing in common: they were all human. She couldn't name a single person she'd seen up close that was anything else.

She drew her hands together, squeezing them. Just being an elf was enough to draw attention to herself. This is not how she thought this would go.

To her relief, the drunkard simply gave them a lopsided smile and moved on to drink with his party.

She returned her attention to Shem. "But no one knows if they *want* to rule. What if they're of my mother's people? Who sought the freedom to use their magic? That cannot be all bad."

Shem leveled a glare at her. "Whether of your mother's or not, the result of the usage of their magic was the same. Soffer burned. The scales were tipped."

"Everyone is so quick to condemn." she said.

"You are quick to give the benefit of the doubt." Shem said in sharp retort.

Philippa narrowed her eyes. "If someone had given my people the benefit of the doubt, we would not be having this conversation."

"You're kind and wise, Miss Aporo, but sentiments do not end stereotypes or glamour others into seeing what you want to see."

"We're getting off topic. What does the cult want? How do we know it's so bad?"

He gathered his locks to the top of his head and secured them with a tie. She could tell that he was avoiding glancing at Sparrow, as if the action would be humiliating him somehow.

Men and their posturing.

"What they seek, is a vial filled with all the magic of the last stand of the scribes. It is said that, in efforts to keep their magic out of other's hands, they poured it like ink into a container able to hold the very magic itself. It was hoped that those who inherited the vial could write anything into existence. Even an army to retake the lands."

She felt a wave of nostalgia wash over her. Her father had told her some of these stories. Used it as an excuse to make her and Morgana practice so often as children to see if they had the gift.

He lowered his voice further. "So, you ask if society had condemned this cult? I'd say they've done that themselves. No one should have power like that. It would be limitless."

Shem's voice was cut off by the sound of Ole clanking three mugs of ale onto the table, nearly tipping the booth over under his weight as he sat down beside Philippa. She smiled up at him and accepted the drink, though it was so murky she wondered what it could possibly be made of.

Across from her, Shem suddenly jerked with surprise. Philippa only glanced up. Sparrow was suddenly sitting next to him, silent as a ghost.

She almost smiled.

"Not limitless." He murmured beneath his black face mask, the fabric somehow staying neatly in place. "But dangerous, perhaps."

Shem rolled his eyes. "How could that much power not be limitless? The scribes who were said to have put all their magic into that vial, as armies began to break down their door, were the most powerful of their time."

"Magic, scholar, is not free. There is always a balance. One would think, in all your studies, you would know this." Sparrow's voice was like gravel, though he did not look anywhere but the table, head kept low. "Limitless? No. It would be limited to one great act chosen by the writer. The ink in that vial is not immeasurable, but it is invaluable."

"You speak like it is a prophecy," Ole said, and Philippa gaped that his mug was already empty. She gently pushed her mug towards him, which he accepted silently.

Sparrow's black hood shook side to side. "History repeats itself. You give a man a club, he will strike his neighbor. He rules. You give another man a sword, he will strike the ruler. Give a man the choice to rewrite the world?"

He didn't need to continue. A silence fell over the table for a short time. Ole drank Philippa's share, and Shem gagged down his ale.

"But you admit that is what your cult looks for." Shem said numbly.

Sparrow tapped his fingers on the table. It seemed he had no more to say on the matter. Shem looked at her, eyebrows raised, as if to say he knew that he was right. Philippa only shrugged. It didn't change the fact that they still needed Sparrow, and whether or not they wanted him there, he was going to be.

She could hardly stand the tension.

Philippa cleared her throat. "Let's play a game." They all stared at her. "A game. You know, an activity friends use to pass the time?"

"I know what a—" They all said in unison, before cutting off at the realization. It was Ole who finished. "It does not feel like a time for simple games."

Philippa put a hand on his massive arm and smiled. "That's exactly why we need one."

With a resigned sigh, Shem nodded. "I'll play."

"Games are exactly what I expect out of you." Sparrow grumbled.

Philippa was ready to tear her hair out. She slammed a hand on the table, exasperated. "Can any of you keep from each other's throats for *five* minutes? Please?"

As if it took physical effort, they each agreed. Ole noted that he was offended to be lumped in with the two 'fighting children'.

"We'll go in a circle. What would you do if you could use the magic vial?" she asked.

A beat passed. "Is this a test?"

She groaned and buried her face in her hands. "No, Sparrow, this is not a test."

"A ship. A ship that sailed without the need of a crew." His voice had turned rather soft, contemplative. Philippa smiled at him, which she couldn't tell if he returned.

"See? How hard is it to have just a moment without—"

Shem cut her off under his breath. "I'm surprised you wouldn't use it to kill me."

Sparrow jabbed his elbow into Shem's gut. "I wouldn't need magic for that."

She slammed both of her hands down onto the table. The booth rattled under her weight. With a pointed glare at each of them, Philippa stopped at Ole, who thankfully was at about eye level as she stood on the seat of the booth.

"Ole, walk with me," she huffed, "I need some air."

"Just Ole?" Shem asked, already starting to rise.

Ole smiled widely as he made room for Philippa to slide out of the booth. "What can be said? I am the favorite."

With that, he slid an arm underneath Philippa and hoisted her up. She swallowed a scream, and suddenly was placed atop his shoulder. She felt like a parrot.

Ole turned, whisking out of the bar with ease. No one tried to get in his path. With that, they both ducked through the slight doorway, and into the street.

<hr>

They returned a short time later to the bar, having cooled off. Philippa was still on Ole's massive shoulder, her arm resting on his head. He'd explained to her when they'd left that the Wahanar would carry their children on one shoulder when they were tired, even when they would become teenagers. She couldn't imagine a younger Heru draped over her father's shoulder, tired as a toddler, clinging to him like he was all that mattered in the world.

Her lips pursed. She couldn't imagine herself clinging to her father, either. He wasn't an unkind man. Just… set in his ways. He often spoke of his son, from his first marriage, about how powerful he would become. But it seemed that Titus Aporo was destined to be disappointed in all of his children. Morgana never presented the gift, and Calix left in a frenzy, speaking about things that even their father thought was unseemly.

Then, there was Philippa. Youngest and smallest, presenting the *chance* of becoming powerful, and yet, it never seemed enough for him.

Their mother wanted her to stay as far away from the gift as possible.

"Do you remember your parents, Ole?" she asked as they waited by the door.

He nodded, her arm bobbing with his head. "A harsh pair. Why do you ask?"

Why *did* she ask? Philippa chewed on the inside of her cheek. "I suppose I'm just wondering what mine would expect me to do right now. This seems like the exact situation they'd be arguing with me about. I know it seems silly, but… I don't know. I wish I could ask them. Even if I didn't like their answer."

She peered down the street from her perch on his shoulder, and though she couldn't see it, she was looking towards the lavender shop. Maybe it was all in her head, but she swore she could still smell it.

"I too would ask my parents questions, if I could." Ole said softly.

Philippa looked down at him. "Even though they were harsh?"

"Even though they were harsh." Olekashan confirmed, his voice wistful and far away.

She pondered on that, rolling her shoulders and clamping her hands together. The world had opened up to her, and now she was *homesick?* She wouldn't tuck her tail and run, not when she was so close to righting wrongs. But Levanta sounded beautiful right about now. Morgana's embrace and Raff's laughter could bind her soul up.

"I'm sorry you lost your parents." Philippa finally said.

Ole shrugged, and she had to squeeze her legs on his shoulder to keep from toppling over. "You lost yours too, Little Pip. It is not so bad to miss someone."

The empty pit in her chest didn't quite agree with that sentiment. "I think I would rather have them. Even if I didn't agree with what they had to say."

"We can only strive to take what we liked from our parents and leave the rest behind. Hope to be better."

Hope. That word that he so often tied to her. Despite his various explanations, she still couldn't grasp the weight of *how* he thought she was so capable. She wouldn't ever be able to express her gratitude enough. What he said was so simple, yet so profound. Philippa didn't know if she felt capable enough to be better than her parents. She was so small when they were taken from her that… maybe she couldn't be like any good parts of them at all.

Ole cleared his throat. "You said you would ask them some things. What would you ask?"

A sigh left her lips in a small plume of white air as night fell on the city. "I know that I'm grown. I should be able to figure all of these things out for myself. But is it possible that some of our pages never fully turn when we miss something from our childhood? I feel so lost. How is it that I deserve this power, can wield it, but not understand it? I don't know, Ole. A twenty-two year old who misses their mommy and daddy? I'm supposed to save us? All because… because I want to? Because I ruined your life—" her voice broke off. She hadn't realized she'd begun crying. Quiet sobs began to rack her body, leaving her shaking on his shoulder like a lost child.

Warmth was suddenly at her sides as his hands grasped her, before he set her solidly on the ground. No one else was in the streets at this hour, and the bar was still loud with patrons to drown out their conversation in the road.

Ole knelt before her, and his frame that at one point seemed huge and imposing, was protective and gentle.

His brow formed a stern line as she cried. "You have not ruined my life, Little Pip. My family was broken before you. It was *I* who called for *you* to be brought before us. I sought a simple fix for my family, my people.

Magic to rewrite wrongs set by our parents before us. My error has led us here."

She covered her mouth to quiet her cries, when suddenly a roughness crossed underneath her eyes. Philippa froze, opened her eyes wide as Ole gently swiped his calloused fingertips to wipe away her tears. This giant man, as gentle as a mouse, comforting her like she was but a child.

"Magic has called to you before we met, Little Pip. You have said so before. Maybe my error and your power needed to meet."

A broken laugh escaped her lips. "Oh, Ole. How can you believe in me this much?"

He gripped her shoulders then, drawing her attention to his determined face. "I believe in you, Little Pip, because you're *you*. That can be enough, if you let it."

His words struck her right in the heart, in a small corner of her soul that usually screamed *worthless, worthless, worthless,* and that corner quieted, ever the slightest.

"But I've made you lose so much." She thought of Taz, of his daughter Heru.

Ole straightened, one hand firmly planted on his knee like a soldier pledging allegiance to a queen. "If I have lost, then I have gained."

She didn't understand what he said, not at first, but then he took her tattooed hand into his and held it to his forearm. As he pushed up their sleeves and pulled away his shirt, it became as clear as the oceans of her home. The swirling patterns of her fingertips bled into the design of his arm, which traced up his neck and over the left side of his chest, where his most intricate designs were tattooed. Heru's face tattoo beheld similar patterns.

This is a part of the Wahanar that even someone as studious as Shem could never understand. He did not want to be a *part* of their people, only understand them. In one's pursuit of understanding though, they would have to toss aside being an outsider. Every time he had reminded her that when she exceeded her worth, they would throw her away, melted from her mind. No, this was a people of deep heart and immense feeling. It's why they were so drastic in their punishments, in defending their beliefs. Foreign rulers came to take everything from them, so instead of glowing, they became fiery defenders.

What good had Philippa done to deserve the defense and honor of the chieftain who stood before her, a leader of his people who would bend a knee to her?

But it didn't matter if she *performed* goodness. That's what he was trying to tell her. It mattered that she *tried,* and that was enough for him.

Her mouth worked itself, trying to find the words, but none surfaced. Her eyes met Ole's. In a flash of memory, in the shadows of the alleyway, she saw her father, felt that pang of hollowness in her chest from longing. She saw Morgana and their mother, she saw Raff and Tazmireth hiding in Ole's dark eyes. And finally in them, she saw herself. She saw Ole.

And it was enough.

She took his face into her hands and brought his forehead to hers.

"What is it you would ask them, Little Pip?" His voice sounded thick, as if he were about to cry.

"I would ask if I'm doing the right thing. If I'm still going to be me at the end of this."

Ole pulled away, and patted her on the head. "The only person who can answer that, is you."

With that, he stood tall, and she quickly wiped away the rest of her tears as Shem came out of the bar. She waved lightly at him, but her focus was still on Ole. His not-answering gave her the best answer of all.

He was right. In loss, there is something to be gained. But that pit was still in her stomach as she wondered just how much more she would have to lose in order to keep what she'd found.

CHAPTER FORTY ✧

"The cultist said that too many people had asked questions about Ole." Shem offered by way of explanation as they walked through the quiet streets, away from the bar. "We could keep walking until morning. Try and make it closer to Aresef."

Philippa nodded, ready to agree, when Sparrow reappeared. His face was still clothed in black, save for the cut of grassy eyes that were illuminated by the moon above. In the alleyways, the hanging lanterns cast gauzy shadows over his form. She had so many questions about him, now. When was he born? How many others made it off of their isle before it was too late?

It was wishful thinking. Her eyes scurried over him, swathed in black and armed to the teeth in sheathed daggers. If others had made it out with him, he wouldn't have been in that cult.

Maybe this is where he found his purpose. Revenge. Saving others from Soffer, like her. It made enough sense.

"Come to contradict me again, have you?" Shem's voice was rueful, hands on his hips. Philippa stepped closer to him and looped her arm through his, at which his posture immediately softened.

Leather ached as Sparrow crossed his arms. "Staying on the move is best for the night. At least to get out of this district of the city."

No one argued, especially when in the distance they could hear a metallic footstep of soldiers starting their rounds for the evening.

They walked down the main streets and alleyways for hours that night, long enough for darkness to enshroud them all. In the distance, there seemed to be the sound of the ocean, though she knew it was impossible. As they drew nearer to the sound, she realized that they must've traversed into the art district of the city; the sound wasn't the ocean, but marbles running over reeds and tracks bolted onto the sides of houses, mimicking nature. Others sounded like birdsong, hanging flutes that caught the breeze and whistled like the wind in a forest.

Shem's arm grew heavy looped in hers, and though she could see he was tired, there was a lazy smile on his face as he looked down the street. This was part of what home meant for him, she realized. The bustle of the city, the artificial noise. He enjoyed it.

Philippa squeezed his arm, which earned her a rather romantic gaze from his golden eyes.

"It's beautiful out here." Philippa said, pressing her side against his. He wrapped his arm around her shoulders, his body warm against hers.

"Trying to steal a moment with me again, Miss Aporo?"

"All we're doing is walking. What's the harm?" Her voice was low, full of mirth and exhaustion.

Shem gently tugged on her, drawing them both to a stop as Ole and Sparrow continued on ahead of them. Then, he cupped both sides of her face, stroking her cheeks with his thumbs. His lips met hers in a soft, tentative greeting. Despite the arguing, the difference in opinions, he felt right under her grasp. He was such a good *person* despite everything they differed on. A man written for one thing and trying so very hard to be another. To be better. He whispered her name on her lips, making her fingers curl around his shirt. What was the harm, indeed?

Then the commotion began.

A door slammed open, rattling shutters. The sound repeated down the street. Footsteps filled the street as metal clanged in the doorways, shouts of indignation rising into the air. Philippa tore away from him, but he held fast, backing them towards a wall to avoid the crowd.

They carried lanterns of all colors and torches of red, blue, and yellow. Dozens of people had filled the small courtyard, effectively separating Shem and Philippa from the others in their party. Panic flared in her chest as she clung to Shem, staring at the mob before them. The mob took one glance at them, and just smiled.

Strangely, music began. Harps and flutes, guitars and drums. Those holding the colorful light sources encircled the courtyard, and stomped their feet to the music. As if practiced, they swapped places with the dancers that had gathered in the center, and became a living serpent of light and bodies.

Shem chuckled darkly behind her. "Of course. It is festival night for the inner cities of Sapria."

She softened against his chest, watching the people dance and scurry around in a wild fray of music and light.

It was beautiful.

"We should probably go around to find the others," Shem said over the sound of the music, tugging her arm, "they won't find their way through this. I can shortcut us through the backstreets."

He tried to pull her away, but she was enamored by the sights and sounds. "Let's wait here."

"But they won't catch—"

"They will. You know Sparrow will, and I doubt he'd leave Ole after their last conversation."

Shem tensed behind her. "This isn't a festival you'd like, Miss Aporo."

The lights danced in her eyes, and her chest stirred with longing. "How should I know? I've never been to one."

"Believe me, Philippa…"

"What is the danger of dancing?" Ole's voice cut over the noise as he strode towards them, tiptoeing around the crowds, who just smiled and waved for him to join their dance. Ole waved and nodded his head, but came to stand beside them. "We are in dire times. A little light in our hearts is not such a bad thing."

Philippa wordlessly nodded in agreement. She felt as though she were a fish on a lure, drawn towards the center of the music. It suddenly did not matter to her that she perhaps looked ridiculous, for in the arts center, everyone had the air of a vagabond. Layered shirts and frilly tops, the men wearing long drapes of color over their shoulders and loose trousers that moved like beautiful skirts when they shook their hips.

They were singing about a journey, a foe vanquished, love protected.

Stay, stay, stay.

Whatever danger lay in the dark corners outside of the festival isn't what kept her there. No, the beauty, the magic of these people kept her planted where she was.

One of the dancers passed her blue torch to a man as she danced to the outside of the circle. Her face was painted in black and ocean blue paints, highlighting the ethereal beauty of her dark skin. The blue of her lips parted in a warm smile as she twirled in place, clapping her hands to the beat.

Her eyes caught Philippa's, with a wild joy that felt raw. The woman gave Philippa a once over, then extended her hand towards her.

Philippa could only nod. *Yes.*

Without thinking about it, her feet were moving, joining the fray. The woman grabbed both of her hands and spun her in a wide circle, before jumping up and stomping both feet onto the road below. The sound was like thunder from the crowd.

It only took a moment to find the beat inside of her chest, to let her body follow the movement of those around her. Philippa closed her eyes, letting herself be passed from dancer to dancer, who all spun and twirled her about.

A laugh escaped her lips as she caught sight of Shem watching her, mouth agape, staring. On a nearby rooftop sat Sparrow, watching, his green eyes glistening as if full of tears. Her confusion about that only lasted a moment as she caught Ole stomping and clapping along with the drums.

Warmth cupped her cheek, and as she opened her eyes, the beautiful dancer from before stared at her, before ushering her to one side of the square. Half of the dancers stood across from them, holding the torches, while the other half stood beside her, painted in all kinds of beautiful colors.

The drums began to change to a steady, almost frantic rhythm that made her heartbeat quicken. Flutes were high and whining. Harps were plucked and deliberate.

Her hand was still clutched in the dancer's, who squatted as if ready to leap into battle. The action was mirrored by all of those on their side of the street.

Slowly, she turned to look across, and saw that those holding the flames had changed their adornments. They replaced flower crowns with head wear formed to look like curling horns, wore bracelets and rings that clawed their fingers. Their face paint wasn't beautiful, Philippa realized, it was horrific. Giant white and red slashes were cut out to mimic curling snarls, their foreheads painted with slanted yellow shapes to mimic beastly eyes.

Flashes of slaughter filled her mind, her hand quaking in the dancer's. She saw her mother's head hit the beach as those monsters pulled her limbs apart.

Then, slabs of wood painted to look like open pages were thrown into the middle. Those wearing the beast paint tore forward, yelling, lighting the wood on fire with their colorful torches.

In response, those on her side began to wail, acting as though they were on fire, crumpling to the ground in a mass heap. Even the dancer holding her hand fell to the street below, screaming as if her actual life book was being burned.

Philippa stood along among the fallen dancers, her chest heaving. They were celebrating the end of the scribe wars. The monsters burning Soffer to the ground. The execution of her people, the burning of the scribe's life books.

Singers told of the great leader their king married to help end the plague of the scribes.

Among those dressed as the monsters, a man drew a painted arrow with dyed feathers on the end. He aimed it into the sky, before firing it almost straight up into the air.

She heard it *whoosh,* and took a quick step back. The arrow whistled by, lodging in the street right at her toes.

Philippa whipped her head up. The music had stopped. Not only dancers stood across from her, but soldiers, who poured in from the dark alleyways. They were nondescript and wore no symbols of allegiance to any kingdom.

All the hair on Philippa's neck stood up. She took a shaking step backwards. This wasn't just a festival - this was a trap. They knew where she would be.

Then, between dancers and soldiers, she recognized a face. The old woman who had been selling lavender. She was sneering at her, and pointed a condemning finger in her direction.

Soldiers raised another volley.

As they loosed the arrows, someone grabbed her ankle and drug her down. Her head smacked against the road, bouncing, and she saw stars.

The dancer rolled on top of her, grasping her face in her hands. "Get up!"

Philippa's vision swam, but she obeyed, leaping to her feet as the dancer pulled her through the screaming crowd. Arrows flew, and Shem was calling her name. Ole lifted a soldier and literally *threw him over* a building. His scream echoed through the night.

The dancer shoved her underneath a wagon filled with fireworks, and quickly ducked under after her.

"Why are you helping me?" Philippa whispered. Feet ran by as chaos erupted around them.

The dancer looked at her incredulously. "Not everyone hates scribes."

"How did they know I was one? How did *you* know that they'd want me?"

The woman's face darkened, the streaks of paint smeared from sweat. "Queen Aura has gotten word that a scribe has murdered Wahanar and now enters the city to take her crown."

Philippa gaped. "I don't want a *crown*! And I didn't murder—" Her voice cut off as booted feet trudged by, chasing one of the dancers. It saved her from correcting herself, too.

There was no time for guilt. They had to survive.

"How many did you bring?" The woman asked.

"It's me and three men. Can you help us?" Her elbows dug into the road beneath them. The wagon above suddenly creaked, and it was lifted away, exposing them entirely. The woman reached for Philippa, as if to cover her, but she only smiled.

"I'm glad the big one is yours!"

Ole waved them out from underneath the wagon, letting it fall to the ground unceremoniously.

The woman smiled up at Ole, and Philippa swore she was blushing. "I can get you all somewhere safe for the night. But we have to hurry."

"Where's Shem and Sparrow?"

"Quite the names," the dancer remarked.

But Philippa hardly heard her. Shem had his sword out, fighting two soldiers, holding his ground but desperately looking for an escape. He wasn't as skilled in fighting as he was, say, reading, and it was showing.

Across from him, a soldier grabbed a crying child and hoisted them up by their arm. "It has the curse! It was writing with the paint!"

It. Not *her.*

Anger flared in Philippa's chest, her hands tingling with untapped power. Then, Sparrow appeared. Philippa reeled back, not wanting to be taken away when others needed help, but he leapt right over her head.

His boots were lethally silent in the chaos of the attack, and he slashed through two soldiers with daggers as long as his forearms. They fell silently to the ground. Moving like water through the shadows, Sparrow jumped at a soldier who was running toward him, used the soldier's neck as a stepping stone, and propelled himself over the next two who were already swinging their swords. They ran into one another, stunning themselves. He rolled across the street, slid through the soldier's legs who held the child, and yanked the soldier's decorative loincloth as he came to his feet. The soldier tripped over himself, face planting into the street with a crunch.

Sparrow appeared under the child as if it were nothing, catching her, and tucking her to his chest. His mask had been replaced. Feathers cascaded down his back as he swung madly at oncoming soldiers.

The haunting mask didn't scare the child, though, who clung to its feathers like her life depended on it.

They were going to kill that girl, for potentially being the scribe. Philippa's nails dug into her palms, drawing blood. Her entire body shook. She could see now how small she and Morgana had been when this fate befell them. How the soldiers could think to kill her without a second thought was *mad.*

"Ole, I need you." Her voice was stronger than she anticipated. She wiggled out of the dancer's grasp, who was trying to pull her down another street. More soldiers could be heard coming.

He stepped up beside her. "As you say."

"He needs help." she said.

"Understood." Ole cracked his knuckles, and flames appeared around his fists. The dancer gaped, but if anything she seemed to like finding this out about Ole. Shem had dislodged himself from the conflict, and was already shaking his head as he ran to her.

Shem grabbed Philippa's arm. "You can't fight through that. He'll catch up."

Philippa pushed his hand off of her. "He's saved me my entire life. Go with the dancer. *We'll* catch up."

She turned, not wanting to hear any more protests. Ole nodded at her. At that, they took off into the fray. Ole took the brunt of the soldiers and panicked performers, knocking them out of the way, or simply scaring them with the threat of his fire.

Soldiers poured into the courtyard, encircling the chaos.

Sparrow fought off two more adversaries, when his gaze suddenly locked onto Philippa. She could see it then. Whatever caused him to save her every time. The compulsion to get to her. He took a step towards her, leaving his back exposed.

It was enough.

A *crack* echoed through the courtyard as a whip tore into Sparrow's back. He gasped. Actually gasped. A sound so raw and unrestrained, so unlike him, that she knew how badly it hurt.

But he was coming to get her.

She whirled around, and screamed as she ducked out of the way of a swinging sword. Ole's flaming hand *caught* the blade, and it began to drip molten metal onto the street. The soldier screamed, and Ole hoisted him into the air, before bringing his head down onto the soldier's mask.

More cracks rang out, and tears pricked her eyes as she saw the whips tear back from Sparrow's body. He crouched over the child, shielding her, forcefully holding her hands together on his shoulder to cover where she'd been hanging onto him.

Her mind was racing. She wasn't a fighter. What could she do? How could she get them both out?

Blood danced around Sparrow as he fought one handed to keep soldiers from harming the girl with blades as the whips tore into his flesh.

A plan wasn't needed. She just had to go.

Ole threw a fireball at a soldier, sending him into a building in a burst of flames as Philippa took a step forward. A tinny clang came from under her foot, and she looked down, realizing she'd knocked over a can of face paint.

Instantly, she dropped to her knees, filling her palms with the blue paint. "Ole! I need a boost!"

She swiped her finger across her sandals and prayed she wanted it enough that it would work. Without hesitation, Ole grabbed her by the shoulders and threw her straight up into the air above the fight.

Wind gushed past her, her hair flying up around her, the air in her lungs whooshing out as she stared down at the blood and beauty below.

This is a very bad idea.

Then, she fell. Right on top of Sparrow. Her sandaled feet nearly bounced as she landed, as if the cobbled roads were plush and blanketed. The soldiers paused and stared down at her feet, which read in part, *soften.*

She grabbed hold of Sparrow, who barely seemed to register she was there. Her painted palms mingled with the crimson of his back, and she quickly took the child from his arms. A fireball burst past their heads as she grabbed underneath Sparrow's arm and began to drag him away.

The soldiers regained their composure quickly. Thankfully, Ole was giving them cover fire. Literally.

Sparrow was groaning inside his mask, but he kept a quick pace with her. Only, her feet were sluggish, like walking through mud.

She hopped on one foot, kicked off her sandals, and tore off as fast as she could, leaving her softened footwear behind.

The bustle of armor was at their backs, and she knew they didn't have much time. As they reached Ole, he took the child, and Sparrow made no protest as Ole scooped him up, too. Philippa waved him off, and used the paint on her hands to write on her arm, *speed.*

Her feet were suddenly barely touching the ground. She couldn't quite control it, and skirted directly into the toppled wagon of fireworks.

Skinned elbows dragging across the ground, another outfit from Sparrow ruined, she wiped the scribed paint off of her arm and reached the edge of the wagon.

Ole had reached Shem and the dancer.

Pushing exhaustion from the output of power, Philippa stared at the oncoming soldiers hazily.

She breathed deeply, inhaling the blood and paint and smoke from the scene, opening up a doorway inside of herself.

Her tattooed palm extended. Flames danced on her fingertips. Fuses lit and sparked.

"Stop hurting my friends."

The courtyard exploded in color.

CHAPTER FORTY-ONE ✧

There was no hiding their presence in the inner cities now. Through all the smoke and debris of the explosion, the only place they could go was down. Philippa's eyes watered horribly, the scent of the fireworks thick down her nose and throat. If not for the dancer coming back to drag her into the darkness, she probably wouldn't have been able to find her way out of the brawl.

Wiping her eyes, she tried not to think about the sludge they were walking through in the sewers. If the dancer could soil her gorgeous skirt and sully her bare feet, so could Philippa.

Shem offered her a hand to step up a lifted part of the sewer where the water ran off like a soiled waterfall. She took it, letting herself be hauled up against his chest. They hadn't had time to speak since she ran off to get Sparrow, effectively leaving him in the dancer's company. He didn't seem to mind, though, and like the rest of them was more grateful that they had a way out instead of questioning how.

The dancer held her blue torch high, sending indigo shadows across her and Ole at the front. "There's a bench to walk on just up ahead," she said quietly.

Philippa's mouth quirked. Surely no one could hear them down there.

Still, seeing the bench as they traveled down was like a beacon in the night. She couldn't help but rush forward to the front, taking the little girl from Ole, and passing the small form to the dancer who was already on the solid stone. The child had long since fallen asleep, head lolling to the side.

Philippa pressed her palms against the stone and pushed herself up.

Still hunched from the narrow sewer, Ole carefully shifted Sparrow from his back to his arms. Sparrow, his bird mask still obscuring his face, groaned faintly, clearly unconscious. The crimson stain soaking Ole's shoulders explained why.

Philippa held out her arms, and Ole positioned Sparrow against her so he didn't slide to the bench below. She strained against his weight, her arms hitched under his armpits, and couldn't imagine that someone hardly taller than her could weigh so much. But this close, she could feel that the black fabric was covering some kind of thick, almost armored material. Perhaps meant to be arrow proof or to deflect a few slices from daggers, but it wasn't enough to stop the lashes of bone laden whips from tearing right through.

Muscle and torn skin lay against her palms as she wrapped around his back. Her throat tightened. He survived poison, he could survive this. He had to.

Philippa's ears twitched as her mind welcomed a hazy, distant voice, whispering into the dark: *alive, alive, alive.*

At that moment, Sparrow inhaled sharply, but did not otherwise stir. Philippa leaned her head against his matted hair, letting the scent of his sweat and blood wash over her. Mixed in with the aroma of the ambush, she could smell salt and sea spray, as if he'd just been swimming and not trudged through a sewer.

Ole had to bend over even more once on the bench, but still offered his hands to carry Sparrow.

"I can take a turn," Philippa said, straining.

He shook his head. "He is keeping Panu safe. I will carry him."

Her eyes darted to the sack of sand Olekashan had tied around his neck to keep from soiling it in the dredges. She wouldn't take this from him. Loosening her grip, she allowed Sparrow's limp form to fall into Ole's arms, but he was moaning more, hands twitching.

She grabbed Ole's hand to stall him, before hovering over Sparrow's body. Gently, she tucked her hands underneath his head, fingers tangling in his blood soaked hair, and unclasped his mask. It was made of hollowed bone, but the weight of it nearly sent Philippa to her knees. That, or the sight of his battered face underneath.

He still wore his black coverings, only exposing his eyes, but horror burned through her. The feathers had hidden a huge gash across his shoulders and neck, all the way up to the side of his face. Fresh crimson blood flowed over the dried flakes that had already turned coppery in color.

She wanted to rip the fabric mask off of him, tear his hood away, to find out where the new blood was pouring from. But he hadn't trusted them enough to take it off in front of them. He would have to forgive her.

The dancer placed a hand on Philippa's shoulder. The feathers of his mask trembled in her shaking hands.

"Just another city block. Then we'll be safe for the night." she said.

Philippa grabbed Shem by the hand and practically drug him forward. Despite having survived Dagna's poison, she couldn't reason with herself that Sparrow would simply just survive again. If the dark, whining feeling inside her gut was right, then they didn't have all night.

Not much later, the dancer shoved the sewer cover off with surprising ease. One by one, they crawled out into the quiet street. Ole grunted as he managed to squeeze through the manhole. This part of Kamath was completely asleep for the night, no sign of performers or musicians anywhere.

At every little noise, even a whisper of her own feet on the ground, Philippa glanced over her shoulder, expecting soldiers to be hot on their heels. They never were.

If the queen was bent on finding the scribe, Philippa thought assassins would wait in every corner. Just like Sparrow had said, and if she'd listened to him better from the start, maybe he wouldn't be cut apart in Olekashan's arms.

A sudden dread curled in her stomach, almost making her stop in her tracks.

The Queen collects stories...

What if the queen had Philippa's life book?

Silence enveloped Philippa like a wet cloth on a fire, snuffing out any courage she had. Her fingers tingled in horrible expectation. The rulers of tread could be watching her every move, right now, waiting for her. A lion in the brush waiting for the prey to draw near enough to strike. What was it the dancer had said? That the queen made up a rumor that she wanted the crown?

The queen knew that she'd killed the Wahanar, but evidently hadn't mentioned the Visage. Maybe because if the queen had scribes of her own, she didn't want the public to know that they were creating monsters. Or… she didn't know how the Wahanar scouts died. Which meant she either had an informant, or Heru was willing to set aside her distaste for the rulers of Sapria in order to get Philippa's head.

Nothing she could come up with seemed more likely. And if they had Philippa's book, why not have a scribe alter her book, force her to walk until her feet bled, until she reached the palace?

There was no confirming that her life book was safe, but she drew upon what her mother taught her about life books. They were supposed to appear right where a baby was born, in the household or space where the child was. That way it would be safe, like a family heirloom. But during the Scribe Wars, that had changed.

For control, a sect of scribes altered the very magic they possessed. Now, life books did not appear when a baby was born, at least not on the continent of Sapria. They had to exist, otherwise the child would not, but as far as everyone knew now, life books simply appeared in the great libraries in Aresef.

According to her mother, when one was close to their own life book, they *felt* it. Philippa inhaled sharply, trying to focus her senses. She didn't know *what* a life book was supposed to feel like, but she certainly didn't feel different. Just exhausted.

Shem touched her shoulder, and she jumped. He smiled at her, rubbing her arm, before pulling her along to catch up with the rest of the group.

Quiet as mice, they followed the woman down completely unlit alleys, darkness swallowing them whole as she snuffed out her torch.

The dancer rounded a tall, thin building in a group of spindly homes, before they were met by a tall stone wall. Philippa ran her hand across the craggy protrusions, dust and pebbles falling free under her touch.

Shem was at her side, and leaned down, his breath warm at her ear. "She brought us to the wall separating Kamath from Aresef. Beyond these walls lies the palace and the great libraries."

Her skin prickled. Nothing about the woman made Philippa feel like this was a trap, but they certainly needed more information out of her.

Philippa nodded at Shem and squeezed his hand. The dancer ushered them over to a basement stairwell that was semi hidden by bushes and flowers. She produced a key from her skirts and opened the door.

They all quickly followed her into the darkness.

Philippa noticed the scent first. Cinnamon and ginger, floral scents that hung in the air as they gathered inside.

Light bloomed to life from Ole's free hand, revealing what appeared to be an apothecary or botanist's office. Unsealed face paint pots lay scattered across a nearby table, along with a curled wanted poster that bared a striking resemblance to Philippa. She swallowed her fear, pushing it down.

The dancer lit candles hurriedly, then unceremoniously shoved all of the items off of the wooden table, ushering Ole over.

"Lay him here. Then bathe."

Ole obeyed, laying Sparrow as gently as he could onto the table. Philippa followed, while Shem took in the entire room, entranced by all of the research that scattered the walls and floor. Every shelf was coated with materials and studies that he surely was itching to take a look at.

"We don't have time to bathe," Philippa protested.

The dancer leveled a glare at her as she gave Sparrow a once over. "You want to put infection in his wounds? Be my guest."

"Thank you for saving us, but I still don't know you." Philippa's voice was tight.

The woman's eyes searched hers, narrowing ever the slightest. Then, she sighed. "I don't have a name. Not anymore. Call me whatever you like, but you need to wash. I'll help you tend to him, but this little one needs to go home, too."

Philippa started. She had forgotten all about the child, which still rested neatly on the dancer's shoulder.

The dancer adjusted the little girl's weight in her arms. "The entire tower is yours to use. Bathing chambers are behind the stairs, two of them. Get cleaned up. I will take the child upstairs to bed until it is safe for her to go outside. When you're done, we'll clean up your friend."

She could only stare at Sparrow's unmoving form, the blood that now seeped onto the table below him. If this woman practiced medicine as she seemed to, then she wasn't worried about him dying. At least, not urgently.

With a resigned sigh, Philippa nodded. The dancer gave Ole a sultry glance, gesturing to the bathing chamber, before disappearing up the stairs with the child.

"Ole and I will share the first chamber, Miss Aporo," Shem offered, gently guiding her to the second door behind the stairs, "take your time."

Despite the grime, he cupped her face and stroked her cheek. Philippa felt tears burn at the back of her eyes. "They were singing about my family's death like it was beautiful."

"I know. I tried to warn you."

That he did. Leaning against his palm one last time, Philippa pushed open the bathing chamber door and locked herself inside.

CHAPTER FORTY-TWO ✧

Hot water sprang from the faucet like magic. There was no need to warm buckets over fires or burners, it simply leapt out of the pipe like fire from a dragon's mouth.

Philippa eased into the scalding water, letting it burn away the dust and grime from their travels. Bathing in rivers only every few days did not quite do the job, and she realized just how badly her clothes and hair had begun to smell from their journey. Sliding down the copper basin, she let her chin and lips delve underwater, singeing the tender flesh as if it would cleanse her thoughts as well.

Her fingers tangled through her curls, strands of hair being plucked free from her carelessness.

She lay here, in a warm bath, while Sparrow was lashed apart like meat on a butcher's block. While Morgana and Raff were in Levanta, worrying for her, undoubtedly scorned by superstition since her *grand* reveal. At the same time as Herunavira and Dagna sent Wahanar assassins after them, as Tazmireth's glass heart lay unbeating in her crystalline chest.

Water covered her head. She slid to the bottom of the deep basin, letting the warmth bury her. Hiding herself away in a chamber far from danger, from scrutiny. She allowed the pressure to choke her. To panic her. Even in the oasis, she remembered the dread of falling overboard and drowning. Despite living in a fishing town, Philippa refused to go on the boats. Would not wade past her waist. She could swim well enough, but fear was a funny thing. She let it consume her now. Let the panic flare within her, let her arms thrash in the basin. But even watery darkness could not spare her from her thoughts.

Worthless, worthless, worthless...

Her eyes squeezed shut so that she might not remember the waves rolling over her head, how decent it felt to be alone in the waves of the ocean, surrounded by the impossible silence of death. Then how life bringing hands flung her to a cold beach, how lips forced air into her lungs before slinking away when Morgana approached. She could see her father's face, all harsh lines and angles. The stoniness of his voice as he commanded her to write, to create, to *become.*

How obsessed he was to have a child who was powerful in the gift, and how badly her mother prayed at night that their children would be *normal.*

Water filled her mouth as she gasped for air. Philippa sprang up in the tub, splashing soapy water over the sides, her hands like claws along the edges.

I am not that little girl anymore, she told herself, teeth clenched. *I am not normal, and I am not nothing. They need you. Get up.*

Though her voice was strong, she wasn't sure that she believed herself. Before doubt crept in, she had to act while courage filled her. Quickly, she scrubbed the bar of soap over her entire body, foregoing the razor against her legs, and plunged under a second time to rinse herself.

When she stood, her hair clung past her breasts to her rib cage, curls reforming after the proper bath. Her lips smarted at seeing how dark her hair had become. The ashen color still bothered her. It reminded her all too much of the young girl who had lost everything.

Her eyes flicked to the shears on the stool beside Sparrow's mask. Her hands twitched, fingers curling. The hair could wait. For now.

Dressing quickly and tying back her hair with a ribbon, she headed for the basin door... and she hesitated. Her magic could heal Sparrow's wounds. It could be fast, as she'd learned in the festival, that even small scribing could be effective. She had to open herself up, like summoning a flame, and want it as much as she wanted anything before. By the stars, she wanted to heal him. He was harsh, and he was arrogant, but he had been saving her for her entire life. It was time to repay those favors. Perhaps that is why she lingered by the door, hands pressed against the wood, dressed in dancer's clothes that were too long for her. Or perhaps it was because she knew that if he had the choice, he wouldn't want her to lay hands on him at all. That in his crass demeanor, she knew that there was a barrier. They weren't friends. He followed her out of some perverse obligation.

She rested her forehead against the door, inhaling deeply. He would just have to forgive her. Absently, she reached behind herself and grabbed his mask. Glared at it. Looked back to the door.

Curling her fingers into fists, she pushed open the washroom door. The candles had dimmed low, wicks beginning to smoke at their bases. No matter. She didn't need light to write on him.

But, she would need *him,* and when she looked to the table, only blood and cloth lay there. Philippa whirled around, taking in the entirety of the room. Had someone broken in? Stolen his body?

The dancer appeared on the stairs. "He's in a room."

Philippa's shoulders relaxed. She nodded absentmindedly. Of course he would haul himself upstairs to get away from the rest of them. Maybe he disappeared into his portals, however he did so, just to hide away for a time. He didn't need her. No one did, really.

Philippa turned, starting to ease into a chair, when the dancer cleared her throat.

"He's asked for you."

The stairwell walls had been painted ornately, clearly by hand, in florals and clouds and animals of all shades. It was as if the home had been plucked from a storybook and laid to rest in reality. Philippa ran a finger over the walls, each groove and rise of paint telling a story.

"Thank you. For everything. I'm sorry about my attitude, earlier." Philippa said in a low voice as they strode up the stairs.

The dancer smiled at her, and Philippa was again amazed that someone could be so beautiful. "Forgiven. You're allowed to have an attitude, I suppose. Being an orphan of a people and all."

Her ears twitched at that. "How much do you know about scribes?"

Hand clenching a candle holder, the woman pursed her lips and shrugged. "Enough to know that I don't want you all dead. The queen is just spreading rumors that someone like you wants her throne. It's not right. You people just wanted to raise your families. But that queen doesn't have any children or hardly let her husband make public appearances, so what does she know about family?"

Though her voice hadn't risen or gotten an edge to it, there was a sour familiarity with the way she spoke about all of this. Philippa kept quiet for a moment as they climbed the tall staircase, legs aching.

"Why say I want her crown? How does she know I'm a scribe who's coming into Aresef at all?" Philippa asked.

The dancer paused, and leaned against the wall. "She has ears everywhere. She may be glad that the Scribe Wars ended, and that the scribes were put to death, but she's… fascinated by them. Wants to know everything that she can about them. Saying you're a threat to her makes it more likely a civilian or soldier wanting a promotion will bring you in under suspicion."

"But you knew that I would be there, at the festival. Like she did." Philippa couldn't keep the wavering out of her voice.

Across from her, the woman's face hardened. It only made her more striking. "I'm not selling you out to her. She's not the only one with spies."

Her eyes widened. "Are you… like my friend? Part of the c—"

"No cultist here, missy. Listen… you need to be careful. Whatever you want in Aresef, it's probably not worth your life, or your friend's. This queen is bent on something, and it can't be good. Anyone fascinated with a type of person as much as she is, cannot be trusted."

Philippa's lips drew into a tight line, but she nodded. She would be careful. She needed to be, for the part of her plan that she hadn't told anyone yet. The part that would likely make them want to turn back if she told them.

They'd reached the door where the dancer had said Sparrow had moved himself to. Philippa tried not to wince at the blood droplets on the floor, her hands clutching the strap of his mask that hung loosely from her fingers.

She met the dancer's gaze, firm and full of life and secrets. "I know that you said you don't have a name you go by anymore, but I'd really like to thank you personally. If you wish."

The woman swayed, a silent pendulum of grief and contemplation, her gaze fixed on the worn floorboards as if seeking answers in their ancient patterns. "My husband possessed a touch of your gift, missy." She finally murmured, her voice low. "Not as potent as the power that courses through your veins, but enough. Enough to bring joy to the children of our streets, making painted figures dance and twirl with an unseen hand. Enough to imbue medicine with a potency that defied understanding, healing wounds that refused to close. And through his gentle explorations, he unearthed a truth, something ancient and profound about the very essence of your powers. He discovered that the magic you wield isn't a rigid, unyielding force, bound by inflexible laws. No, he learned that every scribe can scribe differently. You, for instance, used paint to turn the tide of a battle in the streets. Yet, the old legends, the whispers passed down through generations, spoke only of ink and quill, of words etched onto parchment, as the sole means of scribing at all."

A soft, almost imperceptible breath escaped Philippa's lips. "You loved one of us."

The dancer's nod was curt, a sharp, decisive movement. "The queen found him."

"I'm so sorry—" Philippa began, her voice thick with empathy.

But the dancer raised a hand, a silent command that stilled Philippa's words. "She was captivated by his discovery. Utterly fascinated. She demanded his presence, his service in her opulent court, for what she termed 'research purposes.' He refused. He declared, with a quiet strength that contradicted his gentle nature, that he would rather embrace death than serve her. And so, in her fury, she unleashed hordes of soldiers into the streets, a relentless tide of steel and malice. They scoured every alley, every hovel, searching for his family, for leverage, for me. My husband, a man of unparalleled kindness and unwavering courage, offered himself before the queen and her soldiers in the very streets where he had brought so much joy. He promised to work for her, to bend his gift to her will, if only they would cease their relentless search. But it wasn't enough for her. He had committed the unforgivable sin of defying her, of turning her down the first time. And so, to punish his insolence, she demanded that he perform his powers in the streets for all to witness, to make a grand spectacle of his humiliation. Does that sound familiar?"

Philippa didn't know how this woman, this nameless dancer, could possibly know the torment she had endured in Levanta, the public shaming, the ostracization that followed a mere display of her power. She could only nod, a silent acknowledgment of the shared agony. One show of power, and then the bitter taste of being cast out by all.

The woman's hand settled on Philippa's shoulder, a firm, comforting squeeze. "So he gave her a demonstration. He took paint from our old shop, the very paints he used to make his whimsical figures dance, and with them, he wrote on a stone. A simple stone, but one imbued with a profound purpose. He then buried it deep within the earth, in the very heart of the art district."

"What did he do?" Philippa asked, her voice barely a whisper, a sudden chill tracing its way down her spine.

"He took away my name," the dancer explained, her voice devoid of a trace of self pity, only a quiet, resolute strength. "Buried it underneath the city, made it utterly unsearchable, unreadable, even in my life book. He erased my name so no one could ever find out who I was ever again. The queen would never be able to even remember he *had* someone to harm, someone to use against him."

Philippa gaped, her mind struggling to comprehend the magnitude of such a sacrifice. "You… you truly have no name. You do not even know it."

The woman nodded, a small, knowing smile playing on her lips. "And so I am no one but a friend. The queen, though she knew he had hidden *something* from her, something profound and significant, was nevertheless impressed by the sheer raw power of his display. Yet, her spite, her insatiable need for control, remained. She ordered that he be strung up in the morning for *theft* – the theft of her power, the theft of her authority, the theft of a knowledge she desperately craved."

Philippa brought a hand to her mouth, a silent gasp escaping her lips. Stars above, what a tragedy.

"So," the dancer continued, her gaze softening, "I try to honor my husband's people. He protected me, his final act an enduring shield against her wrath. And now, I want to protect his kin, too. That's all I have left of him, the memory of his kindness, the legacy of his courage."

Philippa's heart ached, a profound sorrow swelling within her for the dancer. To lose her husband, the very foundation of her world, to lose her home, her sense of belonging, and then, most devastatingly, to lose who she was, her very identity… It sounded like the loneliest existence imaginable. Yet, Philippa witnessed the unwavering strength in the woman's voice, the proud squareness of her shoulders, the resolute set of her jaw. She did not let herself feel worthless or forgotten. She had forged something new from the ashes of her past. She had found meaning in the very act of living, of enduring, of protecting.

Philippa reached out, taking the dancer's hand, her grip firm and resolute. "I *have* to go into Aresef. Even if it's risky. People are counting on me."

The dancer smiled, a genuine warmth radiating from her eyes. "You sound so very much like him."

"And I promise you," Philippa's voice, though thin and wavering, held a fierce conviction that surprised even herself. "I will find your book. I will return your name to you, whole and untouched."

The woman, a wisp of a figure against the flickering candlelight, slowly shook her head, her grip loosening on Philippa's hand. A faint smile, tinged with an old sadness, graced her lips. "I don't require repayment, missy. This moment brings me peace. Do not make so many promises. They are like unruly children; they will catch up with you, demanding attention and leaving chaos in their wake."

"But I *can* do it." Philippa insisted, her voice gaining strength, a spark igniting in her weary eyes. The idea of restoring something so profoundly lost, of righting a wrong, resonated deep within her. It felt like part of her mission, a tangible way to mend a broken world.

Suddenly, the woman was a hair's breadth from Philippa's face, her eyes narrowed to piercing slits, reflecting the dancing candle flame. Her slender frame seemed to expand, eclipsing Philippa's, casting her in a sudden, unsettling shadow.

"Ability does not mean you *should.*" The woman's voice was a low, resonant hum that vibrated through Philippa's bones. "Giving to others, even with the noblest of intentions, will not give you what you truly seek. It is a hollow well, perpetually thirsting."

"You don't know what I seek." Philippa retorted, a defensive heat rising to her cheeks. She felt exposed, as if the woman could see the deepest, most hidden corners of her soul.

The woman slowly backed away, the oppressive closeness receding, allowing Philippa to breathe again. Her chest rose and fell steadily, a testament to an inner calm that belied the intensity of their exchange. The candle flame, held aloft in her hand, wavered slightly, a subtle tremor that betrayed a hidden vulnerability.

"You're not so mysterious, child. Your soul, though cloaked in fierce independence, sings a familiar tune. Collecting debts and other lost souls, like so many discarded treasures, to fill your own emptiness. Look me in the eye and tell me what you seek is not a sense of meaning, of purpose? A quiet, aching yearning for belonging that you believe others can provide?"

Philippa's jaw tightened, a knot of resistance forming in her throat. Her eyes were burning, hot with a mixture of frustration and a dawning, unwelcome recognition. Her heart raced a frantic drum against her ribs. So much for all the courage she'd painstakingly mustered in the basin. It felt as if the woman had stripped her bare, leaving her vulnerable and exposed.

Turning to descend the creaking, shadowed stairs, the dancer paused, looking over her shoulder at Philippa. The candlelight cast long, shifting shadows that distorted her features, making her seem ancient and ephemeral. "Others cannot give you what you seek, Philippa." she said, her voice a soft, echoing whisper that seemed to hang in the air long after she was gone. "Remember that. The answer you crave lies not in what you collect from the world, but in what you cultivate within yourself."

Then, with a final, lingering gaze, she disappeared into the darkness below, leaving Philippa alone with the flickering candle and the profound, unsettling weight of her words.

CHAPTER FORTY-THREE ✦

Her knock was unanswered, but that wasn't a *no* either. Trembling, her fingers wrapped around the knob and turned, the door responding with a creak. She set his mask by the door.

Philippa wasn't sure what she expected, but it wasn't the scene before her.

Lanterns illuminated the room. The walls were covered in chalky paintings, in the same style as the stairwell and hallway. Foxes, horses, little figures in flowing clothes, all painted with few delicate lines. In the center of the room, Sparrow was sitting on the bed, his head in his hands, which were clutched in his hair as if it were all that was keeping him together.

His breathing was so ragged. Had he even noticed she'd come in?

But that was a silly question. The way his breathing evened out, the gentle incline of his head, waiting for her to speak. He knew.

She let the door close with a soft click. "The dancer said you asked for me?"

Blonde locks fell over his face as his shoulders shook with effort. "But you would have come anyway."

It wasn't a question. "You were in my head. In the tub."

Sparrow groaned.

"That's why you called for me. You thought I was going to—"

He lifted his face from his hands, only to stare forward, letting the lantern light cast odd shadows across his face. "You were thinking about it. I keep you alive. That's my job."

Philippa's hands shook slightly. "Let me try to help you."

To her surprise, he didn't deny her request. Her hands shook slightly as she walked across the small room. He'd given her no real reason to be scared of him, but the last time they were this close, she'd been dying… and he'd *died.*

The dress she'd gotten from the bathroom whispered across the floorboards, pooling around her feet as she paused at his side. Her throat and eyes stung at the sight of his back. The blood had stopped, but his flesh was in ribbons. Flaps of skin and muscle were flayed open, and with every breath, his back seemed to shudder. He made no move to get away from her, and so she stretched out her hands and laid them on his shoulders. His body tensed under her touch, trembling, as if even the slightest pressure was agony.

"I knew you had a bigger heart than you let on." she whispered. He only huffed in response. "Thank you for saving the child."

Sparrow's head shifted, but he didn't look at her. "You didn't need to pull the arrows from me before, and you don't need to heal me now. I'll live."

"Yet you called for me." she said, voice tight. He sighed and she knew that she'd won the argument. "You're hurting. I can help. That's all that matters."

Removing her hands, she scanned the room for anything she could use to write on him with. There was a barren nightstand, which revealed only dust and a few children's toys when she pulled open the drawer. Other than that, the room was rather empty. She sighed.

She turned to tell him that she would go look for material, but she froze. His hands no longer cradled his face, but rather were working on unclasping a layer of his dark clothing on his chest. Underneath a buckle, with a swift flick of his fingers, he pulled a tiny glass vial. He offered it up in his outstretched palm, green eyes intent on her. It didn't even register to Philippa that he'd been hiding ink this entire time, not when his face was bare for her to see. It was all she *could* see.

His cowl and cover had been removed. It was like seeing him for the first time. Blood and dirt caked against his ashen skin, but it didn't take away from his presence. Everything about him told a story; from the slope of his high cheekbones, the anguished set of his jaw, to the bags and kohl that shadowed his ever intense eyes. As she neared, taking the vial from his warm hands, she saw the jagged scar that ran from the underside of his jaw, up his chin, that ended in a slash that pulled his top lip up slightly.

An assassin. A cultist. A son of Soffer.

He really is one of us, her thoughts raced, *of my people.*

Are you really so surprised?

The voice startled her. She nearly took a step back, but when she looked at him, his eyes seemed elsewhere. Absent. Could he hear her, but not realize that she heard him sometimes, too?

She cleared her throat. "Thank you. For this."

"Thank you for wanting to." he said, which surprised her. She couldn't think of a time he'd ever been thankful. Then again, she hadn't really done anything *for* him before.

"Take off your shirt." she said gently.

In an instant, he obeyed, unclasping and untying so many layers that kept his dark suit together that she wondered how he might ever get any rest. Perhaps he did not. When the last buckle came free, he pulled the covering over his head, wincing and groaning.

Her heart ached for him. This man hadn't complained about being shot with poison, and yet, this whipping was making him desperate.

Rounding to the other side of the bed, her light skirts flowed over her legs as she settled behind him. She pulled the cork with her teeth, setting it aside on his pillow. The smell hit her instantly.

Inside the vial, the scent of the sea and lavender filled every crevice, every crack of glass. It wasn't ink inside, not really, but rather crushed lavender and water, perhaps mixed with an oil or another binding agent. Tears pricked her eyes. This was fresh and homemade. Slowly, her eyes drug to where he'd discarded his shirt, and found a bundle of half plucked lavender inside a pocket.

He'd bought the lavender from the shop. It wasn't a question of for *whom.*

Sparrow would only grow agitated if she mentioned it, so she bit down her thoughts and swallowed the lump in her throat.

The lavender ink was cool against her fingertips as she poured it on, dribbling over her finger and dripping onto the bed sheets. Quickly, she pressed it against the base of his neck and closed her eyes. He would live through this, but she didn't want him to be in pain anymore.

She wanted to thank him for everything he had ever done for her. For saving the child. For saving her, many times.

And so, she wrote the word that would not have saved Elodie, but could close the gashes in his skin.

Heal.

Heal.

Heal.

She rewrote it across every tear and wound, watching the muscle slowly begin to stitch itself back together. The process was slow, and he sharply inhaled every time a wound began to close. He needed a distraction.

"So," she began, "it has been you saving me since I was small."

Sparrow groaned in what sounded like agreement.

Philippa chewed on the inside of her cheek. "When I arrived in Levanta, you saved me from drowning. Then, there was the house fire. And the bandits. Of course, every time since then. But... there were other times, too? When I wasn't going to die, you were there."

He made a noncommittal sound. "I only have to keep you from dying."

Have to, he'd said. A commitment was there, some promise or obligation. She tucked that piece of information away for later.

Her chest constricted as she healed another opening, and built up the courage to ask what she'd suspected was the truth.

"But there were other times. When you didn't have to. I'm sure you know, but I was seeing a man in Levanta for some time. We were so young, and I... I just wanted someone to want me. He'd snuck in one night when Morgana was out. Do you know this story?" Her voice waned, and she watched the words on his back grow increasingly shakier as she spoke.

Sparrow turned, looked at her. His eyes were dark and his jaw feathered.

"I do."

"He was going to kill me that night?" she asked.

"No. But he was hurting you," his voice was thick, and he shrugged as if it explained everything.

Philippa felt like someone had struck her in the gut. He quickly averted his eyes from her to stare at the floor again. He may not have wanted to have this conversation, but she needed it. "Something compels you to keep me from death, but I suppose I just thought you hated me. That tells me that I was wrong."

His voice was no more than a whisper when he spoke. "I can hate someone and still not wish them harm."

So simple and true. He twitched under her fingers as she passed over an old scar that had risen from her healing. She could promise to try and help him, but the dancer's words twisted around in her mind. There had been so many that she'd made, and could she really make good on any?

Her fingers trailed over the cords of muscle in his back, the tension that had seemingly never been massaged out. A body made of strain and torture.

As she dipped her head to pour more lavender ink onto a fingertip, a spiral of black caught her eye. The air seemed to go stale. She dragged her eyes back to where she'd been writing on him. As flesh stitched itself back together, her own ink faded, revealing the intricate inked patterns, spiraling and looping across his skin. These weren't simply tattoos. They glimmered faintly in the firelight, alive with a magic she could feel in her bones. Her fingers hovered over the markings.

There was a time, not so long ago, when scribes would write onto others. Turn the tide of their choices in favor of those holding the quill.

She stared at his back. A time not so long ago, indeed.

"These… These are alters," she whispered.

Sparrow shifted slightly, wincing as her hand brushed his shoulder. "Don't." he said, his voice rough but steady. "Leave it."

But she couldn't. Her eyes darted over the patterns, tracing their meaning like threads in a tapestry. The words etched into him, the binding magic woven into his very being. They all pointed to one undeniable truth. It was suddenly as if she were back in the Wahanar camp, her first day arriving, watching the elder carve tattoos into a man's back. The way memories that she knew weren't hers had flooded her mind.

She saw them now.

Hands forcefully holding a boy to a burning slab of stone, fire cascading around the binding site as monsters bellowed in the distance. A bite of metal into his flesh as his back was written upon, altering his life. Binding him. Trapping him.

Her voice broke as she whispered, "these were written to tie you… to me."

Sparrow said nothing. His silence only made the realization hit harder. He'd wanted her to know. That's why he called for her.

"You wouldn't have believed me before…" he cut himself off. He knew that was a lie once he'd said it. She would've believed him. Would've wanted to help him. Which is why he had said nothing.

Her hands clenched into fists at her side. "How long have you known?"

He stood, turning away from her to find his discarded shirt. As if it would cover anything now. "Long enough."

His answer was curt, but it carried a weight that made her heart ache. She hurried off the bed, moved to face him, her green eyes blazing with equal parts anger and guilt.

"Who did this to you?"

For a moment, he didn't respond. Then, he turned his mirthless eyes to hers, unflinching. "Your father."

The ground beneath her feet seemed to shift. "What?" She breathed. "No. That's not… he's dead. He couldn't have—"

"He could. And he did," Sparrow said, his voice calm but filled with resignation, maybe even bitterness. "When the monsters came to Soffer, he thought it would be clever to tie my life to yours."

In the pause he took, her mind spun. Her father wasn't with them when they tried to escape Soffer. Her mother had been alone in trying to get her and Morgana out. A memory of acrid smoke filled Philippa's nostrils as she pictured herself in Vaelith's mind, watching the glimpse of time when Vaelith had seen her father. Philippa, Morgana, and their mother had never known where he'd gone when the attack started. In his absence, he'd done this.

Philippa's fingers clawed through her wet hair. Why did he want to protect her when he thought she was so *worthless*? Why condemn another to this existence?

Sparrow reached for her almost consolingly, but stopped before he made contact. Philippa thought at first it was because he thought she was poisonous, like her father, but the way Sparrow looked at his own hands made her realize that it was quite the opposite.

The assassin before Philippa hardened his voice and clenched his fists. "I don't know if he saw it as protection or punishment. But either way, it's done."

She stared at him, horror creeping into her expression. "This is why you're always there. The execution. Following me, before I even knew it."

"I didn't have a choice." Sparrow's voice was quiet now, eyes darkening. "Every time you're in danger, it pulls me back. Every time you wander too far, it drags me along."

"Why tell me this *now*? You've hidden it all this time. Were you working with my father? Are you of the sect of scribes that wanted to rule? Did he intend for you to keep me safe until they could see if I had any worth to their cause?" She charged at him, jabbing a finger to his chest, before recoiling, as if this would be the moment he abducted her. Half of her expected an evil smile to creep across his face, for his scar to suddenly make him ugly, for the dark truth to come out.

"I was a child when Soffer burned, same as you," he deflated. "I did not work for Titus Aporo. I ran to him for help. Instead, this. I am not your guardian, Philippa, I am your leash."

The words struck her like a blow. She stepped back, her mind racing. As a child, they were taught about altering other's stories, but she'd never seen it. Until now, she did not know what it could do to someone.

"I am telling you," he continued, "because you are set on going into

Aresef. Into the mouth of the beast that wishes you dead. So if things go awry, I will pull you out. It will not be up to me."

Something inside her hardened. "I don't want you getting yourself killed over this. Have you just accepted this? We could have been fighting it—"

He was suddenly all harsh lines and sharp angles, nothing soft left about him. He laughed, a hollow, bitter sound. "You speak so foolishly about our people, our practices."

Her hands trembled. "This isn't fair. It's not right. You shouldn't have to live like this!"

"Fairness doesn't matter." Sparrow interrupted. His voice was sharper now, but not cruel. Just tired. "What's done is done. I was a fool for trying to get you to turn back, to want you to understand. The only thing that matters is keeping you alive. Whether I want to or not."

The room felt cold and sterile. A numbness crept up her arms as she absently reached again for the vial, to continue to wrap up his wounds.

He brushed her away. "Give it a night and it'll close on its own."

She pressed a palm to her forehead, trying fervently to calm herself down. "I don't understand that. I don't understand *this.* Maybe it makes me a fool. But how does being bound to me enslave you so? How does it mean that you'll heal?"

He looked at her like she'd stabbed him. "Enough of this. I was a fool for thinking you'd turn back if I told you. Give me my mask."

Philippa lunged for it almost instinctually. She crushed it to her chest so he couldn't grab it. "You're not disappearing tonight."

His gaze narrowed, and for the first time, she thought the scar on his face marred his appearance. As he sneered, it pulled against his lips, creating the animal underneath he'd been warning her about. He said nothing, and moved all of an inch.

"Sparrow. I don't want you to keep doing this. I want to free you. Maybe my naivety of all this makes me a fool, but I don't want you getting yourself killed protecting me."

"That's rich."

Her ears tingled. "Excuse me?"

"Give me my mask."

"Not if you're just going to get yourself killed over me." she countered.

He moved so fast that all she had time to notice was the glint of a blade being pulled. Sparrow's dagger was in his shaking fist, his emerald gaze wide with fury.

"Don't you understand?" His voice was a shadow, a curling wisp of smoke that barely registered in the quiet of the room. "Healing me won't help, Philippa Aporo. Our people were very thorough. So, don't worry about me dying." He took a step towards her and the blade flashed. He shoved the hilt into her palm. "Try it."

"No."

He took her wrist with surprising gentleness, but in her spiking fear she let herself be guided. His hand directed the blade right under his neck, at his collarbone, pressing against his flesh.

Philippa ripped her hand away. He caught the falling blade. "I will not hurt you!"

Sparrow's chest rose and fell rapidly. The dagger shook in his fist. In a quick movement, he swung it around and drove it straight into his stomach.

She nearly screamed, but blood did not pour. His wrist was tremoring, as if a giant were holding him back. He drew the blade back again, pulling it towards himself, and it was then she noticed the faint glow from his back and shoulders. The alter was stopping him.

Tears pricked his eyes as he turned over her palm, his hands hot, and placed his weapon back into her hand. "Do not worry about me in all of this. Because I am altered to forever keep you alive. And. So. I. Can't. Die."

His smile was wry as tears began to well in his haunted eyes. He gestured vaguely to himself with one hand, the other still cradling hers. "All of this, to save Philippa Aporo."

It was all too much. She let the weapon clatter to the floor and put distance between them. All she wanted to do was curl up and hide. To disappear. He remained silent as she lifted his mask up before her, and she let her back hit the wall, before sliding to sit on the cold floor.

As her forehead came to rest on the cool inside of his mask, she opened her eyes, and stared through the slits. Inscribed words were written in several languages all around the inside of the mask. Commands. Portal guides. Other instructions she couldn't understand.

The Cult of Scribes doing. The mask helped him fall through the world and reappear around her. It gave him freedom, she realized. He was pulled to her when she was in danger, but other than that, he could fall through the world and potentially live some semblance of a life.

She couldn't imagine that he had a family waiting for him with how often he was getting pulled away.

Her stomach felt hollow.

He told her this because he didn't want to get hurt. He didn't want to be ripped apart for her sake.

Pulling away, she let the feathery mask fall to the wooden floors. Her throat tightened, and for a long moment, she couldn't speak. She stared at him, at the weight he carried in silence, and something inside her hardened.

"No." she said softly, but there was an edge to her voice.

Sparrow frowned, took a step closer. Cocked his head to the side in question, blonde waves falling over his shoulder.

"No." she repeated, meeting his gaze. She forced herself to her feet, to step closer to him. "You might not have a choice, but I do. When we get to Aresef, I will find your book."

His eyes glinted, just for a moment as he considered it. He knew what she was implying. "We don't even know if it's there."

"Then after."

"No."

"Why not?"

He grimaced. "I'm not supposed to tell you anything that could unbind me from you."

Philippa clawed her hair. "I don't know why my father did this to you—"

"Because you are worth so very much." Sparrow cut her off with a surprising softness that only made her entranced by the tears that still sat in his eyes.

Philippa grimaced. Her fingers curled and uncurled, fighting for purchase in the conversation. She filed away what he'd said and continued. "I'm going to find a way to undo this. To set you free. I don't care what it takes." Philippa clenched her teeth. "Even if I have to rewrite the entire library, I'll do it. You don't deserve this."

He looked away, his expression unreadable. For a moment, the silence stretched between them.

Finally, he said, "right. Sure you will."

But she saw the flicker of something in his eyes. Hope, or maybe the fear of it, and she held onto that. "I will fix this, Sparrow," she said firmly, "I swear it."

He didn't respond, but the tension in his shoulders eased every so slightly. Silently, he sat on the floor, resting his back against the bed. She joined him without a word. This was all so *much.* Were all life stories this complicated?

Even if he were bound to her, to keep her alive, she had to try with him. He wasn't some heaven sent savior, and he wasn't an anomaly. He was a person. Someone who had lost everything like she had, and more.

He flipped his dagger in his palm. Over. And over. And over.

Philippa reached out and snagged his wrist, which made him go rigid. As tenderly as she could manage, she weaseled her fingers into his palm and wrenched his grip free of the blade. Sparrow let her have it. She held it up to her eyes, which still stung from watching him try to stab himself, and she grimaced. Blades did awful things. But words could, too. She let the dagger fall to the floor with a heavy *twang.*

She kept her eyes forward, as his were, as if the paintings on the walls were the most interesting things they'd ever seen. She thought again of how hard he'd tried to use the blade on himself. At the sheer willingness he had to do it.

Her throat felt swollen. "You weren't in my head at all in the bathing chamber, were you?"

Out of the corner of her eye, she saw his thick eyelashes flutter. His breathing was strained, and she wanted so very badly to look at him. But that would drive him further into silence.

"I was not."

She gestured to the discarded blade. "That's how you knew what I was thinking. Because you… you think similarly, too. Sometimes."

He gave a stiff nod.

She knew that this moment had changed something between them, had seen the burden he carried, and was now determined to share it. She could start by being his friend.

"I'm sorry you feel this way." she said.

Sparrow laughed bitterly. "You speak like you've overcome it yourself. You haven't. That much I can see inside your head."

A breeze from the open window caused a candle to shudder against the wall, and they both jumped. Ah, so he could be distracted. Philippa glanced down and smiled faintly when she realized that he'd stuck his arm out to block her from the phantom danger of the night air. But her smile faded. He did not want his arm to reach out to protect her.

Instead of drawing attention to it, she cleared her throat and finally looked at him. "You confuse me."

Sparrow's curls bounced as he shook his head with a devilish smirk. It was just another mask, Philippa thought, to act half crazed and impish when his real mask was unavailable. It was a way to hide the pain. She absently touched her own lips, knowing she wore a smile like her own facade.

Then, he looked at her. Really looked at her. His lips were tight, but his eyes were open, and for the first time, it felt like he was really speaking to her. His voice sounded like when she'd thought he was a dream in the caves. "I am not meant to make sense to you. But I do believe you are going to try and unravel me whether I want you to or not."

Philippa rolled her eyes and settled her head on the bed behind them. "You know me so well. It's only fair I get to know you, too. Sparrow, you do not want to hear it, but I want to help you. I really do."

His shoulder shifted to rest against hers. An unspoken understanding passed between them. They were in this together, even though they were both strangers and companions at the same time, and they needed each other to fix their problems.

Sparrow groaned inwardly. "I believe you."

Philippa smiled then, a soft, tired one. But she trembled.

Can I make good on this?

CHAPTER FORTY-FOUR ✧

When the first rays of sunlight crept into the room, she was already awake. Her thumbs drummed absently on her chest, eyes wide and tired. Sleep had eluded her again, her thoughts wild and frantic about what today would bring. A gnawing anxiety had taken root in her stomach, a cold knot tightening with each passing moment. Every rustle of the leaves outside, every distant bird call, seemed to amplify her unease. She longed for the solace of deep slumber, but the darkness held no comfort; only a constant replay of her conversation with Sparrow.

Philippa had left him shortly after their brief admissions to each other. She wanted to stay, to talk, but he only continued to stare at the wall and hum a tune she didn't know. When she'd gotten up to leave, she'd told him to sleep well.

"If you're near, I won't be sleeping."

That's all he'd said as she closed the door. She wondered if he knew that she wouldn't be sleeping, either.

Shaking away the thought, Philippa flung her legs over the side of the bed. Squeezed her toes into the boots the dancer had provided with a curl of her lip. *Soon,* she promised herself, *I will bury my bare feet in the sand again.*

Downstairs, everyone was already standing, ready to go. Ole was hunched over a small hand mirror, expression drawn. Philippa rolled her shoulders and narrowed her eyes. In the reflection of the glass, she caught the orange of a flickering flame. Her lips quirked into a soft smile when she realized he was checking in on Panu.

A throat cleared. She turned, finding Shem standing by the table, which had been cleared of any remains of Sparrow's blood.

The assassin cultist was notably absent.

Shem unfurled a map, waving Philippa over. The dancer hovered nearby, wringing her hands nervously. When Philippa got close, she saw why. The map had been hand painted, and it was like nothing she'd ever seen before. Colors and notes everywhere, each corner covered in pastel, like a fairy tale book come to life on paper. Philippa put a hand on the dancer's shoulder and squeezed reassuringly. Shem was careful, placing small stones on each corner to hold it open.

"It's not a long journey now, but…" his voice trailed off.

"Shem Tetra, are you at a loss for words?" she asked, trying to keep her voice light.

He gave her a wan smile. "Much of the time around you."

Then he schooled his features and called Ole over. The chief covered the glass with both of his hands, and with soft flames coming to life, he squeezed the small portal until it became grains of sand one more, softly piling into the bag on his lap. As he stood, he bent his head and joined them over the map. The dancer wiggled her fingers at him, her brow lifted suggestively. Ole only smiled.

Shem traced a path with his finger along the roadway. Through the gates that connected this city to Aresef, and along the main road until they reached a courtyard.

"We'll continue until the road curves, that's on purpose. Everything here is laid out in spirals and circles," Shem explained, his finger hovering so as to not disturb the pastels.

He then lingered over a fountain at the center of the courtyard. His eyes flicked up to meet Philippa's, and she understood what all the other buildings surrounding it were. The libraries.

"The palace is across the inner city, north of the fountain, straight up the Great Stair. The libraries are in the eastern spiral. Once we're there, you'll have to tell us which one Panu's book is in. I can get us an entry."

She nodded along, shifting her weight. "I know which library Panu's book is in."

All eyes locked onto hers.

Philippa adjusted the belt, her loose trousers from the dancer swaying as she twisted about uncomfortably. "If the queen has had scribes under her thumb, then at some point they've gone in. Whichever library they managed to open for her, that's where it will be."

Shem swallowed. "That would be the Great Library."

Her heart sank to her toes. Of course it was. If Queen Aura was as greedy as she sounded, then it made sense she would go there. The Great Library was said to house the most stories, the most books and of course, the inner sanctum. Which is exactly where Philippa intended to go.

"You're all in for a treat," the dancer said with a sigh, "you'll be glad if you're quick. But take extra clothes before you leave. I'm guessing you won't be coming back anywhere near Kamath once you're done there."

Philippa's chest tightened. "I'm sorry. I wish we could come back to thank you."

The dancer smiled brightly, her plump lips the color of red wine. "Believe me, I don't need you coming back here with all of your trouble. But it would be thanks enough if I could tell my associates that there is still a scribe with a good heart in Sapria."

Shem groaned and shook his head sharply. Philippa just rolled her eyes and grasped the dancer's shoulder. "Your friends aren't of the Cult of Sparrows, right?"

"I already told you that they weren't. Besides, your friend is one of them. Why would I need to tell them what they likely already know?"

Philippa's ears twitched. "Why do you want to tell them?"

The dancer leaned back on her work table, her fingers tracing designs onto her thigh absently. "Because not everyone wishes things to stay the same. And knowing that a scribe is willing to fight would mean a great deal to those of us who are tired of being stepped on."

It was a gamble, giving this woman permission to share about Philippa's existence. But then again, she could tell them whatever she wanted and Philippa would never know. Inhaling, Philippa nodded slowly toward the dancer.

"But you cannot say I am willing to fight. I'm not a fighter," Philippa said sternly, "I don't want to be involved with any of this after today."

The woman twirled a lock of her hair and nodded. "I won't say you're a fighter. But you are taking a stand. That may be enough to inspire people. Now, you best get going. The gates are always crowded in the mornings, and I must return the girl to her family."

With the gracefulness of a performer, the dancer began to glide out of the room. Philippa wasn't sure what came over her, but she reached out and grabbed the woman by the arm. Ole grunted in surprise, and maybe a bit of pride.

The dancer's ethereal eyes settled on Philippa with surprise.

"Please. Tell me what to call you, and what to call your friends. Then, I'll give you permission to tell them what you want about me."

In a motherly way, the dancer placed her hand over Philippa's and squeezed. She then leaned into Philippa's ear to whisper. "You can call me Ballerina, if you need a title. My associates will know what it means. As for what to call them, simply call them Silvers."

At that, Ballerina removed Philippa's hand from her arm and sauntered out of the room.

Guards stood watch when the gates opened in the morning, but they took note of no one in particular as the crowds on both sides rolled through. Even if their eyes seemed lazy, Philippa knew they had to be on alert after the festival incident. There was no way that they would be so dull as to just let her waltz into the Great Library.

All around them, there were people trying to push their way through the gates. Many were merchants, others performers, some scholars - who Shem ducked his head around - and every sort in between. Philippa and her traveling party were dressed in clothes the dancer had left over from herself and her husband.

Philippa begrudgingly wore a light pair of boots, with a simple tunic top and loose trousers. Shem had just cleaned his old clothes in the basin, unwilling to give up the tunic that had been on all of his travels. Philippa fought a smile as she remembered how the dancer smiled having dressed Ole in her husband's old clothes. Surprisingly, they fit him, if not a little tight. The dancer did not seem to mind at all. Ole had indulged her, though he didn't really respond anytime she gave him a suggestive glance.

As they moved like cattle through the gates, Philippa felt a shiver run down her spine. This was Aresef, the great city of Sapria, where rulers were born and decrees were made. Where her people once ruled, once took note of all the goings on of the world, before things changed.

It wasn't very long before there was a breath at her back, and she knew Sparrow had caught up with them. Wherever he'd gone before now, he didn't share, and she hadn't expected him to. Her gut twisted as she pondered over the fact that she knew he would be back, though not his choice.

They walked in silence, as if it would help take the weight off her shoulders, somehow. Before long, they had entered the main courtyard that Shem had described. She glanced at him, his hand fiddling in his pocket. His eyes were roaming everywhere, jaw feathering, clearly on edge. Gently, she reached for his hand, but stopped. Her breath caught as she heard the bubbling of the fountain they were to meet at as the crowds departed in several other directions.

Sunlight filtered through carved golden latticework and broad leafed palms, casting patterned shadows on burnished stone. In the center lay the vast obsidian fountain that rose in tiers like a stepped pyramid, each level overflowing with crystalline water that shimmered with traces of alchemical minerals, pooling into a basin like a coiled serpent. The air was thick with the scent of sun warmed orchids and incense that curled from braziers like jackal-headed beasts.

Four broad sandstone paths, inlaid with mosaics of sapphire, jade, and sunstone, led away from the fountain toward silent monoliths of knowledge: the libraries. Their doors were sealed with bronze plates inscribed in forgotten script.

It amazed Philippa that these once stood open to all, and now they sat in wrapped creeping vines, guarded by sentinel statues of the old scribes with eyes that watched unblinkingly.

Opposite the libraries, a monumental stairway ascended like the backbone of the world, flanked by colonnades etched with seemingly celestial glyphs. At its peak rose the palace, an immense structure of gold veined stone and lapis domes, where banners of deep crimson fluttered in the breeze, bearing a sigil of a snake swallowing a single glyph: *knowledge.* The courtyard pulsed with quiet reverence, its grandeur both awe inspiring and foreboding; an echo of a once living belief system that now lingered like a ghost in the bones of the city.

She blinked several times. Tears threatened to fall at the sheer reverence she had for this place. She didn't know what she expected to feel when she arrived, but there was a sense of ancient gratitude that settled in her fingertips, that begged to run over every crevice, every set of stone. It was meant to be a place of beauty and knowledge. Now it sat quietly, caged and guarded against those who wanted to take what was inside.

Philippa stood at the head of their party, staring straight forward. The air was thick with heat, and the perfumed blossoms flitted down from their perches when the breeze blew between columns. This was it. The crux of her journey, the solution to all that had gone wrong.

Her boots struck the pavers that were glittering with stones and minerals, which pulsed faintly under her feet. She followed the curling path, which was not designed for speed, but for reverence, heeding her instincts on where to go.

There were no guards in the courtyard. Why would there be?

No one was left alive who could enter here, and no one was stupid enough to do what they were doing.

The moment her foot touched an offshoot of the path, something shifted, like a chord drawn taut beneath the stone, resonating deep in her bones. The air around the library shimmered faintly, the heat warped not just by the sun but by old magic stirring awake. She had never stood here before, but the place *knew* her.

They ascended in silence, her companions trailing behind, each of their weapons slung low but eyes sharp. Quiet or not, they could not trust this place. Not with the palace so near.

The stairway leading up to the main doors felt longer than it should have been. To Philippa, it was like each step a question, each breath heavy with expectation. Around them, faded murals lined the walls: masked scribes, solar beasts, rivers of ink running from open hands. She reached out once, letting her fingers brush the ancient stone, and felt it hum in return.

Then they reached the doors.

The bronze seals that had bound them shut that had been beautiful, solemn things etched with protective writings were gone. Melted, broken, *undone.* Only scorched markings remained where the great bands once crossed. She paused, something twisting in her chest.

"It wasn't supposed to happen like this," she murmured, her voice far off, as if in another time.

Shem shifted behind her uneasily. "Queen Aura ordered a scribe to open it. She said it was *time.*"

"No." she whispered. "My people sealed it. To protect everyone from someone like her… from someone like ourselves."

The doors hung slightly ajar now, just enough to reveal the shadowed maw beyond. It felt like a wound. A breach. And yet the library called to her with a distinct presence, with that deep, rhythmic pulse of something ancient and patient and waiting.

She stepped forward, placing her hand against the cool metal edge. It didn't resist her. It welcomed her.

The darkness inside was thick, layered with dust and memory, but as she crossed the threshold, it parted gently before her, veils lifting. The air was rich with the scent of old paper, dried herbs, ink, and something older still. Light from high, stained glass windows pierced the gloom in silent beams, illuminating a vast, tiered chamber of shelves and forgotten altars.

For a heartbeat, she couldn't move. The place breathed around her, slow and immense. Somewhere, in the quiet above, a voice she had always known whispered her name. Taking another cautious step, she passed the entryway. She felt Sparrow behind her, felt Ole's steady presence at her side, and Shem's unease rippling around them. She exhaled, and took another step—

Right into the bustling side of a robed servant.

Philippa caught the scream in her throat, and Sparrow had his blade out, already drawing it above his head to silence the servant.

But the old man just stared at them with big, empty eyes. Philippa's breath came in uneven gasps, ready for him to sound the alarm at any second. Even Sparrow was frozen, his black fabric covering his face once more, leaving his eyes to tell her that he too was confused. As he straightened, feathers rustled from where he'd clasped his mask to his shoulders like the antlers of a kill.

Tiny taps echoed off of the columns of the entryway. They collectively glanced down. The servant's foot was tapping at a rather odd pace. He still stared at her with a glaze over his eyes.

"What is the creepy man doing?" Ole asked, his voice low.

Shem's tension was palpable. "He's counting."

As if on cue, the man turned, and continued on the path he had been walking in a distinctly straight line. She followed him with her eyes, until he disappeared through an archway where she could see the beginnings of stone shelves.

They all turned to Shem.

He sighed. "He won't tell a soul we're here. He's blind and mute. He was counting his steps."

"Seems like the perfect fellow to keep as a librarian," Sparrow huffed, his blade plinking as she sheathed it on his chest.

Shem's unease quickly shifted to a great annoyance. "You were ready to kill that man for *nothing*. Speak with more honor. The queen keeps them mute and blind so they cannot act out."

Philippa stepped forward, towards Shem, as if pulled by a string. Her chest was tight, breath shallow.

"She *keeps* them like that?" she repeated, her voice barely a whisper.

Shem didn't answer. He didn't have to. The weight of the truth pressed down like a cold iron.

She moved toward the archway, eyes fixed on the space where the old man had vanished. Her body trembled with something that she'd tried to keep at bay for a long time. Sparrow's eyes shifted toward her, but he said nothing.

"I didn't see it," she murmured, shame seeping into her voice. "I looked right at him, and I didn't see it."

Ole tilted his head. "See what, Little Pip?"

She gestured vaguely, at the air, at the place the man had been, at nothing and everything. "The stillness. The *thrumming.* The scribes carry it - *we* carry it - even when it's been buried. Even when it's broken."

She turned to Shem. "How many more like him?"

Shem didn't meet her gaze. "Enough to run every archive between here and the palace. Enough to light a thousand lanterns while never speaking a word. Keeping them like this makes it easier for her to send them braille decrees they simply sign and make into truth."

Philippa swallowed hard. Her hands were fists now, her fingernails digging into her palms. "She took everything from them, but their power. Clipped them down like birds in a cage."

She could see her parents in her mind's eye, picture her mother's despair at seeing this, her father's rage. The anger swelled hot and quick, and then just as quickly, it cracked open to sorrow. "We're not meant to be used like this. We're not... tools. My people didn't seal off the libraries for us to be forgotten relics to abuse."

Sparrow suddenly stepped to her side, close but not touching. "You didn't forget this man, Philippa. You know of him now."

She turned to him, her eyes wet and furious. "It's not enough."

"No," Sparrow said softly, "but it's a beginning. Now lead us. Use that anger to smoke out Panu's book, and then we can hit back where it hurts the most."

There was an awful lot of *we* in his words, but she tucked the thought away. He was right. She couldn't promise to save that scribe right now. They were close, so close, and they had to hurry.

Her eyes drifted to Shem, her gaze lingering on his face, a mixture of hurt and frustration swirling within her. He hadn't told her the true condition in which the scribes were kept under Queen Aura's cruel and unforgiving rule. It was a bitter pill to swallow knowing that he thought he was shielding her, but in reality, his sugarcoating the truth only hurt her more. He had to stop trying to protect her by keeping her in the dark. It only made her feel more vulnerable, more exposed. The skin on her arms, neck, and face began to prickle.

Philippa averted her gaze. "Ole, go with Shem. Sparrow and I will search the first floor. Start above us. How much time do we have to look?"

Shem rubbed his neck. "Perhaps an hour before it becomes apparent to her that someone has entered."

She nodded. "In an hour we will meet back together. We'll adjust from there."

"The inner sanctum is located at the very center of the first floor. It'll be the easiest place for us all to find." Shem said.

She heard the steadiness in his voice, how he emphasized the inner sanctum. Shem still promised to help her get to it when they had the chance, and today was the day. She let Ole gently squeeze her face before watching him depart through an archway with Shem, as the weight of her task settled in her gut. The part of the plan that she'd kept to herself all this time.

Sparrow jerked his head, and she followed him down the main hall, towards the first section of shelves carved from ancient stone.

Once she reached the inner sanctum, it was time. As soon as she found a way in, she would take what her people had whispered was there, and change it forever.

And strip every last scribe of their powers. Down to the letter.

CHAPTER FORTY-FIVE ✦

The library opened like a cathedral carved from the bones of the world. Columns of pale stone rose in the dim, vaulted heights, each veined with shimmering threads of crystal - violet, emerald, and pale gold, just like in the caverns - catching the light in a quiet defiance of the gloom. With the library's keepers being blind, there wasn't much use for lit candles. Arched windows stood high above as she craned her neck back, but the glass was colored and warped, letting in slanted beams of amethyst and jade that painted shifting mosaics across the floor.

This place had been designed for beauty, once. For welcoming. Now it was…

Worthless, worthless, worthless.

Philippa's footsteps echoed in the hush, softened by the dust and the reverence hanging in the air. Sparrow was idly at her side, eyes shifting up and down the shelves in search of the boy's book. In the back of her mind, she tried to picture what Tazmireth's book would look like. Just in case.

She inhaled, tracing a finger over a shelf. The smell was dense with parchment, beeswax, and the faint mineral sharpness of magic that had soaked into the stones over centuries. She had never thought a place built of magic to have a *scent.*

Shelves stretched endlessly in rows that curved like ribs around the heart of the building, and the books themselves were bound in everything from cracked leather to metal scales. She swore some hummed faintly as she passed.

Light filtered from hovering orbs, some still, some slowly circling like planets, casting soft halos over the ancient desks. Cobwebs shimmered in the corners, undisturbed. At times, blind servants would come clear of them with a duster, always tapping their feet, counting.

Every now and then, she passed statues of nameless scribes: faceless figures with styluses pressed to stone, their features long worn away by time or intention.

The deeper they walked, the quieter it became. Not just quiet in sound, but in feeling. A hush that felt alive, like the library itself was watching.

She trailed her fingers along the edge of a shelf, eyes searching, mind sharpened. Somewhere in this vast place were the books she needed. Single volumes hidden among thousands.

Wait, wait, wait!

Her feet obeyed, her frame going still. Sparrow crept up beside her, his blonde curls whispering past her ear as he took another step in front of her.

He cast his eyes about, searching. A metal *twang* let her know that he sheathed his dagger.

"We are no longer alone in this library," he whispered. He stood up straighter, looking around cautiously.

"How do you do that?" She asked.

Sparrow rolled his eyes. "I have ears."

Philippa dragged a hand down her face. "No. I meant talking to me. In my mind."

At that, he put a palm to her back and gently ushered her forward, around the shelves. "I am not. A side effect of having to save you, it seems. My thoughts to yours, to keep you safe."

She pondered on that for a moment as she quickly scanned the next shelf for the books. "So you cannot hear my thoughts all the time."

He grabbed a book from the shelf, turned it over in his hands. Replaced it. Shook his head.

Well, that was a relief. Just because he had to protect her, she still didn't know why he would've run off to join a cult. There were things he wasn't telling her, or couldn't.

"Do you still have that lavender ink?"

Sparrow shimmied up the shelf to reach the top. Ran his fingers over the spines. She felt a thrumming in her chest. "It won't change the boy's book if it's been altered like you think. You'll need real ink."

His footsteps were barely audible as he leapt down from the top. Philippa followed him around another corner, to an alcove built into the wall.

The shelf before her was old, and notably, not stone like the rest. Its wood was splintered, but stubborn, thick with the scent of old ink and forgotten things. Philippa reached out without thinking, her fingers trailing along spines of every size and material.

And then… a stillness.

A break in the rhythm. One book among the hundreds didn't hum, didn't crackle with old magic. It waited, silently, as if trying not to be found at all.

She froze, her fingertips hovering over the narrow black tome wrapped in cracked hide. Its spine bore no title, no gilded letter. But the moment her skin brushed it, warmth pulsed up her arm, not burning, but familiar. It was like touching the edge of a dream she'd once lived. Her tattoo pulsed against her skin. Magic touching magic.

She pulled it free, heart racing. The air around it shifted, ever so slightly, as if the library itself leaned in to listen.

Opening it, she saw lines that shimmered and sank, half written glyphs that dissolved when stared at too long. But the first name etched inside remained. A single word, marred by magic and left unreadable.

She knew whose it was without a doubt once she flipped to the back of the book, and saw words appearing at that very moment.

"The assassin in black reached for another tome, his anger and anguish blinding him to the scribe holding his very life in her hands."

Sparrow.

Her breath caught. Her fingers gripped the book tighter.

"Philippa?" a voice hissed, sharp and urgent.

She whirled, clutching the book to her chest. Footsteps echoed above. For a heartbeat, her fear spiked. Another servant? A soldier?

Then Ole and Shem leaned over the stone railing of the upper floor, eyes wide.

"I found it!" Ole whispered hoarsely. "Panu's!"

Relief crashed over her like a wave, but she didn't move. Her eyes were still fixed on the book in her hands.

So were Sparrow's.

He suddenly closed whatever book he'd been holding, letting the sound snap through the quiet of the library. Deftly, he slid down the ladder he'd been on and trudged past Philippa without a word. She was stunned into silence, her head swimming. How had it been this easy to find Panu's book, and to stumble across Sparrow's? It felt like a trick. But then again, if one was supposedly able to feel their own life book's presence, then maybe she could feel his if they were truly bound to one another's story.

They moved in silence towards the heart of the library, toward the inner sanctum, as planned. Philippa still clutched Sparrow's book, her fingernails digging into the spine like it might disappear if she loosened her grip.

He knew she had it, but said nothing. It was eating at her. When she finally spoke, her voice was quiet but certain. "I'm going to free you from it. From this."

Sparrow didn't look at her. They'd had this conversation before. "Let it go."

She swallowed hard. "You said it yourself: our stories are bound. That doesn't mean they have to stay that way."

He stopped walking. "The only way to free me," he said, flatly, "is to burn my book."

She stared at him. "Burn your book?" she echoed, voice faint.

He still didn't meet her gaze. But the silence was solid. Final. They both knew what burning a book did to a person. When he didn't speak again, she knew he hadn't been dramatic. He'd spoken, not a fact, but his truth, cold and immovable. Despite the churning it caused in her stomach, she understood what he meant. Philippa wouldn't lie and say that there weren't days where she'd wished her book burned in Soffer.

"Is that what you want?" she asked. Her voice broke on the last word.

Finally, he lifted his eyes to hers, startled. "You would do that?" he whispered. "If I had asked? Are you insane?"

Philippa looked away, chewing on the inside of her cheek. Her ears flattened to the sides of her head. "No one deserves to serve a soul they didn't choose," she murmured, "I don't want your book to burn, Sparrow. But if you asked me… and your freedom was in the ashes, I would help you."

He gave a dry, humorless laugh. "How tender. You know even less than I thought about scribes and their magic." He shook his head, bitter. "Maybe I should've trusted your promise, not for your wisdom, but for your naivety."

Her eyes sharpened. Here she was, trying to be vulnerable with him, and he was spitting venom back at her. She couldn't forget that this was the same man who'd spat atrocities at her, Shem, and Ole the first time he'd gotten the chance. "You're attacking me out of pain. I'm being serious."

Sparrow moved sharply, taking the book from her, and placing it on a nearby table with a thud that somehow sounded louder than any scream.

"You think I *wouldn't* take you up on it if I could?" he snapped. "Our stories are *bound,* Philippa. Words woven together. Eternal." He looked her dead in the eye. "The only way to burn my book—"

"—would be to burn them together." She finished in a whisper.

He nodded. His jaw clenched. "And since I cannot let you die," he said through gritted teeth, "I can *never* let you do that."

His voice shook with fury, with grief as he continued. "If you tried, I would stop you. Time and again. For all eternity, if I had to. Because these words, they're not just in ink. They're etched onto my skin. Carved into my soul. My life is yours." He stepped closer, his voice dropping low. "For once," he said, "stop being selfless and *take* something."

Philippa blinked. Confused. Angry. Hurting.

"I am your greatest gift." he said. "Life eternal, at the cost of mine." Philippa wanted to reach out and hold his arm to steady the trembling that had crept into his voice. "Stop trying to save everyone. Stop throwing yourself into every flame. Take, Philippa. Just once. As anyone else would. Hold something so precious, just because you can." His final words came quiet, like an old wound breaking open. "Why do you think you aren't worthy of that? Of a gift? Of your father's love? A love so fierce he would condemn an innocent boy to save his child?"

Philippa stared at him, breath shallow, her heart pounding against her ribs. His pain was a fire, scorching and bare, but it wasn't what made her hands tremble. It was the truth buried inside it, the one she wanted to pull out and rewrite, but couldn't.

"That's not love." she said, her voice rough with hurt.

Sparrow flinched, just barely. But she saw it.

"That wasn't love." she repeated, louder now, stepping closer. "What my father did to you wasn't mercy. It was desperation. It was power. Love doesn't shackle someone to a life they didn't choose. It doesn't steal your will and call it protection." Her eyes burned. "Don't you dare call that a gift."

Sparrow looked away, his jaw rigid, but not before she saw his grief, so old and tangled that she knew that he didn't have the words to respond. She didn't touch him. She just let the silence press between them, heavy with all the things neither of them had chosen.

Then, softer: "You don't have to be grateful for your cage just because someone painted it gold."

He drew in a sharp breath. There was a war in his eyes; he wanted to hate her, she knew it, but he didn't. And that broke her in a way that didn't have a name, didn't have a feeling strong enough to describe it. They could've been friends. Might've had the chance to grow up together. He could've been a painter, or a dancer, or a hunter. Not an assassin to a cult bound to her like a dog.

Before either of them could speak again, a deep, metallic groan echoed ahead of them. Shem had knocked at the inner sanctum, as planned.

They turned together, the moment between them still raw and unhealed, and walked toward what came next.

CHAPTER FORTY-SIX ✧

They moved deeper into the library, past the final ring of shelves and into a space seemingly untouched by time. The air grew cooler, heavier, as if they were descending not into stone, but into memory. Philippa felt like words were heavy on her tongue as Shem and Ole pressed in at her sides as the steps widened, curving gently downward into a grand, circular chamber set in the heart of the library floor.

At its center rested the sanctum.

It was not a room in the usual sense. It had no walls, no doors. It was *held* in place. A great orb of clouded glass, easily twice the height of a man, floated just above the stone, suspended within six golden arms that reached up from the marble like branches of a mechanical tree. Each curved band was etched with words; some faint and worn, others glowing faintly like something still lived inside them.

Philippa's breath caught as she stepped closer. The orb shimmered with a subtle light, cloudy and swirling like stormed water beneath ice. Once, perhaps, it had been clear. A window to something vast. But now the fog clung to the inside of the glass, like a breath on a mirror.

The closer she got, the more it felt like standing at the edge of the dreams of those who came before her. Philippa's hand floated up, hovering above her head to get closer to the orb. It felt like something only her people should have seen, something sacred, something sealed.

Sparrow and Shem stopped beside her, and even Olekashan seemed dwarfed by the orb's presence. No one spoke.

The sanctum was not open. But it was waiting. Philippa's fingertips tingled like someone was running their hands along her spine, an awareness of being watched without anyone actually around. Is this what it felt like to feel close to your life book? Her heart was hammering, her body filling with that familiar thrum of magic begging to be used as she stood directly underneath the orb. She turned her head upwards, staring at her distorted reflection in the misty surface.

Philippa narrowed her eyes, honing in on the way her reflection warbled as if the inside of the orb was filled with murky water. The way it showed her mahogany hair, her bright green eyes, her crown…

Philippa gasped out loud, earning everyone's attention, but she did not speak. With a shaking hand, she grabbed a lock of her hair and held it before her eyes. It was ashen brown, as she expected. Though she knew the truth, Philippa felt her forehead. No crown.

Uneasily, she looked back up into the orb. Her reflection was the same as it had been, her hair purpled and her brow adorned in a circlet made of light and mist and floating shards of colored glass. Then, a dark hand swallowed her visage, drowning it as her reflection seemed to fight, until there was nothing but the ugly truth of how she actually looked.

A bitter tang coated her tongue. Whoever designed a Visage got the idea from this, she was sure. Whatever magic lay inside the orb was showing her a possibility, one that had now been trampled down by the truth.

She turned to face everyone, regarding them with reverence. It could take years to find out how one was to enter an *orb* where the oldest laws and functions of the scribes were kept. But here and now, there were those she'd made promises to.

Ole's flinty eyes were watery, his expression drawn. He was staring into the orb, his appearance warped. He turned to Philippa, his giant shoulders turning in on himself. She watched as his chest expanded gently as he inhaled deeply. The library's floating sprites of light gathered around him, as if waiting for an announcement. A chief he had been, and presence he still carried, it seemed.

He took a knee before her. "It is time, Little Pip, to make good on our promises."

Philippa took him in. This giant of a man, on his knee, bending to her. If the queen saw her now, she'd take her head. Philippa nodded, taking the book that looked so small in his palms.

Her hands trembled as she opened Panu's book beneath one of the smaller reading lamps. The others stood by, giving her space, though she felt the weight of their eyes. Flipping through the pages, she was looking for clues. For signs of tampering. If there weren't any, then… then she simply hadn't been strong enough to help.

She frantically thumbed through the pages, a mark blurring under her touch. With a loud slam, she stopped the turning pages, inhaling deeply. Slowly, she fumbled through the parchment, sweat dampening the sheets, searching for something that might not even exist. But there it was.

Ink glistened across the bottom margin, shaky and oddly shaped, like it had been written under duress: *and so he fell into an eternal sleep.*

She touched the line carefully. The page dipped unnaturally where the words had been forced in. Margin space had been stretched, as if the sentence pulled the rest of the writing downward, warping the story to make room for itself.

This wasn't here before, she thought to herself.

She flipped the page. There should've been more that was written in already, though he was asleep, but there was a deep sense of wrongness about it. Even as she read, the sentences were moving unnaturally, spreading out the added sentence from what was naturally occurring.

No matter what was happening now, it all ended in the same, added text written in red ink.

It did not make a difference if the current activity of his life read: *Panu stirred uncomfortably on the ground of the cavern...*

It didn't move the last, added sentence when the words appeared: *A Nazheris, filled with great concern, pressed her muzzle to his cheek. He could feel the heat, like a distant fire...*

No, nothing being added mattered at all.Not when the angry, hasty, capitalized letters someone wrote at the end read: *THE SLEEP WILL CLAIM THE BOY'S LIFE.*

The words hit her like cold water. She'd been right. She spun on a heel. Earned all of their rapt attention. "Someone wrote him to die in his sleep."

It hadn't been a matter of inability, or healing tactics of the Wahanar, no, this was evil. This was a toxic, throbbing strike against an innocent boy.

Ole moved.

Sparrow stared at him, something like concern in his cut of eyes. Shem still fidgeted uncomfortably with his pocket.

The chief moved beside her. He didn't say anything at first, just stared at the page, his body motionless. Then, without warning, he sank to the stone bench beside her like a man whose legs had given out.

"Panu…" he rasped. His voice cracked, low and gravelly, like it had been buried under decades of strength. "Who? Why?"

It was Sparrow who responded, anger palpable. "People don't need a reason to tamper. If they had the power to play, they did."

"There were more books up there, likely altered as well. The scribes had been stacking them," Shem added quietly.

Ole groaned.

Philippa looked at him. The bravest, strongest man she knew looked small.

"We can fix it," she said, "I can alter it back. Remove the roadblock. Scribing is finicky… there's an unforeseen outcome if you don't write things *ever* so carefully."

Ole didn't answer. But he nodded once. Slowly. Then, he took Philippa's hands. He pressed one to the pages of Panu's book. The other, he placed the glass he'd reformed into her palm, their window to Panu. His hand was warm, and his voice a whisper:

"Let us be done with this!"

***

Sparrow had gone on a scout of the library twice in the time it took Philippa to try and study the alteration of Panu's book, as well as the events leading up to it. The cultist hadn't mentioned any new foes coming into the library, but each time he reappeared, his shoulders were squared, his fingers dancing by his sheathed daggers.

Shem approached Philippa slowly, his touch just a whisper on her arm. "I'm going to sweep the library. I know your… friend keeps going but…"

"But you still don't trust him." she said.

Shem nodded, his brows drawn with stress. "I'll be back. You can do this."

He pressed his warm lips to the back of her hand before stalking out between the shelves to look for any danger. As soon as he was out of eyesight, Philippa heard a ruffling of feathers. She could almost hear Sparrow in her mind saying, *well, there's no point in both of us being gone.*

Philippa turned back a page and saw something worse than just an alteration. Halfway down, as the fresh ink appeared, it flickered weakly, as if struggling to exist:

Philippa Aporo carried this book into the heart of the library. Her company was unaware that they were fulfilling larger wishes by holding this book…

The ink *warbled.* That was the only word that fit. The sentence wavered at the edges like it couldn't decide whether it had the right to exist.

Sparrow leaned over her shoulder.

"Going to tell me that I'm naive for this?" she asked shortly. Her back ached from poring over the book on the stone altar.

He shrugged, curls framing his face swathed in black. "I was going to ask if you had any idea what that meant."

By his tone, she was meant to laugh, but there was no humor left in here. Panu was deemed to die, by who? The queen? For what purpose? Was it possible that Panu had the gift, and she was trying to kill him quietly without starting a war between herself and the Wahanar?

It made enough sense. But that kind of power, used for something so ugly… It churned her stomach.

Philippa focused on what she could control, her fingers tightening around the edges of the book. It was hazy, thinking about the lessons her father had been trying to teach her. Sometimes it felt like the horrors she saw were *all* she could remember, instead of the menial memories. Her eyes were closed, thinking back. There was something, a block, keeping her from fully remembering.

Her tattoo tingled against her skin. She inhaled. Imagined a doorway opening inside her. Instead of filling it with thoughts of fire, she imagined herself as a child. She tried to imagine her father, to picture him wholly.

The memories hit her like a brick. For a moment, it was too much, and she was sure that she was screaming. Her eyes cracked open. No time had passed. Sparrow was looking at the book over her shoulder, waiting for her answer.

She only got fragments from her father's voice, his lessons. But perhaps that was enough.

"It means that alter isn't stable. Something is… resisting it." she murmured. "Either me, trying to fix it, or…" Sparrow's eyes widened in recognition and question. Her voice dropped. "Or maybe the book is rejecting the lie."

She snapped the book closed and turned to Sparrow. "You said that I need real ink, right? You would know the right kind by looking at it. Sealed, undiluted. Can you find some here?"

He nodded immediately and peeled off the pack he always wore hidden somewhere on his back. "Take this. In case you need to run."

With that, he slipped on his mask, crossed his arms, and fell through the floor. A single feather drifted towards the ground.

Philippa set his pack on the ground, and reached for the second book that she hadn't let out of her sight. She tucked it into the deepest pocket and strapped it to her back. Ole nodded at her. Full of so much trust. She smiled at him.

She just hoped that the alteration at the end of his book wouldn't make anything they tried meaningless in the end.

CHAPTER FORTY-SEVEN✦

Shem paced around the circular sanctum entrance, arms folded. Evidently, he'd run into Sparrow in the library and hurried back to keep watch over Philippa and Olekashan. Philippa knew that Shem would probably never appreciate Sparrow's presence, but there was something off about him. She kept glancing at him. He was so stiff, so quiet.

"You're very still for someone on the lookout." Ole said, watching him. Shem didn't reply.

Philippa pursed her lips. With a soft voice, she asked, "are you alright?"

Shem looked over, and his expression softened at her in familiarity. "I'm fine. I'll keep watch. It makes me… uneasy, to be so close to the palace."

They waited a moment longer in the dim hush of the sanctum, the locked orb looming over them. Philippa crouched under the lights as more floating sprite orbs gathered as she studied the pages. Her focus drifted as she heard Ole speak again.

He was standing a few paces off, watching Shem still. Not with suspicion, but something softer.

"I don't pretend to understand your ways, scholar." Ole said, voice rumbling and low. "Or what you still run from."

Shem barely acknowledged him. His head was on a swivel. It had to make him nervous, this whole endeavor. To live a life dedicated to quiet perseverance, to trust others with your secret truth, knowing it could cost you everything. In a way, Philippa thought, he was being braver than most of them right now.

Ole shrugged, but there was weight behind his words. "But I have come to care for you."

Shem froze. Didn't meet Ole's gaze, but turned his head to listen to him.

"You are risking your life for my family. That is not a small thing. When my watchmen found you, I thought, *look at this man of polish who wants to study my people.* I thought you were small. But you have much greatness in your bravery. You were not given the life you wanted. I live a good life."

"Pardon me, chief, but you are currently wanted and exiled by your people," Shem said coolly.

Ole shrugged, like it would soon be remedied. "If you ever meant what you have said, about leaving your court, you would not have to disappear like sand in the wind. You could return with me. Right things. Stay."

A long silence passed. Philippa watched as Shem looked at Ole, really looked.

"You would trust me, just like that?" he asked, his voice just above a whisper.

Ole gave him a crooked smile. "You lived with me once before. This time, imagine no chains."

Philippa's chest ached. She didn't speak. She felt the moment press into the quiet like the final line of a story not yet written.

Darkness yawned open between the three of them. They each took a step back as Sparrow seemingly fell *upwards* through the opening, before the shadow closed. She could hear his breathlessness in his mask, but in his gloved hand, he held out a small glass vial.

"Real scribe ink." he confirmed. "Sealed with salt wax. Untouched."

Philippa popped the seal. The ink shimmered inside like oil and flame. She was about to dip her finger into the bottle, when someone cleared their throat. Shem pointed at the desk, and as she dragged her eyes to it, she hesitated. A stone stylus, one a real scribe would use. Practiced and carved for the hands of those who knew exactly what they were doing.

Worthless...

She grabbed the stylus. As she dove it into the inkwell, she felt it burn gently up and into her skin.

Her eyes found the disgusting alteration in Panu's book. Watched as what was currently happening was trying to be written, but struggling. Just as Panu's breath would be, as his heart and lungs begged to live.

The ugly sentence in red glared at her: *THE SLEEP WILL CLAIM THE BOY'S LIFE.*

She pressed the stylus to the parchment. Slowly, deliberately. In the time she'd been searching his book, trying to find answers, her mind had pinwheeled in the efforts to find just the right cure. Simply crossing out the alter could kill him.

Philippa exhaled. This would be the hardest thing she would ever have to do. But she held the ink of her ancestors in her hands, had the power in her veins from her parents, and more than anything, she wanted to right these wrongs. She opened herself up and filled the void with every wish she could.

Her hand moved.

Ole stood by somewhere, she could feel him, anxiously thrumming his fingers on his legs. In his other hand he clutched his reformed looking glass.

She saw Tazmireth in her mind, smiling at her.

Thought became written word. A cost was determined.

With fire, the alteration was cleansed. Panu stirred. THE SLEEP WILL CLAIM THE BOY'S LIFE...

A sudden gust of heat bloomed in the chamber. Philippa jerked her head up just in time to see the faint shimmer of golden flame spiral across the ceiling. It coiled downward like smoke in reverse, weightless and alive. In the Wahanar glass, Vaelith had awoken next to Panu.

Sparrow opened up his shadow and disappeared. In the blink of an eye, the Nazheris and Panu were before them in the chamber, near the sanctum orb.

The wind and fire blew Sparrow across the room, and Ole caught him, dragging him back to the floor. Shem hid behind a column against the elements. But none could hide their eyes. They all watched in morbid curiosity.

From the shadows above, Vaelith moved silently, her flame-engulfed eyes fixed on the boy's sleeping form. She stalked across the phantom wind, her gait like that of a royal steed. She did not roar, or strike, but she met Philippa's gaze and bowed her head. The Nazheris brayed quietly and turned her eyes to Panu as she lowered herself back to the ground where Sparrow had laid the boy. The storm was alive now, wisps of fire circling around like debris caught in a tornado. Nothing stopped the monster, the beast Philippa had been so afraid of her entire life. The beautiful creature that now was looking at Panukirah like a mother saying goodbye to her child. Philippa knew that look. Philippa wanted Vaelith to look at them, to offer an explanation, but none came. Even Philippa's mind was quiet, no trace of the Nazheris' consciousness within herself. Vaelith only lifted a talon, and with impossible gentleness, pressed a single glowing claw into Panu's chest.

"What is she doing?" Philippa cried out.

Ole's voice boomed across the hall. "She is family."

The glow sank into Panu, and the flaming wind died immediately. The book fell into Philippa's lap as she gasped for air. The stylus had broken in two next to her.

She pushed her hair from her eyes frantically, chest heaving. Staring down, her eyes widened. She waved Ole over wordlessly. The text had changed.

THE SLEEP WILL CLAIM THE BOY'S LIFE... when his heartflame no longer burns.

Philippa read the line twice. Silently held the book up to a panicked Ole. He dropped it and ran for his grandson.

The book hit the floor with an unceremonious thud, falling closed. The magic had bent. The alter held, but the meaning had been twisted. Not death for Panu, not now, perhaps not ever. She had no idea what a heartflame was, other than that Vaelith had given it to him.

She closed her eyes, trembling with the weight of what she'd just done... and what it may have cost. What did it take from Vaelith for Panu to live?

It didn't matter for the moment. Not when Panu coughed and gasped for air.

A weary, uncontrollable laugh filled the air as Philippa threw her head back, her elbows almost giving out. Sparrow was at her side, catching her head and laying her to the stones below. Stars, her body ached.

"You laugh now? Did you trade your sanity?" he asked, voice pooling in his mask.

She shook her head softly. "I laugh, because it worked. Do you realize what this means?"

He did. She could see it in the way he stiffened, and she could practically see him putting the pieces together. If she could alter the work of a real, trained scribe, she could fix everything.

"You did it…" Shem's voice cut over her delusional laughter.

She turned her head, hair plastered to her cheek, as she stared at him standing on the circular steps of the sanctum. Now, together, he could get her inside the sanctum orb, and she could do what she intended to from the start.

"You fixed an alter." he said, his voice low and toneless, as if completely stricken by awe.

Rolling to her stomach, Philippa pressed herself up on her arms to look at him better. Somehow, she smiled. "Now we can finish all of this, Shem."

He walked up the stairs to draw close to her. But something was off. His shoulders moved like they were suddenly very heavy, and his legs were moving like a mechanical soldier's.

Sparrow silently put a hand to his blade. Philippa stared at him in confusion, sat down so Sparrow's backpack didn't weigh her back down. Or so no one could try to take it, with his book inside. She wasn't sure why she felt the need.

"No, Philippa, I don't think we will." Shem's voice was ice.

Then, with inhuman speed, he reached out and took Sparrow by the throat. Philippa shrieked. Sparrow flailed. There was a sound, like sticks breaking.

Ole bellowed. With a wave of his arm, Shem sent Sparrow's limp body straight into the sanctum orb, which cracked like a bell being blown apart.

The sanctum grew quiet again. But it wasn't the same as before.

It was the silence right before something broke.

430

CHAPTER FORTY-EIGHT ✦

The cost had been her sanity, just like Sparrow had said.

That was why she could not stand, could not speak, could not look Shem in the eye. This was all some horrid hallucination, a dive into the subconscious that whispered only intrusive things. Yes, that was it. It explained so very much, and so very little.

She was insane. That was the reason her eyes were filled with tears, and she could not rise to grab Sparrow by the shoulders and shake him awake. That is why the thought about how he tried to convince her not to come because he was scared to get hurt was rattling around in her skull.

No.

Insanity would be blissful, an incoherent fever dream of cross stitched events blurring into one, hazy life.

It would not feel like this.

Her hands fumbled dumbly with the pages of Panu's book, as if to find where she had gone wrong. Had she ruined them all by doing this? Where had her words left room for such ugly interpretation?

Ole yelled something about how Shem would be going to Nyxveil if he moved. Philippa could only partially hear. Her ears were ringing, tears falling onto Panu's pages, simply being soaked up by the parchment and leaving the ink unbothered.

She had to have done something wrong. She was supposed to be entering the inner sanctum now, finding the old scribe laws, changing them. Then she could go home. To Morgana. To Raff. Wrap them up in her arms and never let go. There would be no facing them now, not if this was her fault.

Her ears twitched. Her body sang in discord, in panic.

Something was coming.

She began to slide Panu's book under her knee to protect it. Shem's boot came down hard. Just missing her hands. When she looked up at him, his edges were hazy, as if she was drunk.

"I'm sorry about this, Philippa. I didn't know you could actually do it." he said, as if it explained everything.

It did not.

She clutched Morgana's locket.

Ole began to leave Panu's side to step between them. Philippa shook her head, raising her hand to stall him. He froze mid-step. The air turned sharp.

A sound followed… no, not a sound. A *pressure.* Like glass crackling in her chest. Philippa's hand dropped.

From the dimly lit shelves behind Shem, light spilled inward, thin and deliberate, like a spotlight meant only for a queen. Philippa saw through it; the orb sprites gathered in a stead, heralding an arrival.

Gold dust scattered through the air as if drawn by her presence, like even the dust knew to kneel.

And then she was there. There would be no denying her.

The Queen of Sapria stepped into the inner chamber, and the world hushed around her.

She looks too young. That was Philippa's first thought: *too young to hold so much power.* Skin smooth and bronze, lips dark and precise, her eyes a shocking pale blue that caught every flicker of lantern light. Her hair was bound in thick braids laced with pearl-thread and crowned in a fire forged gold. She didn't wear armor. She didn't need to.

She moved like a storm that already knew the outcome.

"How touching." The queen said, her voice smooth and deliberate, folding over the silence like silk over a blade. Her gaze passed over Philippa, over Ole, pausing only briefly at Sparrow's fallen form. "Though I expected more dignity from a daughter of my realm than tears on my floor."

Shem turned toward her and dropped to one knee. Not out of fear, but something worse. *Conviction.*

"My Queen."

"Rise." she said, barely sparing him a glance. Her eyes returned to Philippa and held. "So. You are the scribe."

Philippa didn't answer.

The queen tilted her head to look down her nose at Philippa. "You changed an alteration. A stubborn one. You rewrote *death.* That takes power... and arrogance." She stepped closer, inspecting the way a collector might ponder over a stolen relic. "You've made quite the mess."

She smiled then, beautifully. Coldly. "Such a beautiful tool that you were born with. A tool that now, little woman, belongs to me."

***

Philippa sat there feeling stupid for what felt like an eternity. Slowly, she scooted away from Shem, away from the queen, and tucked Panu's book into her pack silently. Shem had been informing his master of what she'd missed, and she didn't seem to think that any of them were a threat while she was distracted.

Ole was crouched over Panu and Vaelith, too scared to leave either of them.

Queen Aura looked at Shem with half lidded eyes, long eyelashes brushing her cheeks anytime she blinked. Even her lids were coated in gold.

But Philippa could only stare at Shem.

"You used me." she whispered, her voice trembling with the weight of the realization.

His golden eyes slid towards her, slowly. But he did not deny her. Queen Aura's shoulders shook slightly, like she was suppressing a laugh. She turned away, waving her hand, as soldiers began to pour through the shelves. They were armed to the teeth, as if she expected an all out brawl. Except, she'd made her grand entrance by herself. Everything was screaming that this was all for show, just to prove that even if Philippa *did* think about running, that there were others to stop her. An army, if the queen wished. Philippa still didn't know why Olekashan hadn't lit the place on fire yet, something she desperately was hoping for. Part of her must've been delirious if she was praying for fire to rain down where she sat.

"Philippa, I don't have much of a choice." Shem began again, reaching towards her, as if to pull her to her feet. Philippa inched away.

"You always had a choice. Instead you led me here, like a lamb to the slaughter."

A slight commotion began as the soldiers discovered Ole's large frame had been covering an entire body - Panu's - and as they understandably balked at the sight of Vaelith. Queen Aura seemed more interested in that, and sauntered over to watch.

Philippa kept her eyes on Shem.

"I can tell you why. I can explain everything." he said, his voice in a hush.

Her eyes narrowed to slits. "How."

He rubbed his neck, then his shoulder, as if they were hurting. As if he didn't just snap someone else's neck. His expression was taut.

Philippa tried to keep herself from sneering. Anger and hatred were blooming in her chest, two things she fought so very hard not to feel. How could he be surprised that she didn't care *why?* It only mattered that it happened. Her head was still swimming, her body still weak from the scribing. Her body was thrumming in the way that scared her again. That tight coil, ready to spring as soon as she lost control. She just had to keep him talking.

Silently, Shem reached into the pocket he always fiddled with. When his palm came out, she flinched.

He drew back. His mouth was agape, his eyebrows knit together, eyes wide with hurt, as if to say, *do you really think I would hurt you?*

Involuntarily, she stole a glance at Sparrow.

Yes, I do.

Instead of speaking, he uncurled his long dark fingers from around what he'd been hiding the entire time. Through every stolen moment, every shared secret, every kiss, he'd had this. Nothing had been private at all.

In his palm, sat a fat, refined crystal of jade and violet, heinous in all its crystalline glory. Suddenly, she knew what the Wahanar people had been telling her. Though the crystals could not speak, they could listen.

Queen Aura wore what Philippa had thought were diamond earrings. She knew better now.

"You needed me. You needed me to enter the inner sanctum, and the other libraries, for *her.*" Philippa knew that if she pretended to sound heartbroken, he would at least hesitate. Except, she wasn't pretending. Her heart felt like it had been torn in two. She was so stupid to have trusted anyone, to think someone like Shem could want a creature like her...

Worthless, worthless, worthless...

He nodded. Didn't deny a word. "I tried to tell you not to come."

"What was all this? Helping me, just to let her have me?"

Shem tucked the crystal away. Anxiously toyed with one of his blue braids. "If you were strong enough to change an alter, she wanted you alive."

His words sank in. Bitterness settled on her tongue. The alternative, if she had failed, was plain. Either she was an asset to the queen, or she was a threat. The way that Aura circled them all, observing, made Philippa think that the monarch had yet to decide which.

Philippa's hand absently touched her lips. "This is why you pretended to care."

Shem's breath caught. "Those moments weren't pretend, Miss Aporo, I swear it."

"Enough."

The queen's voice cut through the chamber. She folded her hands together as she stalked back towards Philippa, the soldiers fully encircling them now. Philippa's eyes darted around. She needed to keep them talking. Just a little while longer.

"Such sentiment, Shem, my dear scholar. But you have done well. You will be rewarded." The way Queen Aura smiled at him, how she lingered on the last word, made Philippa's skin crawl.

He never was interested in Philippa at all. How could he be, when this twenty year old tyrant with perfect skin and all the power of the continent at her golden-tipped fingers, could let him play with her.

The queen clapped her hands together twice, drawing attention to herself as her golden nails flashed. "I want this one bound in scribed chains and brought back to the palace. Strip her bare and leave her without water for a few days. Take the brute back to the dungeons. Scald his tattoos with acid so they are not potent enough to make flame."

Bile rose in Philippa's throat. The queen spoke with such ease, like she was making dinner plans. Assigning servants to make dresses. Simple tasks for a needy woman.

One soldier cleared his throat. "What do you want done with the bodies, your Highness?"

Philippa's head jerked. *Bodies?* Had Panu not woken? No. She had heard his breath, had seen the heartflame appear from…

Vaelith.

Philippa's hands formed fists, her fingernails digging into her palms as more tears threatened to fall. *I am so sorry,* she thought to Vaelith, to Morgana, to Raff, to Taz, to all.

Queen Aura tapped her cheek in thought. "The Nazheris were creatures of *design,* not nature. Shem, what shall we do with one of your kind?"

His head bowed, ever so slightly. Of course this woman would remind him that he had no family, and was not a true human. Despite herself, despite everything, Philippa felt pity.

"She would make a very nice centerpiece, my Queen." Not *your highness.* No, she was his ruler. His queen. He still took ownership of his servitude to her, even right in front of Philippa.

Queen Aura stalked over towards Vaelith, who Philippa could now see was lying on the steps of the inner sanctum. With a snap of her fingers, Queen Aura ordered Shem to bear down on Philippa's shoulders, holding her in place. She wanted to wretch free, but she needed more time.

The queen took a knee, inspecting Vaelith's head. She reached out, as if to caress Vaelith's horn, when Vaelith brayed incoherently, desperately. The queen reeled back, the first crack in her facade. Philippa almost smiled.

"Don't you touch her!" Philippa yelled.

Fury rose in the pale eyes of the queen, and when she snapped this time, Shem was dragging Philippa to kneel at the queen's feet.

"Touch her?" The queen asked, incredulous. "Oh, Philippa, you misunderstand me. This creature is no threat to me. You, on the other hand," she knelt, and lashed out, grabbing Philippa's face. It was so unlike the Wahanar. What she had thought were gold painted nails, turned out to be solid gold caps on her fingertips, which drew blood from both sides of her face. She thought she heard Shem bottle up a gasp. "You have *potential*. Real potential. But from what I've heard, you've always been too soft. Too weak."

"I'm not weak." Philippa retorted. She had to draw this out, even if she was trembling.

Queen Aura's laugh belonged to a tea room, not here. "Oh, but you are. You surround yourself with people who lie to you. People who use you. Even your precious shadow," her eyes flicked to Sparrow's prone form, her smile sharpening, "has kept secrets from you."

Philippa knew that, but for some reason, it stung to hear it from someone who wanted to bottle her up like a drug and use her when convenient.

"I know what Sparrow is. I know why he's here."

Nails dug further into her cheeks, biting past her skin, skewering her as the queen looked to Shem like they were sharing a great joke. "You were right, my dear scholar, she is adorable." Then, the queen released her grip and all of her humor faded away. "You don't even know what questions to ask him. Didn't question *who* it is in his little cult that he works for."

Before anything else could be said, Vaelith cried out in the most sorrowful sound that Philippa had ever heard. The Nazheris was dragging herself, head lolling, towards Panu. Panu, whose chest still was alight with her heartflame.

Philippa's heart fluttered as her mouth fell open. The flame between Vaelith's horns was gone. Not dimming, not fading, *gone*.

It felt like the library crashed around her when she put together what a heartflame was.

Ole was crouched over his grandson, shielding him, and reached out gently with his massive hand. Vaelith fought to raise her head, to lay her maw into Ole's palm. With the gentleness only a father could possess, the former chief of the Wahanar squeezed the creature of myth's head, drawing their foreheads together.

A soldier moved to separate them, but the queen held up her hand. Her icy eyes were full of wonder and intrigue, as if she'd never seen someone honor another before. Not willingly.

"You didn't tell me they all were so interesting." the monarch whispered, clearly to Shem, though she only had eyes for Ole and Vaelith. "They are all so broken. So insignificant. But interesting. Guards! Take a letter for one of my little library mice. Instruct them that I wish to have all the books of those here in this room."

Ole's onyx eyes snapped up. "You will not."

Queen Aura pouted her lips. Said nothing. Clicked her tongue. Ridiculous little creature, she must have thought. She could not have known she was one ruler speaking to another.

For the first time since the queen had entered, Ole stood to his full height. He towered over the soldiers, over her, over everyone. Philippa felt her skin warm in his shadow.

The queen rolled her eyes, but her arm was up defensively. "You believe in her? You think she can stop me from having what I want?"

"Your husband may not agree with what you wish to do. He outrules you." Ole countered, carefully positioning himself in front of Vaelith and Panu. The Nazheris had gone frightfully still, her nostrils only flaring every few seconds. Philippa didn't fight these tears.

Clapping her hands together, the queen giggled, like a little girl. "Oh! That. Tell me, oh brute of the sand dunes, who is my husband?"

Ole opened his mouth, fists shaking, but did not speak. Did not move. Closed his mouth and titled his head in thought. "The self proclaimed king."

Philippa wished she could smile. Of course Ole wouldn't recognize the king's claim to power over his own lands.

Queen Aura waved her hand. "His name, if you please."

The room fell silent again, save for some light shuffling. Philippa's knees were biting into the stone floor, Shem's hands on her shoulders, but she closed her eyes. Reached out into her deepest thoughts. That slight sound may save them all yet.

"Can no one answer? Really?" Silence was the queen's answer. She giggled again, hopping in place like a little schoolgirl. Philippa's stomach felt hollowed out as she watched the self proclaimed girl-queen prattle about, and as she looked around, she saw everyone, including the guards, watched her like a malformed animal lolling around.

"It worked! It really worked outside of Aresef!" She chanted and repeated that three times before she seemed to realize that she could compose herself. Her lack of control almost frightened Philippa more, because no matter how juvenile she may let herself seem, she was very much holding all the cards. "Tell her the first thing I ever had a scribe do, Shem! Tell her. Tell her so she knows the shoes she must fill!"

Philippa refused to look up at him. His fingers in her flesh were burning her enough.

Shem's voice was like a string pulled too tight. "My Queen had the king's book unwritten."

She could've thrown up right then and there. Her shoulders quaked at the thought, at someone killing someone down to their very soul, stripping them of all their genetics, their personality. To unwrite someone was to undo their very being. It was worse than death.

Philippa slowly felt herself come out of the brief shock. She had never remembered the king's name. Not once. The people remembered there *was* a king, but did not question his absence, his unchecked admittance of whatever his foreign wife wanted.

When Philippa looked up at the woman, all she saw was a hunter.

"Now tell me," Queen Aura repeated, "do you believe she can stop me from having what I want?"

Philippa didn't answer. Couldn't. Her chest was too tight, her breath too thin. Shem's grip on her didn't loosen, and the queen - no, this *monster* - just smiled at her.

"Why the boy?" Philippa asked.

The queen's eyes narrowed into slits, but that smile was still on her face. "What boy?"

Her hands shook. "Panukirah. Panu. Son of the Wahanar, heir to their throne. The one you had altered. Why? Why hurt a child?"

With a severe lack of emotion, the queen knelt before Philippa, her caplet cascading around her on the ground. Her pale eyes took Philippa in like a wounded animal. Or like she was going to eat her.

Queen Aura twirled a lock of her golden hair around a finger - and it was *golden.* Inhumanly so. "You're mad at me for that. But you don't understand the bigger picture here, little woman."

"I'm older than you," Philippa said, her voice shaking.

The queen smiled wider. "I'm glad it still looks that way. Imagine what a scribe of *your* ability could do for me. As for the boy, I needed the Wahanar to be distracted. I didn't foresee a scribe stumbling upon them, but it was a lovely surprise."

She blinked at the woman, who was evidently older than she seemed. No wonder she wanted scribes, she was *vain.* Why did anyone like her want power anyway, other than to benefit themselves?

Swathed in gold and crystals, the queen stood and took stock of the situation. "Now that the Wahanar *are* distracted, my scouts can roam more freely in their lands."

Ole growled. He cradled Panu, whose chest was rising and falling steadily, though he did not seem fully awake yet. "Why want my land when you have your Sapria?"

She seemed insulted that Ole spoke directly to her. "Why rule land when you can rule *lives?*"

The Queen collects stories... the stacks that Shem had seen. He had known what they were. Had known where Panu's book would be kept. It's why Ole had found it so quickly. Whatever the queen's long-term game was, she was right. Philippa hadn't seen the bigger picture. Her skin crawled as she took in what was really going on here: something that stretched ages into the past, into the wars that determined the order of how things were now.

"Now, Philippa, was it? You seem a bit agitated. But take note! This is your salvation. You were born to be used. You are the greatest tool mankind has ever received. You're going to help me make this continent a beautiful place." The queen spun on a crystal heel, clapping lightly, her smile twitching unnaturally, as if it wasn't really her skin.

Philippa ground her teeth together. This is the kind of person she was taught to run and hide from as a child. A user. But there was nowhere to run, and her fear was molding into something that her people warned her about far more than users. That uncontainable *thirst* to make someone feel exactly how they made others feet. To show the boot over the ant a bigger boot. Philippa was too exhausted to have the power to unleash everything she wanted to. But she wouldn't run, and she certainly didn't have to close her mouth.

"I am not a tool to be *used*. None of us are."

The queen seemed to like that. She laughed. She crouched again and tried to pat Philippa on the head. Out of desperation, Philippa turned her head and tried to bite her hand. The queen pulled back, giggling.

"You're scared. That's okay. Many of your people were scared when I first found them." Queen Aura smiled that unnaturally beautiful smile and reached out, grabbing Philippa by the face and drawing close.

Philippa spat.

The ruler recoiled, about to scorn her, when Philippa spat again. "Scared? Like how the painter was scared when he defied you in the middle of your own city?"

At that, Queen Aura's eyes widened. The soldiers even made noises in response, some murmuring that it was true. The queen raised her hand, golden dagger nails glinting in the lantern light, ready to strike.

"The rest of my scribes are blind," The queen snarled, "maybe it's what keeps you filth *docile*."

But behind her, something crashed.

Not quite a natural sound. A sensation. Like bones reknitting themselves under force. Shem's hand twitched. A shadow flickered at the corner of

Philippa's vision. A sound like a breath drawn backward into the lungs of the world. And then there was movement.

Sparrow stood.

Neck twisted, eyes wild, strange smoke pouring out from underneath his mask. His blade was already in hand. He didn't speak. He didn't groan. He charged.

The queen turned just before his blade would have struck her in the shoulder, he dropped to a knee, slammed his hand to the floor, and the shadows swallowed himself and Panu whole.

Gone. Vanished into the dark. Safe. Philippa shook.

The queen blinked, her smirk widening. "Sloppy."

Then her chest jerked forward. Sparrow was already back and up, already slashing. The edge of his blade scraped across the queen's shoulder, sparks flying where steel met enchanted silk.

Queen Aura growled, not in pain, but *disdain.* Shem suddenly let go of Philippa in an instant, lunging to defend his ruler.

That was the only moment Sparrow needed. He turned, not to fight, but to steal. His hand was on Philippa's wrist before she even realized what was happening.

"Don't look back." he whispered.

The shadows opened wide. They began to fall through the floor, when claws sunk into her shoulder, tearing muscle, and she was ripped free from Sparrow's grasp like a paper doll.

CHAPTER FORTY-NINE⋄

Philippa screamed as claw-like nails tore into her shoulder, and her body was yanked forward with horrible force, out of the shadows, out of Sparrow's reach. Morgana's locket snapped free from her neck.

Sparrow vanished beneath the surface of the dark, a feather falling, his fingers just brushing hers before the portal sealed with a sound like cracking ice.

She hit the stone floor hard, breath gone, ears ringing. Blood dripped down her face and arm. The world spun. Was her shoulder torn open?

Shem stood above her, but he was different. He wasn't the scholar she knew anymore. If she wasn't so dazed, she would've thought he looked down at her with remorse. With regret for what was to come.

The queen smiled, slow and satisfied. If Philippa closed her eyes, she would've thought a snake was speaking. "Yes. Show her what you were really written to be."

Philippa held her breath, staring bleary eyed up at Shem. For a moment, nothing happened. Then his back *arched,* violently, his shirt splitting open with the sound of tearing fresh as something beneath the skin erupted outward. His faint shadows of a tattoo she had once thought she saw, were now coming to life. Philippa was frozen, her breath caught in her throat, watching the man who had been her ally, her friend, maybe more. The air crackled with an unseen energy, pressing down on her like a physical weight. Then, a low, guttural growl rumbled from deep within his chest, a sound that was less human and more beast. The thin fabric of his shirt, already strained, split fully open, revealing taut, dark skin beneath. The tattooed lines deepened, pulsing with a faint, internal light, and began to shift, coalescing into something far more intricate and terrifying than any ink could achieve. She could almost feel the raw power emanating from him, a primal force stirring beneath his skin, ready to erupt outward and consume everything in its path.

Wings, feathered and vast and *wrong.* Not like any creature of the sky. They shimmered black and indigo, like his hair, each feathered edged with a sort of silver fire. They curled inward, then snapped open with a thunderclap.

Philippa crawled back, choking on her own breath.

His nails blackened and curved, becoming claws. His skin shimmered with faint magic, and as he lifted his face to her, horns curled from his temples, glowing faintly with the same golden-red as the Nazheris' flame.

Shem had never looked like the Nazheris. Now, he was their echo.

The queen's voice purred behind him. "He was of the first ever made. A prototype. Made to walk among you, among scribes. Meant to tear you apart."

Philippa couldn't move. The wings, the claws, the horns, they were all too familiar. Smoke. Screams. The sickening sound of steel meeting bone. The fire that swallowed up her village hadn't just come from flames, it had come from creatures like this.

Her hands dug against the stone, trying to push herself away from the thing Shem had become. But she couldn't outrun the memories that swam over her.

This wasn't just any kind of monster. His kind had beheaded her mother. Had her sister dragged through rubble. Had burned her people's names from existence.

Her breath stuttered in her throat. She shook her head, trying to find *him* beneath it all. Shem. The conflicted scholar. The one who had once looked at her like she mattered. The young man who had saved her from falling prey to the Wahanar and stood beside her before anyone else had.

But those beautiful, golden eyes, had nothing left in them that she wanted. For the first time, they looked like fool's gold. Without a trace of humanity.

Not like the Nazheris.

Nazheris had been born to obey, to destroy, but they had broken their chains to protect. They had found gentleness, chosen mercy. Shem wasn't breaking free. He was *becoming*.

Despite it all, he was still the most beautiful person she'd ever seen.

Tears blurred her vision. Her voice was hoarse, but she forced it out anyway. "You're one of them."

His expression didn't shift.

"You killed my family." she whispered. It didn't matter to her if he hadn't held the blade. He was there. Relished in their deaths. "You… you ruined my world."

Still, no flicker of remorse. Only the cold, steady rage of something that had always waited to be unleashed.

"You were never confused," she said, her voice trembling, "you were hiding."

Shem took a step forward, his wings spreading wider. But behind him, a roar shattered the stillness.

Ole.

His palm was raised, and the fire pooled like liquid sun in his hand. His face was that of a man who had nearly lost everything, and gained tenfold back in return. He had the expression of a determined chief, of a king, returned to the throne of his heart: he was Olekashan, He Who Is Seated By The Flame.

"You want to play god?" he bellowed. "Then burn like one!"

The fire exploded outward, engulfing the guards that had flooded the chamber, curling around the shelves but burning the banners, throwing chaos into the library like a match into dry hay.

Still, Shem advanced.

His wings carved the smoke like scythes. The shadows seemed to cling to him, thickening as if the room bent towards his will. The sprite orbs scurried away from him. Philippa's breath came in shudders. Her shoulder throbbed. Blood dripped to the stones below. Her body screamed to stay down. Hide. Disappear.

But she couldn't. She remembered the backpack she wore, what it contained, who she couldn't stand to lose.Her tattoo buzzed on her hand, quiet at first, then growing sharper, deeper, insistent. She closed her eyes.

Open the tunnel. Make room. Let it fill you.

Philippa didn't feel full. She felt hollow.

She pressed her palm flat to the floor. The ink on her hand ignited, glowing like molten gold. Her teeth clenched as the magic poured through her, raw and stinging, like sunlight forced through a wound.

Not fire. Not yet. Light.

It burned behind her eyes before she even summoned it. The memory of Tazmireth's execution, how the world had gone white in her grief. She called it back. The air around her split with a high, sharp shriek as a blinding flash burst from her hand: pure, white light tearing through the smoke and striking across the chamber like lightning born from sorrow. She recoiled, and the queen flinched.

Guards cried out, blinded, stumbling.

Philippa forced herself to her feet, vision swimming. Her legs buckled once, but she caught herself. Her hand burned, *actually* burned, but she didn't let go of the magic. She turned, palm still glowing, and this time, she let the flame burst through.

Not much. Just enough.

It burst from her fingertips in a narrow, twisting threat, like a snake of fire launched straight towards Shem's shoulder. It caught and flared, giving Ole just enough room to shove back another wave of guards with a roar of heat.

She had never battled. She wasn't strong. Not right now. But she could still fight.

The queen screeched for Shem and her soldiers to get her, to bind her hands together, to tie her down. "I want her!" she screamed over and over.

Philippa gagged. It was not a pleasant feeling to be wanted any longer.

She dove behind a bookshelf, grabbing her wrist with her other hand and shaking it violently. The light wouldn't disappear, wouldn't go away. Her eyes were squeezed shut until she felt the draining stop, felt her heartbeat slow. The library around her was in chaos. Soldiers were literally *toppling* shelves to find her. No doubt they were the same who burned open the bronze plates holding the library closed.

She pressed her palm to her chest, trying to breathe.

I am alive, and this is my life, she kept thinking to herself. Nothing felt real. Nothing felt like it mattered. Not until Morgana and Raff's faces came to mind, his pudgy hands and her sister's sharp-toothed grin.

Then the first soldier found her. He must have not heard the orders to bind her, because his first motion was to draw his short sword and try to stab her. She rolled out of the way, barely, feeling her top get snagged by the tip of the blade. She let it tear, scrambling down another curling path.

Her legs ached as she ran, wincing with every loud footstep she caused. For a moment, she saw a flash of movement, hoped it was Ole, and then came to realize it was just another guard. The armored man turned, without a sword, but he was holding cuffs linked by chains of gold. The manacles had a glow about them that made her think she should *absolutely not* let them get put on her wrists.

The sword wielding soldier appeared behind her. She was boxed in. Had no weapons. Had no ink or paint or dirt to scribe with. She wasn't sure her body could express any more magic without her heart stopping.

So she threw herself against the stone bookshelf.

Her feet found purchase immediately, her hands sinking into the alcoves and pulling with all of her might. She imagined Raff and Elodie under the crates, how the ropes had been cut, and now realized that someone was trying to draw a scribe out. Her teeth ground together, and she pictured the ropes, pictured Morgana and Raff and everyone she loved under the falling shadow of the queen. And so she pulled.

Heaving up onto the next shelf, trying to ignore the bite of metal at her heel, she clambered all the way to the top, running along the shelves as guards on both winding sides followed her from below. Heavy footsteps were shaking the floor, shaking the shelves, books falling off and tripping some of the guards. As if the library listened to Ole's giant feet and prayers and was trying to help them escape.

For Ole it was, pummeling his way through the shelves, firing small blasts at duos of soldiers as more hurried in for backup.

He did not know where she was.

She didn't think much about this, at first, until he threw his weight into the ancient shelves. Her feet slid right over the edge, a sensation of falling, followed by her chest hitting the next set of shelves as the first collapsed. Ole had completely smothered some of the guards. He paused, chest heaving, as he looked rather apologetically at the books he had toppled.

"Ole!" she cried out.

His eyes snapped up, searching, before he found her. He waved.

She waved back. Shook her head. "Get out of here!"

"Not without you, Little Pip!" he yelled back, punching a guard so hard in the face that their faceplate shattered.

Gross.

"Sparrow will get me! Go, so *I* can go!"

He somehow had time to put a finger to his face in thought. Then, he nodded, and ran off towards the staircase he and Shem had first traversed when they arrived. The stained glass windows cast shadows across the tops of the shelves, light patterns and mosaics that used to be beautiful. Now it all looked like stains.

Her heartbeat slowed to a crawl, and she found herself limping across the shelves in the library she had so recently revered. It stunk of death and bloodshed. The dancer's husband must have felt the same as she did now.

Except, he did something useful about it.

Worthless, worthless, worthless...

She shook her head to rid the thoughts. Tried to center herself. The dancer's husband earned death by taking something that the queen wanted. If Queen Aura wanted her power, then she would have to take it. Philippa looked back over her shoulder.

Somewhere, in the depths of the toppled spirals of endless shelves, lay the inner sanctum. She hadn't had the time to study the orb, to determine how to enter, but it couldn't have been more different than the Wahanar glass portals. Sparrow's mask had runes that allowed him to enter and exit at different intervals. The orb could function similarly. But Aura wanted in there badly that she wrote her husband out of existence to rule without question.

So Philippa had to get inside first, and strip everything down to the bare bones, before Queen Aura found her way inside, or forced her to open it. Surely, Philippa thought, she would choose death over entering the sanctum for the queen. But something about those icy blue eyes told her that the queen wouldn't kill her. No, she'd hurt. She'd maim. She'd behead mothers and bury children.

Philippa thought of the tattoo, not on her hand, but on her shoulder, the one she'd had as long as she could remember. She thought of Morgana's shoulder, twin to hers, how they never spoke of it. How they chalked it up to culture. How it could somehow be related to the inner sanctum, her father's obsession with power. Perhaps, the very power locked away in the sanctum, the power that Queen Aura also desired.

Her jaw set. She didn't have the time to think about this now, to make a plan. If she could just—

"There!" called a shrill voice.

Philippa turned just in time to see golden darts flying straight for her. She ducked, but one still buried itself in her ankle, the others plunking against the pack.

White hot pain seared through her foot, radiating up her leg. She collapsed to the top of the bookshelf, head smacking, as she saw Aura's outstretched hands. Philippa's eyes dragged down to her cradled ankle, and she sneered. Queen Aura's clawed fingertips were not just decoration.

Philippa could not fight her. So she ran. She drug her useless ankle, leapt to the nearest balcony of the second floor, scurrying like a mouse as more flurries of golden dagger nails and crossbow bolts buried themselves after her.

Her arms ached as she tried to throw herself over the railing, to climb higher, but she just felt so *heavy*. She couldn't tell if the nail bolt was poisoned, or if she was simply at the last dregs of energy she had. Magic burnout was real, she'd seen it, and she absolutely could not risk trying to heal herself now.

Philippa's ears twitched. Soldiers had climbed to the tops of the shelves. She could feel it. Could hear them readying their next volley.

They fired their weapons.

A thick, padded feeling came against her back as she dangled there, and the *thunking* of metal on metal shook her core. Then, the pressure was gone, soldiers grunted, and someone grabbed her by her belt and flipped her up and over the railing. More bolts buried themselves behind her as she was nearly flung to the floor, but caught by a hairsbreadth.

She flung her arms around his neck without having to look at who he was. "You couldn't have come sooner?"

He groaned, pushing her back by the shoulders. His mask was still on, but a crack had formed under the beak of it, stretching towards its eye. He reached over to his back, pulling the shapely metal forward. "I needed supplies."

"One would think an assassin had a shield on hand," she countered, as he pulled her to her feet.

Sparrow's head fell forward slightly as he rose along with her, which he simply righted by cracking his neck. He still wasn't fully healed. He was in pain.

"Didn't need one until today."

"Shem knows about the glass portals. We can't just disappear."

He shoved the shield into her hands as Ole rounded the stairs, blockading the massive hallway with the nearest wooden bookshelf. "I brought a distraction."

He sounded too pleased about that. Ole and Philippa exchanged glances, before they heard two women shriek.

"Oh, stars above, what is that *thing?*" the queen's voice shook like a disgusted child.

In response, a slew of Wahatan curses came out in angry screams. Ole tensed. Philippa smacked Sparrow in the arm, despite his broken neck.

In the chaos below in the library's maze, a shadow portal was closing as Dagna stared in disorientation at the Queen of Sapria, the sworn enemy of the Wahanar. Olekashan and Philippa turned slowly, both of their mouths agape.

Sparrow pulled his hair to keep his head upright. "I told you, I had to get supplies."

Dagna and Queen Aura exchanged blows almost immediately. Dagna was armed to the teeth with poisons, but something about Queen Aura makes her able to deter at least some of the effects.

The three of them, all bleeding, stood at the edge of the balcony, watching in morbid curiosity. Ole did not seem sad per say, but certainly conflicted. It was clear he and Dagna had no love for each other. Whether or not that was a recent development, Philippa couldn't say. She couldn't picture Ole as a wild, angry young man that fit Dagna's superstitious rage. At any rate, he made no sudden movements to aid his wife in her fight against Queen Aura.

Sparrow, masked, was indifferent, catching his breath and continually resetting his neck.

As Queen Aura raged against Dagna, throwing her own golden darts, there was another commotion, near the back center of the library. By the inner sanctum.

Wing beats filled the air as Shem rose towards one of the glass domes of the ceiling. Philippa winced at seeing him rise as if on those wings, he weighed nothing, a malformed phoenix in a forgotten holy place. The uppermost level of the library loomed like a hall of silence, broken only by the echoing flap of massive wings. Shem hovered at its pinnacle, tall and transformed, the crown of the library behind him like a twisted halo.

"Come out!" he roared. "I know you're still here!"

In his hand was proof of his victory: Vaelith's severed head, still glowing faintly with traces of flame, like embers refusing to die. He hurled it down into the chamber below. It landed with a wet thud, flames curling around it in a dying crown.

Philippa gasped, stumbling back into Ole's arms. Her eyes blurred, her stomach hollow. She had only just earned trust with Vaelith. She hadn't known she could mourn what was once a monster.

Sparrow turned to her and caught the movement in her hands, her twitching fingers inching towards her tattooed palm. "Don't. Not yet."

He reached inside his layered tunic, and handed her what remained of the vial from before. It felt more delicate now, a smoky glass with the ink writhing in it like a storm. He must've added something to it.

"Break this against the outer wall. The wards will collapse. It'll get you out."

"Sparrow…"

"What will you do?" Ole asked, voice low, full of mixed grief and desperation.

Blonde curls bouncing, Sparrow nodded towards the inner sanctum. "Deal with him."

"But your magic, your healing—" Philippa couldn't finish. He moved quickly, but it was enough to shut her up.

He lifted his mask, revealing a necklace of bruises and nail bites along his neck. He smiled faintly, before tightening the straps of his tattered assassin's tunic. "Is more than enough to buy you five minutes. Maybe more. Go."

Olekashan gave him a stiff nod. Philippa wanted to argue, but didn't have the strength. Her entire body felt like it weighed a thousand pounds, her heartbeat an inconsistent rhythm in her chest. She let herself fold up under Ole's arm as he tucked her away, hurrying along via Sparrow's instruction to find a way out.

As soon as they were out of sight, Sparrow sighed. Righted his head. Climbed the balcony barricade, and leapt.

CHAPTER FIFTY

Sparrow shot through the aisles, weaving between collapsed ladders and fallen books. A shame, this place, being ruined this way. He would've liked to tear it down entirely differently.

Bygones, bygones.

Shem descended from above, a harbinger of ruin, wings splayed wide, scattering paper like ash. He landed hard, cracking the stone beneath him, cornering Sparrow, and immediately lashed out.

There was no love lost here. Sparrow had hated him since the first time he saw him. Granted, he had a general dislike for most people. But Shem had rubbed him the wrong way. Shem had choices, had gotten to *choose* friends and family and purpose, but he'd been too comfortable with the ugly truth of his existence that he had done *nothing*. Sparrow grit his teeth as he dodged low, slicing upward with his dagger, which glanced off of the base of Shem's wing. He wished he had the luxury to be so lazy in a world that needed change.

His dagger drew sparks from Shem's wing, but barely pierced the skin. Shem snarled, and swung his other wing like a club, catching Sparrow in the ribs and sending him flying into a column.

Sparrow coughed up blood, stumbling upright. "So you *were* always hiding how strong you were." he growled.

"I hated hiding it from you the most." Shem snapped back.

Their blades met again. Shem now wielded elongated claws like razors, which Sparrow had to block with both arms, elbows locked for balance. Shem had the height, the literal wingspan, the reach. Sparrow smiled, relishing in the fact that it was hidden in his mask. He knew he was faster, more deliberate. More trained for the tactical kill.

When Shem lunged again, Sparrow sliced beneath him and cut across his leg, just enough to make him snarl. The corridor was too narrow for Shem to fully take flight, but his wings allowed him to move with impossible speed and dexterity, darting between walls as Sparrow slashed.

Shem's strength in this form was starting to wear on Sparrow. Each strike sent vibrations up his arm, every flick of his wing felt like bones breaking. They had fought their way through the levels of the library, rising and descending like madmen out for blood. Books tumbled around them, Shem vaulted with his wings, and Sparrow kept leaping between ledges to stay close but out of reach.

"You're wasting time." Shem snarled as soon as he caught Sparrow by the back of his hair, ripping him backwards and dragging him up into the air of the library. "When the queen catches you, she'll tear you apart." Shem brought his head and horns against Sparrow's mask. Once. Twice. Broke the beak clean off and split Sparrow's lip open. Blood flowed freely down his chin, coating his teeth as he smiled idly at Shem.

This was the part of fighting he *did* enjoy. Getting under their skin, seeing them squirm. Because nothing, *nothing,* could stop him from saving Philippa Aporo. Even if he wanted to be stopped. Sparrow's head lolled, but his voice was pure ice. "And every time she does, I'll come back for you." Then, he unsheathed a hidden dagger, plunging it into Shem's shoulder.

Shem roared, and in his agony he hurled Sparrow away, straight into a stained glass mural. Glass exploded. Colorful shards rained down. Sparrow fell further, his dagger swinging, catching a torn banner and cushioning his fall to the second floor.

He rolled to his feet, spitting blood. It had been a long time since his hands had shaken like this, from pure exhaustion, from torn ligaments and broken bones. He lifted them to his mask, felt the leaking of the magic that opened portals and hid him away when he needed to heal. Though it was a cage, it was his, and he would miss it.

But Philippa needed time. Shem may not murder her now, but the queen would torture her to the brink, something he could not allow. He told himself it was because of his binding that he did not want to see her suffer.

That is, he told himself this for all of ten seconds as he ripped the mask free, and glared at its empty, powerless eyes for the last time. Then, his eyes reflected in the blackness of the mask's orbs, he told himself the truth.

Philippa Aporo was good. She was good despite loss and abuse, and he would have very much liked to know her without a book telling him that he had to. In another life, he could've seen himself pledging allegiance to her willingly. But this was not another life, and he could save her now.

He threw the mask to the ground. Took one last look at his beautifully carved leash, pulled a miniature crossbow from his hip, and splintered the avian facade into oblivion.

He felt Shem land behind him, the floor cracking under his talons. "Bound to her like a *dog*. Does she even care for you? Or are you just another tool for her?"

When Sparrow turned around, he saw the beastly form of Shem hesitate. As if, for a split second, he did not quite think this was a fight he could win.

Blood ran down Sparrow's temple.

Shem readied into stance. "Nothing to say about that?"

Sparrow drew a blade from his back that Shem had never seen before. It was rare that he used it. A scythe, long and curved, meant for one purpose only: heads hitting floors. He angled it up, looking down his arm at Shem. Then, he pulled back the collar of his tunic, revealing the necklace Shem had given him earlier, as the last of the bruises disappeared and his bones knit back together.

"You will not find me to be very quippy."

They clashed. Claws ran down Sparrow's sides. Blade reached under and sliced Shem's arms.

Anger began to run through Sparrow. Shem's slashes hurt more than the whips, but felt less humiliating. Anger would do. It inspired him. This had become more than bound-duty. This was personal.

"You made *no choices* when it came to her!" Sparrow yelled. He jabbed his blade, jumping over the swing of Shem's wing. "I only have to save her. I didn't have to come back in here to kick your—"

A horn found its way into Sparrow's gut. Claws dug into his arms, stretching him apart from his torso. Time slowed. He gasped, unable to keep the rush of pain from stealing his breath.

Shem flipped Sparrow's blade out of his hand and kicked it away. "Tell me. Will you revive if your body has to head to control it?"

He angled his sharp horn against Sparrow's throat. Sparrow grinned, pursing his lips. He spat blood into Shem's face. If Shem wanted to kill him, he'd make him earn it.

Before Shem could make the killing blow, his golden, wild eyes darted to a nearby staircase. Philippa stepped out, hands outstretched, ankle dragging, and her voice was steady despite the fear in her eyes.

"Shem! Please."

Shem hesitated. He really only needed her. Sparrow cursed. That woman could follow no direction.

The Evirian form Shem was now in seemed to be pushed aside as a softness came out in his voice. "I'm doing this *for* you, Miss Aporo. You'll live if you go with her."

Sparrow rolled his eyes, fingers itching to keep fighting, to get Philippa out of there. But whatever capacity she had for goodness was loosening Shem's grip, and out of pure morbid curiosity, Sparrow let himself stay in the Evirian's grip.

"No, you're not." Philippa said, voice strong. "You're doing this because you think loyalty to her is all you have. But I won't be used by her, or by you."

Shem's wings drooped slightly, and for a moment, it seemed like the man beneath the beast was breaking through. But the queen's voice echoed faintly from somewhere above, and his resolve hardened.

"I can't let you go." his claws flexed. Sparrow grit his teeth.

Philippa's bright eyes softened. "Then I'm so sorry."

She meant it.

Then she smashed the vial against the wall. Her tattoo was aglow, sending tendrils into the vial. It released a blinding, surging light towards Shem. He roared in pain, his wings folding protectively around him as the magic drove him back. Sparrow seized the opportunity, twisting away from Shem and grabbed Philippa's arm to pull her toward the staircase. Ole was waiting at the bottom, his massive frame blocking the exit until they arrived.

"Where's Shem?" Ole asked, his voice grim. Despite everything, he still expected Philippa to get through to him. Maybe he thought that he had, too.

"Not coming." Sparrow said shortly. "Nice trick with the vial. Now how do we get out of here?"

Ole crossed his arms and mimed falling backwards, then gestured to Sparrow, as if asking where his mask was. Sparrow only groaned.

Philippa chewed on the inside of her cheek. "I can open up the wall. But I won't be able to do anything after."

"I won't let you die." Sparrow said, as if he needed to. He never knew why he felt like he had to remind her, but when she nodded at him with wet eyes, he promised himself that he would remind her a thousand times if it kept that look off of her face.

Having been inside her head rather unwillingly, he knew that she usually pictured a tunnel to fill with her magic. Sparrow tried not to invade her mind, but their connection bloomed within him, and he sneered. Philippa Aporo did not picture a tunnel when she looked at the wall barring their freedom.

No, she pictured the queen waiting for her, cackling and torturing. Sparrow winced as he felt Philippa see her mother's head hitting the beach, with Shem in his Evirian form standing over her.

But then Sparrow smiled, pride swelling within him strangely. For then, Philippa pictured a battering ram and swung, flames to white hot that the very stones of the library cellar melted as her consciousness dissolved. His arms were under her before her knees even gave way. Sparrow grimaced at seeing his blood drip onto her kind face. But the queen's voice was ringing above them, and so he moved through the wall Philippa had blown open without cleaning her up, without worrying that his blood would mar her. It didn't matter the pain he was in, or that she was heavy in his battered arms. His heart could be torn from his chest and it would not stop him. Because he would save her.

Every time.

CHAPTER FIFTY-ONE ✧

Roars and screams of agony rippled through Aresef that evening. As the sun began to fall behind the cities, no one could block out the horrific, amplified cries of the Evirian thrashing around the Great Library.

His screams were rattling around in Philippa's mind, tormenting her. She wished he'd been brave enough to just *stop*, to come with them and figure it out as they went. Even in her dreamless sleep, Philippa felt that Shem wasn't truly lost. But neither was he someone she could trust, ever again.

The hilltop wind stung her cheeks, but Philippa didn't flinch. The smoke trails from the library had begun to dissipate, embers of the walls scattered to the dirt. Already, word had rippled through the cities that no books had been burned, miraculously. She dug her fingers into the dirt. Miraculous, maybe, but intentional.

Sparrow crouched nearby, fingers busy crafting something from a few broken wires and a leather strap - remnants of his mask, sloppily pieced back together. It would have no power for him now. Ole watched over them, one hand near the hilt of his blade. None of them stated the obvious; without Sparrow's mask, wherever he placed Panu, is where the boy would wake. Alone. But he would be alive, and that seemed enough for Ole.

Philippa didn't speak. She stared down at her palm, where the underside of her tattoo still shimmered faintly, as if locked between inaction and action. Even more than that, she felt the markings on her shoulder, felt them rumble with the urge to *go*. She'd finally put together that her constant thrum to leave, to explore, came in part from the ink on her shoulder. For what reason, she could not remember. Could not begin to wonder.

Her eyes were frozen open, looking at her bloody, twisted ankle. She hadn't tried to heal it. The pain felt earned, sharpening her focus. If she thought of everything wrong in the world now, she'd break apart.

Everything slowly fell into place. It all made sense. Shem had known she had a sister, had known her name, had pieced together so much about her that she had convinced herself that she'd told him. The way he would've let her drink the poison tea from the old woman, even trying to haul her into the shadows in the streets of Kamath where soldiers were waiting. Even if he looked like a monster now, he was a scholar, ever learning and observing. Except he didn't want to write about her - she was his prey.

On the hilltop, the three of them had no fire. They had to leave soon. The queen would send soldiers, more beasts, anything she could to get Philippa back. That woman's only error was thinking that she had Philippa caught the moment she laid eyes on her. Something in Philippa's gut twisted. Queen Aura would not make the same mistake again. She thought of the dancer's husband, hanging limp from a noose in the courtyard.

Movement shuffled beside her. Sparrow settled in the long, dry grass, his wounds beginning to close. He didn't look at her when he spoke. "You don't have to run back towards this."

She glanced at him. His voice was rough, from battle, and from something inside himself that had grown weary. Cautious.

How could she run back towards any of this? She was nothing. Amounted to the highest degree of failure in every sense of the word. Panu was healed, but she'd let Shem lead her straight to the one who would either have her power or her head. And Shem knew *everything* about her now. Her family. Levanta.

When she didn't speak, Sparrow looked at her more keenly. Waiting.

"I must be the worst scribe that there has ever been," she murmured, pressing her lips against her arm as she held herself.

"No."

She didn't even look at him.

"Philippa."

He groaned, and rocked to his knees, before crawling to look at her straight in the face. His eyebrows were furrowed, his mouth a tight line, the scar on his chin pulling up his top lip.

"Can you hear me?"

She mustered a nod.

"There have been worse scribes." he said softly, so only she could hear. She pictured his back. Thought of her father. "Even I did not know what he was. But we do now. An Evirian."

Philippa cradled herself, wanting to rock to sleep. "There was no way to know."

"Then there is no reason to blame yourself," Sparrow brushed his bloodied hair from his brow, eyes still locked on her. "You said it yourself. You felt like we were together for a reason. Now is not the time to accept that your book is written, Philippa. You want to wallow? Do it later. Do it when that wench's blood has been spilled. Don't let her take your heart. Run. Fight. Pick a path. Do not freeze now."

A sob worked its way into her throat. The intensity of his eyes, two fields of green that bore no sympathy for the weak. The tell-tale sign of great emotion among elves, the twitching of his long ears. A man knelt before her, an assassin of great skill, who had lived a life in forced dedication to her, and *he* was encouraging *her?*

"No one commands your book, Philippa. Choose your ending. Whatever it may be."

A wry smile crossed her face as she was reminded of what Shem had told her before this. *If there is an after.*

There wouldn't be. But she would make one.

He cleared his throat. "I'll get you back to your family. Vanish. You'd never have to think of all this again."

Philippa didn't answer right away. She traced the edge of her tattoo with a finger. Then she looked out towards the horizon, the direction of the city they shattered, the library's spire turned black just barely visible in the haze of smoke and gold.

"If I go back to them now, she'll find them. Use them to control me."

"You don't know that." he said.

She turned to face him. "She did it with Shem."

He didn't argue there. The truth sat between them, a silent weight.

"I didn't want to go to the inner sanctum just to survive all this." she said at last. Her voice had sharpened, smoothed out the tremble from before. "I came to change it. Everything and anything that lets someone have outright control over others, or turn them into a bludgeoned tool. Or worse."

She pictured Shem's beautiful eyes. Even when he transformed, when part of him was eaten away, he was ethereally beautiful. She rubbed her stomach, trying to push the feeling away.

When she continued, her voice cracked, but she didn't turn away from him. "I wanted to unwrite it all. To give control back to the ones who have been silenced. I still do."

Sparrow leaned back, watching her in the fading light of day. He nodded once, slowly. Something like resolved passed over his face. She at first thought he would ask her if she was ready to give up her own power, what could've made her special, but he did not. He knew her better than that.

"You're powerful, Philippa. But you are one. You'll need help."

She picked at the grass. Leaned closer to him. He did not seem to care. "I know where to start looking."

He blinked at her, like a cat. "The cult won't accept you outright. They've spent generations learning what even the earliest scribes were written to forget."

"Then we better get going." she said.

A long silence followed. Sparrow nodded sharply. He put his finger to his mouth, pulled his gloves off with his teeth. Revealed ashen, pale hands that longed for the sun to turn them bronze again. His emerald eyes bore down at his own hands, like he was seeing everything they had ever done, everything they might never do.

Slowly, he offered his hand to her. She stared at him. He never touched her voluntarily.

"Try to keep your heart, Philippa. The world is out to get it."

For a moment, she didn't think she could swear that, even shake on it without believing it. But his eyes bore into hers, and here was a man who had lived one life begging for release, and who had foregone any wishes at all. His freedom would be in ash and ruined parchment. What was one more promise in the sea of those she had already made?

He didn't have to help her find the cult, could let her wander aimlessly, keeping her alive, as she sought them out. But this was his small price. Try to stay who she was, as he knew her.

In a twisted, selfish way, she could've smiled at the thought that he didn't hate her as much anymore, if at all. She reached out, but he pulled back.

"There is more. If you want this, no more blind kindness. Feel everything. There is a time for mercy. Now is the time for fury. Kindness is your greatest strength, but for this, you will need to be stronger. It's time to get angry."

Philippa stared at him. Slowly, she nodded, and offered her hand again. He had no idea that she felt way past *mercy.*

His hand was warm as it cradled hers. He shook her hand as if she were a lady of court, not like they were making a deal that would probably get them both killed. She felt like it was because he knew the truth about his request: none of them may be the same by the end of this.

Ole stepped closer, trapping both of their hands in his massive fist. His face was soft, but determined.

Philippa gave him a tired, grateful smile. "You're not done with us yet?"

"Not by half," he said, "you saved my boy, Little Pip. Wherever he is, his heart is aglow. He will be safe. I have not forgotten this already. Where you go, from here, I go too."

She thought of Vaelith, whose body was now lying cold in the Great Library. It was she who'd saved Panu, not Philippa, but staring into Ole's dark eyes, Philippa couldn't bear to mention it. The chief too looked like he was dancing around mentioning what had happened.

The three of them stood in the glow of the dying sunlight, the weight of the broken world pressing in from all sides. The world had called her out, and it yawned open to be so much bigger than she expected. So much deadlier. Now, she would give the world a response.

Philippa looked up at the dawning stars, and for the first time since she was in that canoe leaving Soffer, she didn't feel small beneath them.

"Let's finish our story."

The wind shifted. Ash curled upward from the scorched edges of Aresef, catching in the breeze like whispers of what had burned. Above them, the stars blinked faintly through a veil of smoke and alterations undone. Somewhere, far below them, the queen's wrath stirred.

Philippa didn't look back.

The trio walked toward the tree line, the shadows long behind them. Sparrow lifted his eyes skyward. Ole held a small shard of what remained of his Wahanar looking glass. And Philippa - her tattoo tingling against her skin - touched the strap of the pack she still wore. Sparrow made no mention if he knew that she had smuggled his book out, along with Panu's.

She could feel it pulsing now, slow and alive. Still writing, despite it all. But this time, the story would be theirs to tell.

They disappeared into the dark. Far below, deep in the dungeons beneath the queen's court, something stirred in chains.

Waiting.

EPILOGUE

Only the back wall of the cell was stone. The rest were smooth crystal, all light edges and etched with writing that burned when he touched them.

Shem didn't move. He sat in the center, in the mosaic light, wings curled around him like a shield. His queen had not spoken to him since the battle in the library. Of his failure. He heard how the guards spoke as they passed him. How he could only be waiting for beheading, since he could be marked a traitor.

He felt this is how a child in trouble with their parents must feel. He had never known that feeling, not really. Never having parents really made the concept of childlike guilt unfathomable. Until now.

A shiver ran over his skin, goosebumps rising from his dark flesh. Tunics and shirts did not fit anymore, not with his wings on full display. Only trousers kept him warm, and the spurs on his feet made shoes impossible.

The dungeons did not have to be cold. Often, they were warm. This was punishment.

He drew his wings closer, insulting himself. A stray feather brushed his cheek, and for a moment, he thought of *her*.

The one he'd been sent to find. When he'd first been given this assignment, he didn't know he would think twice about her. All he knew is that there was a scribe woman hiding in an immigrant town by the shore, and there was always a way to draw a scribe out. Force them into action, like a lion roaring into the ground to scatter a herd, to find the stray, the one who couldn't keep up with the rest.

No, he did not even think about cutting the ropes that nearly killed those two children. They did not matter to his queen, so they did not matter to him. Then, all he had to do was hide. But the Wahanar had found him first, and he could not risk his true form being seen, so he allowed it. Then, she was brought *to* him.

Even then, she at the time meant nothing to his queen, so what could she mean to him?

That is the way it had always been. Until he heard her speak. Saw the way she moved without even a touch of malice. Filled with indignation at others' mistreatment.

The assassin was right. It could not have been the blooming love he felt for her, could it? She treated him with decency, even when she found out that he was not *real,* written from ink and greed, not of love and family. But she looked at him like he was beautiful. He *felt* that. In his bones. He felt beautiful around her. Felt seen. Felt real.

His queen would tell him it was part of Philippa's scribe magic, an illusion to draw him close, for who could ever truly love a scribe? Who in their right mind would keep someone so near to their heart, who could overtake them in a moment?

This was the first of the lies he would continue to tell Queen Aura, he determined. If she tried to convince him that Philippa Aporo was malicious or using him, he would agree. He would lie. Because no matter what Queen Aura said, Philippa Aporo had shown him love.

Even in the moment when it was twisted into horror and disgust - when he'd *hurt* her - she came back. Offered him a chance. Gave him a split second to determine what he would do. Before she smashed that altered vial of ink against the wall and blinded him, not with light, but with memories.

Whatever was in that bottle, he never wanted to see again. Whatever magic she'd infused into the ink vial had shown him things he'd never known he had done. Terrible things. Stories parents would be too frightened to tell their children before bed. His fists clenched and unclenched. A monster is not what he wanted to be, but with the newfound memories rattling around in his head, Shem resigned that if he were to be a monster, he'd prefer to be a dead one.

An Evirian's memory was meant to be wiped clean when ordered to. He knew it was coming. It had happened countless times since being written into existence.

At the very least, he thought, taking stock of his circumstances, it felt good to stretch his wings. When his queen first figured out that she could have them hidden into tattoos on his shoulders, it was like being put into a straitjacket. Some of the residents in the dungeons still wore them as they cackled.

But that was not enough. He didn't want to forget Philippa. He could not have her, and he did not agree with her ideals. But she had been real, had been tangible, tasted like the salt of the sea and the sweetest berries. She would accept him back, if he came to her. That was who she was, he decided. She was kind. She had been kind to him before she trusted him.

He ground his teeth, and nicked his lip with his elongated canines. He opened his palm, staring at the necklace he'd torn from her neck when he ripped her away from the assassin. It took a great amount of effort to gently touch the button on the top to flick it open. Inside was not Philippa, but a woman who looked like her, with two children. A sketch rendered so realistically that he could see where she got the gentle downward curve of her nose, the fullness of her lips. He didn't want to forget her.

It was not that he wanted Queen Aura to rule forever, no, but he had known nothing else. He was a creature born of the scribes, turned into their condemnation. His queen gave him direction. Did she have to?

He shook his head. Traitor's thoughts.

Human thoughts.

He closed his eyes. In this form, rage bubbled just under the surface, always. He hated being like this. He couldn't even read, or focus long enough to study like this. His queen was doing this to him. Once he got his hands on her…

The cell shimmered, and he tucked the necklace away between rivulets of his feathers, exposing his face to the queen.

"You were written for so much more, Shem." she said, her voice neither cruel nor kind. "You failed. But failure has its lessons."

She stalked towards him, observing him. Correcting him.

"What of the woman?" he asked hoarsely.

Queen Aura smiled. "So eager to win her back for me, are we?" she turned, her eyes burning with a fury she didn't bother to hide. "She will come to me. They always do. Just give her time to believe she has a choice."

With that, she knelt before him. He did not move, just stared at her blankly. She reached out, her golden-tipped fingers gently tracing along his cheek, until her palm cradled his face. Her expression was sorry, lips pursed and eyebrows tight.

"Now, Shem. I don't want you to have to remember this failure." she said it lovingly. Then, her beautiful lips were on his.

It was not so much a kiss, but she made it one. He had never remembered when this happened before, but this time, he knew she tasted bitter. His mind addled, and he relaxed as she pulled away, his wings drooping around him as her effect took hold of him.

She turned before he could ask for his next assignment. Left him there, her heels clicking as she walked away.

Shem just turned around, to stare at the stone wall, as the lights went out in the dungeon, leaving even the glass walls to conjure darkness for him. Absently, he reached for the necklace hidden in his wings, letting it weigh down his palm.

He did not know who was inside. But they all looked kind.

There was a sound, like a stone being carved. His eyes adjusted to the darkness as his head snapped up. The Queen may have left, but her punishments were never so easy. No, he was not alone in that cell at all. He pressed the necklace to his chest, whispering the name he could not fully remember.

And from the shadows, someone whispered it back.

LOG 14

A GROUP OF WAHANAR ⊢ "FIRE BRUTES", IF YOU'RE
UNFAMILIAR ⊢ UNFORTUNATELY SPOTTED ME OUTSIDE OF
THEIR CAMP.
I WAS ATTEMPTING TO LURE THE SCRIBE INTO THE DESERT
WHEN I WANDERED TOO CLOSE TO ONE OF THEIR DOORWAYS.
I WAS UNPREPARED FOR A COVER STORY.
I'M NOW BORED TO DEATH, WRITING ON THIS HIDDEN PAD OF
PARCHMENT WITH A CHARCOAL STYLUS I BROUGHT WITH ME
ON THIS MISSION.
I'M REDUCED TO DRAWING TO PASS THE TIME IN THE
PRISONER'S TENT UNTIL THEY FIND OUT WHAT TO DO WITH
ME.
I HOPE THEY DON'T TRY TO KILL ME.
I'M ACTUALLY QUITE CURIOUS ABOUT HOW THEY LIVE.

TAZMIRETH;
SHE APPEARS TO BE THE CHIEF'S NIECE.
THUS FAR, SHE IS THE ONLY ONE TO SPEAK TO ME.

LOG 16

THEY CANNOT READ THEIR OWN WRITINGS.
THIS IS AN ADVANTAGE.

LOG 19

I CANNOT REVEAL MYSELF TO THEM. MY QUEEN WOULD NOT
WANT THAT.
SO, LIKE ANY SCHOLAR, I RETURN TO MY HABITS.
THE WAHANAR ARE A FASCINATING SPECIES.
MANY CALL THEM "BRUTES" OR "FIRE BRUTES", STRICTLY
BECAUSE THEY LACK UNDERSTANDING.
AND, WHEN YOU WANDER INTO THE DESERT AND SEE A
GIANT LUMBERING TOWARDS YOU, SLINGING FLAMES, YOU
HAVE LITTLE TIME TO DESCRIBE THEM AS ANYTHING ELSE.
THAT, PAIRED WITH THE UNFORTUNATE TRUTH THAT OFTEN
THE NATIVES OF A LAND ARE PAINTED IN QUITE A HARSH
LIGHT.
THEY ARE OUTWARDLY WARY OF ME, BUT THEY HAVE NEED
OF ME.
THEY WANT ME TO TRANSLATE OLD WRITINGS OF THEIRS.
ONE OF THEM CONTINUES TO WATCH ME LIKE I'M HER
NEXT MEAL. SHE HAS VITILIGO AND IS THE TALLEST ONE I
HAVE PERSONALLY SEEN, SAVE FOR THE CHIEF.
THE CHIEF HIMSELF IS A KINDLY IMBECILE. HE'S OVERCOME
WITH GRIEF, THAT'S PLAIN ENOUGH DESPITE THE LANGUAGE
BARRIER.
THEY SEEM TO BE A VERY EMOTIONAL PEOPLE AT THEIR
CORE.

AT TIMES IT'S ALMOST HARD TO REMEMBER WHAT I LOOK
LIKE. SO MUCH HAS CHANGED SINCE I WAS LAST RELEASED
ON A MISSION. THE CELLS AT THE PALACE DO NOT HAVE
MIRRORS.

LOG 2Ø

THERE HAS BEEN TALK OF FINDING A SCRIBE AMONG THE
WAHANAR PEOPLE.
I'VE DECODED MANY OF THEIR WORDS. IT'S NOT A
PARTICULARLY COMPLEX LANGUAGE, THOUGH IT IS THROATY
AND MANY OF THE WORDS HAVE MULTIPLE MEANINGS.
POINT BEING, THEY KNOW OF A SCRIBE.
MY QUEEN HAD A BOY HERE ALTERED. I DIDN'T REALIZE IT
WAS THIS SECT OF WAHANAR THAT SHE HAD CHOSEN TO
TARGET.
AS ALWAYS, THE QUEEN'S PLAN FALLS PERFECTLY INTO
HER LAP. I WONDER IF SHE HAD ONE OF HER SCRIBES
ALTER THIS VERY MOMENT INTO OCCURING, OR IF IT WAS
JUST A STROKE OF LUCK.

THEY HAVE FINALLY DECIDED TO FEED ME.
AS A WHOLE, MOST OF THEM EAT CRUSTACEANS AND LARGE
SCORPIONS THAT THEY HUNT. THEY SLURP THE MEAT FROM
THE INSIDE, OR IF THEY HUNT AN OCCASIONAL MAMMAL,
THEY DRY THE MEAT IMMEDIATELY.
AFTER BEING CONFINED TO EATING PALACE FOOD FOR THE
LAST TWO YEARS, I'M RATHER EXCITED TO EAT THE FOOD
OF OTHER PEOPLES.

NOTE: DO NOT EAT THEIR FOOD IF YOU ARE UNACCUSTOMED TO
SPICE. OR POISON. THEY EAT MANY POISONOUS THINGS. I
AM WRITING THIS IN BETWEEN BURYING MY HEAD IN A
HOLE IN THE SAND TO EMPTY MY STOMACH.

LOG 20 - CONTINUED

FURTHER NOTE; DESPITE OUR LANGUAGE BARRIER, ONE OF THEM WAS ABLE TO EXPLAIN TO ME THAT THEIR STOMACHS ARE ESSENTIALLY IMMUNE TO SPICE AND HEAT.
THAT IS, IF I WAS ABLE TO TRANSLATE CORRECTLY. THEY CAN ALSO BREAK DOWN POISONS AND TOXINS FROM NATURALLY OCCURING SOURCES, LIKE THE CREATURES THEY EAT. THEY HAVE ALSO LEARNED TO SIMPLY GIVE ME THEIR DRIED MEAT AND FRUIT THEY'VE GROWN.
THEY HAVE ALSO GROWN FOUND OF CALLING ME AN UNSAVORY WAHATAN WORD THAT, IN ESSENCE, CALLS ME A DONKEY.

QUESTION; ARE THEIR INTERNAL ORGANS LINED WITH EXTRA MUCUS OR CASING TO ALLOW THEIR HARSH DIET?

LOG 21

I SAW HER IN PASSING IN LEVANTA. BUT UP CLOSE... SHE'S
ALARMINGLY STRIKING.

LOG 23

THE CHIEF'S DAUGHTER, HERUNAVIRA, HATES THAT
THERE IS A SCRIBE HERE.
IT IS ONLY A MATTER OF TIME BEFORE I CAN RIGHT
THAT FOR HER, ALTHOUGH IT WON'T BE DOING HER
ANY FAVORS.
I NEED TO GET THAT SCRIBE BACK TO ARESEF, SOON.
MY QUEEN WAITS.
IMPATIENTLY.

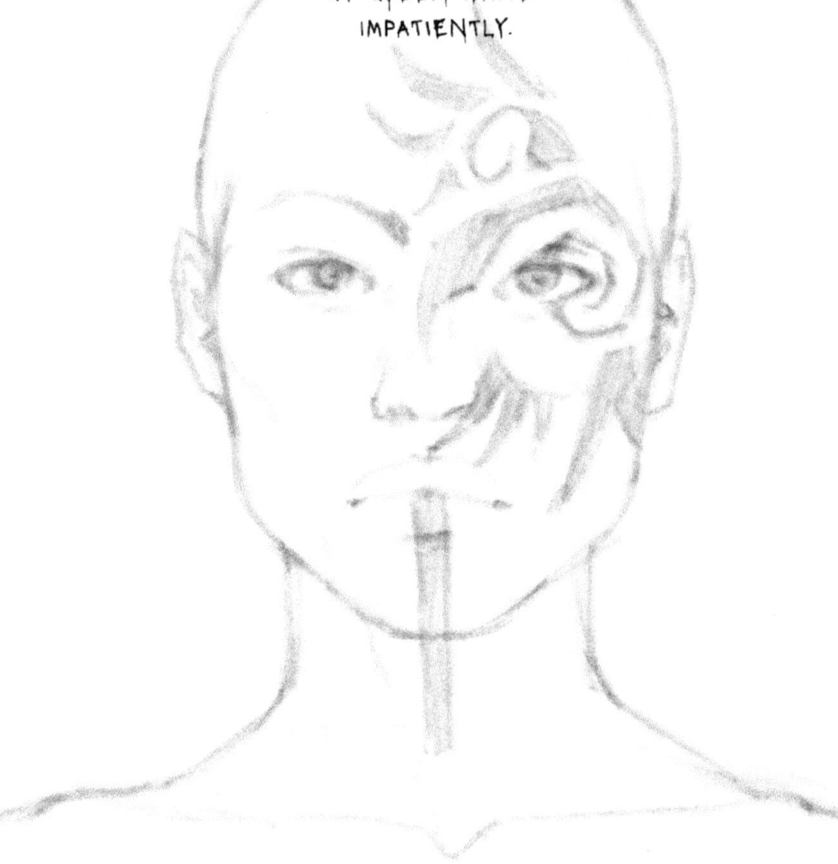

LOG 24

THE SCRIBE...
SHE WANTS TO WORK WITH ME.
IT'S CURIOUS, BUT IT WILL ALLOW ME TO GET CLOSER
TO HER.
MAYBE I CAN CONVINCE HER TO HAVE A BACKUP PLAN,
TO NOT GET TOO COMFORTABLE HERE.
EARN HER TRUST.
HAVE HER COME WILLINGLY.

CHIEF OLEKASHAN "HE WHO SITS BY THE FLAME"

LOG 25

IT'S LIKELY BEEN WEEKS SINCE I'VE WRITTEN
ANYTHING DOWN. IT'S HARD TO REMEMBER.
I'VE BEEN DISTRACTED.
THE CHIEF'S DAUGHTER CAME TO SEE ME IN PRIVATE.
HERUNAVIRA WANTS TO GET RID OF THE SCRIBE. TO
HER, IT'S THE ULTIMATE UNCLEANESS TO HAVE HER
HERE.
FROM WHAT I CAN TELL FROM THEIR OLD RECORDS,
SINCE THEY DO NOT EVEN REMEMBER WHY THEY
THINK SCRIBES ARE UNCLEAN, IT DATES BACK TO THE
SCRIBE WARS. THERE ARE HUGE CHUNKS OF HISTORY,
ENTIRE LENGTHS OF TIME, THAT ARE UNACCOUNTED
FOR IN THE RECORDS OF ALL PEOPLES. THE WAHANAR
PEOPLE SEEM TO HAVE SOME KNOWLEDGE TO FILL IN
THE GAPS.
SOME TIME AT THE BEGINNING OF THE WARS, THE
WAHANAR SEEM TO HAVE ALLIGNED THEMSELVES WITH
A SECT OF SCRIBES. THEY WANTED BOTH THE OTHER
SECT OF SCRIBES, WHO WANTED TO RULE, AND THE
FOREIGN RULERS TRYING TO ESTABLISH SAPRIA AS A
CONTINENTAL KINGDOM OUTNUMBERED, TRY AND
SCARE THEM INTO LEAVING.
THE WAHANAR WERE SOMEHOW BETRAYED. IT IS
UNCLEAR FROM THE RECORD WHAT HAPPENED.
HISTORICAL RECORDS HAVE BEEN SO MUDDLED.
BUT NOW THEY CONSIDER THEMSELVES UNCLEAN
WHEN EVEN COMING INTO CONTACT WITH A SCRIBE.
TO ME, THE MOST LIKELY EVENT SEEMS THAT...
PERHAPS THE WAHANAR SPECIES DID NOT COME INTO
EXISTENCE WITH THE ABILITY TO WIELD FIRE.
BUT PERHAPS THE COST OF THIS GIFT WAS THEIR
BETRAYAL.

LOG 25 - CONTINUED

ALL OF THIS TO SAY, HERUNAVIRA WANTED TO KNOW
IF THERE WAS ANYTHING TO BE DONE ABOUT THE
SCRIBE BEING HERE AND STILL HEAL HER SON.
SOMETHING DRASTIC.
I INFORMED HER THAT TO KNOW FOR SURE, I WOULD
HAVE TO SEE THEIR OLDEST LAWS IF SHE WANTED TO
ABIDE BY THEIR HONOR.
IN AN EFFORT TO KEEP HER PEOPLE CLEAN, IT SEEMS
AS THOUGH SHE IS WILLING TO DO SOMETHING
UNCHARACTERISTIC. SHE WOULD BE SOMEONE MY
QUEEN WOULD VERY MUCH LIKE TO WORK WITH.
IF I CAN GET THE SCRIBE DOWN TO WHERE THEIR
LAWS WERE FIRST WRITTEN, MAYBE IT CAN CONDEMN
HER WITHOUT IT SEEMING LIKE IT WAS MY FAULT.
HERUNAVIRA PROMISED ME THAT I WOULD BE
REWARDED.
I THINK SHE IS LYING TO ME.
IT DOESN'T MATTER. I NEED TO GET PHILIPPA DOWN
THERE, SO WE CAN GET OUT OF HERE.
I KNOW THE QUEEN WON'T READ THIS UNLESS I FAIL.
SO IN ALL HONESTY, TO KEEP MYSELF SANE, I MUST
ADMIT TO MYESLF THAT... I NEED TO GET HER OUT OF
HERE.
AS FAR AWAY FROM THIS AS POSSIBLE. SOON.
THE SCRIBES MY QUEEN KEEPS ARE LOWER CLASS. IT'S
HARD FOR THEM TO MAKE ALTERATIONS. IT HAS BEEN
SOME TIME SINCE MY QUEEN FOUND A NATURALLY
OCCURING SCRIBE.
THE LAST SCRIBE SHE FOUND, SHE FORCED THEM INTO
TRYING TO DISPERSE THEIR GIFT AMONG HER
LIBRARIANS.

LOG 25 - CONTINUED

THEY ARE KEPT MUTE AND BLIND, SO THEY'RE EASY TO CONTROL.

BUT IT DID NOT WORK IN THE WAY SHE ANTICIPATED. IT UNMADE THE NATURAL SCRIBE.

FRACTURED THEIR GIFT INTO SEGMENTS AMONG HER LIBRARIANS. HE WAS THROWN IN THE DUNGEONS UNTIL HE WAS HANGED.

SO, THESE NEW ONES OF HERS, THEY ARE REALLY SCRIBE OFFSHOOTS. THEY CANNOT MAKE SOEMTHING COMPLETELY NEW, LIKE AN EVIRIAN. IT'S WHY THEY COULD TAKE THE SKETCHES OF OLD SCRIBES' DESIGNS AND MAKE THINGS LIKE A MIRROR TOUCHED, BUT NOT GIVE IT A FULLY DEVELOPED FORM. THEY ARE EASILY CORRUPTIBLE.

THE SCRIBE HAD BEFRIENDED A WAHANAR SOLDIER, ONE STRIPPED OF RANK. I'VE SEEN HER BEFORE. THEY CALL HER TAZ-MIRETH.

THEY ARE VERY CLOSE, AND I FEAR THAT ~~PHILIPPA~~ DON'T WANT TO LEAVE HER BEHIND WHEN WE MAKE OUR ESCAPE.

SHE'S WHO I PLAN TO PIN THIS WHOLE THING ON.

WHAT IS HE?

LOG 26

I LET HER KISS ME.
MAYBE I KISSED HER.
WHAT AM I DOING OUT HERE?
I NEED TO ABANDON THIS LOG UNTIL MY NEXT ASSIGNMENT.
IF THERE IS ONE.

LOG 1

I AM NOT ALONE IN THIS CELL.
IT IS NOT WHO I WISH IT TO BE.

AFTERWORD

Oh, my, STARS! If you've made it this far, or even started the book and somehow wandered your way back here, thank you. Creating the world of the *Legends of The Unbound* has been such a special treat for me, and I am so happy to share with you the first entry with *Tale of Philippa*.

As a debut novel, I understand there are things in this novel that will not be my strongest work ever, but it is beloved to me. I've had these characters with me for a long time, and finishing writing this at twenty-two years old is a feat in itself. We have to praise our small wins.

Philippa is a part of myself I grew up really trying to keep pushed down. I never wanted to be seen as too emotional, too soft, or like I needed help.

So, in a way, Philippa is the very soft parts of myself that I wish I knew that the time *were* strengths. Mercy, kindness, choosing to let things go, those are strengths in a world that is "me first" always. But, she must learn to balance. Boundaries are what make kindness and forgiveness beautiful and worthwhile.

Each character in this I feel like is a part of myself or someone I love. Olekashan knows how to be a good father, even to those who aren't his, and simply finds meaning in caring, despite cultural or societal traditions. Shem is fundamentally an intellectual, who only knows how to operate within the realm of logic and meaning, while fighting to want a deep interpersonal connection. Sparrow is bound to obligation, to serving, to making sure someone feels more safe than he does, because he quite literally *cannot* speak up otherwise or choose his own needs.

Thank you for letting me share them with you. I hope you'll continue to take part in their stories in the vast world of *Legends of The Unbound*!

About the Author

Well, hello. My name is Portia and I have always loved creating characters and worlds that I thought would help me connect to others, or let me explore something I simply may never get to do.

I live with my beloved husband, our two cats, and our absolute tank of a golden retriever named Peaches. (We call her Phat Peaches).

I love creating art, traditionally and digitally, and love a good bit of snarky humor. Honestly, I think I'm just a big sensitive soul wrapped in barbs to make sure people know that I can stand up for myself, before they see me all melty and tired.

I come from a beautiful, loving family, and there really isn't anything in my life I would change. Not even the hard things. With support, we learn, we grow, and we love.

You can connect with me on:
- https://portiahbooks.weebly.com
- https://www.tiktok.com/@portiascorner